Praise for

MYSTERY WRITERS OF AMERICA
Presents
VENGEANCE

"Stunning, shocking, and unforgettable.... Each contributor has brought his or her 'A' game to the proceedings, and the results will keep you reading one after the other. There is much to love here.... As always with a collection of this caliber, the question arises: Which story is best? And, as often occurs with an MWA collection of original stories, it's tough to pick a winner.... *Vengeance* is a collection you will want to read, keep, and reread."
— Joe Hartlaub, Bookreporter.com

"A pretty impressive showing."
— Barbara Hoffert, *Library Journal*

"This is one of those rare original anthologies where the authors highlighted on the cover are the obvious attraction, but where the works of the 'ten others' linger in your memory as strongly as those of their famous counterparts. Whether you read the contents of *Vengeance* front to back, or skip back and forth, all are well worth your time. Bottom line: This is one of the strongest and most impressive original collections to appear in a long time. Add it to the list of 'must-have' anthologies you read this year."
— Alan Cranis, Bookgasm.com

"Jam-packed with dark and violent stories by twenty-one different authors.... There aren't any light and fluffy tales or whodunits; instead there are many encounters with nasty characters. While most of the action is set in the United States, foreign locales are deftly used. The variety of authors is excellent—a brief biographical section offers insights into other talented efforts of the individual writers.... It's easy to make this collection of short stories last about three weeks—just limit yourself to one a day."

—*Lansing State Journal*

"These are great reads dealing with the consequences faced by taking 'vengeance.'"   —Dave Biemann, MysteryOne.com

"High-quality anthology.... The writing is top-notch, especially in Lehane's 'The Consumers'.... Brendan DuBois's especially satisfying 'The Final Ballot' features an unsophisticated woman's quest for justice when a powerful politician with national ambitions victimizes her daughter.... But Meyer delivers the biggest jaw-dropper in 'Blood and Sunshine,' about an evil five-year-old boy."

—*Publishers Weekly*

MYSTERY WRITERS OF AMERICA
Presents
VENGEANCE

MYSTERY WRITERS OF AMERICA
Presents

VENGEANCE

Edited by
LEE CHILD

MULHOLLAND BOOKS
LITTLE, BROWN AND COMPANY
NEW YORK • BOSTON • LONDON

Compilation copyright © 2012 by Mystery Writers of America, Inc.
Introduction copyright © 2012 by Lee Child

Mulholland Books / Little, Brown and Company
Hachette Book Group
237 Park Avenue, New York, NY 10017
mulhollandbooks.com

Originally published in hardcover by Mulholland Books, April 2012
First Mulholland Books paperback edition, April 2013

Mulholland Books is an imprint of Little, Brown and Company, a division of Hachette Book Group, Inc. The Mulholland Books name and logo are trademarks of Hachette Book Group, Inc.

The Hachette Speakers Bureau provides a wide range of authors for speaking events. To find out more, go to hachettespeakersbureau.com or call (866) 376-6591.

Copyright notices for individual stories appear on page 385.

Library of Congress Cataloging-in-Publication Data
Mystery Writers of America presents Vengeance / edited by Lee Child. — 1st ed.
    p. cm.
  ISBN 978-0-316-17634-7 (hc) / 978-0-316-17635-4 (pb)
  1. Detective and mystery stories, American.   2. Revenge — Fiction.
 I. Child, Lee.   II. Mystery Writers of America.   III. Title: Vengeance.
  PS648.D4M99 2012
  813'.08720806 — dc23   2011040552

10 9 8 7 6 5 4 3 2 1

RRD-C

Printed in the United States of America

CONTENTS

Introduction by Lee Child   ix

THE FOURTEENTH JUROR *by Twist Phelan*   3

LOST AND FOUND *by Zoë Sharp*   20

THE MOTHER *by Alafair Burke*   29

BLIND JUSTICE *by Jim Fusilli*   50

THE CONSUMERS *by Dennis Lehane*   61

MOONSHINER'S LAMENT *by Rick McMahan*   80

RIVER SECRET *by Anne Swardson*   104

HOT SUGAR BLUES *by Steve Liskow*   119

THE FINAL BALLOT *by Brendan DuBois*   133

AFRICA ALWAYS NEEDS GUNS *by Michael Niemann*   156

THE UNREMARKABLE HEART *by Karin Slaughter*   177

IT AIN'T RIGHT *by Michelle Gagnon*   213

CONTENTS

SILENT JUSTICE *by C. E. Lawrence* 217

EVEN A BLIND MAN *by Darrell James* 240

THE GENERAL *by Janice Law* 262

A FINE MIST OF BLOOD *by Michael Connelly* 276

LEVERAGE *by Mike Cooper* 296

THE HOTLINE *by Dreda Say Mitchell* 318

BLOOD AND SUNSHINE *by Adam Meyer* 337

IN PERSONA CHRISTI *by Orest Stelmach* 354

THE HOLLYWOOD I REMEMBER *by Lee Child* 372

About the Authors 379

Copyrights 385

INTRODUCTION

Editing this anthology was a lot of fun—not least because Mystery Writers of America's invaluable and irreplaceable publications guy, Barry Zeman, did all the hard work. All I had to do was pick ten invitees. And write a story. And then later on read the ten winning stories chosen by MWA's blind-submission process. Piece of cake. Apart from writing my own story, that is, which I always find hard, but that's why picking the invitees was so much fun—I love watching something difficult being done really well, by experts.

It was like playing fantasy baseball—who did I want on the field? And just as Major League Baseball has rich seams of talent to choose from, so does Mystery Writers of America. I could have filled ten anthologies. Or twenty. But I had to start somewhere—and it turned out that I already had, years ago, actually, when I taught a class at a mystery writers' conference in California. One of the after-hours activities was a group reading around a fireplace in the motel. A bit too kumbaya for me, frankly, but I went anyway, and the first story was by a young woman called Michelle Gagnon. It was superb, and it stayed with me through the intervening years. So I e-mailed her about using it for this anthology—more in hope than in expectation, because it was such a great story, I was sure it had been snapped up long ago. But no—it was still available. Never published, amazingly. It is now.

One down.

Then I had to have Brendan DuBois. He's a fine novelist but easily the best short-story writer of his generation. He just cranks them out, one after the other, like he's casting gold ingots. Very annoying. He said yes.

Two down.

And I had Twist Phelan on my radar. She's a real woman of mystery—sometimes lives on a yacht, sometimes lives in Switzerland, knows about oil and banks and money—and she had just won the International Thriller Writers' award for best short story. I thought, *I'll have a bit of that.* She said okay.

Three down.

Then there was the overtalented but undersung Jim Fusilli. He wrote two great New York novels that I really loved, and then four more just as good, and he's the rock music critic for the *Wall Street Journal.* We make lists together, like the top three bands most dependent on their drummers for their sound. (Led Zeppelin, the Who, and the Beatles, obviously.)

I asked; he said yes.

Four down.

And then, purely by chance, in the course of a conversation Karin Slaughter told me she'd just finished the nastiest story she'd ever written. Which had to be something, right? With Karin? I didn't ask. I just told her.

Five down.

Alafair Burke was next. I've followed her novels from the very beginning and loved them all. Then she went and wrote a terrific story for Michael Connelly's MWA anthology a few years ago. I thought, *Hey, she did it for him, she can do it for me.* I asked. She said yes.

Six down.

Then, because I'm a transatlantic person, I thought about a couple of great writers from the old country. First up: Dreda Say Mitchell. She's five novels into a terrific career, and I find her narrative voice completely fresh and utterly addictive. I asked; she said yes.

Seven down.

Then, Zoë Sharp. If I were a woman, I'd be Zoë. If Jack Reacher were a woman, he'd be Zoë's main character, Charlie Fox. A natural fit. I asked; she said yes.

Eight down.

Two spots left.

I thought: *Let's complete the lineup with a couple of heavy hitters.* I waited until both of my targets were drunk and happy at the Edgars, and I asked. Michael Connelly first. A busy guy, but a nice guy. He blinked. He said yes.

Nine down.

Then I turned to Dennis Lehane. Equally busy guy—he'd just had a kid. But equally nice too. He blinked. Twice. But he said yes.

Bingo.

So then it was about sharpening my editorial blue pencil and waiting for their stories to show up. They did, but I didn't need the pencil. I think there was a spelling mistake in there somewhere, but authors like these don't need help. So then it was about waiting for the MWA winning stories to arrive.

The way it works is that any paid-up MWA member can submit a story; the author's name is replaced with a code number, so the judges read each story blind. The selection panel evaluates them all and chooses the ten best. The panel for this anthology was Heather Graham, Tom Cook, David Walker, Joe Trigoboff, and Brendan DuBois (pulling double duty, which was good of him—he could have written another nine or ten stories, probably, in the time it took). I thank them all for their hard work, and for their excellent judgment—the ten they came up with are first-class, and when the numbers were matched to the names, it turned out we had an interesting bunch of people.

Ladies first: Anne Swardson submitted from Paris, where she's been living for fifteen years as a heavy-duty financial journalist. Tough gig, but hey, someone's got to do it. C. E. Lawrence is a multitalented New Yorker—writer, performer, poet, composer, and prize-winning playwright. Quite irritating. Janice Law is already an Edgar-nominated short-story writer (but the panel didn't know that—remember the code numbers). She's had stories published all over the place, so it's no surprise she made the top ten.

And the men: Rick McMahan is a special agent with the Department of Justice, so he walks the walk, and naturally he's also published here and there. Adam Meyer is an accomplished movie and TV writer and novelist and short-story writer who comes from New York but lives in DC. Michael Niemann is a German guy who lives in Oregon and is mostly a nonfiction writer specializing in African and global issues. Orest Stelmach is a thriller writer from the Northeast. He's fluent in four languages, which is four more than me on an average day. Darrell James lives in California and Arizona and is a multipublished and award-winning short-story writer, and also a debut novelist. Steve Liskow lives in Connecticut and is also a published novelist and short-story writer. And finally, Mike Cooper is a former financial guy from the Boston area whose stories have won a Shamus Award and been selected for *The Best American Mystery Stories* annual anthology.

So, ten high-quality invitees and ten high-quality competition winners, plus me. We all got the same brief: Write about vengeance, revenge, getting even, maybe doing a bad thing for a good reason. Or a bad reason. It was a loose specification; a tighter one would have been ignored anyway. Writers are like that. Their imaginations run along unique and uncontrollable paths, as you will see. Or maybe as you've already seen. I know some people read anthologies back to front. If you're one of them, thanks for reading. If you're not, I hope you enjoy what follows.

Lee Child
New York

MYSTERY WRITERS OF AMERICA
Presents

VENGEANCE

THE FOURTEENTH JUROR

BY TWIST PHELAN

Thi two detectives stood in the reception area of the judge's chambers on the fifth floor of the county courthouse. Ebanks made the introductions.

"We have an appointment to see the judge," he said.

The secretary smiled at them. She was a discreetly elegant woman with assisted blond hair and not too much pink lipstick.

"His Honor is expecting you," she said. "He shouldn't be too much longer. He's just finishing up a JNOV hearing."

Ebanks had to cough.

"May I get you something to drink?" the secretary asked.

Ebanks cleared his throat. "No, thank you," he said.

"Coffee would be good," Martinez said.

Ebanks was pinning his hopes on Martinez. The guy was no genius, but once he got an idea in his head, he was relentless. If Ebanks could get him pointed in the right direction on this case, the rookie's doggedness would pay off even after Ebanks retired next month.

Ebanks wasn't looking forward to turning in his shield. Some retired cops spent their days fishing or golfing or motor-homing to Arizona in the winter, but Ebanks didn't own a motor home or play golf. He did like to fish, but he wouldn't be getting up to the lake much. He'd be staying put in the house he'd grown up in. He and his wife lived there now.

The two cops sat down on a long sofa. An abstract painting hung on the wall facing them, its vivid reds and bright oranges warming the room. Martinez ran a hand along the plump leather arm of the sofa. "Nice."

Ebanks glanced around. Smooth parquetry floors gleamed with wax. The government-issue fluorescent overhead fixtures had been replaced with incandescent models. Magazines—current issues only—were lined up equidistant from the edges of the cherry coffee table. The lone plant, a ficus tree, had been trimmed into perfect symmetry, its leaves polished to a glossy green.

"Hmmm," he said. The rookie was observant, but he usually drew the wrong conclusions.

"How's Sheila?" Martinez said.

"Sonia," Ebanks said. He didn't really mind the mistake. After four years, hardly anyone on the force bothered to ask anymore. "Better," he lied.

Just then, the door behind the secretary's desk opened. A woman and a man wearing suits walked out. The woman smoldered with unhappiness. The man bore the dazed grin of a lottery winner.

The justice system at work, Ebanks thought.

———

THE JUDGE STOOD to greet them as they entered his chambers. His lean, intense face was incised with deep vertical grooves. His body was long and angular. Metal-rimmed glasses were perched on his nose and disapproval was apparent in the set of his mouth, like the preacher in the Pentecostal church Ebanks had attended as a kid.

"Sorry to keep you men waiting," the judge said. "JNOVs are never easy. But it's something that has to be done."

"JNOV?" Martinez said. "What's that anyway?"

The judge shook his head solemnly. "Of course—you're from the criminal side. I wish I could do more work over there, but I go only when they need me to fill in. *JNOV* stands for Latin words that mean 'judgment notwithstanding the verdict.' If a jury comes back with a decision that's contrary to the evidence, the judge has a responsibility to reverse it. The two people you saw leaving were a plaintiff's attorney, who just lost a two-million-dollar punitive-damage award, and a very relieved defense counsel."

Ebanks massaged the bridge of his nose. Sonia hadn't done well last night. He'd barely gotten two hours' sleep.

"Too bad crim court judges can't do that," Martinez said. "Some of these juries come back with the most half-ass—" He stopped himself, cheeks reddening.

The judge smoothly stepped in. "What you're saying is that jurors are often dazzled by attorney antics or irrelevant issues and so they don't focus on the evidence."

"Yeah," Martinez said gratefully.

"As long as the Constitution says 'jury of our peers,' that's who decides our cases," the judge said, "but my fundamental duty is to see that justice is done. That female lawyer you saw ran rings around the defendant's man; she bewitched the jury with her short skirts and PowerPoint closing argument. I can't let that kind of thing stand. It's my duty as a judge, in civil court at least. It's my responsibility."

Ebanks noted the confident righteousness in the judge's

baritone voice. He looked around the office. The room was large enough to hold not only the judge's desk and leather swivel chair but four guest chairs and a loveseat. The judge indicated they should take a seat in the guest chairs. He chose the leather swivel one.

There was a tray of dry fly-tying tools on the credenza, with hooks, thread, hackle pliers and guards, scissors, whip finishers, and a vise all lined up in a precise row alongside small containers of feathers and what looked to Ebanks like white goat body hair, usually used for wings. Ebanks preferred Swiss straw.

The photos on the wall behind the desk showed various images of the judge: proudly displaying a shoulders-wide trout; standing beside his partners—all wearing dark suits and rep ties—in the law firm he'd headed before ascending to the bench; and sitting stiffly with his wife in a room furnished in Modern Hunting Lodge (log timbers, antler chandelier, Black Watch plaid on the chairs).

The mountain range visible through the window in the last photo told Ebanks the house was in the new development on the north shore of the lake. The environmentalists had screamed, but high-priced lawyering had won the day. A small gated community of million-dollar homes had been built in the remote area. Ebanks had once had a place near the lake, a decades-old A-frame.

He used to fish the lake in a sweet little eighteen-footer. Sometimes Sonia went with him. She'd pack thick sandwiches and iced tea in the cooler, and she'd bring a book. Wearing her floppy sun hat, she was content to read while he dropped his line. He'd sold the A-frame, his boat, and most of his gear when Sonia couldn't go with him anymore. All he had left from those times was the nice Sage fly rod Sonia had given him one birthday.

Ebanks studied the photo of the judge at his lake house. He

noted the judge's blond wife, the modern painting over the fireplace, the polished wood floors.

Class, Martinez would say.

Ebanks knew there was something else. The decor of the judge's chambers matched the interior of his house. The shade of blond on the judge's wife was nearly identical to the color of his secretary's hair. The coffee table was cherry. The flowers in the vases were all trimmed to the same height and were the same shade as the red accent pillows.

His Honor was a man who made sure everything was in order. Ebanks understood that.

The judge regarded the two detectives, his gaze direct. "How can I help you gentlemen?"

"We need to ask you a few questions about the Dolan case," Martinez said.

UNDER THE SPEEDY Trial Act, a criminal defendant has the right to go to trial within seventy days of his indictment or his initial court appearance, whichever comes first. If the trial doesn't begin within that period, the charges are dismissed.

Overworked defense attorneys usually ask for, and are readily given, extensions. But occasionally the system logjams, with too many trials and not enough judges to hear them. When that happens, the presiding judge requests that the civil bench jurists assist their criminal colleagues. Civil proceedings are delayed while judges used to hearing securities-fraud claims and divorces preside over robbery and assault trials instead.

This judge had been drafted for such a criminal proceeding two weeks ago. Kenny Dolan was charged with second-degree murder for allegedly stabbing his wife during a domestic dispute. The case had gotten some pretrial coverage in the local press—Dolan was a catcher on the resident minor league team with a real chance of moving up to the big leagues.

The evidence of Dolan's guilt seemed insurmountable—his fingerprints on the knife, blood spatter on his shoes, his 911 call that was more a confession than a plea for help—but in the middle of the trial, it was revealed that one of the cops assigned to the investigation, an old bull named Borosovsky, had been convicted of planting evidence in another case. Despite a vigorous closing by the prosecutor and absolutely no indication of police misconduct in Dolan's case, the taint couldn't be eradicated in some jurors' minds. After four days of deliberations, the jury had hung, nine to three in favor of conviction.

"Speaking off the record, I believe Mr. Dolan was guilty." The judge made a face. "Never underestimate the power of celebrity, no matter how minor."

"Too bad you couldn't've done one of those JN-whatevers," Martinez said.

"I assure you, I would have entered the order in a heartbeat," the judge said.

"The way it turned out…" Ebanks said.

"Justice was done," the judge said briskly.

After the jury failed to reach a verdict, the judge had dismissed them and concluded the trial. During his posttrial press conference, the prosecutor vowed to retry Dolan. He'd wanted Dolan returned to jail pending the filing of new charges. But the baseball player's lawyer had argued that his client should be released on bond, and the judge had agreed. It all became moot two days later when Dolan was discovered dead at his lake house. The coroner hadn't released his final report yet, but the blogosphere had reported the furnace in Dolan's house had been leaking carbon monoxide.

Ebanks looked over at the tray of fly-tying paraphernalia. The judge noticed.

"Do you fish, Detective?"

"Not so much anymore," Ebanks said.

"How can you live without it? I get up to the lake every weekend. You should've seen the rainbow I caught the day after the Dolan trial — it was at least a foot long."

"Hmmm," Ebanks said. "So you tie your own flies?"

"I do." The judge held up his finger to display a Band-Aid. "Although it has its hazards."

"Like everything else," Ebanks said. He checked his watch. "You know, we're not focusing on Kenny Dolan right now."

"I don't understand," the judge said.

Ebanks nodded at Martinez. The rookie said, "One of the trial jurors was killed."

"Oh?" the judge said. "Which one?"

Martinez looked toward Ebanks again, and the older detective nodded once more.

Martinez consulted his notebook.

"Eric Shadid. He didn't even make it to the hospital. The car that hit him was going pretty fast. Witnesses said it aimed right for him, didn't brake, and *bam!*"

The judge furrowed his brow in concentration. "Mr. Shadid was the foreman, wasn't he?"

"Right," Martinez said.

"When did this happen?" the judge said. "Why didn't I hear about it?"

"A day after the trial ended," Ebanks said. "It didn't make the news."

"I would have missed it anyway. I'm always at the lake house after a trial." He grimaced. "This time it was a damn good thing

I got up there so fast. There was a burst pipe in the laundry room. I fixed it myself—a foot of half-inch pipe, some solder, a propane torch, and about two hours of labor." He turned to Martinez. "So you think this hit-and-run is related to the Dolan trial?"

"Maybe," Martinez said. "At first we just figured Shadid was in the wrong place at the wrong time."

"What changed your mind?"

Martinez looked embarrassed. "That magazine writer called."

"Writer?" the judge said.

"Leonard Lunney. He's one of those true-crime guys. Said he was writing about the Dolan trial. He got a copy of the jury list and started calling 'em to see if they'd talk. When he found out Shadid thought Dolan was innocent from the get-go and then Shadid's killed in that hit-and-run..."

"Journalists are rightly skeptical of coincidence," the judge said.

"Police too," Ebanks said.

"I've read some of Mr. Lunney's pieces in *Vanity Fair*," the judge said. "It's his job to spin the suspicious into the sensational."

"According to Lunney, the first vote was eleven to one to convict," Martinez said. "Shadid was the holdout. He ended up getting two other jurors to go along with him."

"I've seen some heated deliberations," the judge said. "That one was among the most acrimonious. I could hear the shouting in my chambers. The bailiff had to break up a scuffle at one point."

"You catch what the fight was about?" Martinez said.

"From what I heard, a juror in favor of conviction accused Mr. Shadid of being blinded by Dolan's status as an athlete." The judge spread his hands. "Of course you'll talk to the rest of the panel."

Ebanks frowned. "You're thinking maybe a juror who argued with Shadid wanted to kill him because Shadid thought Dolan was innocent?"

The judge looked at Ebanks over the top of his glasses. "Remember Jack Ruby? People have done worse in the name of justice, especially when they have some tangential involvement in the situation."

"The thing is, we checked into that," Martinez said. "All the jurors had alibis for when the car hit Shadid."

"So if a juror isn't a suspect, I'm not sure how I can help you," the judge said.

"We'd like to ask you about Mrs. Dolan's family," Martinez said. "Specifically, her brothers."

————

THE PROSECUTOR, AS usual, had made a point of extolling the victim's virtues at trial. Tina Lucchese Dolan was a loving wife who supported her husband's baseball career, cheerfully moving from town to town as he worked his way up from Class-A to Double-A to Triple-A ball. She sang at church and did volunteer work.

Tina's only blemish was her maiden name. The Luccheses were a second-tier New Jersey crime family. Dolan's lawyers, trying to create reasonable doubt, made some noise about Tina's death being payback for a sanitation-contract dispute, but that's all it was—noise. They didn't have any evidence to back up their claims, only innuendo, largely in the form of Tina's two brothers, who attended the trial every day. They sat in the first row behind the defense table and glared daggers at Kenny Dolan's back, tough guys stuffed like sausages into shiny suits. No one would sit next to them.

The judge blinked. "You think a *Lucchese* killed Mr. Shadid?"

"We talked to the Jersey police. The Luccheses really are pretty Old World when it comes to justice." Martinez leaned back in his chair and hooked his thumbs behind his belt. "Make that more like Old Testament. You should see their rap sheets."

"I'm not surprised," the judge said.

"Shadid didn't exactly keep his views to himself," Martinez said. "Right after the trial he told a blogger the police had planted evidence to frame Dolan. So when the prosecutor said he was going to retry Dolan, we think maybe the Luccheses killed Shadid."

A hung jury didn't mean a defendant walked. The prosecutor could try the defendant again, either immediately or after collecting more evidence, as long as the statute of limitations hadn't run out.

"But why now?" the judge said. "The trial's over. Mr. Shadid won't be a member of the new panel."

"To send a message to the next jury," Martinez said.

"You're saying the Luccheses killed Mr. Shadid to intimidate prospective jurors into voting for conviction at the second trial?" The judge steepled his fingers. "I don't know. Sounds a little far-fetched to me," he said.

"Fits the Luccheses' m.o.," Martinez said. "Besides, we're kinda running out of suspects. We've talked to Shadid's family, friends, business associates, enemies." He ticked them off on his fingers. "Everybody's got an alibi."

"What about Dolan?" the judge said.

"Dolan was already dead," Ebanks said.

"No," the judge said. "The Luccheses. If they were going to kill someone, I would have thought it'd be Dolan."

Police work was a lot like fishing. You stuck your best fly on your hook and waited for the hungry trout to come along and strike. The fish thinks he's the predator, but he's really the prey.

Sometimes an even bigger fish comes along and snags your catch right off the hook before you can reel it in.

"Funny you should say that," Ebanks said. "Because we just got the word that Dolan's death was no accident."

The judge looked surprised. Martinez looked confused.

At the press scrum on the courthouse steps, Dolan had expressed his faith in the justice system, refused to answer any questions, and announced he was heading for his lake house to chill. He then drove off in his black SUV.

When he didn't show for a meeting the next day, his lawyer was annoyed. Later that afternoon, when he couldn't reach Dolan by cell phone, the lawyer got worried. The next day, the lawyer called the cops. Dolan's body was found in his bed. He had died of asphyxiation.

"The furnace at the house didn't malfunction," Ebanks said. "Someone tampered with the heat exchanger and disabled the CO detectors. Dolan was murdered."

Now Martinez looked totally stunned. Ebanks shot him a look, and the rookie recovered his poker face.

After a trout bites, you have to set your hook. You can't allow any slack in your line, but you have to make sure not to pull too hard. Otherwise the fish can throw the hook.

"Let's talk some more about Tina's brothers," Ebanks said to the judge.

He asked a few questions, then let Martinez take over. The rookie led the judge through his prepared queries on how the Lucchese boys had behaved during the trial. Ebanks paid little attention to the questions or the answers. He spent the time reminiscing about past trips to the lake. Romance novels and cookbooks—that was what Sonia liked to read. He wondered where her sun hat was now.

After five minutes or so, Martinez closed his notebook.

The judge said, "Do you have any other suspects?"

Ebanks said, "We'll be working hard on that."

"I don't pretend to know your job…" The judge hesitated.

"It's okay," Ebanks said. "What's on your mind?"

"Well," the judge said. "Have you considered Mrs. Batista?"

"The pitcher's wife?" Martinez said. "Why would—"

Ebanks broke in. "What's your theory?"

————

CRIMINAL DEFENSE ATTORNEYS know it isn't enough to say their clients didn't do it. The jury always wants an alternative suspect for the crime, and if one suspect is good, two are better. In addition to offering the Luccheses' mob enemies, the Dolan defense team served up Nikki Batista, wife of Dolan's best friend on the team.

"The evidence will show Kenny and Nikki Batista were having an affair," Dolan's attorney announced in his opening. The "evidence" included several months of late-night phone calls and lunch meetings at out-of-the-way restaurants, but no hotel bills or photos of the tabloid variety. Claiming Dolan broke off the affair because he'd come to realize how much he loved his wife, the defense trotted out the "hell hath no fury/scorned woman" maxim and asserted that Mrs. Batista had no alibi for the time of the murder.

The prosecutor called a tearful Nikki to the stand to deny the affair, and to explain that the clandestine meetings and phone calls between Dolan and Nikki were to organize a surprise birthday party for Tina Dolan. As for the night of Tina's murder, Nikki said she'd driven up to the lake area to visit a friend, who turned out not be home. A PhotoCop shot dug up by the prosecution proved that she'd been doing fifteen over the limit while Tina was being killed.

"I didn't believe that birthday-party story," the judge said. "I think Dolan was having an affair with Nikki Batista. With his wife gone, Nikki expected to be the next Mrs. Dolan, but Dolan dumped her. Hell indeed hath no fury. Mrs. Batista knew Dolan was going to his lake house. She went there too, and rigged his death."

"There's only one problem with pointing the finger at Mrs. Batista," Ebanks said. "We did the background investigation for the prosecutor. Turns out she *was* having an affair, but not with Kenny Dolan. Apparently third basemen are more her type. They were in bed together fifty miles north. That explains the PhotoCop shot."

The judge slowly shook his head. "I must say, my brethren on the criminal bench have a challenging time sorting the sinners from the innocents."

Ebanks slapped the tops of his thighs. "Well, that's it, I guess. Sorry to have taken up so much of your time."

"I'm always happy to do whatever I can in pursuit of justice," the judge said. "Let me ask you this: What about the forensics? Tire tracks, paint transfer..." The judge permitted himself a smile. "My wife is a fan of those television shows," he said. "I suppose some of it has rubbed off."

Ebanks imagined the judge and his pretty blond wife in a large, tastefully decorated room, sitting in nice chairs like the ones he and Martinez were sitting in, watching TV. Sonia and he used to watch old movies every Friday night. He'd make popcorn and they'd curl up on the old plaid couch together. Sonia couldn't watch TV anymore. Fast-changing images triggered the seizures.

"Too bad we don't have a lab like the one on *CSI,*" Martinez said. "But we need a lot more big-city crime before that happens. Right now, we have to process the crime scenes ourselves. If we want something tested for prints or DNA, we ship it off to the FBI."

"We better get going," Ebanks said. He stood, and Martinez followed his lead. The judge pushed his long frame out of the swivel chair.

While his partner shook hands with the judge, Ebanks bent over to tie his shoe. In the wastebasket beside the tray of flies, a partially constructed Parachute Adams lay on top of a piece of Kleenex. Both the fly and the Kleenex were stained with what looked like blood.

Lucky break, Ebanks thought. He hadn't expected to find something literally soaked with DNA.

Martinez and the judge had walked over to the wall, where the judge was pointing to one of the photos. After making sure they weren't paying attention, Ebanks reached into the wastebasket and scooped up the bloody fly and the Kleenex. He slipped them into his pocket and straightened up.

The judge showed them into the reception area. The secretary was on the phone. She waved and smiled at them.

"Let's catch some lunch," Ebanks said, "but first I want to ask her something."

The secretary finished her call. "May I help you?" she said.

"About those JNOVs," Ebanks said. "Aren't they usually kinda rare?"

The secretary nodded. "They are, except for with this judge. You could almost say he's famous for it — some of the lawyers call him the 'thirteenth juror.' He takes his work very seriously. He always says if the jurors don't do justice, it's up to him."

"The thirteenth juror," Ebanks repeated. "Hmmm."

He and Martinez got into the elevator. As the mahogany-paneled box descended, Ebanks said, "Well, that was a bust. We didn't learn anything we didn't already know about Shadid."

"How'd you know about Dolan being a homicide?" Martinez said.

"I got a text when we were waiting for the judge," Ebanks said. "I thought you did too."

"Nope. But hey, no problemo." A few seconds later, Martinez said, "You know, that got me thinking about some of the stuff the judge said."

Ebanks kept his eyes on the numbers over the door. They lit up as the car passed the floors. "Such as?"

"Such as when you told him Dolan was murdered, he was pretty quick to finger Mrs. Batista, and when that didn't pan out, he tried to hand us the Luccheses."

Ebanks shrugged. "You heard him. He was just playing at *CSI* or *Law & Order.*"

"Maybe, but did you notice that his house is on that same lake as Dolan's?"

"So? I used to have a place near there too."

"Yeah, but the judge was at his house when Dolan was killed."

Ebanks folded his arms across his chest and made an effort to look thoughtful. "You know, you're right."

The elevator doors opened on the ground floor. The two detectives walked across the lobby. The rookie's thick eyebrows scrunched together whenever he was thinking something through. They were like that now.

"We had it backward," Martinez said. He pushed forcefully through the revolving door at the courthouse entrance, and Ebanks followed him. When they were out on the street, Martinez said, "We thought Shadid was murdered and what happened to Dolan was an accident."

"It does look like Shadid was just in the wrong place at the wrong time," Ebanks said.

"You mean, it was only a coincidence?"

"Hmm," Ebanks said. He nodded at the hot-dog cart on the corner. "Feel like a brat?"

"As long as they have mustard and kraut," Martinez said.

The two detectives walked down the sidewalk.

"You know, I think the judge is as Old World as the Luccheses," Martinez said. "All that JNOV stuff. What if he did let Dolan out on bail so he could, you know..."

Ebanks blew out a dismissive breath. "What the judge said about justice being done was just a joke."

"He strike you as the joker type? All I'm saying is, anyone who can fix a busted pipe would know how to rig a furnace."

Ebanks rolled his eyes. "You really think the judge killed Dolan?"

Martinez slowed to a stop in the middle of the sidewalk, forcing the other pedestrians to flow around him like water around a rock. He turned and stared back at the courthouse.

"Yeah, I do. After lunch, let's start at Dolan's place at the lake. I'd like to look around some more."

"Fine by me," Ebanks said. "But I think you're wasting your time."

"I don't," Martinez said.

The rookie's face expressed the joyful anticipation of a fisherman who'd just snagged a big fish... or of a big fish who'd just swallowed a hand-tied fly. Peace settled into Ebanks's soul, not unlike what he used to feel when he and Sonia were in his boat on the lake.

They ordered their brats, enjoying the thin warmth of the sun while the vendor assembled them. The scent of cut grass and freshly turned earth wafted on the breeze. Spring had finally arrived.

Ebanks had been a little worried that the judge might recognize him from Sonia's trial, although it had been four years ago. He remembered their day in court, even if the judge didn't. The jury came back after two hours with a seven-figure verdict against the trucking company whose driver had been amped on speed when he broadsided Sonia's car. The money would have paid for the experimental treatment the insurance company refused to cover. Ebanks still couldn't figure out what their lawyer, a chubby little bald guy in a bargain-basement suit, had done to offend the judge's sense of order and justice. Whatever it was, the JNOV killed their chance at the miracle cure. Now his wife was serving a life sentence in a prison of pain, and the judge was still spending every weekend at his lake house.

Ebanks chewed his hot dog and thought about the half-finished Parachute Adams in his pocket. He knew exactly where he'd leave it when they went back to Dolan's place. There'd be no stopping Martinez once he found it.

The only time he'd been back to the lake since Sonia's trial was the night the Dolan jury hung. Maybe after his retirement was official, he'd take his Sage rod up there and see if the trout were biting.

LOST AND FOUND

BY ZOË SHARP

H e waits. No hardship there—he's waited half his life. But now, tonight, finally you provide him with that perfect moment.

The one he's been waiting for.

In the alley, in the dark, just the distant glitter of neon off wet concrete. And he's so scared he can hardly grip the knife. But anger drives him. Anger closes his shaking fingers around it, flesh on bone.

He tries not to know what the blade will do.

But he knows. He's seen it too many times. He remembers them only as a slur of violence, swirled with a lingering despair.

And he can't remember a time before you. A time when he was innocent, trusting. You taught him misery and guilt, and he's carried both through all seasons since. A burden with no respite.

Tonight, he hopes for respite.

Tonight, he hopes finally for peace.

There should be lights in the alley, but he's taken care of them. Something else you taught him—not to let anyone see.

It's fitting you should die here in the dark, amid the rats and the filth and the garbage. You are what they are—the detritus of life.

And he is what you made him.

He hopes you're proud.

But right now he just hopes you're ready. That he's ready. He's dreamed of this so often down the years between then and now that he feels suddenly unprepared, naked in the dark.

Shivering, he's a seven-year-old boy again, with all the majesty fresh ripped out of him, howling as he's punished for truth, punished for faith.

Punished for believing, when you told him you would take very special care of him indeed.

He's punished himself and those around him ever since. Lived a life stripped to base essentials, where "refinement" means cut with stuff that's only going to kill you slow.

Lost.

And now he's found you again, and he thinks, if he does this right, he may find himself again too.

He hears the footsteps, familiar even loaded by the drag and stagger of the years. He folds his hand tighter around the knife, takes in the sodden air, feels the pulse-beat in his fingertips.

Feels alive.

It's a privilege only one of you can share.

Attuned, he sees your figure sway into the open mouth of the alley, hesitating at the unexpected gloom. A stumble, a smothered curse, but he knows you won't play it safe. You never have. Going the longer way around will take time, and you're loath to be away from your latest pet project, whoever that might be.

He wonders if he will be in time to save them—not from what's been but from what's to come—even as he steps out of the recess, a wraith in the shadows, the knife unsheathed now and eager for the bite.

At the last moment you hear his lunge of breath and you begin to turn. Too slow.

He is on you, fast with the lust of it, strong with the manifestation of his own fear. His hand grasps your forehead, tilting your head back for the sacrifice. Is it instinct that tries to force your chin under, or do you know what's coming?

Too slow.

He can smell soap overlaying sweat and tobacco, the garlic of your last meal. Garlic that failed to keep this vampire at bay.

The knife, sharp as a butcher's blade, makes a first pass across your stringy throat. It slips so easily through the skin that for a moment he almost believes you are the demon of his childhood nightmares, to be slain by no mortal hand.

Then he remembers a laughing boast—that the first cut is for free.

The second cut, though, is all for himself.

He goes in deep, hacks blind through muscle, tube, and sinew, glances across bone. The blood that gushes outward now is hot, so hot he can almost hear it sizzle.

Your legs run out on you. Shock puts you down and sheer disbelief keeps you there. He steps back, hollowed out by the skill, watches your eyes as the realization finally sets in. *Your heart still pumps but you are dead, even if you don't know it yet.*

He expected a fierce joy. He feels only silence.

He turns his back, not waiting for your feeble struggles to subside, and walks away. At the mouth of the alley he drops the knife into a drain, and walks away.

The rain starts up again, like it's been waiting, like it's been holding its breath.

———

THE RAIN CLEANSES him. His feet take him past the gang tags, the articulation of alienation that forms the melody of his daily life, to the crumbling church. Not the same church, but another very like it. They have all become one to him — a place of undue reverence. A place where he was found and lost, and maybe found again.

A penance. And now a place of twisted sanctuary.

Approaching the altar, he makes jerky obeisance, slides into the second row. The wood is polished smooth by long passage of the tired and the hopeful. And the building smells of incense and velvet, wax dripped on silver, and the pages of old books lined with dusty words.

Still damp from the rain, he finds no warmth here.

Still restless from the act, he finds no comfort.

He wonders if he was expecting to.

You first came upon him sitting alone like this, all those years ago, scuffed and crying, pockets emptied and pride stolen. You comforted him then. He remembers a pathetic gratitude. *Salvation.*

The blood rises fast in him. His hands are clasped as if for prayer, the knuckles straining to release a plethora of fury and regret.

There was no release then. He had nowhere to take it other than the river, was so close to letting go when strangers wrestled him, a child demented, from the railing's edge. They were shocked at his vehemence, his determination.

They brought him back to you.

And you smiled as you told him suicide was the gravest sin. That he would go straight to the depths of hell, where he would be raped by every demon up to Lucifer himself.

So he chose to live rather than die, although it seemed to him that there was little to choose between one and the other.

———

LYING JUMBLED IN the alley, the truth of what's done finally descends on you, soft as snow.

You see the lights of passing cars, buttoned tight, oblivious. Flashes of colored sound made distant by the glass wall of your dysphonia. Out of reach. Out of touch.

You are nearly out of time.

But still you grip to the coattails of life with the stubborn savagery that is your nature. Logic tells you that you should already be dead, that somehow the blade has missed the vital vessels. You have gotten away with too much to believe you will not get away with this, if you want it badly enough.

After all, by will and nerve you have survived exposure, excoriation, excommunication.

Someone will come.

A stranger, a Samaritan. Someone who doesn't know you well enough to step over your body and move along through.

If he *doesn't come back to finish you first.*

Only a fatalist would believe this is some random act of violence, but not knowing *who* scratches at the back of your mind. There have been too many likely candidates to narrow it down.

You are troubled that he did not speak. You expected the bitter spill of self-righteous self-pity. Of blame.

See what you made me do, old man.

Killing you without triumph is pointless.

But the face...you don't remember the face. You are not good with the faces of men, although it's different with the boys. Unformed and mobile, fresh. You have never forgotten one of your boys.

Your special boys.

It tore your heart out to have them taken away from you. To be taken away from them. But they underestimated the number, and few came forward to be counted.

They called it shame.

You call it love.

Maybe that is the reason you are lying here, bleeding out into a rain-drummed puddle smeared with oil, in an alley, in the dark, alone.

Maybe he loves you too much to see you with anyone else.

———

HE IS ON his knees when the cops come for him. They shuffle into the church snapping the rain from their topcoats, muting radio traffic, hats awkward between their fingers. Like they've seen too much to believe in the solace of this place. Like they're embarrassed by their own lack of devotion.

For a moment panic clenches in him and he teeters on the cusp of relief and outright despair. He should have anticipated this.

He rises, crosses himself—a reflex of muscle memory—and turns to them with empty hands.

The cops don't need to speak. Their faces speak for them. It is not the first time they have come for him like this. Not here. He doesn't stop long enough to pull on a coat before they hustle him out, through the slanted rain to the black-and-white angled by the curb, lights still turning lazily.

The ride is short. The cops exchange muttered words in the front seat. He reads questions in their gaze reflected from glass and mirrors but has nothing to say. This is the place of his choosing, and they cannot understand the choice.

He stares out through the streaked side window at the passing night, at the tawdry glitz of hidden desperation.

The rain comes down with relentless fervor. Water begins to

pile up in the gutters, flash-flooding debris toward the storm drains. *If only sins were as easily swept clean away.*

The car slews to a halt beside two others just outside the crime tape. The lights zigzag in and out of sync with more urgency than the men around them.

Hope plucks at him.

The cops step out; one opens his door. They lift the tape to duck inside the perimeter, though there is nobody to keep at bay. Violence is too common here to draw a crowd in this rain.

A detective intercepts them with a doubtful glance, hunched into the weather. He has a day's tired stubble above his collar, and a tired suit beneath his overcoat.

"This him?"

One of the cops nods. "All yours."

"Let's go." The detective steps back with a spread arm, an open invitation tinged with mocking—for what he is, for what he represents.

"Wallet was still in the vic's hip pocket—how we knew he was one of yours," the detective says as they walk toward the alley. "But we would have made him sooner or later."

The detective waits for a response, for a simple curiosity that's not forthcoming.

"I do what needs to be done."

The detective shrugs. "Sure you do. For the sinners as much as the saints, huh?"

"That's always been the way of it."

"Sure." The detective's face bulges, bones pressing against his skin as if engorged. "This guy's a convicted pederast. He fucks boys—kids. The younger the better. And he was a priest when they sent him down. A goddamn priest."

"He'll be judged."

They reach the throat of the alley and the detective stops, as if to go farther will leave him open to contamination.

"Well, I'd say he's had his earthly judgment." And if the voice is ice, the eyes are fire. "All that's left for him is the fucking divine."

———

ADRIFT IN YOUR own circle of confusion, you catch only snatches of words you recognize but can no longer comprehend.

"...amazed he's lasted this long..."

"...nothing more we can do..."

"...had it coming..."

And you're colder than the sea, locked inside a faltering body and a breaking mind, locked into a tumult of regret and the terror of going to meet a vengeful Maker.

The medics rise, retreat, leaving the clutter of their futile effort strewn around you.

You want to cry for them not to leave you, not to let you die alone, but you lie muted by the blade, stilled by the approaching darkness. Darker than the alley, darker than the earth. The devil prowls the shadows, waiting without tolerance, watching with lascivious eyes. Soon he will engulf you, rip apart your body even as your last breath decays, and devour a soul already rotten.

Unless...

"...he's here..."

Your eyes flutter closed.

Thank God.

It takes effort to open them again, to see the priest approaching. The medics have moved back a respectful distance, clustering with the detective at the mouth of the alley, superfluous. The priest bends over you.

You prepare yourself for Penance, Anointing, Viaticum. He'll hear no spoken confession from your lips, but absolution assuming contrition surely must be granted.

You prepare yourself for a ritual worn with consoling familiarity. One you carried out often enough, back in a former life.

But as the priest bends low, you catch sight of his face, and this man's face you *do* remember, from behind the blade all the way back to his boyhood.

He was a special boy, all right.

Your first temptation on the path of sin.

And now your last.

The fear writhes in you, but he touches your forehead with a gentle finger and when he speaks, his voice is gentle too.

"God, the Father of mercies, through the death and resurrection of His Son, has reconciled the world to Himself and sent the Holy Spirit among us for the forgiveness of sins; through the ministry of the Church may God give you pardon and peace..."

Impatient, your mind runs on ahead:

...and I absolve you from your sins in the name of the Father, and of the Son, and of the Holy Spirit.

But the expectation is not fulfilled. The essential words do not follow.

Your eyes seek his, frantic, pleading. The devil growls at your shoulder, taking shape out of the umbra, exulting as he solidifies. Closer. You feel his talons pluck at your vision, begin to pull the fetid shroud across your eyes. You are sinking.

Quickly! Finish it!

The priest bends closer still, his voice a whisper in your closing ear.

"You found me, and I was lost. Now *you* are lost, because *I* found you..."

THE MOTHER

BY ALAFAIR BURKE

Diane Light closed the file folder and added it to the heap on her desk. At nearly a foot high, the pile began to wobble. She rested her forearm on top of the tower to hold it steady.

She resisted the urge to separate that last file from the rest. It was special. It deserved to be carried into court on its own.

"Jesus, I thought *I* was late." Diane heard harried footsteps rush past her office door, her coworker's generic voice fading as he moved farther down the hallway. "Stone's a stickler about time, you know."

She knew.

She stole a glance at her watch as she scooped the stack of files against her chest. Two minutes until Stone would be seated at his bench, tapping the face of his own watch, eager for the deputy district attorney to start calling cases.

Judge Stone was a stickler for promptness, but he was also a stickler for facts. She'd memorized the contents of Kiley's file, from start to finish.

———

Two hours in, Stone finally commented on the time. "Nice job this morning, Miss Light. You could teach your colleagues a thing or two about docket management."

Her previously foot-high pile was now down to two inches. Three more cases. Two more before Kiley's. And still an hour to go before Stone's hardwired lunch alarm would sound. The strategy was working.

She rushed through the next two cases. They were easy ones: Mothers complying with conditions. Social workers report progress and recommend continued monitoring and treatment. No request for immediate disposition, Your Honor.

Forty-five minutes to go, and only one more file. *The* file. Kiley's file. She called the case number and watched Kiley's father approach the opposition table with his court-appointed counsel. Kiley's assigned guardian ad litem stood between the two lawyers.

"Your Honor, you may recall this case. The State originally moved to terminate parental rights ten months ago, after police learned the child had been sold sexually by her parents. She was only twenty-two months old at the time." Twenty-two months sounded much younger than two years old. Somehow it sounded even more babylike than a year and a half.

"Objection." It came from the dad's attorney, Lisa Hobbins.

Hobbins pretended to care about her clients, but Diane knew for a fact that last Cinco de Mayo, after too many tequila shots at Veritable Quandary, Hobbins had puked her guts out in the gutter of First Avenue, crying about the scumbag parents she represents. "Miss Light is well aware that only the mother was convicted of those charges," Hobbins said now. "My client was estranged from his wife at the time the crimes occurred. He wanted to get clean. She didn't. He wouldn't have left Kiley with his wife if he'd known—"

"We dispute all of that, Your Honor. A grand jury indicted the father as well after finding probable cause for his involvement. The defendant was acquitted at trial after his wife testified about her sole responsibility, but the State's position is that his wife, a battered woman and not estranged from her husband at all, protected Mr. Chance—"

Judge Stone held up a hand to cut her off. "The State lost at trial, Miss Light. The jury must have rejected your theory."

"But this is a separate case, Your Honor. As an independent finder of fact, you can make a fresh assessment—"

"So where are we now?" He didn't try to mask the long glance at his watch.

"The mother has stipulated to a termination of parental rights, but Mr. Chance has not. The case has been continued seven times over the past ten months. At the third hearing, Judge Parker found grounds for termination but wanted assurances that Kiley would have a permanent home. The State objected to the condition and has continued to object since, but the case has been set over at each subsequent hearing pending further monitoring of the situation and while Kiley's foster mother, Janice Miller, decided whether to enter into a legal adoption."

Stone was rifling through the court's file, still trying to understand the procedural posture. She didn't want him thinking about continuances, hearings, and orders held at bay. She needed him to care about Kiley. That little girl was not just a number. She was not just the last case of the day. Maybe Diane should have called the case first. All that work. All that planning. And now she was blowing it.

"To cut to the chase, Your Honor"—she knew that was Stone's favorite phrase—"Kiley was not an easy child to place.

Adoptive parents are reluctant to take on children who have been through the kind of trauma Kiley experienced. In addition to having been subjected to repeated molestations, she was born drug affected. At the time of her parents' arrest, she was under-nourished and suffering from PTSD. But after nearly a year as a foster parent to Kiley, Miss Miller was sufficiently comfortable with Kiley's physical and emotional progress. This was to be a hearing to finalize the termination of Mr. Chance's parental rights with a simultaneous adoption by Miss Miller."

"But?"

"But Miss Miller was struck and killed by a drunk driver two nights ago as she was jogging across Powell Boulevard." Judge Stone made a *tsk* sound. "The State is still seeking termination of parental rights. Although counsel notes that Mr. Chance was acquitted, it cannot be ignored that one of the men who was paying for sexual contact with the child was a former cellmate of Mr. Chance. At Mr. Chance's trial, that man testified that—"

Hobbins interjected on her client's behalf. "Your Honor, that man was a child rapist who testified in exchange for leniency. Given how child abusers are treated in prison, he would have said anything to get in the prosecutor's good graces."

The man's name was Trevor Williams. His status as a convicted felon was the primary reason the State's criminal case had come together. A neighbor in the Chances' apartment building called the police after she saw blood on a child's pair of pants in the communal laundry room. A fan of *CSI,* she went so far as to seize the evidence and seal it in a Ziploc bag. Police found not only blood but also seminal fluid. A search warrant executed at the Chances' home turned up a set of pajamas with a different man's fluids. Thanks to the state's DNA data bank for convicts, they linked the second sample to Williams.

Cutting a deal with that pedophile was the hardest bargain

Diane had ever struck. They might never identify the other man—or men—to whom Kiley was traded off, but they had Williams, and Williams was willing to give them both of the parents. It was the only way to protect the girl in the long run.

Judge Stone wasn't interested in the details of Williams's testimony, however. He raised an impatient palm again. "I'm not going to relitigate the criminal case here, ladies. You should both know that the standard is the best interests of the child."

And how the hell was it in Kiley's best interests to live with a man who sold her as a two-year-old to support his crack habit?

Diane knew her argument would only go downhill from there. The State had not yet secured a new foster placement for Kiley. She was staying in a group home, the youngest of all the children there.

Then it was Hobbins's turn. The conviction of Chance's wife and initiation of TPR hearings had been the wake-up call the father needed, she said. After some initial relapses, he had been clean for five months. He still denied all knowledge of his wife's crimes, but he had been willing to let Kiley go with Janice Miller because the woman had been there for his daughter when he had not. But now Miller was gone, and he was finally in a position to parent.

"Miss Hobbins, does your client live in a residence suitable for the child to be there now?"

Now?

"Yes, Your Honor. He has a private apartment with subsidization through Section Eight. It is a one-bedroom; Kiley would have the bedroom, and he would sleep in the living room. Were he granted custodial status, he would qualify for additional subsidization. He has a social worker through his drug rehabilitation program, and she would assist him in securing a two-bedroom. He is working part-time as a janitor at Portland State, but his sister has agreed to watch Kiley while he is at work."

Diane remembered the sister. She'd refused to take Kiley in because "my food stamps barely cover my own three kids, and you people don't pay foster parents for shit."

"And what does Kiley want?" The judge directed his question to the guardian ad litem.

"Your Honor, she's not even three years old," Diane said.

"I didn't ask if she wanted to run off and live with Santa Claus. I'm simply asking a question of our assigned guardian ad litem, since presumably she needs to justify her public-interest salary here today. Is that all right with you, Miss Light? Am I allowed to ask a question?"

The guardian ad litem's role was to advocate directly for Kiley, but in this case, Diane believed that the prosecution was doing precisely that.

Diane took a deep breath and forced herself to nod deferentially. She waited while the guardian ad litem rushed through the basics. In some ways, Kiley was lucky to have suffered the abuse at such at a young age. The psychiatrists said she was unlikely to retain any conscious long-term memory of the incidents.

She tested at below-average intelligence—most likely a consequence of her mother's prenatal drug use—but the experts attributed her delayed speech to the lack of environmental stimulation prior to her placement with Miss Miller. She had recently shown some willingness to vocalize but had become distracted and unresponsive in the two days since her move to the group home. She had seen her father six times during the last three months with the consent and supervision of her foster mom. According to the monitoring social worker, she demonstrated a "natural fondness" for him and "clearly recognized that he played some role in her life."

Kiley's father said, "I just want one more chance to be her

dad, Judge. I promise you on my life that I will not mess it up this time. Please, sir. *Please.*"

"Baby steps, Mr. Chance. We'll start with five-hour days with you, one hour supervised. She'll remain at the group home at night. We'll hear again from all parties in two weeks and make a decision then."

"Your Honor, that's four hours a day without supervision," Diane protested.

"I'm aware of basic math, Miss Light."

"But the best interests of the child —"

"— require some consistency for this little girl. The biological mother is in prison. The foster mother just died. She has one person left, and he stands here by all accounts a changed — and acquitted — man. You have nothing to offer but a group home filled with juvenile delinquents."

"I can offer myself, Your Honor. I'll take her if that's the only option. You can't put her back with this man."

"Good Lord, Miss Light. Get control of yourself. I recognize your indignation, and it's on the record. There's no need to be hyperbolic."

"It's not hyperbole, Your Honor. I've been on this case for ten months. I handled the criminal prosecution. I have shepherded the case through the family court process. I went to Miss Miller's home multiple times to talk to her about the adoption. He's seen Kiley — what, six times since this all happened? I've seen her on at least twenty occasions. Does he even know her favorite stuffed animal? It's a raccoon. Its name is Coo-Coo. It was one of the only times Kiley repeated after her speech therapists — she tried to say *raccoon,* and she said *coo-coo,* so that became the toy's name. I was there for that, not him. Kiley *knows* me. I know Kiley. I will take her."

The courtroom fell silent. Even Diane could not believe her

outburst. In all those hours studying the file, she had never once considered the possibility. But suddenly every piece fell into place. There was a reason she had been the major-crimes attorney assigned to the trial. There was a reason she had requested the transfer from criminal court to the family law unit. Maybe there was even a reason Janice Miller had been hit by a drunk driver.

Diane could do this. She could be a good mother to that girl. She and Kiley could be a family. The two of them, together.

Stone cleared his throat before speaking. "Well, that's very noble of you, Miss Light, but the best interests of the child value biological connections. Let's give Kiley a chance at a life with her father. I hope I'm not wrong about you, Mr. Chance."

"You're not, sir. I promise you, you're not. Thank you. Thank you so, so much."

Chance grabbed both of Hobbins's hands and shook them hard. Diane saw the defense attorney's eyes tear up and wanted to slap her.

———

THREE WEEKS LATER, Kiley officially moved in with her father full-time. Kiley's clothing and Coo-Coo were packed into a black Hefty bag at the group home. A social worker drove her and the bag to Chance's recently rented two-bedroom apartment, outfitted with a new twin bed for Kiley, and left her there.

———

DIANE STARTED HER car engine, searching for the comfort of the radio. All that silence made the minutes tick by too slowly. Where the hell was Jake?

The guy leaving the Wendy's was looking at her. He saw her notice him. He smiled.

She still wasn't used to that kind of smile from a man. She had spent her entire life as the type of girl men looked away from. Or if one looked, the glance would be followed by a nudge of his buddy, then a wisecrack and guilty giggle. *Dude, that's just wrong.*

At least they usually had the courtesy to keep their voices down. Well, not that one time, back in law school. She'd worn her knee-length purple sweater tunic to class. Even with the black leggings, it was a bold fashion choice. She'd thought she looked pretty good until she heard the male voices singing in the undergrad quad, "I love you, you love me..." Maybe she would have managed to forget the incident — the day abandoned somewhere in the recesses of her mind like that enormous sweater discarded in the bathroom garbage can — but someone had yelled, "Barney!" as she walked the stage at commencement. To this day, she couldn't see that big purple dinosaur without wanting to eat a pint of Häagen-Dazs.

Her cell phone buzzed on the console. A text message illuminated the screen. It was from Mark. *Will u pls change cable bill to ur name? Mindy tried 2 add Showtime. Mix-up b/c 2 accts under mine. Thx.*

Mark and Mindy. Just the sound of it was ridiculous. Diane had spent nearly thirty years with the man, and now her relationship with Mark was nothing but logistics hammered out through misspellings and abbreviations. She hit Delete.

Where the fuck was Jake?

Maybe pulling Jake into this had been too big a risk. At one point, they'd had something resembling a friendly relationship, albeit based on reciprocal compensation: He was her favorite informant; she was his benefactor in the drug unit. Relying on and rewarding the cooperation of criminals was one of the ugly realities of her job, but as drug dealers went, Jake wasn't so bad.

He sold only to adults and only in small quantities. Most important — for her purposes, at least — he always kept his ears and eyes open for information that he could trade for a get-out-of-jail-free card.

Jake was so well connected to Portland's white crack trade that she'd gone to him last January hoping he might recognize Kiley's parents. Maybe he was selling to them or had seen them in the usual spots looking to buy. Jake had never seen either one of the Chances, but Diane had mentally added a chit to his account, just for the time he spent studying their mug shots.

Jake the Snake had been popped fourteen times, but because of the chits, he had never taken a conviction.

That track record made him a good informant, but not a good ally. A senior deputy district attorney's head on a silver platter was some pretty hefty currency in Jake's trade, much more valuable to him than yet another IOU from her.

She wondered how the office would respond if she were tainted by the whiff of scandal. She'd been with the office for nearly eighteen years; she'd known colleagues who had DUIs, arrests for so-called domestic disturbances, even coke problems. Some had jobs waiting for them after the appropriate amount of rehab. Others got shipped off, their cases referred to the attorney general for investigation.

A year ago, she would have gotten the kid-glove treatment. She'd been a team player. Kept her head down. Put the office first, always.

And then Mark left her. The boy who'd taken her to the high school prom. The guy she'd shacked up with in college. The man she'd married the weekend after graduation. The asshole left her.

When he'd asked her to prom, she was already approaching two hundred pounds. She was nearly at three when he told her there was someone else.

Her weight was never really an issue for him. That's what she'd thought, at least. He was big too. They both liked to eat. They both said they were happy in their bodies and wished other people would accept them as they were. Instead, they had accepted each other. Now she wondered whether they'd loved each other only because no one else would.

Everything started to change about five years ago. They'd gotten married so young that they just assumed a baby would come along eventually. Before they knew it, their thirties were almost over. The doctors said her weight might be the reason she hadn't conceived.

She and Mark went on a diet together. They joined the gym. Success came faster to him than to her.

So did pregnancy.

Ironically, it wasn't until Mark broke the news that he was expecting a child with someone else—Mindy from spin class, naturally—that her own weight finally started to come off. It was as if that one conversation changed her physical makeup. Her metabolism, her glucose levels, her fat cells—all transformed. It was like waking up in someone else's body.

But by then, the body was too old. She was forty-four. On a government salary, she didn't have the money for in vitro, private adoption, or a surrogate. She'd always assumed she was lucky to have Mark, even when he'd looked like Jabba the Hutt. Now she couldn't believe the person she saw in her mirror every day. She was finally the kind of woman who was appealing to men, but to what end?

It wasn't just her body that changed. So did her determination. Before the weight loss, though she worked in an office filled with athletes and health nuts who viewed physical fitness as a measure of character, she had nevertheless excelled because she was like an uncaged tiger at trial. But the anger and indignation that had propelled her courtroom performances had somehow burned away with all those pounds. She found herself cutting corners. Winging opening statements. Last December, she'd snapped at a rape victim: *What do you think happens when you smoke meth with total strangers?* She rang in the new year by oversleeping on the final day of Kyle Chance's criminal trial, then delivering her closing argument in a groggy haze.

She'd barely had the energy to cry after the acquittal.

And so, after climbing the prosecutorial hierarchy for eighteen years, she'd asked for a transfer out of the major-crimes unit, the most coveted job in the office. She knew the rotation out of downtown and into the wasteland of family court was intended as punishment, a message to the rest of the attorneys that they requested changes at their own peril.

But now she realized the move had allowed her to stay in Kiley's life. Who else would have protected her?

She finally spotted Jake, who looked only in the direction of oncoming traffic on the one-way street before he dashed across Park Avenue. This was the kind of thing a mother noticed.

She rolled down her window halfway.

"Sorry, Light. No dice."

"You didn't find him?" According to the social worker, Chance worked janitorial duty at the campus until nine o'clock.

"I found him a'ight. Dude dipped." Jake's skin was white as Casper, but not his voice. She once tried getting him to drop the affect for his trial testimony, telling him he sounded like a twenty-first-century minstrel show. He responded by asking what religion had to do with it.

"Are you sure you talked to the right guy?" She hit her overhead light and showed him Chance's mug shot again. If only Jake had recognized this photo in January. If only he'd had some connection to Kyle and Rachel Chance. Testimony placing the couple together near the time of Kiley's abuse would have debunked their bogus story that the mother acted alone during a desperate binge brought on by their separation. "This picture's a year old. He's put on a little weight since then."

"I did my thing, you know? Acted like I was working the park blocks. Saw him coming. Sidled up to him. Asked if he was looking for rock. Dude just said no, thanks, and kept on walking."

"I'm not buying it, Jake."

"You're my girl, Light. Liked you better with that junk in your trunk, fo' sho', but you know I want to he'p you out. You think I'd cross you? I know better than to get DiLi mad."

She smiled, remembering the nickname he'd conjured up for her when J.Lo first hit the cultural lexicon, a decade earlier.

"I want to trust you, Jake, but I don't believe for a second that this guy turned down the opportunity to get high."

"Hey, whatchu want me to say?"

"That you just sold the man in this picture some dope."

"Then you send your man in there to frisk him down but he don't find no rock. That would make me a liar, and you know I only speak the truth. I bathe in the light of honesty, girl. I might sell folks to the law, but only if they did the crime, you know? Hey, don't get so upset, Light. I never seen you so down. It must be that diet. Get yourself some cheeseburgers and onion rings, you know what I'm saying?"

"You're *positive* it was the same guy?"

Jake looked back toward the park, but she could tell he was just buying himself time to answer. "If it makes you feel better, I could tell he was craving it. Real tempted, you know? Like pondering and shit. But—I don't know—maybe I made it seem too easy. I knew you wanted him, so I floated a half ball at a hundred. Price was too low; he probably figured I was po-po. Maybe try again in a few weeks? I'd do anything for DiLi."

A few weeks was too long. A man like Chance could break Kiley all over again in a few hours.

"No, that's all right. You want a ride back uptown?"

"Nah, I'm good. Might hang down here for a bit."

"Dumb question, Jake, but any chance I can persuade you to get into another line of work?"

"You cute, girl. And, seriously, you look good, Light. Maybe a little too *light,* if you get it. But good. Hang tough."

―――

THE NEXT NIGHT, Chance showed up at home close to eleven o'clock. Diane watched Kiley hold his hand as they stepped from the bus onto McLoughlin Boulevard. From the university to the aunt's house to here should not have taken him the nearly two hours it had. Chance was definitely up to something. Not to mention, what kind of father let a three-year-old stay up that late?

She watched from her car as they walked together, hand in hand, to their apartment complex. She saw Kiley's bedroom light turn on. Five minutes later, it turned off. She waited another twenty minutes before stepping from her car out into the darkness.

The chill of the night was perfect. Her quilted black hat felt snug on her head. Her neoprene gloves provided just enough compression to make her fingers feel extra alive. She placed her hands in her coat pockets, felt the knife against her left hand, the brick-shaped wad of paper against her right.

He opened the door for her. Of course he did.

It was over fast. She knew it would be. He was a lifelong junkie with slow reflexes and no idea what was about to happen when he turned to get that glass of water she asked for. Blade into the carotid artery, the results of which she'd seen in so many autopsies. He never even touched her.

The hardest part was waking Kiley, but she had no choice. She lifted the girl from her bed. Was it her imagination or was the child lighter than the last time she'd held her at Janice Miller's house? Chance had probably been trading food stamps for drugs instead of feeding the poor thing.

She held Kiley close to her chest and grabbed the stuffed raccoon from the bed. "Shhh," she whispered. "It won't be long, baby girl."

She set Kiley on the worn linoleum of the bloody kitchen floor and then started walking backward toward the living room, waving the stuffed toy in front of her as she moved. "Come here, sweetie. Come play with your Coo-Coo. Yeah, good girl. You're such a good girl. Now you're safe. No more bad things in the kitchen, okay?" Kiley followed her. Diane gave her the stuffed animal.

She dialed 911 and let the receiver fall to the floor.

"Don't be afraid, Kiley. Someone will be here in just a few minutes. We're going to be all right." Diane tried not to cry as she looked one last time at Kiley, alone on the living room rug with nothing but a blood-smeared acrylic raccoon.

———

"THE FINAL CASE on the docket, Your Honor. Kiley Chance."

Stone nodded as Diane reminded him of the court's decision to reinstate custody of the child to her biological father, Kyle Chance.

"Mr. Chance's body was found in his apartment late Wednesday night." Stone emitted multiple *tsk* noises as she outlined the facts. Fatally stabbed. A wad of paper found at the scene. Not money, but a twenty-dollar bill folded around strips of newspaper cut to resemble bills. The police believe it was likely a drug deal gone bad. Chance tried to bilk the seller. Got a knife in the neck in return. The perpetrator at least had the decency to dial 911 before leaving.

The judge said, "I guess we'll have to chalk this up to a lesson about the fragility of recovery from addiction."

"Yes, Your Honor." As if she hadn't warned him.

"And what do you need from me today, Miss Light?"

"Nothing imminent. I thought you deserved the earliest possible update on the case status. The child is back in the group home where she resided prior to placement with her father, and the State is trying to secure a foster home for her."

"Sad stuff. All right, we're done here?"

She had expected Stone to at least ask about the chances of a foster placement before calling it a day.

"It won't be easy to find a home for this girl. The prenatal drug exposure, the sexual abuse, and now having apparently witnessed the murder of her father—she was covered in his blood—well, the deck is stacked against her."

I'm so sorry, Kiley. I'm so sorry for waking you. For putting you through that. For the blood. But I couldn't take a chance. According to dispatch, it was only six minutes before police arrived. Six minutes I hope you can't remember. Six minutes that were nothing compared to what your parents put you through.

"I thought there was an aunt or something?"

"The father's sister. Even she won't take her. Potential parents assume she's damaged goods."

"What about that offer you made, Miss Light? I don't suppose that door is still open?"

Stone laughed, mocking what he still considered her overly dramatic objection to his initial ruling. She joined him with an awkward giggle.

"Actually, Your Honor, I suppose I should put my money where my mouth is. Yes, I guess if it's acceptable to you, I am willing to take her home. Just temporarily. The child does know me, after all. Maybe something else will come through in a week or two. And if worst comes to worst, once she starts making progress with speech therapy, it will be easier to find another placement for her."

"Well, I'd say that's very generous of you, Miss Light. You're sure about this?"

"Sure, Your Honor. Why not?" Not one of the million little goose bumps she felt beneath her sleeves revealed itself in her voice.

———

THAT AFTERNOON, DIANE'S cell pinged as she strapped on her seat belt. She pulled it from her purse and saw a new message on the screen. From Mark again. He couldn't call or even e-mail like a regular adult. He was like a teenager with the texting. *Mindy in Seattle so I'm mister mom this week. Any chance you're willing to meet Nicole? Know it's a lot to ask. Trying to find a way to be friends.*

Nicole. At least Mark and Mindy hadn't named their kid some stupid matching M-name.

She hit Delete and looked at herself in the rearview mirror. Behind her she saw last night's purchases: a child safety seat and the biggest, best stuffed raccoon she could find. Maybe they'd call him Coo-Coo Two.

She was careful as she backed out of the parking space. She was in a hurry but would need to be a more cautious driver now. She was picking up her daughter.

———

"WHAT COLOR IS this one?"

"Red!"

"How about this one?"

"Yellow!"

"And this?"

"Ahnje!"

"That's right. Orange. And all of these flowers are called *tulips*. Isn't that a funny name? *Tulips*."

Kiley smiled and pointed at Diane's mouth. "Two lips."

She and Kiley had been together nearly six months. The adoption wasn't quite finalized, but Diane had nevertheless succumbed to the calls from her old downtown colleagues to bring her daughter for a visit. It was a rare dry day in April, so after leaving the office, they'd gone over to enjoy the bloom of tulips on the Portland Park Blocks. The area's potpourri of college students and homeless people shared the lush green grass and an occasional park bench.

She reached into the brown sack in her purse. "What's this, Kiley?"

"Coo-kie."

Maybe someday her daughter would talk her ears numb, but for now, Diane cherished every word. In light of Kiley's progress, her speech and cognition therapists said she might even be ready to start kindergarten with her own age group.

Diane broke off an especially chocolaty piece of cookie for Kiley and kissed her on the forehead. "That's right. And you are my little cookie monster." She allowed herself a bite as well. She wasn't worried about the few extra pounds. It was normal to gain weight with a child around.

She heard her cell phone beep in her purse. She recognized the office extension on the display screen.

"Light."

"Hey, Diane. It's Sam Kincaid." Kincaid was the major-crimes attorney who'd inherited Diane's caseload last year. "I hope you don't mind my calling your cell, but I hear you and your sweetie were doing the rounds on your old stomping grounds."

"Yeah, we just headed out." Kincaid was a good lawyer but a little high maintenance for Diane's taste. They'd never been close.

"Shoot. I was hoping to catch you. Do you remember your case against Kyle and Rachel Chance? It was a rape one, compelling prostitution, bunch of other charges involving their two-year-old daughter?"

Twenty-two months.

Diane had told her friends she'd adopted a daughter but hadn't mentioned Kiley's connection to the earlier criminal trial.

"Not the kind of case you forget."

"I didn't think so. You flipped one of the men — Trevor Williams. He was the father's former cellmate?"

"Yeah, sure."

"You ever doubt him?"

"What do you mean?"

"Sorry. I mean, obviously, you wouldn't have put him on the stand if you doubted his testimony. I guess I'm just digging around here for more information about him. He's serving the seventy-two months he got as part of his deal with you and is trying to whittle it down by handing us his current cellmate. Williams says the guy confessed to a home invasion last year, but the cellmate doesn't match the vic's description. Looks like the story might be bogus."

"Well, it wasn't bogus in my case. Williams's DNA was found on Kiley Chance's clothing. That's why he's doing six years."

"Yeah, I saw that. But he would've been looking at nine, minimum, if it weren't for the plea. As I understand it, the mom said she was the one who made the agreement with Williams after seeing him at a bar and recognizing him from her visits to the prison. Wasn't Williams the only person to say that both the mom and dad knew what was going on?"

Rachel Chance had confessed but steadfastly refused to turn on her husband. If only Diane had found another witness. If only someone other than Williams could have placed the parents together during that time window—she would have had a second witness to contradict the Chances' fabricated story about separation.

"The mom's a piece of shit. So's the dad. And so is Williams. Maybe he's lying now, but he wasn't then."

"All right. I was all set to cut him loose. Wouldn't be the first time a jailhouse snitch lied to me. I'll take a closer look at the cellmate, just in case. Thanks for the info."

As she zipped her purse, Diane caught sight of a familiar face near Market Street. She was too far away to hear his words, but after eighteen years as a prosecutor, she could spot hand-to-hand drug transactions across a football field.

Once the customer had left, she waved in Jake's direction. Kiley turned to look, then held on to Diane's leg. Her sweet little brown eyebrows were furrowed.

"That's just a friend of your mommy." She'd have to ask Kiley's psychologist whether a lingering fear of men was to be expected.

Jake nodded, but then turned away to walk farther south. She supposed the presence of a deputy district attorney wasn't good for a drug dealer's business.

"You want some more cookie? Can you say *cookie?*"

Kiley was still clinging to her leg, but the worry in her eyes had transformed to panic. Her breath quickened, and Diane recognized all the signs of a serious meltdown.

"What's wrong, sweetie? Is Mommy's cookie monster all full? Is it nap time?"

Her daughter's gaze moved south, and her grasp tightened. "Jake."

"What did you say?"

Kiley's lower lip trembled, but her next words were unmistakable. She pointed to a spot between her legs. "Jake. Snake."

"How do you know—"

Snippets of images replayed in Diane's visual cortex. A pair of Kiley's soiled pants in a Ziploc bag, the source of the bodily fluids still unidentified. Jake's frantic banter when she'd approached him about the Chance case. His utter certainty when he'd finally said, "Sorry, DiLi, never seen either one of these ugly crackheads." Fourteen pops, no convictions. No convictions meant no blood sample for the DNA data bank.

She tasted bile and chocolate at the back of her throat. What else had she been wrong about?

She pictured Trevor Williams on the stand, promising to tell the whole truth. Rachel Chance's insistence of full responsibility: *I'm so ashamed, but I can't blame this on Kyle. I fell apart when he left me.* Kyle Chance hugging his lawyer when Stone allowed him back in Kiley's life. The lawyer for once appearing pleased to have helped a client.

As if Chance were standing before her, Diane remembered the clarity on his face when he'd opened the apartment door that night. She saw her daughter on that worn kitchen floor, gazing up with sleepy eyes, oblivious to her father's blood beginning to soak into the bottom of her flowered flannel pajamas.

The grass and the tulips shimmered in the sunlight and went out of focus, as though the laws of gravity had been set in abeyance and would not be restored anytime soon.

BLIND JUSTICE

BY JIM FUSILLI

A ngie and Turnip were best friends for as long as either could remember, beginning when Angie came to Turnip's aid, grabbing Weber by his pale hair, bloodying his nose with a roundhouse right, then dribbling his skull on the sidewalk. Bobby Weber was in the first grade, Angie and Turnip in kindergarten at St. Francis of Assisi in downtown Narrows Gate.

That was twenty years ago, the winter of 1953, and since then nobody picked on Turnip twice.

Though they were unemployed, neither Angie nor Turnip lacked: Their widowed mothers, both of whom were born in the Apulia region of southern Italy, received pension checks from Jerusalem Steel as well as Social Security. They gave the boys what they wanted and then some, provided they spoke not of the source, figuring if anyone knew they received so much for doing nothing, the flow would be tapped. Whatever extra Angie and Turnip had, the neighborhood figured it came from those little jobs they did on the side.

Entering Muzzie's one afternoon, Angie and Turnip were surprised to find, lounging on a platform above the round bar, a woman wearing only a purple boa and shoes that seemed made of glass. Last time they were here, they had seafood with a marinara sauce so spicy Angie knew Big Muzz was hiding two-day-old scungilli.

"Muzz," said Turnip as he mounted the three-legged stool, "what happened to the scungilli?"

"There's the scungilli," Little Muzz said, nodding up at the stripper. He was checking pilsner glasses for cracks.

Propped on an elbow, the droopy blonde filed her nails.

Turnip held up a finger. "Yeah, but what's she do?" he asked the bartender.

A Ping-Pong ball shot from her *fica*, just missing his head.

"That," Little Muzz said.

"Who says?" Turnip asked.

Inching away, Angie already knew the answer.

"Who?" Little Muzz replied with a dark shrug. "Like you don't know who."

Big Muzz's voice rumbled from where the kitchen used to be. "Turnip," he bellowed. "Soldato wants you. Now."

Turnip frowned as he faced the red-velvet curtain.

"Muzz? Now? I ain't here for three months," he said. "What's 'now'?"

Little Muzz spoke soft. "Maybe he seen the car."

Turnip drove a '69 canary-yellow Super Yenko Camaro 427 with a V8, an M-22 four-speed manual transmission, and custom-made spoilers front and back. Zero to sixty in 3.7 seconds on the ramp to the turnpike. Now it was parked in the bus stop on the sunny side of Polk Street.

"Soldato wants me?" Turnip whispered. Without thinking, he tapped the .45 in his jacket pocket.

"Apparently," Angie replied, knowing full well the car had nothing to do with it. Big Muzz made a call. Which meant Soldato had an eye out for Turnip. For what, who knows?

———

TURNIP GOT HIS handle when some roly-poly ice cream man translated his surname to impress the other kids on line. That evening over dinner, he asked his father why the wiseass threw him a new hook. His father, who knew damned well *rapa* was Italian for "turnip," said, "Because you look like a fuckin' turnip, that big fat ass you got."

Later, Angie told Turnip his old man must've been thinking of a butternut squash or an eggplant, a turnip being more or less round. Either way, Turnip was displeased and he took to weight lifting to change his body shape. It worked, even if the name stuck, and now he looked like he didn't need Angie knocking the Webers of the world off his back.

At about the same time, Angie realized that he wasn't going to be much bigger than his old man, who went about five and a half feet in work boots. Also, he'd have to wear eyeglasses. But by then, he'd been discovered to have an IQ of 154 and was in a class for the advanced. Soon, it was common knowledge that Angie, the toughest kid in Narrows Gate, was also the smartest.

About fifteen years later, it dawned on Silvio Soldato that Angie and Turnip were a dangerous duo. *Very dangerous, these two,* he mused. Brains and brawn. Mind and muscle. Hmmm.

The problem in this case, he noted, was that usually when you had a Hercules and an Einstein, at the same time you had a moron and a weakling. Not so with these two. Turnip had a fresh head, especially with numbers and mechanics, and little Angie was *pazzo* times three—everybody in town knew he'd crammed those turnips down the ice cream man's throat when he was ten years old. Each time a guy turned up on the waterfront with his shins shattered or his ears pinned to his cheeks, Soldato made Angie for it, wondering how he always walked away clean.

Soldato wanted them broke up, now and forever, and for six weeks he thought about how to do it. Killing them both would look desperate, he reasoned, and killing one would send the other one seething toward revenge. He considered having the brakes go on the Camaro as Turnip and Angie headed down the viaduct, careening them to a fiery death at the Getty station. But then he started thinking maybe Turnip could figure some way out of the crash, twisting and maneuvering, tires squealing. Kid drives like he was born behind the wheel, that son of a bitch, him and his Camaro.

Then he decided, the lightbulb going bright.

Now Soldato was sitting in his booth at the Grotto, enjoying a late-afternoon meal of *zuppa di vongole* over linguine, and here comes Turnip. Alone and more or less right after Big Muzz said. A good sign, he thought as he watched Pinhead frisk him, concluding by giving his nuts a threatening tug.

Turnip shivered as he shook off the September chill.

"Mr. Rapa," Soldato began. "How's the Camaro? And Angie?"

———

"Two questions, and there was the entire plan," Turnip said. "The shit heap gave it up before I had my ass in the seat. What a fuckin' *babbo*."

"So he said that? Just like that?" Angie asked.

"Not in so many words, no. Different words."

"What words?"

"Ang, how the fuck do I know? I got the gist of it, all right?"

They decided to play it safe, leaving the Camaro in Turnip's garage. Angie had a beat-up burgundy Impala, one of about three thousand in Hudson County. He drove it north on Boulevard East while Turnip took the 22 bus up to Cliffside. Now they were in the Bagel Nosh in Fort Lee, figuring nobody was eyeing the joint.

"The one sentence," Angie insisted. "Repeat that one—"

"He said, 'I don't want to see him no more.'"

"Meaning what?"

"Well, I don't think he wants you to move, Ang," Turnip chuckled.

"And you don't take me out, he'll blow up the Camaro. What's wrong with this guy? Did you tell him they made a lot of Camaros?"

You had to be half a fag to drink Tab, but Turnip liked the taste. "In fact, Ang, they ain't made that many Super Yenkos."

Angie narrowed his eyes and sat back in the orange booth.

Silence hung heavy. Soon Turnip wondered if his friend could kill him with a plastic spoon covered with chicken liver.

"I'm saying, that's all."

Angie tapped his fingers, one after the next, and Turnip began to squirm.

"Ang," he said finally, palms up. "What the fuck..."

Angie adjusted his eyeglasses. The color began to return to his face.

"Let me guess your plan," Turnip said. "You let me guess?"

"Yeah. Go guess," he replied, dabbing at the corners of his mouth with his thumb and forefinger. He'd noticed the knockout behind the counter. A schnoz on her, but those dark curls and like an hourglass under the Bagel Nosh uniform. A streak of mischief too: He could tell she liked that he wouldn't return when they were done.

He had to ask if she had a friend. A friend with a car didn't mind driving Turnip down to Narrows Gate after.

"You want to find out where they got another '69 Camaro," Turnip said, sucking on a lemon slice.

Angie stood. "No. Jesus…"

Looking up, Turnip frowned. "What then?"

"When I come back, you tell me how Soldato's connected," he said. "Let me know if there's somebody maybe who wouldn't want to, you know, make a move, given his misstep."

———

THOUGH IT WAS a short ride under the Hudson from Little Italy, Narrows Gate no longer drew much attention from the Five Families. The Gigentis still had a slice via the creaking waterfront, but the shipyards had closed, the Great Atlantic and Pacific Tea Company moved, Venus Pencil too, and now the city's population, once as high as sixty thousand, was down to less than half that. And half of those left were *melanzane* who'd turned the projects into Little Harlem.

Seeing the Mob now thought the place an ass pimple, Soldato had moved in and set up his own operation, running a numbers racket that catered to the old-time Italians, the coloreds, and the *Irlandese*. Soon, come eight thirty at night and almost everybody left in Narrows Gate was throwing elbows, grabbing the bulldog edition of the *Daily News* for the total mutual handle at the track to see if the last three numbers matched their bet.

Given it's a thousand-to-one shot to hit on the nose, Soldato needed a rake to collect, taking in maybe two large a week in small change and paying out less than 7 percent. Most of that went to his army of bookies, all blue-haired grandmothers who knew everybody on the block who wanted in. Somebody gave him shit he'd send Pinhead to bruise her sensible. Grandma in

JIM FUSILLI

ShopRite with a fat lip and a shiner, and soon everybody's back in line, the thing almost running itself.

Angie knew the *donnaccia* with the Ping-Pong ball at Muzzie's was a sign that Soldato wanted to expand. But the Gigentis sent hookers through the Lincoln Tunnel for action all over the county: One Saturday 4:15 a.m., Angie and Turnip counted sixteen *zoccolas* waiting for a New York–bound bus outside a motel only a mile from Muzzie's platform.

Clear, Soldato asked nobody what he could do.

Angie got his meet at two thirty in the morning at Sal Rossi's on Houston Street with six feet of poured concrete named Bobo. Him and his giant melon coming out of the kitchen and Angie wondered if he'd made the right play.

Adjusting his sunglasses, Bobo passed on the handshake and said, "What?"

Angie was no pigeon. "It's about propriety," he said.

Bobo went, "Uh?"

"He put the *puttana* two blocks from a school. Muzzie's is the place. It used to be a nice restaurant. Long row of brownstones around the corner. Two, three generations in the same building."

"Muzzie's."

"Now you got mothers going by with their little kids, teenagers hanging around...It's not a class move and people are thinking it's you."

"Me?"

"The family." Jesus.

"Yeah, right, and..."

"And the cops come, and the newspapers," Angie said, "and soon they're closing down the York Motel and half the whorehouses on Tonnelle Avenue. In time, it blows over and he moves in on your territory."

Bobo thought. Then he said, "Who is this guy?"

"Soldato. Right now he's under the protection of nobody. But after he makes his move, he seeks an accommodation..."

"And you got a hard-on for this guy why?"

Angie sat back and lifted his palms. "Why?" he asked, feigning surprise. "Because he figured *this*. You and me. So he tells some guy he doesn't want to see me anymore."

"Maybe you hop a Greyhound or something."

"No good. Not for the long run."

Bobo agreed. Then he rubbed his chin. "You want in?"

"Hell no. It's yours and God bless you."

"But what?"

"One, Muzzie's goes back to scungilli and calamari."

"Two is...?"

"Nobody misses this guy."

Bobo couldn't decide on his own, Angie knew, but how the big guy left the table told him he was going to get his way.

———

He waited until "Mala Femmina" ended on the jukebox and joined Turnip at Sal Rossi's horseshoe bar.

"So?" Turnip asked.

"It's done. You're off the hook. Drive in peace."

Turnip smiled his relief.

"So what happens?"

Angie said, "Stay out of the Grotto until I tell you."

They wandered onto Houston. Traffic to the FDR was backed up to Mulberry Street.

"Ang, I'm surprised at that guy, to tell you the truth."

"How so?" They turned up their leather collars in unison.

"If he gives you a hard time, I'm sitting there," Turnip said. "I can put two between the third and fourth buttons before he knows what hit him."

"Not likely," Angie said as they headed toward the garage on Elizabeth Street. "The guy at the bar with the wavy hair, black suit, resoled loafers? Playing with his onyx pinkie ring?"

Turnip frowned. "Three stools down? You're shitting me."

"Carrying double. On the right ankle and the ribs."

"How'd you — your back was to him. How'd you make him?"

"My guy's sunglasses," Angie said. "Plus your guy got up when the genius scratched his chin."

Turnip shook his head in wonder. "How you like that."

As they walked in silence toward the Camaro, Turnip pondered how much his friend could achieve if he had a speck of ambition.

———

PINHEAD WENT PAST the bar and poured himself a big cup of hot clam broth, dropping in a couple shots of Tabasco. Screaming at the widows gave him a scratchy throat, so he threw it down, thinking a Schlitz chaser.

"Yo, Pin," said Milney, the night bartender. He wiggled a crooked finger.

Pin said, "What?"

Milney leaned over. "The senior center on Fourth Street," he whispered. "Some bullshit in the lounge. Take a cab, but go."

Pin understood and he threw Sally B a fin.

Milney slipped it over the half a yard Turnip gave him a half hour ago.

Outside the Grotto, Pin flagged the first cab that rolled the corner. He didn't notice Angie behind the wheel.

Soon, they were on their way toward the Jersey City end of the viaduct, taking the cobblestone road behind the last horse stable in Narrows Gate.

"Angie, you got some set of *coglioni* on you, you know that?"

Pin said. "But I admire that. I do. Tells me we can do something, a guy like you."

Angie looked in the rearview, seeing if the barbed wire he'd used to tie Pin down was making a mess of the vinyl seat.

"Pin, there are five stages of receiving catastrophic news," he said. "You blew through anger—wisely, if you ask me—and you're bargaining now. Which means depression is next."

"Hey, Ang, smart is smart, but sometimes what's smart in books—"

"You don't hurry, there's no time for acceptance."

Fourteen minutes later, Pinhead went over the rusted rail atop the viaduct and landed two hundred and thirty feet below, smack on a chain-link fence outside the bus terminal, the cops trying to figure how the barbed wire got hooked so thorough around the weasel's neck and hands.

———

"SYMMETRY," SAID ANGIE as he entered Muzzie's, old Maxwell House coffee can in his hand. "I love it."

Muzzie and Little Muzzie came from the kitchen. The asbestos in their hair and on their faces reminded Turnip that soon they'd be coated in flour, making fresh linguine for the seafood and flaming-ass sauce.

Turnip sat next to his friend at the bar and pointed to the nothing where the platform had been. One of the Muzzolinis had spackled the holes.

"What happened to Miss Ping-Pong?" he asked.

Little Muzzie, who now feared Angie more than ever, shrugged. "I heard the Gigentis are opening some new clubs on Tonnelle Avenue."

"Could be," Angie said. "You of the mood to pour a little sambuca?"

Big Muzzie stepped up. "We're closed—"

"No problem," said Little Muzz, going quick to the round bar, yanking back the canvas cover, and coming up with a bottle. With Pinhead two weeks dead and Soldato missing, Little Muzz was looking to the future.

Turnip smelled the anise through the cap.

Two shot glasses, and Little Muzzie retreated as the friends set their elbows down to raise a toast.

"To what?" Turnip said.

"To Soldato," Angie replied, "and to being careful what you wish for."

Turnip didn't get it, but he sipped anyway, expecting a coffee bean to bump his lip. When he put down the little glass, he said, "So you're going to tell me?"

"Tell you..."

"What's in the coffee can?"

Turnip shook it and heard something rattle inside.

"You like to guess," Angie said. "Guess."

A minute later, Turnip said, "I could use a fuckin' clue, Ang."

"What did Soldato say?"

"He said he didn't want to see you no more."

"Which did not mean..."

Suddenly, Turnip recoiled.

"Bingo," said Angie.

"*Madonna mio,* Ang." Then he whispered, "You took his eyes?"

Figuring the Muzzies were peeping, Angie nodded slow.

Turnip blessed himself.

Angie said, "Nobody puts you on the spot, *il mio amico.*"

His head spinning, Turnip asked, "Ang, dead or alive?"

Angie dipped his little finger in the sambuca. "What do you think?"

THE CONSUMERS

BY DENNIS LEHANE

It wasn't that Alan didn't love Nicole. She was possibly the only person he did love, certainly the only one he trusted. And after he'd beaten her or called her all kinds of unforgivable things in one of his black rages, he'd drop to his knees to beg her forgiveness. He'd weep like a child abandoned in the Arctic, he'd swear he loved her the way knights loved maidens in old poems, the way people loved each other in war zones or during tsunamis — *crystallized* love, pure and passionate, boundless and a little out of control, but undeniable.

She believed this for a long time — it wasn't just the money that kept her in the marriage; the makeup sex was epic, and Alan was definitely easy on the eyes. But then one day — the day he knocked her out in the kitchen, actually — she realized she didn't care about his reasons anymore, she didn't care how much he loved her, she just wanted him dead.

His apology for laying her out in the kitchen was two round-trip tickets to Paris, for her and a friend. So she took the trip with Lana, her best friend, and told her that she'd decided to have her husband killed. Lana, who thought Alan was an even bigger asshole than Nicole did, said it shouldn't be too much of a problem.

"I know a guy," she said.

"You *know a guy?*" Nicole looked from the Pont Neuf to Lana. "A guy who kills people?"

Lana shrugged.

Turned out the guy had helped Lana's family a few years back. Lana's family owned supermarkets down south, and the guy had preserved the empire by dealing with a labor organizer named Gustavo Inerez. Gustavo left his house to pick up training pants for his three-year-old and never came back. The guy Lana's family had hired called himself Kineavy, no other name given.

Not long after Nicole and Lana returned to Boston, Lana arranged the meeting. Kineavy met Nicole at an outdoor restaurant on Long Wharf. They sat looking out at boats in the harbor on a soft summer day.

"I don't know how to do this," she said.

"You're not supposed to, Mrs. Walford. That's why you hire me."

"I meant I don't know how to hire somebody to do it."

Kineavy lit a cigarette, crossed one leg over his knee. "You hire somebody to clean your house?"

"Yes."

"It's like that—you're paying somebody to do what you don't want to do yourself. Still has to get done."

"But I'm not asking you to clean my house."

"Aren't you?"

Hard to tell if he was smiling a bit when he said it because he'd been dragging on his cigarette. He wore Maui Jim wraparounds with brown lenses, so she couldn't see his eyes, but he was clearly a good-looking guy, maybe forty, sandy hair, sharp cheekbones and jawline. He was about six feet tall, looked like he worked out, maybe jogged, but didn't devote his life to it.

"It feels so *odd*," she said. "Like, this can't be my life, can it? People don't *really* do these kinds of things, do they?"

"Yet," he said, "they do."

"How did you get into this line of work?"

"A woman kept asking me questions, and one day I snapped."

Now he did smile, but it was the kind of smile you gave people who searched for exact change in the express line at Whole Foods.

"How do I know you're not a cop?"

"You don't really." He exhaled a slim stream of smoke; he was one of those rare smokers who could still make it look elegant. The last time Nicole had smoked a cigarette, the World Trade Center had been standing, but now she had to resist the urge to buy a pack.

"Why do you do this for a living?"

"I don't do it for a living. It doesn't pay enough. But it rounds off the edges."

"Of what?"

"Poverty." He stubbed his cigarette out in the black plastic ashtray. "Why do you want your husband dead?"

"That's private."

"Not from me it's not." He removed his sunglasses and stared across the table. His eyes were the barely blue of new metal. "If you lie, I'll know it. And I'll walk."

"I'll find somebody else."

"Where?" he said. "Under the hit-man hyperlink on Craigslist?"

She looked out at the water for a moment because it was hard to say the words without a violent tremble overtaking her lower lip.

Then she looked back at him, jaw firm. "He beats me."

His eyes and face remained stone still, as if he'd been replaced with a photograph of himself. "Where? You look perfectly fine to me."

That was because Alan didn't hit her hard every time. Usually, he just held tight to her hair while he flicked his fingers off her chin and nose or twisted the flesh over her hip. In the last couple years, though, after the markets collapsed and Alan and men like him were blamed for it in some quarters, he'd often pop the cork on his depthless self-loathing and unleash on her. He'd buried a fist in her abdomen on three different occasions, lifted her off the floor by her throat, rammed the heel of his hand into her temple hard enough for her to hear the ring of a distant alarm clock for the rest of the day, and laid her out with a surprise punch to the back of the head. When she came to from that one, she was sprawled on the kitchen floor. He'd left a box of Kleenex and an ice pack by her head to show he was sorry.

Alan was always sorry. Whenever he hit her, it seemed to shock him. His pupils would dilate, his mouth would form an O, he'd look at his hand like he was surprised to find it attached to his wrist.

After, he'd fill the bedroom with roses, hire a car to take her to a spa for a day. Then, after this last time, he'd sent her and Lana to Paris.

She told this to Kineavy. Then she told him some more. "He punched me in the lower back once because I didn't move out of his path to the liquor cart fast enough. Right where the spine meets the ass? You ever try to sit when you're bruised there? He took a broomstick to the backs of my legs another time. But mostly he likes to punch me in the head, where all my hair is."

"You do have a lot of it," Kineavy said.

It was her most striking attribute, even more than her tits, which were 100 percent Nicole and had yet to sag; or her ass, which, truth be told, had sprouted some cellulite lately but still looked great for a woman closing in on thirty-six; or even her smile, which could turn the heads of an entire cocktail party if she entered the room wearing it.

Her hair trumped all of it. It was the dark of red wine and fell to her shoulders. When she pulled it back, she looked regal. When she straightened it, she looked dangerous. When she let it fall naturally, with its tousled waves and anarchic curls, she looked like a wet dream sent to douse a five-alarm fire.

She told Kineavy, "He hits me mostly on the head because the hair covers the bruises."

"And you can't just leave him?"

She shook her head and admitted something that shamed her. "Prenup."

"And you like living rich."

"Who doesn't?"

Nicole had grown up in the second-floor apartment of a three-decker on Sydney Street in Savin Hill, a neighborhood locals called Stab-'n'-Kill. Her parents were losers, always getting caught in the petty scams they tried to run on their soon-to-be-ex-employers and on the city and the welfare system and DSS and the Housing Department and just about anybody they suspected was dumber than they were. Problem was, you couldn't find dead fucking houseplants dumber than Jerry and Gerri Golden. Jerry ended up getting stomach cancer while in minimum-security lockup for check-kiting, and Gerri used his death to justify climbing into a bottle of Popov and staying there. Last time Nicole checked, she was still alive, if toothless and demented. But the last time Nicole checked had been about ten years ago.

Being poor, she'd decided long ago, wasn't necessarily a bad thing. Plenty of people had nothing and didn't let that eat their souls. But it wasn't for her.

"What does your husband do?" Kineavy asked.

"He's an investment banker."

"For which bank?"

"Since the crash? Bank Suffolk."

"Before the crash?"

"He was with Bear Stearns."

Finally, some movement in Kineavy's face, a flick in his eyes, a shift of his chin. He lit another cigarette and raised one eyebrow ever so slightly as the match found the tobacco. "And people call me a killer."

———

SHE THOUGHT ABOUT it later, how he was right. How there was this weird disconnect at the center of the culture around various acts of amorality. If you sold your body or pimped someone who did, stuck up liquor stores, or, God forbid, sold drugs, you were deemed unfit for society. People would try to run you out of the neighborhood. They would bar their children from playing with yours.

But if you subverted federal regulations to sell toxic assets to unsuspecting investors and wiped out hundreds of thousands, if not millions, of jobs and life savings, you were invited to Symphony Hall and luxury boxes at Fenway. Alan had convinced the entire state of Arkansas to invest in bundled sub-primes he knew would fail. When he'd told Nicole this, back in '07, she'd been outraged.

"So the derivatives you've been selling, they're bad?"

"A lot of them, yeah."

"And the CD, um, whatta you—"

"Collateralized debt obligations. CDOs, yeah. They pretty much suck too, at least a good sixty percent of them."

"But they're all insured."

"Well..." He'd looked around the restaurant. He shook his head slowly. "A lot of them are, sure, but the insurance companies overpromised and underfunded. Bill ever comes due, everyone's fucked."

"And the bill's going to come due?"

"With Arkansas, it sure looks like it. They bundled up with some pretty sorry shit."

"So why not just tell the state retirement board?"

He took a long pull from his glass of cab. "First, because they'd take my license. Second, and more important, that state retirement board, babe? They might just dump those stocks en masse, which would *ensure* that the stocks would collapse and make my gut feeling come true anyway. If I do nothing, though, things might—*might*—turn out all right. So we may as well roll the dice, which is what we've been doing the last twenty years anyway, and it's turned out okay. So, I mean, there you go."

He looked across the table at her while she processed all this, speechless, and he gave her the sad, helpless smile of a child who wasn't caught playing with matches until after the house caught fire.

"Damned if you do, damned if you don't," Alan said, and ordered another bottle of wine.

The retirees lost everything when the markets collapsed in 2008. *Everything,* Alan told her through sobs and whimpers of horror. "One day—fuck, yesterday—old guy worked his whole life as a fucking janitor or pushing paper at city hall, he looked at a statement said he'd accrued a quarter million to live off of for the final twenty years of his life. It's right before his eyes in bold print. But the next day—*today*—he looked and the number was zero. And there's not a thing he can do to get it back. Not one fucking thing."

He wept into his pillow that night, and Nicole left him.

She came back, though. What was she going to do? She'd dropped out of community college when she met Alan. The prospects she had now, at her age and level of work experience, were limited to selling French fries or selling blow jobs. Not much in between. And what would she be leaving behind? Trips, like the one to Paris, for starters. The main house in Dover; the city house twenty miles away in Back Bay; the New York apartment; the winter house in Boca; the full-time gardener, maid, and personal chef; the 750si; the DB9; the two-million-dollar renovation of the city house; the one-point-five-mil reno of the winter house; the country club dues—one country club so exclusive that its name was simply the Country Club—Jesus, the shopping trips; the new clothes every season.

So she returned to Alan a day after she left him, telling herself that her duty was not to honor a bunch of people she didn't know in Arkansas (or a bunch of people she didn't know in Massachusetts, New York, Connecticut, Maine, and, well, forty-five other states); her duty was to honor her husband and her marriage.

Honor became a harder and harder concept to apply to her husband—and her marriage—as 2008 turned into 2009, and then as 2009 turned into 2010.

Outside of losing his job because his firm went bankrupt, Alan was fine. He'd dumped most of his own stock in the first quarter of '08, and the profit he made paid for the renovation of the Boca place. It also allowed them to buy a house she'd always liked in Maui. They bought a couple of cars on the island so they wouldn't have to ship them back and forth, and they hired two gardeners and a guy to look after the place, which on one level might seem extravagant but on another was actually quite benevolent: three people were now employed in a bad economy because of Alan and Nicole Walford.

Alan cried a lot in early 2009. Knowing how many people had lost their homes, jobs, retirement savings, or all three ate at him. He lost weight, and his eyes grew very dull for a while, and even when he signed on with Bank Suffolk and hammered out a contract feathered with bonuses, he seemed sad. He told her nothing had changed; nobody had learned anything. No longer was investment philosophy based on the long-term quality of the investment. It was based on how many investments, toxic or otherwise, you could sell and what fees you could charge to do so. In 2010, banking fees at Alan's firm rose 23 percent. Advisory fees spiked 41 percent.

We're the bad guys, Nicole realized. We're going to hell. If there is a hell.

But what were they supposed to do? Or, more to the point, what was *she* supposed to do? Give it back? She wasn't the one shorting stock and selling toxic CDOs and CDSs. And even if she were, the government said it was okay. What Alan and his cohorts had done was, while extremely destructive, perfectly legal, at least until the prosecutors came banging on their door. And they wouldn't. As Alan liked to remind her, the last person to fuck with Wall Street had been the governor of New York, and look what happened to him.

Besides, she wasn't Alan. She was his wife.

Maybe she was doing a service to society by hiring Kineavy. Maybe, while she'd been telling herself she didn't want to leave the marriage because she didn't want to be poor, the truth was far kinder — maybe she'd hired Kineavy so he'd right a wrong that society couldn't or wouldn't right itself.

Seen in that light, maybe she was a hero.

———

IN ANOTHER MEETING, at another part of the waterfront, she gave Kineavy ten thousand dollars. Over the years, she'd been able to siphon off a little cash here, a little cash there, from funds Alan gave her for the annual Manhattan shopping sprees and the annual girls' weekends in Vegas and Monte Carlo. And now she passed some of it to Kineavy.

"The other ten when I get there."

"Of course." She looked out at the water. A gray day today, very still and humid, some of the skyline gone smudged in the haze. "When will that be?"

"Saturday." He looked over at her as he stuffed the cash in the inside pocket of his jacket. "None of your servants work then, right?"

She chuckled. "I don't have servants."

"No—what are they?"

"Employees."

"Okay. Any of your employees work Saturday?"

"No. Well, I mean, the chef, but he doesn't come in until, I think, two."

"And you usually go out Saturday, go shopping, hang with your girlfriends, stuff like that?"

"Not every Saturday, but it's not uncommon."

"Good. That's what you do this Saturday between ten and two."

"Between ten and two? What're you, the cable company?"

"That's exactly what you're going to tell Alan. On Thursday afternoon, your cable's gonna go out."

"Out?"

He popped his fingers at the air in front of his face. "Poof."

"Alan'll go crazy. The Sox play the Yankees this weekend; there's Wimbledon; some golf thing too, I think."

70

"Right. And the cable guy will be coming to fix it Saturday, between ten and two."

Kineavy stood and she had to look up at him from the bench. "You make sure your husband's there to answer the door."

———

At nine Saturday morning, Alan came into the kitchen from the gym. They'd had the gym built last year in the reconverted barn on the other side of the four-car garage. Alan had installed a sixty-inch Sony Bravia in there, and he'd watch movies that pumped him full of American pride as he ran on the treadmill— *Red Dawn, Rocky IV, Rambo III, The Blind Side.* Man, he loved *The Blind Slide,* walked around quoting it like it was the *Bhagavad Gita.* He was covered in sweat, dripping it all over the floor, as he pulled a bottle of OJ from the fridge, popped the cap with his thumb, and drank directly from the container.

"Cable guy come yet?"

Nicole took an elaborate look at the clock on the wall: 9:05. "Between ten and two, they said."

"Sometimes they come early." He swigged half the bottle.

"When do they come early?"

"Sometimes."

"Name one time."

He shrugged, leaned against the counter, drank some more orange juice.

Watching him suck down the orange juice, she was surprised to remember that she'd loved him this past week. Hated him too, of course, but there was still love there. He wasn't a terrible guy, Alan. He could be funny, and he once flew in her brother, Ben, to surprise her for her thirty-third birthday—Lord knows, he could always be depended on for the grand gesture. When he spent two weeks in Shanghai on business right after her third miscarriage, he sent her white roses every day he was gone. She spent the week in bed, and sometimes she'd place one of those white petals on the tip of her nose and close her eyes and pretend she'd have a child someday.

This past week, Alan had been surprisingly attentive, asking her if everything was okay, if there was anything she wanted, was she feeling under the weather, she seemed tense, anything he could do for her?

They'd fucked twice, once in the bed at the end of the day, but once on the kitchen counter—the same counter he was leaning against now—good and lusty and erotic, Alan talking dirty into her right ear. For a full ten minutes after he'd come, she'd sat on the counter and considered calling the whole thing off.

Now, only an hour (or four) away from ending her husband's life, her heart pounded up through the veins in her neck, the blood roared in her ear canals, and she thought there might still be time to call it off. She could just run upstairs and grab the number of Kineavy's burner cell and end this madness.

Alan burped. He held up a hand in apology. "Where you going again?"

She'd told him about a hundred times.

"There's an art fair in Sherborn."

Drops of sweat fell from his shorts and plopped onto the floor.

"Art fair? Bunch of lesbos selling shit they painted in their attics from the backs of Subarus?"

"Anyway," she said, "we won't be all day or anything."

He nodded. "Cable guy's coming when?"

She let out a slow breath, looked at the floor.

"I'm just asking. Christ."

She nodded at the floor, her arms folded. She unfolded them and looked up, gave him a tight smile. "Between ten and two."

He smiled. Alan had a movie-star-wattage smile. Sometimes, if he put his big almond eyes behind it, tilted his chin just so, she could feel her panties evaporate in a hushed puff of flame.

Maybe. Maybe...

"Don't be all day with the lesbians, that's all, okay? Money's like rust—shit doesn't sleep." He winked at her. "Know what I'm saying, sister?"

She nodded.

Alan took another slug of orange juice and some of it spilled into his chest hairs. He dropped the bottle on the counter, cap still off. He pinched her cheek on his way out of the room.

Nah. Fucking time for you to go, Alan.

———

KINEAVY HAD BEEN very clear about the timeline.

She was to stay in the house until 9:45 to make sure Alan didn't forget he was supposed to stick around for the cable guy, because Alan, for all his attention to detail when it came to money, could be absentminded to the edge of retardation when it came to almost anything else. She was to go out through the front door, leaving it unlocked behind her. Not open, mind you, just unlocked. At some point while she was out with Lana on a Bloody Mary binge at the bar down the street from the Sherborn Arts Fair, Alan would answer the front door and the cable guy would shoot him in the head.

Oh, Alan, she thought. *You aren't a bad guy. You just aren't a good one.*

She heard him coughing upstairs. He was probably sitting in the bathroom waiting for the shower to get hot, even though that took about four seconds in this McMansion. But Alan liked to turn the bathroom into a steam room. She'd come in after him, see his wipe marks all over the mirrors as her hair curled around her ears.

He coughed again, closer to the stairs now, and she thought, *Terrific. Your last gift to me will be a cold. My fucking luck, it'll turn into a sinus infection.*

He was hacking up a lung by the sounds of it, so she left the kitchen and crossed the family room, which would remain an ironic description unless she hired the von Trapps to fill it. And even then there'd be room for one of the smaller African nations and a circus.

He stood at the top of the stairs, naked, coughing blood out of his mouth and onto his chest. He had one hand over the hole in his throat and he kept blinking and coughing, blinking and coughing, like he was pretty sure if he could just swallow whatever was stuck in his throat, this too would pass.

Then he fell. He didn't make it all the way down the stairs — there were a lot of them — but he made it nearly halfway before his right foot got jammed between the balusters. Alan ended his life facedown and bare-assed, dangling like something about to be dipped.

Nicole realized she'd been screaming only when she stopped. She heard herself say, "Oh, boy. Jesus. Oh, boy."

Alan's head had landed on the wood between the runner and the balustrade, and he'd begun to drip.

"Oh, boy. Wow."

"You got my money?"

To her credit she didn't whip around or let out a yelp. She turned slowly to face him. He stood a couple feet behind her in the family room. He looked every inch the suburban dad out on Saturday errands — light blue shirt untucked over wrinkled khaki cargo shorts, boat shoes on his feet.

"I do," she said. "It's in the kitchen. Do you want to come with me?"

"No, I'm good here."

She started to take a step and stopped. She jerked a thumb toward the kitchen. "May I?"

"What?" he said. "Yeah, sure."

She felt his eyes on her as she crossed the family room to the kitchen. She had no reason to think he had, in fact, turned to watch her go, but she felt it all the same. In the kitchen, her purse was where she'd left it, on one of the high bar stools, and she took the envelope from it, the envelope she'd been instructed to leave in the ivy at the base of the wall by the entrance gate on her way out. But she'd never gone out.

"You cook?" He stood in the doorway, in the portico they'd designed to look like porticos in Tuscan kitchens.

"Me? No. No." She brought him the envelope.

He took it from her with a courteous nod. "Thank you." He looked around the room. "This is a hell of a kitchen for someone who doesn't cook."

"Well, no, it's for the chef."

"Oh, the chef. Well, there you go then. Makes sense again. I always wanted one of those hanging-pot things. And those pots, what're they—copper?"

"Some of them, yeah."

He nodded and seemed impressed. He walked back into the family room and stuffed the envelope into the pocket of his cargo shorts. He took a seat by the hearth and smiled in such a way that she knew she was expected to take the seat across from him.

She did.

Directly behind him was an eight-foot-tall mirror in a marble frame that matched the marble of the hearth. She was reflected in it, along with the back of his head and the back of his chair. Her lower eyelids needed work. They were growing darker lately, deeper.

"What do you do for a living, Nicole?"

"I'm a homemaker."

"So you make things?"

"No." She chuckled.

"Why's that funny?"

Her smile died in the mirror. "It's not."

"Then why're you chuckling?"

"I didn't realize I was."

"You say you're a homemaker; it's a fair question to ask what you make."

"I make this house," she said softly, "a home."

"Ah, I get it," he said. He looked around the room for a moment and his face darkened. "No, I don't. That's one of those things that sounds good — I make the house a home — but is really bullshit. I mean, this doesn't feel like a home, it feels like a fucking monument to, I don't know, hoarding a bunch of useless shit. I saw your bedroom — well, one of them, one with the bed the size of Air Force One; that yours?"

She nodded. "That's the master, yeah."

"That's the master's? Okay."

"No, I said —"

"Anyway, I'm up there thinking you could hold NFL combines in that room. It's fucking huge. It ain't intimate, that's for sure. And homes, to me, always feel intimate. Houses, on the other hand — they can feel like anything."

He pulled a handful of coins out of his pocket for some reason, shook them in his palm.

She glanced at the clock. "Lana's expecting me."

He nodded. "So you don't have a job."

"No."

"And you don't produce anything."

"No."

"You consume."

"Huh?"

"You consume," he repeated. "Air, food, energy" — he looked up at the ceiling and over at the walls — "space."

She followed his gaze and when she looked back at him, the gun was out on his lap. It was black and smaller than she would have imagined and it had a very long suppressor attached to the muzzle, the kind hit men always used in movies like *Grosse Pointe Blank* or *The Professional,* the kind that went *pffft* when fired.

"I'm meeting Lana," she said again.

"I know." He shook the change in his hand once more and she looked closer, realized they weren't coins at all. Some kind of small metal things that reminded her of snowflakes.

"Lana knows who you are."

"She thinks she does, but she actually knew of another guy, the real Kineavy. See, they never met. Her father met him, but her father died — what — three years ago, after the stroke."

Her therapist had taught her breathing exercises for tense situations. She tried one now. She took long slow breaths and tried to visualize their colors, but the only color that came up was red.

He plucked one of the metal snowflakes from his palm and held it between the thumb and forefinger of his right hand. "So, Kineavy, I knew him well. He died too. About two years ago. Natural causes. And faux Kineavy — that's me — sees no point in meeting most clients a second time, which suits them fine. What do you do, Mrs. Walford? What do you do?"

She could feel her lower lip start to bubble and she sucked it into her mouth for a moment. "I do nothing."

"You do nothing," he agreed. "So why should I let you live?"

"Because—"

He flicked his wrist and the metal snowflake entered her throat. She could see it in the mirror. About a third of it—three metal points out of eight—stuck out of her flesh. The other five points were on the other side, in her throat. A floss-thin line of blood trickled out of the new seam in her body, but otherwise, she didn't look like someone who was dying. She looked okay.

He stood over her. "You knew what your husband was doing, right?"

"Yes." The word sounded funny, like a whistle, like a baby noise.

"But you didn't stop him."

I tried. That's why I hired you.

"You didn't stop him."

"No."

"You spent the money."

"Yes."

"You feel bad about it?"

And she had, she'd felt so terribly bad about it. Tears spilled from her eyes and dripped from the edges of her jaw. "Yes."

"You felt bad? You felt sad?"

"Yes."

He nodded. "Who gives a shit?"

And she watched in the mirror as he fired the bullet into her head.

Afterward, he walked around the house for a little bit. He checked out the cars in the garage, the lawn out back so endless you would have thought it was part of the Serengeti. There was a gym and a pool house and a guesthouse. A guesthouse for a seven-bedroom main house. He shook his head as he went back inside and passed through the dining room and the living room into the family room, where she sat in the chair and he lay on the stairs. All this space, and they'd never had kids. You would have thought they would've had kids.

To kill the silence, if for no other reason.

MOONSHINER'S LAMENT

BY RICK McMAHAN

Chapter 1

Goat McKnight's hands ached for a gun.

Walking up the mountain path, he yearned for one. The moonlight, where it penetrated the canopy of trees, bleached the open spaces in pools of white and created twisted shadows in the lee of crooked branches. Goat never feared the dark of night. Darkness held no sway over him. Not even while he trudged through the blackest jungles did fear of the dark edge into his heart.

Goat had never feared the law either, not even after he was caught with a load of moonshine. The judge had given him a choice. Prison or the army. Sometimes late at night, freezing on a jungle trail or facedown in a rice paddy under a hot sun as Charlie zinged rounds at him, Goat had thought he'd made the wrong choice. When he got back home, Goat had two options — go down in the mines or go back to hauling whiskey. The thought of the law catching him running untaxed whiskey didn't scare him, nor did it make him yearn for a gun.

A simple smell made Goat's hands ache for a gun. The thick and earthy scent rose up from the loamy creek Goat and Ralphie had waded across at the base of the hill. The primal smell brought back a rush of memories from the not-so-distant past spent hunting Vietcong. As the aroma filled his lungs, Goat found himself scanning the ground, his eyes searching for trip wires leading to bouncing Betties or scuffed earth that signaled an ambush. Oblivious, pulling the wagon, Ralphie babbled on the whole time.

When they were halfway up the path, a movement on the opposite hillside drew Goat's attention. As a figure slipped through a clear spot of moonlight, Goat saw the glint of a belt buckle and a shoulder and arm covered in a tan uniform just before the NVA soldier slipped back into the shadows.

Goat stopped.

He knew it was his imagination projecting the picture like a Friday-night drive-in movie. There were no NVA soldiers stalking the hills of eastern Kentucky. Still, he held his breath as he scanned the woods. He waited a whole minute, not taking a breath until his chest was tight, but the soldier never reappeared.

"Goat?" Ralphie called from up ahead in a low whisper. "Goat." This time louder.

Pushing the phantom soldier from his mind, Goat jogged up the trail. He nodded to his young cousin to keep moving. With the wagon wheels once again creaking, Ralphie continued his one-sided conversation. Goat wasn't sure what made more noise, the banging of the empty wagon or Ralphie.

"Groovy, I'm telling you," Ralphie was saying. Even though Goat had zoned out for a bit, he was sure Ralphie was still talking about what all teenage boys talked about. Girls. Ralphie had a crush on his new English teacher. Ralphie thought she was a hippie, even though Ralphie wouldn't know a hippie if one bit him in the ass. "She drives one of those little German buses painted up like a rainbow with a peace sign. I'm telling you, Miss Love's a hippie."

Goat glanced over his shoulder, searching the trail for the NVA soldier.

"And you know what they say about those hippies," Ralphie intoned. Goat wasn't sure what they said about hippies, but he was sure Ralphie was going to tell him.

"What do they say about them hippies?" a voice called down.

Goat grinned. From up ahead, a yellow glow leaked out around the edges of a tarp hung across the trail. Leave it to Luther to pull Ralphie's chain.

"Come on, Ralphie," Luther called, pushing aside the tarp so the glow from the lanterns and fire pit lit up the trail all the way to Goat and his cousin. "Tell me about them hippie gals like Carrie Love." From farther back in the stand of trees came low laughter.

Ralphie and the Radio Flyer were quiet.

Sliding past his cousin, Goat glanced at the younger man's face. Even in the dim glow of the lantern light, he saw that the kid was the same shade of red as the wagon.

Goat called, "Luther, at least the boy's got the good sense to have a crush on a young teacher. He's not prattling on about Old Mrs. Napier."

"No-Neck Napier." Ralphie gasped. "She has a mustache." There was more cackling from underneath the lean-to, and Luther told someone to shut up.

Luther held the tarp open so Ralphie could pull the Radio Flyer underneath and park it next to the other two. These weren't your kid's Radio Flyer wagons. No, sir. The original wheels had been replaced with thicker, bigger tires to handle more weight, and the wagon sides had been cut out and several-foot-high metal slats welded in so that boxes of full mason jars and plastic jugs could be stacked up. It made it a little easier getting the bootleg whiskey down the hill.

Once the wagon was in, Luther dropped the tarp. The tarp was meant to hide the lanterns' and fire's light. Not that anyone would venture up the mountain, but Luther's daddy was careful.

"No-Neck Napier," Luther said, punching Goat in the arm. "Like I'd ever." Luther was solidly built although shorter than Goat, which Goat thought served the man well down in the mines. Even in the lanterns' flickering light, the black coal flecks ingrained in his skin were visible. Just as the men stripping coal out of the dark holes they'd dug left an imprint in the mountain, the coal left its mark on the men. The coal dust permeated the clothes and soaked into the skin. And if it soaked in deep, it took a man's life.

Farther back in the grove sat the liquor still—all copper tubing and barrels holding the mash being heated by a fire tended by Luther's dad. Nearby, a pair of men sat on wooden milking stools. They were seventy if they were a day, and over time they'd become almost mirror images of each other, both white-headed, grizzled, and skinny in overalls and white dress shirts. One filled the mason jars from the still. The second screwed on the lids, wiped off the jars, and slid them into waiting cases. The sour smell of fermenting mash hung heavy in the air.

"Luther, what're you doing up here with us outlaws?" Goat asked.

"Just helping out." Nearby stacked knee-high were full cases of mason jars ready to go. Ralphie started hoisting the liquor up onto the red Radio Flyer, the glass jars rattling.

"You don't need to be up here. You have an honest job," Goat replied.

"Foolishness," Luther's dad said, stalking toward them, waving a piece of firewood. "Plumb foolishness."

"I took a stand," Luther replied.

"Ah." Luther's dad waved a hand. "Striking from a good job. Unions and such. Causing trouble, and a man won't be able to go back to that job."

"Me? I'm not stepping on Cassidy's toes."

Cassidy Lane was the closest thing Bell County had to organized crime. Though he owned gas stations all the way to Knoxville, everyone knew Cassidy's real money came from the bootlegging, gambling, and whoring he provided up on Kayjay Mountain. When preachers railed about a Sodom and Gomorrah in their midst, they were talking about Kayjay and Cassidy Lane.

"Ah, Cassidy just likes talking big," Luther's dad said, turning away from his son. In the glint of the light, Goat saw the smooth brown grip of a pistol poking out of the old man's back pocket.

Luther opened his mouth and closed it. Shaking his head, he turned away to help load the wagon. Goat figured the two had gone round and round as much about the father's making white lightning as they did about Luther's striking.

Deciding to stay out of the fight, Goat told Luther's daddy, "I'll have your money in two days, as soon as I run this load down to Jellico."

"Mama's wanting you to come to supper," Luther's daddy said.

Goat smiled. "I'll pay you then."

"You're ready," Luther said. Moving to the front of the wagon, Goat took over. Just like in the Pontiac parked below, when there was whiskey onboard, Goat drove.

"See you boys," Goat said. Putting his back into it, he swung the wagon in a tight circle with Ralphie pushing. As they headed down the trail, Goat glanced back in time to see Luther's silhouette raise a hand just before the tarp dropped, blacking out the lanterns' glow. With the wagon loaded, going downhill was a lot quieter. The wheels squeaked less, and the heavy load made Ralphie concentrate more on steadying the wagon and less on talking.

Halfway down the mountain, Ralphie finally spoke in a whisper. "I don't want to cross Cassidy Lane."

"We aren't," Goat answered. "And there won't be any trouble."

The words were still in the air when a distant gunshot cracked the night. Goat's first thought was that a pocket of sap in a log had popped in the flames at the still, but even as he thought this, the whole mountaintop erupted in a flurry of gunfire. The first gun was joined by the deep booming of shotguns and the long burps of a tommy gun on rock and roll, something straight from Nam. A mad minute. Dumping all of your ammo into a kill zone. Pure insanity firing until the wood stocks smoked and the barrels sizzled.

Goat turned the wagon and ran it off the path. Ralphie stood unmoving on the trail. Goat grabbed the teenager's shirt and yanked Ralphie over and down to the ground with him.

"A raid?" Ralphie gasped. Their faces were so close that Goat smelled the sweat beading on the young man's upper lip.

Goat shook his head. Neither the police nor the Revenuers did a raid like this. Sure they'd shoot you, but they wouldn't gun you down. The gunfire rose to a crescendo; then, as suddenly as it started, it stopped, leaving only the echoes bouncing back and forth in the hills.

Ralphie said, "We have to go back. We gotta help."

Goat shook his head. He knew the reality of killing. Up on the hill, armed men were doing the business of murder.

"We got…" The words died. Ralphie's Adam's apple bobbed up and down.

"They're dead," Goat said harshly. "They're all dead and we can't help a bit. What we gotta do is get off this mountain." Pulling Ralphie in his wake, Goat slipped back onto the trail.

In the heavy summer air, gun smoke drifted down the hill like a mist, the smell bringing an adrenaline dump and a rush of memories. Thumping helicopter blades beating the air as they dropped into an LZ. Orange muzzle flashes and the steady climb of an M16 on full auto during a firefight.

With Ralphie in tow, Goat moved quickly down the path, his eyes scanning for the irregular shape of a human. His ears strained to hear the snap of twigs or the racking of a gun. At the bottom of the hill, they paused to catch their breath.

The night was silent. Even the running water in the creek was holding its breath. No animals hooted or scurried.

Without speaking a word, Goat and Ralphie shared the same knowledge.

The four men they had just left were dead.

Chapter 2

Goat drove alone, the moonlight ticking through the trees, blackness and a milky slash alternating across the GTO's hood. White. Black. White. Black.

Goat and Ralphie had slipped down the hill to where the GTO was hidden. With the headlights off, they made their getaway by creeping down the winding road until they hit the main road, where Goat snapped on the lights and sped away. After making Ralphie promise not to tell a soul what had happened, Goat dropped his cousin off at the mouth of his holler.

Leaning down into the car, Ralphie asked, "Was it like that... over there?"

Goat knew what he meant. Vietnam. "Some. And sometimes worse."

Without a word, Ralphie closed the GTO's door and trudged into the darkness.

And Goat drove the night away. The slash of the moon's bone light and the ink of dark night played out across his windshield.

Black.

White.

The windshield awash in light.

Awash in darkness.

As the GTO's tires rolled along eating up the miles, the wheels in Goat's head ate up time. He thought of Luther, not as the man he'd seen just a few hours ago, but as the boy he'd met in a schoolyard wearing hand-me-down clothes and a serious look in his eyes. Goat thought of how Luther's daddy had helped him out, schooling him on making shine and teaching him how to handle a car with a full load. Goat's own father had died in the mine when a slate of coal broke free and crushed him, so Luther's dad helped fill a gap that Goat needed filled as a boy. Then there were the memories of the recent past in Southeast Asia; Goat knew the country had taken part of his soul. Driving, Goat let his mind ramble and bounce about as night gave way to morning.

At daybreak, he pulled into a filling station on a mountain road. As he pumped gas, the road rumbled like a freight train, and he shielded his eyes as a line of big coal trucks thundered down the road in convoy. The trucks were placarded for the Blue Diamond Mine. Luther's employer. Each truck had a driver and a passenger, and the passengers all had rifles poking out the truck windows. Bell County was one incident away from a full-blown coal war. Goat watched the trucks roll past, but his mind was elsewhere, had latched onto a memory. During the Tet offensive, Goat had found himself fighting alongside a unit of MPs. During one of the lulls, he had talked to the lieutenant, a Yankee from Boston named Cuddy, who said he was going to be an investigator. Goat didn't understand much about investigating, and John Cuddy had simplified it for him—you ask questions to find answers, but mainly you kick stuff around, hoping to stir things up.

Goat planned on stirring things up.

Chapter 3

Goat didn't want to go back. He had enough visions of dead men in his head, and he didn't want any more. Steeling himself, he went up the hill. The Radio Flyer was still half on the trail, half off in the weeds, just as he'd left it. Pausing, Goat put a hand on the cases of whiskey and used the tail of his shirt to wipe the sweat out of his eyes. Looking up the hill, he saw the green tarp hanging from a tree and flapping in the breeze. His mouth was dry, his throat constricted. Taking a deep breath, he left the Radio Flyer and slowly walked up the trail, keeping his eye on the edge of the swaying tarp.

Up close, he saw the tarp had been shredded by bullets. It was splashed with brown stains drying sticky, and flies congregated over the blood. The two old men with their well-worn white shirts lay next to their stools. One had fallen right and one had fallen left. One was facedown, and the other on his back with his arm thrown over his head. The still was riddled with bullet holes, and the stack of finished moonshine was toppled over, glass and cardboard scattered on the ground. The raw scent of fermenting mash, the smell of moonshine from smashed mason jars, was overpowered by the copper tang of spilled blood.

Luther and his daddy were farther away from the still. Luther was on his back, arms splayed, a single gunshot in his forehead.

Tears burned Goat's cheeks.

Luther's daddy was a few yards back down the hill, facedown, one arm stretched out toward his son.

Goat knelt in the open space between Luther's body and the old man's. Flies buzzed incessantly, but it was no match for the buzzing in his mind. A sob came from his chest, popping out of his mouth like an air bubble. He drove his fingers into the dirt and rocks and leaves, pushing his anger into the ground. Grinding his teeth. Following the sob came a long moan that turned into a primal scream. He shouted until his lungs hurt and he could no longer make a sound. His outburst scattered a flock of crows in the trees, their black ragged wings flapping as they dove and cawed through the valley.

Silence returned.

Goat pushed the rage back into the dark box in his chest. Calmly, he stood and surveyed the killing ground. Instead of seeing the sunlight streaming through the trees, Goat imagined the scene as it had been the night before. Darkness. Lanterns lighting the still operation.

Luther and his daddy were at the far edge of the light, almost into the trees. Luther heard the killers come. He went to check it out. His father followed. Goat remembered hearing the shot that at the time he'd mistaken for a popping in the fire. Now he saw it differently. That had been the first shot.

Maybe Luther's daddy had pulled his gun and that started the shooting. *No, wait,* Goat thought, looking at the bodies. The brown grip of the revolver stuck out of the old man's back pocket. Untouched. Turning his attention to Luther, Goat again saw his friend had been shot dead center in his forehead. An aimed shot. Aimed shots worked only at the start of an ambush, because once the firing got going, people bobbed and weaved, scrambled away. Luther was killed first. The leader of the killers shot Luther and that had been the signal to open fire. Then the mad minute of pure murder.

Goat moved forward to the crest of the wooded hill, his eyes scanning the ground. His gaze found a cluster of golden brass glistening. Squatting, he checked the pile of brass. There were six empty .357 Magnum casings. A revolver. Probably the leader's whose shot started the ambush. Goat stood and moved farther and found scattered, empty shotgun shells—12-gauge double-aught buck. Man killers. More gold-glinting brass in the grass caught his attention, and he scooped one up, a .45 ACP. This brass was scattered everywhere. Goat knew he was right: One killer had used a Thompson submachine gun. Goat knew the sound of a tommy gun because he had carried one during the Tet street fighting.

He moved back down the hill and knelt beside Luther. Lightly, he rested a hand on his friend's cold chest. He continued on, stopping at Luther's daddy. This time, he pulled the revolver from the dead man's pocket. It was long-barreled Colt .38, the finish dulled and dinged.

"I'm going to kill 'em," Goat said out loud. Tucking the revolver into his belt, he repeated, "I'm going to kill every last one of them."

Chapter 4

"Goat, that's a pretty car," Clarence said. Goat was tilted back in the barber chair, hot lather on his face, Clarence's straight razor glinting three inches above. Poised.

"Thanks." His GTO sat at the curb right next to the striped

barber pole of Clarence's shop. The three wooden chairs lining the wall were held down by a trio of old men who spent their days spreading gossip. Goat needed information and he knew these old men knew more about what was going on than anyone else.

"That's not the one the revenuers took?" Clarence asked.

Goat waited until Clarence slid the razor across his chin, scraping as he went.

"Naw, that was a '61 New Yorker," Goat answered. He had loved that car. The New Yorker had lots of room in the trunk, and with double springs and shocks and a tuned-up engine, the car was fast enough for Goat to outrun any lawman in Kentucky and Tennessee, even hauling a full load of shine. Until the night he ran out of gas trying to outrun the law.

Clarence nodded, looking down at Goat over his half-glasses. "Yup, I remember now." Clarence damn well knew Goat had bought the car from Luther's daddy and hauled the man's shine. After all, Goat had delivered Clarence's stash of shine even before he could drive, pedaling his bike to the barbershop twice a week.

The newspaper in Goat's lap was folded open to the moonshine-murder story. It was two days since an anonymous call had led the state police to the massacre at the moonshine still. Goat thought the story was pretty much right, except for the police's claim that the killer had called in the murders. Goat figured the police were doing the same thing he'd been doing when he called in the murder: stirring things up. Just like he knew coming to the barbershop would cause a stir.

Goat stared out the window across the Pineville town square to the courthouse, where a dozen cop cars sat. The paper reported that the state police were bringing more troopers to Bell County to keep the peace. With striking miners and rumors of northern organizers trying to start up unions in Bell County, there were fears. After all, unions were just a step away from communism. With blown-up coal trucks and miners beaten on the strike lines, tensions were high, and now with the four men killed in the moonshine murders, the state police were trying to make sure things stayed cool in the summer heat. At least that's how the newspaperman had put it.

"A shame about them boys," Clarence said, trying for nonchalant. Goat waited as Clarence did his thing with two more swipes of the razor. He kept his eyes glued to the cop cars across the way, pretending not to be paying much attention to Clarence. "Weren't you and that one boy, Luther, friends?"

"Yup," he answered, feeling the barber's eyes on him. Goat watched as the side door to the courthouse opened and three men in uniforms came out. All three paused to shake out smokes.

"I knew his daddy was making moonshine, but I didn't know the boy was helping—did you?" Clarence asked. The trio of cops fired up their smokes and headed across the square.

Before Goat could answer Clarence, one of the men in the chairs behind him said, "Hell, everyone knew Luther was making deliveries for his daddy."

"I didn't," Clarence said.

"Oh, yeah," said the man Goat couldn't see. "Just a few jars. Like the milkman going door to door. I think everyone in my rooming house, including the teacher, was buying his liquor."

"I thought the boy was one of those agitators," another man said. Goat hated that he couldn't see who was talking behind him, but he didn't dare move with Clarence's straight razor working.

"Luther was no communist agitator," Clarence said. "He just wanted a good job."

"What are you talking about?" Goat asked, perplexed.

"Northerner socialists down here trying to get the miners unionized," the second old man explained. "Agitators."

"The mine owners want the unions stopped?" Goat asked.

There was a snort. "They want it nipped in the bud."

The three cops were on a direct course for the barbershop.

"Shame about them boys," Clarence repeated, taking the last of the shaving cream off Goat's face with a flourish of his razor.

"It is a shame," Goat said, pointedly nodding toward the approaching cops. "Think they'll find out who did it?"

There was another snort from one of the old men.

Clarence took a warm towel and patted Goat's face. "Everyone knows who had them boys killed." He looked to the approaching cops. "Even they know."

One of the men said, "Everyone knew that old man was making shine and not paying his due. If we knew, Cassidy knew."

Cassidy Lane.

The three cops stopped at the square as a farm truck rolled by. Two of them were state troopers in their gray uniforms and Smokey Bear hats. The last man, in a tan uniform, was Aaron Grubbs, chief deputy under the Bell County sheriff.

"You think Cassidy had them killed?" Goat asked.

"There any doubt?" Clarence asked just before the bell above the door jingled.

What Clarence didn't say but every man in the room knew was that Aaron Grubbs ran protection for Cassidy Lane. If Grubbs was involved in the investigation, there would never be any arrests in the murders on the mountain.

Raising his voice, the barber said, "Afternoon, Officers." He pulled the warm towel from Goat's face, threw it over his shoulder.

"How long a wait for a haircut?" the tall blond trooper said.

"We're all done here," Clarence said, spinning Goat's chair so he could see the haircut and shave in the mirror. Goat nodded before he stood.

"I told you Clarence would take care of you," Chief Deputy Grubbs said. Shifting his attention to Goat, he asked, "Is that your hot rod out front there?"

"Yes, sir," Goat answered, standing.

"One of those '65 Pontiacs?" Grubbs asked. His voice was thin and reedy. He rested his left hand on the butt of the big old Smith & Wesson holstered at his hip.

"It's a '66," Goat replied. The blond trooper removed his hat and took a seat in the barber's chair.

"Don't look like she's got much wear," Grubbs said. "But then I've not seen you around. Heard the judge sent you to Vietnam."

"He did," Goat replied as he paid the barber. "Now I'm back."

"Weren't you running shine for that old man that got himself killed?"

"No, sir," Goat lied, forcing a smile. "I'm making up for lost time, chasing girls and driving my hot rod."

"That a fact?" Grubbs said, like he didn't believe Goat.

"That's a fact," Goat replied, staring the older man dead in the eye.

Clarence produced a fresh sheet and wrapped it around the blond trooper with a flourish. The second trooper hooked his thumbs in his gun belt, watching the exchange.

"We found a load of whiskey abandoned halfway down that hill," Grubbs said. "Word going around is that you were driving for the old man."

"Is that a fact?" Goat asked, still smiling.

"That's a fact," Grubbs said. "Why would someone leave whiskey?"

"Don't know," Goat responded, letting an edge creep into his voice. "You should ask Cassidy Lane."

Chief Deputy Grubbs's eyes narrowed, and his lips set into a hard thin line.

"Is that a fact?" the standing trooper said with an amused look.

"That's a goddamn fact," Goat said as he strode past the lawmen toward the door.

Chapter 5

Goat was scared. He had definitely stirred things up at Clarence's barbershop, and now he was going to shove a stick in the hornet's nest. He knew it was insane, and he could think of only one person crazy enough to go along with his idea.

Goat idled the GTO to a stop. A road sign hung by a single nail from a pole. Copperhead Road. The road wasn't more than twin ruts leading up a lonesome holler. Along the way were a few abandoned houses, falling down, left to the weeds and animals. Goat powered the Pontiac all the way to the flat top of a ridge where a simple house with a rusty tin roof sat. All the windows in the house were open, and the Doors' "L.A. Woman" rattled the window frames.

Goat killed the engine and laid on the horn. Jim Morrison and the boys dropped away. The screen door banged open.

The first thing Goat saw was the .45 dangling loose in the man's hand.

"Goat McKnight, is that you, boy?" the man said.

"It's me, Johnny Lee," Goat said, stepping out of the car.

"Come on in the house." The man waved with the pistol.

John Lee Pettimore was shirtless and deeply tanned. He had on tie-dyed jeans; his hair was down over his shoulders.

"Were you expecting company?" Goat asked as he walked into the house, which smelled like fried bologna, incense, and pot.

"Naw," Johnny Lee said, tucking the pistol into his waistband, moving in front of Goat, and leading the way. "But you never know when Charlie will get through the wire."

No one had ever accused John Lee Pettimore of being stable. In fact, people who knew him said he was crazier than a shit-house rat, and that was before he went to Vietnam.

The entryway in the hall was hung with beaded curtains. And there were hand-painted canvases on the wall. One had a dove and a scroll that said PEACE AND LOVE. Another had a psychedelic-colored peace sign.

"What you been up to since you got back, Goat?" Johnny Lee asked as he went through the beaded curtain and headed toward the back of the house.

"Same as before," Goat answered as he followed. "Running shine."

"Gotta do what you're meant to do," Johnny Lee said, opening the door at the end of the hallway. Goat followed John Lee into the room.

"You're here about what happened up on the hill." It was a statement, not a question.

Goat didn't answer. He was taking in the room. There wasn't any furniture. All of the windows were boarded up, and the only light was from a lone bulb hanging from the ceiling. Crowded around were brown wooden boxes with stenciling, green crates, and even a stainless steel coffin. Some of the boxes had U.S. Department of Defense markings, and some had Chinese letters. The open coffin was packed tight with black M16s.

"We going to hunt?" Johnny Lee Pettimore asked with a cracked smile.

"I aim to make things right," Goat replied, picking up a green plastic case that said FRONT TOWARD ENEMY. A claymore mine. Looking up, he said, "Holy shit, Johnny Lee."

"Gotta be ready for when Charlie comes through the wire."

Then Goat started explaining what he wanted to do. The more Goat talked, the wider Johnny Lee's grin grew, until it was a skull's leer, which confirmed what Goat had already known. This was an insane idea.

Chapter 6

Talk about being in the lion's den. The car parked at the bottom of the hill wasn't the one Goat expected. It wasn't the well-washed sheriff's cruiser of Chief Deputy Aaron Grubbs, but rather a battered Oldsmobile with two rough-looking men inside watching the road. All Goat had to say was that he wanted to drink and play poker, and they waved him on up Kayjay Mountain to Cassidy Lane's three-story place, lit up like a roadhouse with bright neon lights. The parking lot was half full, Goat noted as he got out of his car, glancing back once to see Johnny Lee's shadow slither out of the trunk and then disappear into the darkness. The inside of the bar was like any place allowed to sell liquor — and Bell County wasn't one of them — filled with men spending their money on the booze or the gambling in the back or both. And for more money, the women serving the drinks would take the men to rooms upstairs.

Goat scanned the bar and found another rough-looking man sitting on a stool in the corner, not drinking, his eyes sizing up the patrons. Stopping directly in front of the man, Goat said,

"Tell Cassidy that Goat McKnight's here about those four dead men up at that still."

The man looked at Goat, studied his face, and, without saying a word, got up and left. A few moments later the guy returned. "Come with me," he said, and led him to the back of the bar, where they took two flights of stairs to a landing and a closed door. The man knocked.

"Come in," a deep voice said. The man opened the door for Goat.

Goat went into Cassidy Lane's den. Cassidy was a big man, both tall and wide, with a visage that reminded Goat of Ben Franklin's. His hair wasn't as long as Franklin's, but it did grow thick on only the sides and back of his head, and with a pair of half-glasses perched halfway down his nose, Cassidy did resemble old Ben. Cassidy was sitting on a couch looking at some papers, his legs crossed and bouncing lightly to Frank Sinatra playing on the record player behind him. He stared at Goat over his glasses.

"You come to kill me?" Cassidy finally asked in his baritone voice, almost a bearlike rumble.

Before Goat could answer, he heard the click of a hammer and felt a gun barrel pushing into the back of his head. "Careful how you answer," the man behind him said. The man's hand ran over Goat's body until he found the Colt, which he pulled free.

Cassidy kept his eyes trained on Goat. "You here to kill me?"

Hoping his voice wasn't cracking, Goat said, "If you murdered my friends, then I am going to kill you dead."

"That's a powerful statement for a man in your predicament," Cassidy said. Casually, he reached behind him and turned off the stereo; the record slid to a stop. Turning his attention to the man behind Goat, Cassidy said, "Give me the iron."

The man handed the Colt to Cassidy. Nodding toward the pistol in his hand, Cassidy said, "You don't have any play left.

Now, you listen — I had nothing to do with those four men's deaths."

"Why should I believe you?" Goat asked.

"I don't give a damn if you believe me or not," Cassidy said. "I'm telling you the facts. And you best worry if you're going to walk out of here or get carried out."

"One more buried up here won't make a difference," the man behind Goat said, emphasizing his words with a push of the muzzle into Goat's neck.

Goat nodded once. "I don't know if I believe you. But let me tell you one thing."

"What's that?"

"You kill me, and I promise you hell's coming." Goat opened his hand to show a small whistle in his palm.

"What the hell's that?" Goat's captor piped up from behind him.

"In Vietnam, the Cong used whistles since their radios were so poor. It got to be when you heard one of these, you knew Charlie was coming."

"What's that mean?" Cassidy asked cautiously.

"That means John Lee Pettimore is somewhere close." Goat heard the man behind him take a breath. Most people knew of crazy Johnny Lee. "If I don't blow this whistle, he'll be coming to kill every son of a bitch in here."

Cassidy looked at Goat for a moment.

The man behind Goat said, "He's bluffing."

Cassidy looked past Goat and the man behind him and said, "I don't think so." Slowly, he set the revolver on the coffee table. "He's not bluffing."

"No, he's not, son," Johnny Lee said. Goat glanced over his shoulder. Standing in the open doorway was John Lee Pettimore decked out in camos and black face paint, a large Bren machine gun weighing heavy in his hands.

"The plan was the whistle," Goat said.

"I don't like waiting," Johnny Lee said, grinning.

Goat picked up the Colt from the table, tucked it back into his waistband, and asked Cassidy Lane, "You kill my friends?"

"I had no reason to kill them men. Bad for business to draw attention."

"What about the old man not paying you to run liquor?"

"Him running shine didn't hurt me none," Cassidy replied. "I liked the old man, and he brought me a case of his shine once a month. We respected each other. We had no fight."

"People said he wasn't paying your tithe and you were mad."

Cassidy snorted.

"What?"

"Aaron," the man said with a sneer. "He tells folks that."

"Grubbs?" Goat asked. "Why would your man say that?"

"He doesn't work for me anymore," Cassidy said. "He's going legit, running security for a mine."

"Which mine?" Goat asked, things already clicking into place.

"The Blue Diamond," Cassidy said. Goat saw his own epiphany reflected in Cassidy Lane's face. "He's trying to lay these murders on me. I'm going to kill him."

"No, you're not," Goat said. "I am."

Chapter 7

The whole apartment on the third floor of the rooming house was lit up. Goat sat at the small kitchen table keeping company with a jelly glass of moonshine from a jar he'd found under the sink. The apartment was silent, but Goat thought echoes of the woman's crying lingered in the air. Goat and Johnny Lee had left Kayjay Mountain driving like hell for town. Once the pieces came together, Goat saw the whole thing plainly. Just like if you stir up sand and water and then wait long enough, the particles settle and you can see right through. The picture was clear.

The tan of the NVA soldier's uniform that night.

Luther calling Ralphie's teacher by her name—Carrie Love.

Luther telling his father he was taking a stand.

The old men at the barbershop talking about Luther delivering moonshine door to door.

Luther being shot in the middle of his forehead.

The six .357 Magnum rounds found on the hill. A cop's gun.

Bell County miners striking and the worry about northern agitators organizing unions. The mine owners wanting to nip things in the bud.

The North Vietnamese soldier Goat glimpsed on the mountain was actually the tan sheriff's uniform of Aaron Grubbs.

And the fact that Chief Deputy Aaron Grubbs was working for the Blue Diamond mine—Luther's mine.

Goat and Johnny Lee found Carrie Love in her apartment, and between sobs, she confirmed his suspicions. In other parts of the country, every time people had come to help the miners, the mine owners had busted them up, shipped them out, or killed them. Carrie was a teacher but she was an activist first. She'd been asked to come down and help organize the miners, but she was told she had to be careful. Only a few knew of Carrie Love's role. Luther was tasked with carrying messages between Carrie Love and the striking miners. Luther took and delivered messages with the jars of moonshine. Someone had leaked word that Luther was doing more than striking, and Carrie figured the mine owners thought Luther was pulling the strings, that he was the one calling the shots. No one suspected the hippie teacher was the mastermind.

Nip the union organizing in the bud.

Everyone knew Luther was helping his dad make moonshine, so it wouldn't take much for Aaron Grubbs to find the moonshine still. Then he and some hired thugs slipped up that mountain. Goat had spotted Grubbs's tan sheriff's uniform as they were making their way up to kill Luther and anyone else at the still.

The steps outside creaked. Carrie Love's apartment was on the third floor of the building, and it was the only apartment that was serviced by a rickety staircase running on the outside of the house.

The killers were here.

Goat took a swallow of the moonshine, the whiskey cool on the way down his throat but burning once it hit his stomach.

Damn, Luther's daddy did make good liquor, he thought.

Before sending Carrie Love away with John Lee Pettimore in the GTO, Goat had had her make a call to Chief Deputy Grubbs. She told him she knew he had killed Luther. She told him she was scared, and she would give him all the paperwork she had on the miners and the organizers. She offered to trade the information for safe passage out of Bell County. Grubbs promised he'd let her leave once he had the papers.

The doorknob turned slightly as a hand tested the lock.

Then the hand knocked.

"Carrie," Aaron Grubbs said.

Goat glanced at the green square propped against the door. Wires led back to the plastic square in his hand. He pushed back from the table and stood, making sure to be loud. The killers outside would think Carrie Love was coming to answer the door.

Goat stepped behind the refrigerator and pulled the revolver from his waistband. With his other hand, he readied the mine's trigger.

Goat called out, "Grubbs, I'm going to kill you." Outside there were confused voices. Goat pushed the mine's trigger. *Clack-clack.*

The claymore had a warning on it: FRONT TOWARD THE ENEMY. The warning was there for a reason.

The claymore was a shaped charge of C-4 packed with hundreds of steel ball bearings, and they blew out in a scythe-like arc of destruction.

The explosion shook the whole house.

The apartment's front door was blown out and clouds swirled inside. His ears ringing, Goat moved forward, kicking through the remnants of the front door. Outside, part of the landing was shredded. Below, in the alley, two bodies still clutching shotguns were splayed out on the roof of Aaron Grubbs's cruiser. Partway down the stairs was a body, the man's chest pulped by the claymore's ball bearings. A broken Thompson submachine gun was on the step below the dead man.

The blast had knocked Chief Deputy Aaron Grubbs down the stairs, where he knelt as if praying. His face bloody, his body listing to and fro like a bobbing ship.

Goat cocked the Colt.

Grubbs looked up and saw Goat. Tried to stagger to his feet, but stumbled and fell.

With the comforting weight of the Colt in his hand, Goat McKnight started down the stairs.

RIVER SECRET

BY ANNE SWARDSON

She took one tiny step toward me. Another—then hesitated. Her mother leaned down and murmured a few words in her ear. Reassured, the girl toddled forward more confidently and then, halfway to where I was playing, stopped again.

She wore a white wool coat that reached almost to her knees. A few strands of curly brown hair escaped from the fur around her hood, which had been carefully tied at the neck. By her sleek-haired mother, probably. Those dimpled hands were too little to tie anything.

Fortunately for me, they could hold a two-euro coin.

The child looked at her mother again. It was time to reel her in. I ended "Sous le Ciel de Paris" a verse early—kids never went for the melancholy material—and put the accordion down on its stand with a click. The girl turned her eyes back to me. I transitioned into 2/4 rhythm with the foot pedal on the bass drum. After picking up the trombone, I launched into the "Bayrische Polka," keeping the oompah with the drum, adding a cymbal stroke to each downbeat with my other foot, and bobbing forward each time the slide came out with a wailing *mwaa-mwaa.*

A big smile appeared on the little girl's face. She walked confidently to the beret lying upside down on the bricks in front of me and dropped in the coin. I grinned too and gave her another duck, almost a half bow, with a forward slide of the trombone. The girl looked amused, then beckoned her mother to come as she held out her hand for another coin.

"Maman!"

A few more spectators peeled off from the stream of Paris tourists who were coming down the steps of the Solférino footbridge over the Seine on their way to the tunnel leading to the Tuileries Garden. They joined the gaggle of Americans in tracksuits around me and my drums, horns, and stands, attracted by the polka lilt and by the exquisite little girl standing before me.

My location, at the entrance to the underground passage between the bridge and the stairs to the gardens, was the best in the business. When I blew a long note on the trumpet, the tones reverberated off the rounded tunnel ceiling. The cymbals were sharper, the drums crisper because of those acoustics. The river's flowing water gave a sense of space and openness. And with my back to the passage wall, I could spot the oncoming Italians in high-heeled sandals, the rotund British, and the tall Dutch wearing backpacks, and then adjust the musical selection accordingly.

Still, each day I needed something special to get an audience going, something to lure a real crowd around me. I needed that more than most, since I never sang, only played. The more people, the more likely I could pass the hat at the end of a set. It was always more lucrative than just waiting for the coins to drop in one by one.

If I was lucky, that moment had arrived.

But Maman wasn't about to chip in another coin. She was

distracted by a squat woman wearing a kerchief over her hair. In her grimy fingers, the woman held out a dull, gold-looking ring as she sidled closer to her target.

"Mais, madame, see voo play, madame, madame..." The woman didn't pronounce the words properly. Half her teeth were missing. Even though it was March, she was wearing sandals, without socks, along with a moth-eaten sweater and a long skirt with faded yellow flowers.

"Leave us alone, you disgusting thing! We're just trying to enjoy the music!" Maman held up a forbidding hand as the beggar took a step closer, waving the ring and giving a sidelong glance in the direction of the lady's Hermès handbag.

The mother tossed her head, cinched the tie of her cashmere coat, put one hand firmly around the clasp of her purse, and held out the other to her daughter. "Come, Marie-Christine. Let's go watch the boys sail the boats in the basin." The little girl ran to her, and without another look at me they were gone, up the steps and into the gardens. I tried to save the day by playing "Hello, Dolly," replete with plenty of slides and bass thumps, but it didn't help. The crowd melted away. There was silence.

Only the kerchiefed woman was left standing there. She looked at me like a whipped dog, her head down, barely meeting my eyes. I stared angrily. I didn't speak, because I never did. I didn't cross my arms or shake my finger at her, as I had sometimes done before. But she knew she had driven away my clientele, and she knew I was angry. It was one of our agreements. She was supposed to do her job, and I would do mine.

She twisted her hands in her skirt and sighed.

"I'm sorry, Baptiste. I thought I could help. Top us up a little."

Why I had decided to extend a hand to Tatiana I will never know. I had everything I wanted: a city license to play my one-man setup in a rainproof location that sucked in half the tourists in Paris; enough money to pay for my tiny studio in the Eighteenth Arrondissement and for the frozen dinners I bought each night at the Picard store. There was enough to send to my family in the south too, back when I used to do that. Back when I talked to them. Back when I talked. Before my memory told me I should speak no longer.

I nodded firmly toward the gardens and she knew what I meant: "Leave my customers alone. If people pay you for those stupid rings, they won't pay me for my music. And they certainly won't put money in my beret if they find their wallets missing."

She shuffled off slowly, cowering as she went. I turned back to my instruments, my anger passing. She needed the money more than I did, and every coin she pickpocketed in the park reduced the number I felt compelled to slip her at the end of the day.

Maybe I shared with Tatiana because no one else would. Gypsies are human rats, I'd heard the policemen say after they'd chased the beggars, pickpockets, and scamsters from the gardens. Send them back where they came from. Don't touch them; they're dirty. Even American tourists, the most gullible of all the nationalities that walked by me, eyed the rings the Gypsies proffered with suspicion, then turned their backs and patted their wallets.

So Tatiana got a few coins from me each day, coupled with a warning that if she ever stole from me, she'd never see another euro. She understood everything from my face, my gestures. I'd give her a shake of the head when I wanted her elsewhere, a tilt when a good potential mark walked by. I'd bring her the odd bit of *poulet rôti* from my previous night's dinner, a thin blanket when I had bought a new one.

What Tatiana mostly got from me was something no one else

gave her: an ear. As I packed up each night, she'd come by and tell me in broken French about her life: growing up in a camp outside Plovdiv, making her way with others of her kind in a series of ragtag caravans from Bulgaria, across Hungary, over the Austrian Alps, then here. Camping, stealing, camping. Along the way there had been a man, and a child or two. She didn't know where they were now.

———

I SAW THE little girl again not long after that. It was warmer, but she still wore the white coat. She was with her mother, and so was a handsome black-haired young man—younger than the woman. His arm was wrapped around the waist of his companion. His eyes were on the woman's face; his hand was atop the little girl's head, stroking her hair.

I wasted no time in pulling out the trombone and starting up the polka.

"Maman!"

The girl pointed to me and made an excited little jump. The Mother—what else could I call her?—reached for her purse, but the man pushed her hand away. Fishing in his pocket, he pulled out a pink ten-euro note and inserted it in the little girl's fist. He took her other hand in a firm grip, plastered a big smile on his face, and started walking with her across the paving stones toward my waiting beret. I kept up the beat. Tatiana, happily, was nowhere to be seen.

The child lost enthusiasm with each step. The farther she got from her mother, the more her feet dragged, the more she tried to turn back. Her face twisted into a pout. The beret was forgotten. The man kept the smile fixed in place and continued forward, pulling on her hand, trying to ignore her reluctance. The tourists were nudging one another and pointing.

The conflict ended when the girl stopped moving her feet entirely and collapsed on the ground, wailing. The man bent over her, ostentatiously trying to pick her up and get her pointed toward me, wrapping his arms around her and lifting. But she pulled away, dropped the ten-euro bill, and darted toward the Mother. When she got there, she buried her face in the cashmere coat. The woman made a gesture of resignation and picked up the sobbing girl, draping her over her shoulder as the man picked up the money and then rejoined them. They walked up the steps, side by side, the ten-euro note still in the man's hand. I had warned Tatiana away from the mother, but I wished she were nearby now so that I could nod my head toward that prey.

She came to my stand late that day as I was breaking down the equipment. Business had been good, she said. For me too. My pockets dragged with change, from yellow fifty-centime pieces to two-euro coins. I even had a few bills. As we sometimes did, we dragged my drum case and horn bags around the corner and sat on one of the concrete benches overlooking the Seine.

We often ended the day like that when the weather was good and the cops didn't chase us away. The setting sun shone pinkly on the cream-colored stone buildings across the river: the Beaux Arts rail-station structure of the Musée d'Orsay; next to it the squat headquarters of the Légion d'honneur. To the left, upriver, were the towers of Notre-Dame; to the right, the glass-paned cavernous roof of the Grand Palais, French flag flying atop.

The river itself was a sight to see. At this time of year, the Seine was fed by runoff from the mountains. A deep and viscous brown, the water was almost level with the cobbled walkway along the banks. The current slurped against the bridge's pilings and pushed against the prows of the Bateaux-Mouches as they slid up and down the waterway with their cargoes of tourists.

"Look at this," Tatiana said, lifting her skirt and taking her earnings out of a pocket sewn inside. "There was a guy waving a ten-euro bill around and when he put it in his pocket he left a corner hanging out. He never even saw me."

I clapped her on the back.

———

THE MOTHER, THE man—I'd named him Romeo—and the little girl came by on their way to the gardens often in the month that followed. They—at least the child and her mother—probably lived in the Seventh Arrondissement, on the other side of the footbridge, in one of those apartments with ten-foot ceilings. People in those apartments wore cashmere coats and dressed their little girls in clothing from Tartine et Chocolat, the fancy children's store on the boulevard Saint-Germain.

Romeo must have learned his lesson, because he never again tried to bring the girl to the beret. She let him hold her hand across the bridge, the Mother alongside. Then she always walked up to me alone. I'd play the polka and do my bobbing routine. It got to be a game: She'd smile at me and I'd respond with a couple of little dance steps and a trombone wail. More steps toward me and I'd twirl around. The girl would laugh and put a coin in. I felt like laughing myself, for the first time in years. Unlike my older fans, who seemed almost ashamed to be giving money to a beggar, albeit a musical one, the child looked straight into my face. Her expression, a kind of puckery smile with a flash of her blue eyes, made me imagine that she knew how much those coins meant to me.

On a gray day in April, I was just finishing a set with "La Vie en Rose" when I saw that the child was there, standing a bit in front of the usual bunch of tourists. Next to her was Romeo. No sign of the Mother. His hair was slicked back from his forehead in an expensive cut. My audience was with me; they had clapped to the theme from *Can-Can* and laughed when I swayed during the refrain of "I Love Paris." I'd lose them if I played the polka. Instead, I just winked at the child, and she smiled at me. She seemed unperturbed that her mother wasn't there. One hand held on to the hand of the man, who looked down at her as if he couldn't believe he'd won her over. Her other hand fiddled with a heart-shaped locket I'd never seen before and that I could tell was gold.

The girl gave me a bill this time, another ten-euro note from Romeo's wallet, and then they walked up the stairs and into the gardens. As they moved out of view, the man picked her up and whispered something in her ear.

The money flowed in that day. No sooner had one group left after a set than another would form around me, sometimes even before I'd started playing again. By late afternoon, I must have had forty people watching. I treated them to a jazz improv on the trombone, with only the cymbal tracking. I didn't try that often, but the crowd was with me.

Suddenly, sirens wailed from the gardens. A voice thundered from the public-address system; I couldn't make out the words. The *pah-paw* of police cars and fire trucks could be heard in the distance, then on the road above the tunnel. Two uniformed cops raced in from the bridge and rushed up the tunnel stairs, taking them two at a time as the tourists gawked. Just after the cops entered the tunnel, the great grilled gates, the ones that closed the park off from the bridge each evening, began sliding shut.

The tourists scattered in confusion. I could still hear noise from the gardens, but it was a muffled rumble. I was locked outside. This was not convenient: I'd have to drag my stuff along the quay and around the west side of the Tuileries to get to the Metro if I couldn't cross the park. Where was Tatiana? I had never before seen the gates close early. I began packing up.

There was a rat-a-tat, and one more set of racing footsteps sounded from the bridge. I turned and saw that they weren't being made by a late cop. The Mother, her face streaked with tears, coat hanging open, lipstick smeared, a cell phone in one hand, ran across the cobblestones in high heels and threw herself against the barred gate.

"My baby! My baby!" It was more a howl than a scream, a noise like no sound I had ever heard. "Let me in!" She hung on the bars as if without them she would melt to the ground.

Two uniformed policemen trotted down the stairs on the other side of the gate and came toward her. I could hear more shouts; someone was ordering that the gates be opened. The cops reached out through the grille and touched her hands. And I could hear some of the words they said to her:

"So terribly sorry."

"He says he only looked away for a second."

"We will find the villain who did this, madame."

———

MUSIC WAS THE only thing that ever filled me up inside. Even before the memories from my childhood came back and stopped my voice, even before the stairs and the tunnel and the broad river became my only horizons, nothing but music touched the hollow core inside me. That's why I learned so many instruments. Each one—not just my one-man-band ensemble, but the violin, the piano, the plaintive oboe—gave me a different facet of what others get from normal life. When I played, I felt complete.

But on this day, the day after the child, the day after the Mother stopped being a mother, I was just blowing air and whacking drums. The voice my instruments gave me was an ugly, blaring thing.

I had gone back to the bridge to work. What else was there to do? I played the most melancholy songs of my Edith Piaf repertoire. No polkas. I didn't even touch the trombone. It seemed unfair that the park was open as usual and that the beret filled up, even though I wasn't twirling, or bobbing, or smiling. How could those tourists be unaware that my music was crying, not singing? But I couldn't leave, couldn't go away from the last place I had seen her.

Around midday, a hard, thin man with steel-gray hair stepped up to where I was playing. He wore an impeccably pressed navy suit with a tiny square of yellow silk handkerchief poking from the jacket pocket. With him were a chubby sergeant in uniform and a thuggish lieutenant in a leather jacket. The small crowd around me dissipated as soon as they approached.

"I am Commander Bassin," the suited man said. "Are you acquainted with a Tatiana Plevneliev?" He pronounced the name as if his lips had never had to speak such horrible syllables before.

I had assumed the police would question me about the child. But why were they asking about Tatiana?

He got a nod of the head. It was tempting to deny our acquaintance, but the park cops had seen us together too many times.

"How does she make her living?"

I held out my hand, palm upward.

Bassin raised an eyebrow. The sergeant murmured something in his ear.

"They say you don't speak."

I shook my head.

"Are you physically incapable of speech or do you choose not to speak?"

I shrugged.

"I have to tell you, Monsieur...Baptiste, this is a very serious matter."

I put my arm to my side, palm out flat.

"Yes, it's about the child. Did you ever see her with Madame Plevneliev?"

Enthusiastic shake no. It was true. There was nothing in children's pockets to pick. Tatiana would have focused only on Romeo.

"When did you last see her?"

When was it? Had she come by yesterday morning? I shrugged and jerked my thumb over my shoulder in a a-while-ago gesture.

"Monsieur Baptiste, you must search your memory. We know she was in the park yesterday. We want to know if she came this way."

Bassin was standing motionless, looking straight at me as the sergeant took notes. I wondered what you wrote down if the person being interrogated didn't speak.

Raising both hands, I shook my head again. Yesterday was filled with the child. I had no recollection of anything else. All I could see in my mind's eye was the white-coated figure in the arms of the man as he carried her into the park.

"Have you ever seen the Gypsy with children?"

Children? My heart turned cold. I could see where he was heading, and it was very bad. No, I hadn't. I tried to shake my head as definitively as I could.

But I had a question. I clasped one hand in the other, one elbow high, the other low, then made a gesture straight back from my forehead as if slicking back my hair. Bassin looked puzzled for a second, then the sergeant whispered again.

"It's not something you need to know," Bassin told me. "But yes, Monsieur de Marigny says he saw her near the child." That wasn't quite what I was asking. But it sounded like the police had found Monsieur Romeo de Marigny to be a very helpful witness.

Bassin left without a look behind him, entourage trailing along.

It was another two days before a park cop told me what had happened. The child had been strangled, and her body had been found in one of the service closets dug into the high walls enclosing the Tuileries. Romeo had alerted the park police that she had vanished when his attention was briefly distracted by a Gypsy. The girl's gold locket was gone. And when the cops searched every Gypsy in the park, which was of course the first thing they did, they found the necklace. In the pocket that Tatiana had sewn on the inside of her skirt. Which Tatiana was wearing.

———

I DIDN'T VISIT her in prison, even though I was sure she was innocent. Gypsies lied, scammed, cheated, robbed, maybe even roughed people up a bit. I had known dozens during my years by the river. They didn't kill.

But even had I been able to tear myself off the tracks that marked my life—home, river, home—to make the one-hour trip to her holding center in Fontainebleau, there was nothing I could do. Tatiana had no more chance of escaping this charge than she had of growing new teeth. No antidiscrimination group would speak up for her, no well-meaning citizen would collect signatures on a petition for her, no politician would stand up in the parliament building across the river and rail against the false charges. When Tatiana told her questioners about finding the necklace on one of the park's pathways, even she probably knew that they wouldn't believe her.

I could imagine her in her pretrial appearances before the judges, looking nowhere but at the floor, twisting her skirt in her hands. Had they given her clean clothes to wear? Did she try to speak? Did her lawyer even make an effort? The front pages of the crumpled newspapers that the wind blew up on the embankment showed her photo more days than not: climbing into a police van, surrounded by hard-faced policewomen who seemed to be shoving a little too hard.

Until one day the front-page photo was of only her face, and what the article said was that she had died.

A brain aneurysm in the middle of the night. The authorities said she had gotten the best of care. The authorities said the case was now closed. I put the newspaper into the yellow recycling can on the other side of the tunnel and walked back to my stand and played something or other on my trumpet for the rest of the day.

It wasn't long after that that I saw the Mother—the Woman now, I guess. She was standing on the bridge, looking east toward Notre-Dame. She was alone, and silent, and thin. Spring had come and gone; it was July. The sun glittered on the river; it was one of those rare days when the water looked almost blue. The faint chatter of the tourists wafted down to me from the bridge. She paid no attention.

I picked up the trombone and began the "Bayrische Polka," looking straight up at her in the distance, ignoring the crowd of camera-pointing Chinese and sounding the notes as loud as I could. At first, it seemed as if the music didn't reach her. Then she slowly turned her head toward me and stared motionless for a long time. It was not until the last chorus that she lifted her hand and gave me a gentle wave.

Romeo turned up too, a week or so after that. I didn't see him at first. He was hanging back in the crowd a bit, as if he were trying to stay out of sight. As I played, I could feel, rather than see, him circling around the watching tourists, coming to rest behind a family of what must have been Americans. A smile was forming on his lips. They had two children, an elementary-school-age boy and a smaller girl. She had blond curly hair and looked like she might have been in kindergarten.

That was enough.

Right in the middle of "Les Rues de Paris," I put down the trumpet and rose from my stool. I walked through the ranks of astonished tourists, parting them with my hands and breaking through to the back of the crowd. I stood in front of him.

He tried to push by me, but I moved sideways and he stopped, the river on his other side.

I opened my mouth. Breathed in. Made a little cough; breathed again.

"M...M...Monsieur." My voice rasped. "I...I have some information that I think you need to hear about the little g-girl in the white coat."

If I had had any doubt, his expression dispelled it.

"I don't know what you mean." The tourists were staring at us as intently as if I were playing my trombone from the bell end. I said nothing. Stared at him. He shifted on his feet. "The suspect died in prison. The case is closed."

I lowered my voice.

"Monsieur, I think it would be better if you heard what I have to say. Better that I tell it to you than..."

"All right, what do you want?" No smile now. His arms were folded, his head cocked, but his body was rigid with tension.

"Return tonight, at midnight. I will be here."

———

HE CAME NOT across the bridge but from the quay, skulking past the long line of moored houseboats, one behind another, the tables and flowerpots on their decks ghostly in the moonlight. I stood with my back to my instruments.

"I've seen men like you before," I said. "I know what you did."

"Is it money you want?"

"I want to know the truth."

"Truth? I don't know what that is. I loved her. Maybe a little too much — is that what you're asking? I only wanted to touch her for a second. Nothing bad. But if she'd told her mother... Anyway, what will it take for you not to squeal?"

He put his hand into the pocket of the loose jacket he was wearing. As he looked down, I made my move, even before I saw that he was pulling out a knife, not money.

And if someday a body surfaces far downriver from where I still ply my trade, or if the police drag the river for some poor drowned child or missing teenager and turn up the corpse of a young man instead, I hope they notice that the victim is not just another casualty of the muddy waters.

I hope they see on the left side of his head, just above his ear, a deep, slanted wound made with a blow of such force that it sliced, rather than cracked, his skull. A blow struck with the force of love, and pain, and decades of pent-up silence.

I hope whoever finds him will know what went into that blow.

And every day now, the tourists who gather around to see me play and bow and bob can witness the other consequence of that force. My polka renditions are a little tinny, a little off-key. The music just doesn't sound the same now that the bell end of my trombone is bent so badly.

But the notes that come out are still haunting.

HOT SUGAR BLUES

BY STEVE LISKOW

B ish Underwood hasn't told the girl on the couch a single lie yet, which is a very good sign. Of course, she's only been here ten minutes.

Bish has just done three encores to top off a two-hour set in Trenton—our thirty-fifth concert in forty-one days—and he's left them twitching in the aisles. The LP, which came out two days after we left home, has been in *Billboard's* top five ever since, the last three weeks at number one. Bish is in full wind-down-at-the-end-of-the-tour mode, and he's already ordered champagne and bourbon and fruit and ice and God knows what else from room service.

He's ready to celebrate, and the girl looks like she can probably help him. The whole suite—928, because it's his lucky number—is thick with sweat and hormones.

But she insists that business comes first.

No, not like that. Bishop Underwood has six platinum LPs under his belt, so he never has to pay for it. But this chick's a freelancer with the green light for an interview from *Rolling*

Stone, and that means they talk on the couch before they talk on the pillows.

I want to go to bed with someone too, and plenty of women have slipped by security and are patrolling the halls ready to help me do just that, but I'm Bishop's manager and he's never been good at editing his mouth, so I don't go away until this girl turns off her tape recorder and closes her notebook. What happens after that is *her* business.

"You were a folksinger first." She's done her homework. "Why did you switch to electric? Did Bob Dylan show you that was the way to go?"

"Sorta." Bish has his feet on the coffee table and is trying to entice her closer, but she's sitting at the far end of the couch, long legs in tight jeans, ending in scuffed sneakers mere inches from his right hand. Even dressed casual, she can put the groupies outside to shame. A blind man couldn't miss what she's got, and Bish is not blind, especially when it comes to women. He's still wearing the white shirt and leather pants from the show, the debauched-preacher look. And he plays the blues like nobody else can since Michael Bloomfield died in that car last year.

"See, Jack and me, we'd been playing the Village—that's Greenwich Village—and all the coffeehouses in the Northeast for about three years, but we were doing traditional stuff, Kingston Trio, Pete Seeger, the Limeliters, nothing original."

The girl doesn't look old enough to know any of them. Barely old enough to drink, but beautiful. She has skin the color of a sunburst Les Paul, but her delicate nose shows there's some white blood in her too, maybe a while back. All the groupies are doing the big-poufy-hair thing now, but she's cut hers short so it frames her face; eyes like lumps of coal on their way to becoming diamonds. She looks so natural and real that something in me wants to cry.

"Until Dylan," she says again. Her voice sounds a little too deep to be coming from her slight frame under that white silk blouse. She's hung her corduroy jacket in the closet and rolled up her sleeves like she's ready to play some serious poker and wants us to know she doesn't have to cheat.

"Yeah," Bish says. "He showed us we could write our own songs and still be legit. Authentic, you know?"

He tries to untie her shoelaces, but she pulls her feet away. Her flirty-playful eyes tell him to keep talking.

"So we wrote a few things of our own. The first ones were pretty bad, but we started to get a feel for it."

Actually, *I* got a feel for it. Bish sang lead, so people thought he wrote them. What the hell—my name was on them, so I could live with it.

That was until the pigs busted me with a nickel bag in Georgia. Drugs, Deep South, 1964, you do the math. They tossed me in a cell with half a dozen other guys, some of them inbred, most of them black, all of them drooling for a piece of the college kid. Bish wouldn't go my bail until I signed over the rights to the songs, and I knew that one way or another, I was going to get screwed. I still feel a little twinge when one of those songs pops up on an oldies station.

" 'Rainbow Girl,' " the girl says. Shonna Lee, her name is, just a hint of drawl she hasn't quite buried. "And 'Quicksilver Romance.' "

"You've studied up on me, haven't you, missy?" Next to hers, his drawl sounds fake. Well, we both grew up in New England and met at Columbia. But it's his bluesman image.

He's got hold of her foot now, getting the lace untied, and she's not struggling. He pulls her sneaker off and I hear a knock on the door.

The room-service guy rolls in a cart with enough stuff to feed a platoon: sweating silver bucket with a magnum of Moët, a fifth of Jim Beam Black, a cut-glass bowl overflowing with apples, cherries, lemons, oranges, strawberries, melon balls, and sliced pineapple on crushed ice. Plates, silverware, fancy pastries, sliced cheese, whipped cream, a big urn of coffee with one of those little burners under it to keep it warm. Enough napkins to clean up a serious food fight. I slip him a twenty and lock the door behind him again.

By the time I get back to the main event, Shonna Lee's sneakers are under the coffee table and Bish is massaging one little brown foot in his big white hands. She sags back against the cushions, her whole face softening like a kitten's and the notebook sliding out of her fingers, but the questions keep on coming.

"Why did you switch from folk to blues?" Her voice shakes just a tad when Bish finds that spot on the sole of her foot. For a second, he looks like he wants to suck her toes, one at a time, and I can't blame him. Even with her clothes on, she's the kind of girl who makes hit songs shoot out of your pencil.

"The blues is the truth," he tells her. "You can't go wrong with the truth."

It's the first flat-out lie he's told her, and I know that from here on, he's going to pick up speed. He's told the story before.

"In early '65, we heard the Blues Project play in the Village, and the crowd went crazy for what they were laying down. Old Muddy Waters and Howlin' Wolf, but reworked into rock. I'd always loved the stuff, but we didn't think anyone would buy it."

Shonna Lee moves a little closer and lets him run his hands up her calves.

I loved Bo Carter, Blind Blake, and Robert Johnson, and I'd been saying blues was our ticket for over a year by then, but Bish didn't want to know from nothing until Dylan had the

Butterfield Blues Band back him with electric instruments at Newport. Their LP came out and knocked everyone on their ass, and Bish finally heard what I'd been telling him.

Shonna Lee's eyes move over to me like she's heard the whole riff already.

Bish gives her a smile so sticky I expect her to wipe her face. "Then the Stones and the Animals and the Yardbirds started shipping it back to us. I knew there was a fast train coming in and we had to jump on board before it left the station without us."

I go to the cart and sink my teeth into an apple before I scream.

"I'd never played an electric guitar before, and it took Jack a while to persuade me to give it a try. See, I loved Muddy and Elmore James and the others, but I really felt like the acoustic country blues was in my blood."

My apple tastes like wax.

"My soul, more like."

His eyes are starting to glow and I wonder how much longer before he suggests they take this into the bedroom. We've been on the road off and on for twenty years now, and he's still the best there is, and she's one of the perks. In twenty more years, when he's turning into a lounge act or an oldies tour, she'll be able to tell her kids that she banged Bishop Underwood.

Damned if I know why that bothers me.

I break the seal on the bourbon and pour three fingers neat. I hardly taste it before I pour three more.

Then the girl's next to me, stacking melon and strawberries on a plate, squirting a little blob of whipped cream beside them. Two more buttons on her blouse are open now. Barefoot, she's still fairly tall and I'm still fairly not, so I get a good look before I straighten up and we look at each other eye to eye.

She pours two flutes of champagne and dumps a handful of ice into a glass and drowns that in the bourbon, clear up to the rim. Bish watches her walk back to him with everything on a tray, real slow, like honey dripping off a table. When I swallow, Jim Beam burns in my throat.

She and Bish clink flutes, then he drains his. Hers goes on the end table, and I'm not sure any of it even wet her lips.

"So you got a Les Paul," she says. "Any reason you chose that particular guitar?"

"Well, I was playing a Gibson acoustic, an old Hummingbird. It's in the other room, as a matter of fact. I still write songs on it."

Yeah, I catch myself thinking, *and muskrats really do ramble.*

"Maybe you can show me later," she says. This time, her voice doesn't seem to reach her eyes.

"I'd love to." He lets her slide a strawberry into his mouth and plays with it before he takes a swallow of the bourbon. "Anyway, I liked the neck on that Gibson, so I figured it'd be easier to move to an electric guitar if I was already used to the feel of it."

There was more to it than that, of course. I had a Martin D-45, loved it like my mother, beautiful sound, but by then I'd signed over my rights, so he was making the royalties and I was just the sideman, which meant that when "we" decided to go electric, it was my guitar that went. I don't even know what that beauty would be worth now, thirty years later. We've got enough money for me to buy a busload of them, but it wouldn't be the same.

"I tried a Gibson hollow-body first," he tells her. "But they feed back when you crank up the amplifier. Then I found a Les Paul."

Right. He heard Clapton playing one on that John Mayall LP and gave it a shot.

"What is it about that guitar you like so much?" The girl feeds him another strawberry. There's a look in her eyes, like before the night's over, she's going to ask him to cut his hair and wrestle a lion. She sees me raise my glass of bourbon again and shakes her head, just a little.

"Oh, the feel, the tone. I've had it so long, it's like an old friend; it just fits in under my rib cage and I feel like I'm not alone. And it's got that great sustain, you can hit a note and hold it forever, warm and soulful, like a woman crying on a rainy night."

That's one of my lines too. From "Pain of Loss." It went platinum in '74 and I got diddly for it. He's still collecting royalties, seven million dollars from that LP so far.

The girl refills his bourbon so surface tension is all that keeps it from spilling over her fingers. She sits back on the couch, but this time she tucks her feet under her.

"Tell me about 'Hot Sugar Blues.'"

Bish loses his rhythm for just a beat before he picks up the glass. "That song was the little pebble that started the avalanche. Sold two million copies and convinced the record company to let me cut a whole album of my own stuff."

Of our *own stuff, you bastard.*

"I've heard stories that you stole that song."

It gets so quiet I can hear water running in the pipes and the traffic nine floors below us.

"What you saying, missy?" His drawl is broad enough to paint a double yellow line down the middle of it. "I wrote the words, I wrote the music, I sang it."

Well, he sang it anyway. Shonna Lee looks like she's two verses ahead of him.

"Someone took you to court. Claimed he wrote that song and you cheated him out of the money."

"Yeah, yeah, yeah." Bish takes a long swallow of bourbon and I feel my hand put my own glass back on the cart. It's like I'm not even there in the room with them anymore.

"Everyone talks about that. But they don't remember the rest of it. We went to court and the judge threw out the case in ten minutes flat. Some old coot trying to make money off me. Well, we sent him packing."

"An old black musician," Shonna Lee says. "Mattix? Something like that?"

"Some broken-down drunk in Mississippi. Claimed he wrote the song and played it for me, and I took it up north and made the record without his permission. Tried to sue me, but I had the music in a safe-deposit box, dated before he'd had anything."

"Hot Sugar Blues" is the only hit he's had that I didn't write. We were in some little jerkwater town, still doing those Kingston Trio covers, and this guy followed us up on the bandstand and blew us off the stage. Deak Mattix. Best guitar player I ever heard, better than Charley Patton, Reverend Gary Davis, or Mississippi John Hurt, and he sang this song while Bish and I sat there with our chins down around our knees.

"See," I'd said to him, "this is why we ought to be doing the blues."

We bought the guy a few drinks, made him play the song again. Then a couple more drinks and play the song one more time. By then, Bish had watched his hands enough to figure out those weird changes. Actually, they weren't weird, he just had the guitar tuned to A-minor so the voicings were different. That night in our motel room, he wrote it down and mailed it to himself at our apartment in East Orange. When we got back, that's when he traded my Martin for his first Gibson electric.

The song came out three months later, and Deak Mattix sued. Well, try to find a jury in Mississippi in 1966 that's going to believe a black guy. Bish and I flew down there with exhibit A. The judge opened that sealed envelope, looked at the papers inside, and gave the poor bastard thirty seconds to get his ass out of the courtroom.

We flew back to New York the next morning.

"Deacon Mattix," Shonna Lee says. "He killed himself a few days later. His wife found him hanging from a beam in the basement."

"I heard that," Bish says.

"Left her and a couple of little kids."

I'd told Bish he should send the woman some money, but he said it would look like he really was guilty and trying to buy them off. As soon as I could scrape something together, I sent it to them with a letter saying how sorry I was. Never got an answer.

" 'Hot Sugar Blues,' " she says. "You ever eaten hot sugar, Mr. Underwood?"

The way he looks at her now, I want to kill him.

She raises her eyebrows. "You interested?"

Before he can say anything, she's back at the cart, digging through the sugar packets and the whipped cream and the strawberries.

"Pour the man more bourbon, will you, Jack?" she asks. "This always tastes better with a little chaser."

She finds her jacket in the closet while I refill Bishop's glass. When I hand it over, I can feel the heat pumping off him like a midnight freight. The girl comes back to the table holding a little envelope.

"What's that?" I ask.

"Some of my secret herbs and spices." She gives me a smile that would stun a snake. "Old family recipe, just for special occasions. This feels like a special occasion, doesn't it?"

She empties the envelope into her hand, mixes the contents

with the sugar in a highball glass, and puts it over that little flame that's been keeping the coffee hot.

"We need to melt the sugar," she says. "Just like the song, you know."

She adds a little bourbon and uses a strawberry to muddle everything together. When I can see it bubbling and steam rising, she breaks a cupcake in half, pours the mixture over it, and takes the plate over to Bishop. She gets down on her knees in front of him, and his smile glows like toxic waste.

"This is best if you take it all in one gulp, sugar. It's got a little bit of an after burn, but the bourbon makes it all better."

"What is this?" Bish asks.

"It's something my mama showed me. It'll keep you going for a good long stretch. If you get my meaning."

She offers him the cupcake on the plate. "One nice big bite. It's going to be hot, so you have to swallow it right down. Then chase it."

He takes the cake and looks at her. She winks like Delilah probably winked at Samson.

"Go for it, sugar. One time, just for me."

The cake disappears into his mouth, and she's already bringing up the glass and tilting it between his lips. He swallows and coughs a little before he sits back on the couch.

"Whoa," he croaks. "Hot."

"Yeah, it is, isn't it?" She squeezes his hand with the glass in it. "But it's going to be so good in a little while."

"That's what I'm thinking too, honey."

She stands up and looks at me, still over by the cart, most of the bourbon gone, and a lot of the fruit and champagne. She turns back to Bish.

"You like any of the young players out there now?" she asks. "Anyone coming up who can really play the blues?"

"There's a kid out of Texas." Bish taps his chest like he's got a big belch stuck in there. "Stevie Ray Vaughan. I saw him in Houston a couple of years ago. Heard that he's cutting an album now."

He tries to swallow again and she pours him another glass of Jim Beam.

"Funny," she says. "Blues is black music, but now only white guys seem to play it."

"Lots of black singers don't like blues now," I say. "They say it reminds them of slavery. And they think it's too country."

Bish rattles the ice in his glass. "Yeah. They're into rap now 'cause it's more modern. City music."

Shonna Lee offers him a cherry.

"Modern, my ass," he goes on. "It's a fad. A year from now, everyone will have figured out it's crap and it'll go away."

"I don't know if anything ever really goes away," she says. "I think maybe it all just goes underground until the time is right again."

"Sure." Bish chases the cherry and grimaces. "Like Santa Claus comes every year."

"Have you heard of a guy named Robert Cray? He's black." Shonna Lee watches Bish drink, and the bourbon seems to burn him all the way down like the melted sugar did.

"I've heard the name. Haven't heard him play, though. You like him?"

"He's not as hot as you, but he's got a sweet sound."

She looks at him like she's just decided not to trade in the station wagon for the fancy sports car after all. She threads her arm into the sleeve of her corduroy jacket and turns to me. I can feel her eyes from across the room.

"Jack." She sweeps her sneakers from under the coffee table and slides them onto her feet in one flowing motion. "It's getting awfully late. Would you care to walk me home?"

"What?" Bishop's voice rises, and it catches a little at the end. He's still holding the empty glass. "No way, honey, you're not leaving."

"Yes, sugar," she says. "I am. Thank you for the interview. I'll send you a copy when I get it written. And maybe I'll see you at breakfast."

I'm reaching for what's left of the bourbon, but she grabs my wrist.

"What the hell?" Bish slams his hand on the table, and I hear the highball glass crack.

"Oh, sugar, did you hurt yourself?" She moves over and grabs his hand. "You better take care of that cut."

She steers him into the bathroom, closes the door behind him, and smiles at me.

"I still need you to walk me home, Jack."

I'm too amazed to do more than nod. I put my arm around her waist and she leans her head against my shoulder while I walk her two doors down the hall to my own room. Her hair smells so good I almost drop the key trying to unlock my door.

The next few hours could be a dozen songs I'm never going to write, and she's still lying beside me when morning creeps through the curtains. I look at the clock while she's in the shower and wonder how I'm going to give her cab fare home without looking like the jerk of the universe. And if I'm still going to have a job when Bish sees me again.

Shonna Lee comes out of the bathroom in a cloud of steam and drops her towel on the bed like we've been together forever. She gives me a kiss and takes her time putting her clothes back on.

"We should go see Mr. Underwood, shouldn't we?"

"I'm not sure that's a good idea," I say.

"It's better if we're together." She opens the door and starts down the hall, leaving me to catch up.

There's no answer when I knock. I try the doorknob. It's not locked.

That cracked glass is still on the coffee table, the champagne is floating in the melted ice, and the fruit is getting a little brown around the edges. Bishop is nowhere in sight. I stick my head in the bedroom, but the bed hasn't been slept in.

Shonna Lee takes the few remaining bits of ice from the bucket and drops them into the cracked glass. She wraps a napkin around the bottle and pours just a tad of bourbon too, then she flicks the crack with the bourbon bottle, and the glass crumbles so liquid leaks onto the table. She puts the bottle on the table next to the glass and folds the napkin again before she looks at me, then at the bathroom door.

I don't hear the shower or any movement behind it. I knock a couple of times, but nobody answers. I try the knob.

Bish is lying on the floor, blood on the sink, blood on the toilet, blood around his mouth, blood soaking the white bath mat. His eyes are bulging and his face is blue.

I come back into the room and see the girl dipping one of the remaining strawberries in whipped cream. Her face looks like I don't have any surprises for her.

"What was in that envelope?" I ask.

"What envelope?" Her voice is smoother than the whipped cream and I feel a cold lump in my stomach.

"You flushed it down my toilet, didn't you?"

She looks at the champagne bottle leaning against the side of the bucket, then picks up another strawberry.

"I was with you all night, Jack. I'm your alibi."

"I had no reason to want him dead."

She raises her eyebrows and bites into that strawberry. I remember the night in jail when he made me give up my songs. And the day he sold my guitar. And all the rest of it.

"They'll think he was so drunk he swallowed the broken glass."

Along with the hot sugar she hid it in.

"Jesus," I say. "What an awful way to go."

"I imagine." She licks her fingers delicately. "Probably even worse than hanging."

For a second, I think I'm going to throw up. "What's your real name?"

"Shonna Lee."

We look each other in the eye. She reaches into her jacket pocket and pulls out another envelope.

"Shonna Lee Mattix."

My voice feels heavy as lead. "Why not me too?"

She hands me the envelope. It's addressed to the Mattix family in Tillerville, Mississippi, and I recognize my own handwriting.

She's right. Things never go away. They just go underground until their time comes around again.

"I'm your alibi too, aren't I?"

"Only if you tell them my full name." She slides the envelope back into her jacket and her eyes meet mine again. "And why would you do that?"

I pick up the phone and dial the front desk.

THE FINAL BALLOT

BY BRENDAN DuBOIS

ventually the room emptied of the two state police detectives, the detective from the Manchester Police Department, the Secret Service agent, the emergency room physician, and the patient representative from the hospital, until only one man remained with her, standing in one corner of the small hospital room used to brief family members about what was going on with their loved ones. Beth Mooney sat in one of the light orange vinyl-covered easy chairs, hands clasped tight in her lap, as the man looked her over.

"Well," he said. "We do have a situation here, don't we?"

It took her two attempts to find her voice. "Who are you?"

He was a lean, strong-looking man, with a tanned face that seemed out of place here in New Hampshire in December, and his black hair was carefully close trimmed and flecked with white. If he looked one way, he could be in his thirties; if he looked another way, he could be in his fifties. It depended on how the light hit the fine networks of wrinkles about his eyes and mouth. Beth didn't know much about men's clothes, but she knew the dark suit he was wearing hadn't come off some discount-store rack or from Walmart. He strolled over and sat down across from her, in a couch whose light orange color matched the shade of her chair.

"I'm Henry Wolfe," he said, "and I'm on the senator's staff."

"What do you do for him?"

"I solve problems," he said. "Day after day, week after week, I solve problems."

"My daughter..." And then her voice broke. "Please don't call her a problem."

He quickly nodded. "Bad choice of words, Mrs. Mooney. My apologies. Let me rephrase. The senator is an extraordinarily busy man, with an extraordinarily busy schedule. From the moment he gets up to the moment he goes to bed, his life is scheduled in fifteen-minute intervals. My job is to make sure that schedule goes smoothly. Especially now, with the Iowa caucuses coming up and less than two months to go before the New Hampshire primary. In other words, I'm the senator's bitch."

Beth said, "His boy..."

"Currently in custody by the state police, pending an investigation by your state's attorney general's office."

"I want to see my daughter," Beth said. "Now."

Henry raised a hand. "Absolutely. But Mrs. Mooney, if I may, before we go see your daughter, we need to discuss certain facts and options. It's going to be hard and it's going to be unpleasant, but believe me, I know from experience that it's in the interest of both parties for us to have this discussion now."

Anger flared inside her, like a big ember popping out of her woodstove at home. "What's there to discuss? The senator's son...he...he...hurt my little girl."

She couldn't help it, the tears flowed, and she fumbled in her purse and took out a wad of tissue, which she dabbed at her eyes and nose. While doing this, she watched the man across from her. He was just sitting there, impassive, his face blank, like some lizard's or frog's, and Beth knew in a flash that she was outgunned. This man before her had traveled the world, knew how to order wine from a menu, wore the best clothes and had gone to the best schools, and was prominent in a campaign to elect a senator from Georgia as the next president of the United States.

She put the tissue back in her purse. And her? She was under no illusions. A dumpy woman from a small town outside Manchester who had barely graduated from high school and was now leasing a small beauty shop in a strip mall. Her idea of big living was going to the Mohegan Sun casino in Connecticut a few times a year and spending a week every February in Panama City, Florida.

And Henry was smooth, she saw. When she had stopped sobbing and dabbing at her eyes, he cleared his throat. "If I may, Mrs. Mooney…as I said, we have a situation. I'm here to help you make the decisions that are in the best interests of your daughter. Please, may I go on?"

She just nodded, knowing if she were to speak again, she would start bawling. Henry said, "The senator's son Clay…he's a troubled young man. He's been expelled twice before from other colleges. Dartmouth was his third school, and I know that's where he met your daughter. She's a very bright young girl, am I correct?"

Again, just the nod. How to explain to this man the gift and burden that was her only daughter, Janice? Born from a short-lived marriage to a long-haul truck driver named Tom—who eventually divorced her for a Las Vegas waitress and who got himself killed crossing the Continental Divide in a snowstorm, hauling frozen chickens—Janice had always done well in school. No detentions or notes from the principal about her

Janice, no. She had studied hard and had gone far, and when Janice came home from Dartmouth to the double-wide, Beth sometimes found it hard to understand just what exactly her girl was talking about with the computers and the internet and twitting or whatever they called it.

Henry said, "From what I gather, her injuries, while severe… are not permanent. And she will recover. Eventually. What I want to offer you is a way to ease that recovery along."

Beth said sharply, "Seeing that punk in prison — that'll help her recovery, I goddamn guarantee it."

He tilted his head slightly. "Are you sure, Mrs. Mooney?"

"Yes, I am."

"Really? Honestly? Or will having Clay in prison help *your* recovery, not your daughter's?"

"You're talking foolish now."

A slight shake of the head. "Perhaps. That's what happens when you spend so much time with the press, consultants, and campaign workers. You do tend to talk foolish. So let's get back to basics. From my experience, Mrs. Mooney, there are two avenues open to you. To us. The first is the one I'm sure has the most appeal for you. The attorney general's office, working with the state police, pursue a criminal indictment against Clay Thomson for a variety of offenses, from assault and battery to… any other charges that they can come up with."

Beth crossed her legs. "Sounds good to me."

"I understand. So what will happen afterward?"

Beth tried to smile. "The little bastard goes to trial. Gets convicted. Goes to jail. Also sounds good to me."

Something chirped in the room. Henry pulled a slim black object from his coat, looked at it, pressed a button, and returned it to his pocket. "That may occur. But plenty of other things will happen, Mrs. Mooney, and I can guarantee that."

"Like what?"

"Like a media frenzy you've never, ever experienced before. I have, and I wouldn't wish it on my worst enemies, personal or political. Your phone rings constantly, from all the major networks, the cable channels, the newspapers, and the wire services. Reporters and camera crews stake out your home and your hair salon. Your entire life is probed, dissected, and published. Your daughter's life is also probed, dissected, and published. All in the name of the public's right to know. If your daughter is active sexually, that will be known. Her school grades, her medical history, information about old boyfriends will all be publicized. If you've ever had a criminal complaint—drunk driving, shoplifting, even a speeding ticket—that will also be known around the world."

Beth bit her lower lip. "It might just be worth it, to see that little bastard in an orange jumpsuit."

"No doubt you feel that way now, Mrs. Mooney," the man said. "But that will be just the start of it. You see, in a close-fought campaign like this one... the opponents of the senator will see you and your daughter as their new best friends, and they'll try anything and everything to keep this story alive, day after day, week after week, so the senator will stumble in the Iowa caucuses and lose the New Hampshire primary and then the White House."

Her hand found another tissue. Henry went on, talking slow and polite, like he was telling her the specials from the deli counter at the local Stop & Shop. "And that's the senator's enemies making your life miserable. The senator's supporters... they would be much, much worse."

Beth said with surprise, "His supporters? Why would they be worse?"

Henry spoke again, sounding like a bored schoolteacher

talking to an equally bored student. "For more than a year, many of them have been volunteering and donating time and money to the senator. They truly believe—as do I—that he is the best man to be our next president, the man who can bring justice back to this country and to our dealings with the world. But if you and your daughter were to pursue a criminal case concerning the senator's son...there will be threats and accusations against the two of you. Some will say that it was a setup. That you are allied with political groups that are against the senator. That you resent the senator, or your daughter has a grudge against the senator and his family. You'll be harassed at home, at work, and places in between. People on the internet will publish your home address and telephone number, as well as pictures of you, your house, and your hair salon. And it would go on for months...perhaps years."

"But that's not fair!"

Henry said, "That's the state of politics today, I'm afraid."

Beth pushed the tissue against her lips, keening softly. This night wasn't supposed to be like this. It was Tuesday night. Grilled hamburger and rice for dinner. Followed by *Jeopardy!*, the *Real Housewives,* and to bed. This wasn't supposed to be a night with an apologetic phone call from the Manchester police followed by a frantic drive to the hospital, and facing all of this...

She took the tissue away. "All right. You said there's two streets—"

"Avenues," he corrected.

"Avenues," she repeated, face warm, "available to us. What's the second one?"

He said, "One that I, if I were in your place, would find much more attractive. The senator's son is a very troubled young man. I admit it; the senator admits it. And the senator is devastated at what happened to your daughter. You're looking for justice, and the senator understands that. What we propose is this: If you and your daughter ask the proper authorities not to file formal and public charges against the senator's son, we will immediately place Clay in a secure mental-health facility, where he will no longer pose a danger to anyone."

"He gets away, then," Beth said sharply. "And your senator boss doesn't have to answer embarrassing questions."

"The senator isn't afraid of questions, Mrs. Mooney. And his son, no, he doesn't get away with anything. He gets the treatment he needs, in a secure place that is quite similar to a prison facility, with locked rooms, few privileges, and lots of discipline and treatment. And while the senator's son is treated, your daughter will be treated as well. Whatever insurance you have won't be billed. The senator will take care of it all, for as long as your daughter needs it. The very best in care... for life, if necessary, though I believe she'll make a full recovery in time. All future educational expenses as well. And since you, Mrs. Mooney, would no doubt have to take time off to be with your daughter, the senator is prepared to offer a generous monthly stipend to assist you."

"To keep my goddamn mouth shut, you mean."

Henry's face was impassive. "The senator wants to do right by you and your daughter. But by doing this, the senator would expect some... consideration from both of you. I'm sure you recognize, Mrs. Mooney, the delicacy of the situation."

"All I want is justice for my girl," she said.

"And I'm here to make sure justice is done. Among other things."

She sat and thought, and then pushed the wad of soaked tissue back into her purse.

"I want to see my girl, Janice," Beth said. "It's going to be up to her."

———

HER DAUGHTER WAS now in a two-patient room, with the curtain drawn to separate her from a young blond girl, who apparently had a broken foot and who was watching the wall-mounted television while chewing gum and texting on her cell phone at the same time. Beth sat down and looked at her Janice, feeling flashes of cold and heat race through her. Tubes ran out of both of Janice's slim wrists, and there was an oxygen tube beneath her nose. Her face was bruised; her left eye was nearly swollen shut; and her lower lip was split. She looked better than she had when Beth first saw her in the ER; now she was in a hospital gown and her face had been washed.

Henry walked in and said, "I'll leave you be for a while," and then he strolled out.

She clutched Janice's hand, and Janice squeezed back. Beth said, keeping her voice soft and low, "Honey, can I talk to you for a minute?"

And Beth told her what the man from the senator's staff had said and offered, and when she was done, Beth thought her little girl had fallen asleep. But no, she was thinking, with that mind that was so sharp and bright. She whispered back, "Mom . . . take the deal . . . okay? I'm so tired . . ."

"Janice, are you sure?"

Her voice, barely a whisper. "Mom, I'm really tired . . ."

———

HENRY CAME IN after a half an hour and Beth said, "We'll do it. The second . . . whatever it was. Choice. Option."

"Avenue," he said. "Mrs. Mooney, trust me, you won't regret it. Give me a few minutes and I'll have the necessary agreements prepared. All right?"

Beth turned to her girl, who was sleeping. "You know…what I'm really thinking…I wish I could spend the night here with my little girl. But I know the hospital won't allow it."

"Is that what you want, Mrs. Mooney? To spend the night here, in this room?"

Beth said, "Yes…of course. But there's no space."

Henry said, "Give me a few moments."

He slipped out.

Beth heard voices raised, phones ringing, more voices. Less than ten minutes later, two young, burly hospital attendants came in, and the girl with the broken foot yelped about why she was being moved, what the hell was going on, where was her boyfriend as her personal items were placed in a white plastic bag, and then she and her bed were wheeled out. An empty bed was wheeled in; a grim-faced nurse made it up; and the curtain was pulled back, making the room bigger and wider.

And Henry had returned and watched it all while typing on his electronic device. When the room was settled, he said, "Is that satisfactory, Mrs. Mooney?"

"How…how in hell did you do that?"

Henry said, "Problems. I'm paid quite well to solve them."

LATER IN THE evening, in a private conference room down the hall from Janice's hospital room, Beth signed a bunch of papers that she had a hard time puzzling through, but Henry said signing them was just a formality. When she was done, he nodded and smiled for the first time that evening.

"Very good, Mrs. Mooney. You won't regret it. I promise. Here—"

He slid over a business card, which she picked up. On the back was a handwritten phone number. "My private, direct line. You have any questions, any problems, anything at all, give me a call. All right?"

"Thank you, thank you very much," she said.

"And here," he said, putting a white envelope on the conference table. "An initial...stipend for your worries."

Beth looked inside the envelope and saw a number of bills, all with Ben Franklin's face on them. She quickly closed the envelope and shoved it into her purse. She said, "I'd like to ask you a question, if that's all right."

"Mrs. Mooney, the senator and I are in your debt. Go ahead."

"Why do you do this? I mean, I'm sure you get paid a lot. But what's in it for you?"

The question seemed to catch him by surprise. "I guess you deserve an answer...for the troubles you've been through. I'll tell you something, though I'll deny ever having said this. What I want, and what I've worked for my entire life, is to put a man in the White House, to know that I did it, and, in return for my work, to be chief of staff for him. But that's always up in the air until the final ballot. That's something I've learned the hard way over the years."

"Chief of staff...is that an important job?"

He abruptly stopped talking, as if afraid he had said too much. He put on his coat. "Mrs. Mooney, if you don't mind, I need to catch a flight to Atlanta tonight...is there anything else I can do for you?"

Beth was suddenly exhausted, like she had spent twelve hours on her feet at the hair salon. "No, I'm going to be with my girl. Thanks for making it so I can spend the night next to her."

The second smile of the evening. "My pleasure."

———

THE NEXT FEW days went by in a daze of working at the salon, being at the hospital, and then being at the rehabilitation facility when Janice was transferred. There, Beth was pleased to see her little girl—all right, young woman!—recovering well. The bruises faded some, and she could walk up and down the hallway without leaning on someone or having to stop to catch her breath.

Beth should have been encouraged, but so many things were bothering her. Janice was always one to talk her mother's ears off about the latest political scandal, the latest celebrity wedding, and the latest news on whatever online or off-line technology she was involved with at that moment, but now, she just stayed in her bed and watched television or read paperback books. Beth had once offered to bring Janice's laptop in, but with some curt words, Janice said she was no longer interested.

Beth was confused and scared, but still, it was good to see her daughter get better, week after week. And as promised, a weekly check made out to her arrived, and she caught up on all her bills and even managed to start a savings account, a first. But truth be told, she always felt a bit self-conscious depositing the checks, like she was doing something bad. Yet Janice was slowly improving, and Janice didn't say anything more about the senator's son, so Beth let everything be and kept hoping for the future.

And so it would have remained, if it weren't for the night of the Iowa caucuses.

———

It had been a long day, first at the rehab center in the morning and then at the hair salon in the afternoon. Beth had accidentally double-booked two of her clients, so she had to work later than expected. Dinner was a quick takeout from McDonald's and after she got home, she went through the mail—another stipend check and an electricity bill from PSNH—then washed up and went straight into her bedroom.

There she switched on the TV, and instead of her usual *Law & Order,* there was a special report about the Iowa caucuses being held that night. In the dark bedroom, covers pulled up around her neck, she watched the panel for the news discuss the Iowa results, and something chilled her feet when she learned that the senator from Georgia had squeaked out a victory. He was now the front-runner, but as some of the commentators stated, he was still on shaky ground. A win in three weeks in New Hampshire could make him unstoppable.

The view of the camera switched to the senator making his victory speech at an auditorium in Iowa. His face was happy and lit up as he stood in front of a large blue curtain and waved to the cheering crowd, the supporters holding signs high. And there was the senator's man Henry Wolfe standing to one side, applauding hard, smiling as well, sometimes ducking his head to say something to somebody on the stage.

She picked up the remote to change the channel, and her hand froze. Just like that. A young man was there as well, cheering and laughing and looking very, very happy indeed.

The senator's son.

In Iowa. In public. On the stage!

He didn't seem to have a care or worry in the world, looked fine indeed as he applauded and cheered his winning father—

Beth stumbled out of bed, raced to the bathroom, and made it to the toilet before vomiting up her small fries and Quarter Pounder with Cheese. She washed her face with cold water, wiped it down with a towel, refused to look at herself in the mirror, and went back out to the bedroom.

The senator was speaking, but Beth muted the television, stared at the screen. His son Clay...out. Free. Not punished at all.

While her daughter, Janice, was still in rehab, still trying to form words and sentences, still refusing to use her computer.

Beth went to her bureau, roughly pulled out the top drawer, went through a few things, and came back out with Henry Wolfe's business card with the handwritten phone number on the reverse. Hands shaking, she sat cross-legged on her bed and dialed the number.

It started ringing. And kept ringing. With the phone up to her ear, she watched the television, and it was like being trapped in one of those horror movies where you saw something bad happening and couldn't do anything to save yourself, for what she saw was...

Henry Wolfe onstage, listening to his boss speak, and then pausing. Reaching inside his coat pocket. Pulling out his phone or minicomputer or whatever they called it.

From little New Hampshire to busy Iowa, she was calling him, was calling him to find out what in hell the senator's son was doing up there onstage. What about the promise, the pledge, that justice would be served?

She stared at the television, willing herself not to blink, for she didn't want to miss a thing.

Henry Wolfe stared down at his handheld device. Frowned. Pressed a button, returned it to his coat.

And her call went to voice mail.

Later on during the night, she called the number six more times, and six times, it went straight to voice mail.

———

AFTER A RESTLESS night, she woke with her blankets and sheets wrapped around her, moist from her night sweats, her phone ringing and ringing and ringing. She reached across to the nightstand, almost knocked the phone off the stand, and then got it and murmured a sleepy hello.

The voice belonged to Henry Wolfe, who started out sharply:

"Mrs. Mooney, I don't have much time, so don't waste it, all right?"

"What?" she asked.

He said brusquely, "I know you called me seven times last night, and I have a good idea what you're calling about. And I'm telling you don't waste your time. You have a signed nondisclosure agreement with a very attractive compensation package and a very unattractive clause that will open you up to financial and legal ruin if you say one word about the senator and his son."

She sat up in bed. "But he's free! That bastard Clay, I saw him last night! The one who hurt my daughter! You promised me that he'd be sent away!"

Henry said, "And he was sent away."

"For three weeks? Is that all?"

"His doctors judged that he had recovered well, and—"

"Doctors you paid for, I'm sure!"

Henry said, "This conversation isn't productive, Mrs. Mooney, so I think I'll—"

"Is that what you people call justice? Throwing some money around, making promises, and walking away? You promised me justice for my girl!"

By then, she was talking to herself.

———

THE NEXT DAY she met with Floyd Tucker, an overweight and fussy lawyer who had helped her sort through the paperwork when she had divorced Joe. He sighed a lot as they sat in his tiny, book-lined office. He flipped through the pages of the agreement she had signed for the senator, sighed some more, and finally looked up. "Beth, you shouldn't have signed this without running it by me first."

"I didn't have the time," she said.

"This agreement"—he held up the papers—"there's a good compensation package, no doubt about it, but the restrictions... Hell, Beth, if you even hint at breathing what's gone on with the senator's son and your daughter, you open yourself up to lawsuits, financial seizures, and penalties totaling tens of millions of dollars. Do you understand that?"

"I do now," she said, staring at the polished desk. "But I didn't have the time."

"Beth, you should have called me," he said.

She reached over, plucked the documents from his hand.

"I didn't have the time," she whispered.

———

A DAY LATER, she was at her town's small library. Past the rows of books and the magazine racks, there were three computers, set up in a row. She sat down and stared at the screen, which showed a picture of the library and said that this picture and the words on it were something called a home page. She put her hands over the keyboard and then pulled them away, as if she were afraid she would make something blow up if she pushed the wrong key.

Beth leaned back in the wooden chair. What to do? She felt queasy, empty, nervous, like the first time she had approached a paying customer with a pair of sharp scissors in her hands.

"Mrs. Mooney?" a young girl's voice said. She turned in her seat, saw Holly Temple, a sweet girl whose hair Beth cut and styled. She said, "Do you need any help?"

Beth said, "I'm afraid I don't know how to use this, Holly. I'm looking for some information, and I don't know how to begin."

Holly pulled over a chair and sat down next to her. "Well, it's pretty easy. I'm surprised that Janice couldn't help you."

Her voice caught. "Me too."

———

She was driving to the rehab center to visit Janice, who had had what the doctors and nurses delicately called a setback. Physically she was improving day by day; emotionally, she was withdrawing, becoming more silent, less responsive. Beth found that she had to drive with only one hand, as she had to use the other to keep wiping her eyes with a wad of tissue.

At a stoplight, scores of supporters for the senator were gathered at the intersection, holding blue-and-white campaign signs on wooden sticks that they raised as they chanted. They waved at cars going by, gave thumbs-up to passing cars that honked in support. Two young men were staring right at her as they chanted. The light changed to green and she drove by, and she couldn't help herself—she gave them the middle finger.

———

That night, for hour after hour, she dialed and redialed Henry Wolfe's number. Eventually, at two a.m., he answered, and she got right to the point.

"Mr. Wolfe, next Tuesday is the New Hampshire primary. The day after tomorrow, I plan to drive to Concord and visit the offices of the Associated Press. There, I'm going to show them the documents that I signed and tell them what the senator's son did to my little girl."

Voice sharp, he said, "Do that, you silly bitch, and you'll be destroyed. Ruined. Wiped out."

"And come next Tuesday, so will your candidate. I may be silly, but I'm not stupid. I know if he wins the primary with a good margin, he'll be your party's nominee. And after that, he'll be the favorite to be president. So destroying him in exchange for losing my shop and my double-wide and the one thousand two hundred dollars I have in my savings account...that sounds like a pretty fair deal to me."

She could hear him breathing over the phone line. "What do you want?"

Beth said, "The first time we met, you said the senator's life was scheduled in fifteen-minute chunks of time, and that your job was to make sure that time went smoothly. So here's the deal. Sometime over the next two days, I want five minutes with him. And with you. Alone."

Henry said, "Impossible."

"Then make it possible," she said curtly. "After all, you're paid to solve problems."

This time, she hung up on him.

———

Two HOURS LATER, her phone rang. She picked it up and a tired voice said, "A deal. The Center of New Hampshire hotel. Two this afternoon. Room six ten."

"Sounds good to me," she said.

"Look, you need to know that—"

Taking more pleasure in it this time, she hung up on him again. And went back to sleep.

———

LATER THAT DAY, Beth drove to Manchester—the state's largest city—and instead of going into the pricey parking garage, she found a free spot about four blocks away. She trudged along the snowy sidewalk and walked into the hotel, past guests and people streaming in and out. In one corner of the lobby, there were bright lights from a television news crew filming an interview with somebody who must be famous.

She took the elevator to the sixth floor, got off, and within a minute, she found room 610. A quick knock on the door and it opened up within seconds, a frowning and worn-looking Henry Wolfe on the other side. He was dressed as well as ever, but his eyes were sunken and red-rimmed. Beth had a brief flash of sympathy for him before remembering all that had gone before, and then she didn't feel sympathetic at all.

He started to speak and she brushed by him and into the room. *Wow,* she thought. This wasn't a room. It was a palace, bigger than the interior of her double-wide trailer. Couches, chairs, big-screen television, kitchen, bar, and doors that led into other rooms. Flowers and baskets of fruit and snack trays and piles of newspapers.

She turned to Henry. "Is this what they mean by a suite?"

"Yes," he said. "Look, Mrs. Mooney, before the senator comes in, I really need to know that—"

"A suite," Beth said, shaking her head in awe. "I've heard of hotel suites, but to think I'd ever actually be inside of one, well, I never figured."

"I'm sure," Henry snapped. "Mrs. Mooney, we don't have much time before the meeting and I must insist—"

She made a point of looking around again. "All of those nice senior citizens, the retirees who send your senator a dollar bill or a five-dollar bill or whatever they can scrape together to help elect him president, do you think they know that their money is paying for this suite? And all those who donated time and money because they believed in the senator's idea of justice, what do you think they'd say if they knew what his son did to my daughter?"

"Mrs. Mooney—" he began again, and then another door within the suite opened up, and the senator walked in, tall, smiling, wearing a fine gray suit and a cheerful look. The room he was emerging from, she saw, was filled with well-dressed men and women, most with cell phones against their ears or in their hands, and then the door was shut behind him.

The senator strode over, and Beth felt her heart flip for a moment. It was one thing to see him on the cover of a magazine or a newspaper, or on the nightly news, but here he was, right in front of her. *My God,* she thought. *What am I doing?* This man coming at her could very well be the next president of the United States, the most powerful and famous man on the planet. And she was a single mom and a hairdresser. For a moment she felt like turning around and running out the door.

Then she remembered Janice. And she calmed down.

"Mrs. Mooney," the senator said, holding out a tanned hand with a large, fancy watch around his wrist. "So glad to meet you. I just wish it were under better circumstances."

"Me too," she said, giving his hand a quick shake. "And, Senator, I know you're very, very busy. In fact, I can't imagine how busy you are, so I will make this quick."

The senator looked to Henry, who looked to her and said, "We appreciate that, Mrs. Mooney."

Beth took a breath. "So here we go. I'm sure you know your son's actions, what happened to my daughter, and the agreement that was reached between me and Mr. Wolfe."

The senator said, "If there's something that needs to be adjusted in the agreement, I'm sure that—"

"Senator," Beth said forcefully, "I don't want an adjustment. I don't want an agreement. In fact, you can stop all the payments. What I want is justice for my little girl."

The senator's eyes narrowed and darkened. Now she could see the toughness that was inside this man who wanted to be president.

"Do go on," he said flatly.

She said, "You can stop the payments. Stop everything. But I intend to go public with what your son did to my daughter today, this afternoon, unless my one demand is met."

Both men waited, neither one saying a word. So she went on.

"By the end of the day today, I want you to announce the firing of Henry Wolfe," she said. "And I want your pledge that he will never be in your employ ever again, either directly or indirectly."

The senator didn't make a sound, but Beth heard a grunt from Henry, like he had just been punched in the gut. She went on. "That is it. Nonnegotiable."

"Why?" the senator asked. "Why should I fire Henry?"

"To keep me from going to the newspapers," she said. "And because he promised justice for my girl. And she still doesn't have it."

She could sense the tension in the air, something disturbing, as she noted both men looking at each other, inquiring, appraising, gauging what was going on. The senator checked his watch. "Well, our time is up, Mrs. Mooney, and—"

Henry spoke desperately. "Tom, please—"

"Henry," the senator said calmly, touching his upper arm. "We have a lot of things to talk about, don't we?"

Henry continued, "For God's sake, Tom, the primary is in just a few days and—"

The two of them went through another door, and Beth was left alone. She looked around the huge, empty suite, went to a fruit basket, picked up two oranges, and left.

———

THE NIGHT OF the New Hampshire primary, she rented a DVD—*Calendar Girls*—and watched the movie until she fell asleep on the couch. She had no idea who had won and didn't rightly care.

———

Two MONTHS LATER, Beth was in her hair salon checking the morning receipts when the door opened and Henry Wolfe walked in. He wasn't dressed fancy, and his face was pale and had stubble on it. When she looked in his eyes, she was glad there was a counter between them.

"Looking for a trim?" she asked cheerfully.

"You...I..."

"Or a shave?" she added.

He stopped in front of her and she caught his scent. It was of unwashed clothes and stale smoke and despair. "You...do you know what you've done?"

"I don't know," she said, flipping the page on her appointment book. "But I'm sure you'll tell me."

"The senator...he barely won the New Hampshire primary. There was a shit storm of bad publicity when he announced my firing, talk of a campaign in crisis, a senator who couldn't choose the right staff, of chaos in his inner circle. And then he lost the next primary, and since then, he's been fighting for his political life. There's even speculation about a brokered convention. What should have been a clear road to the White House has become a horror show. All thanks to you."

"Gee," she said. "I don't think so."

"But that's what you wanted, isn't it?" he demanded. "To get back at the senator. To hurt his chances of becoming president. All because his son didn't get punished the way you wanted. You knew that firing me, his most trusted fixer and adviser, days before the New Hampshire primary would cripple him."

The phone rang, but she ignored it. The door opened and her newest employee walked in, nodded to Beth, and then got a broom and started sweeping near one of the chairs.

Beth said, "You just don't get it, do you?"

He gave a sharp laugh, and in a mocking tone, he said, "I'm sure you'll tell me."

She picked up a pen. "I didn't know much about you when we first met. So after I saw the senator's son up onstage in Iowa, and after you blew me off on the phone, I did some research. I goggled you."

"You did what?"

"I goggled you."

He shook his head. "Stupid woman, it's *Google*. Not *goggle*."

Beth smiled. "Well, whatever the hell it is, I had a friend at the library do research for me. And I found out that you've tried four times to get a man elected president, and each time, you've lost. You have a reputation as a political loser. But this time, you were the closest you've ever been. Years and years of political failure, and you were now so very close to having your dream come true, to be chief of staff. The most powerful man in Washington, right after the president. Four, maybe eight years in the White House as chief of staff, and then millions of dollars doing consulting and lobbying work. It looked like your losing streak was finally about to break. And then the senator's son started dating my daughter."

She paused, looking at his drawn face. "I could give a shit about your senator. Or any other politician. But you promised me justice, and you didn't deliver. So I gave you a taste of what it's like to be betrayed after so many promises. And I was the one to cast the final goddamn ballot."

Beth was surprised to see him wipe at his eyes. It looked like he was weeping.

"Was it worth it, then?" he asked, his voice just above a whisper. "To destroy me like this, to hurt the senator, maybe even prevent him from getting to the White House?"

She looked over at the corner of the store, where her daughter, Janice, was quietly and dutifully sweeping up the floor, her hands holding a broom, the same hands that still hadn't gone back to her computer.

"Yes," she said calmly. "It was worth it."

AFRICA ALWAYS NEEDS GUNS

BY MICHAEL NIEMANN

Some days everything works out. Valentin Vermeulen hadn't had one of those days in a while. He brushed a damp strand of blond hair from his broad forehead, a forehead inherited from generations of Flemish farmers. Like these ancestors, he waited for his luck to change.

There was a slim chance it might. If, that is, the Antonov An-8 cargo plane was sufficiently late.

He looked over the shoulders of the Bangladeshi air traffic controller. The radar scope's scan beam raced in a circle, like the hands of a clock on fast-forward. No blips. The plane was about an hour and a half behind schedule.

The reality of his assignment stared back at him through the dirty windows of what passed for the control tower of the Bunia airport. The humid bush, a single asphalt runway, white UN helicopters parked on makeshift helipads, white armored personnel carriers at strategic positions, soldiers in blue helmets milling about, a peacekeeping operation at the edge of the world.

The usual Congolese hangers-on—were they Hema or Lendu? He never could tell the difference—sat in the shady spots, hoping for a small job, cash, or food. A quiet day in a very unquiet part of the world.

Vermeulen pulled a Gitane Papier Maïs from its blue pack and lit it. He was used to air-conditioned offices in New York, to pulling together evidence from files and interview transcripts. Sure, there were trips to the field—Kosovo, Bosnia, even Cambodia once—but he always had his office in New York. Until he'd stepped on some important toes during the Iraq oil-for-food investigation. Next thing he knew, the UN Office of Internal Oversight Services sent him to the eastern Congo.

An ancient air conditioner rattled in its slot above the door, blowing humid air into the room. It wasn't any cooler than the air outside. He wiped the perspiration from his forehead and took off his jacket. It had dark spots under the arms. The Bangladeshis didn't seem to mind the climate. Their uniforms looked crisp.

"There is the Antonov now, sir," the air traffic controller said with the lilt of South Asians. He pointed to a blip on the radar. The timing was just about right.

"How far is it?"

"About ten miles, sir."

"How long until it lands?"

"Fifteen minutes, give or take. Maybe more. Depends on the approach Petrovic takes."

"Is he usually late?"

"Sometimes Petrovic is on time, sometimes he isn't. This is Africa."

A loud voice crackled over the radio.

"Central Lakes Air Niner Quebec Charlie Echo Juliet requests permission to land."

The voice had a strong Slavic accent.

"Niner Quebec, this is Bunia air control, Bangladeshi Air Force controller Ghosh. Permission granted for runway ten. Visual flight rules in effect. Westerly winds, about three knots."

"Ghosh, you dumb Paki. When're you gonna get a decent radar to guide me in?"

"When you fly a decent aircraft, you lazy Chetnik."

Ghosh smiled and scribbled something into a logbook.

"Can I intercept the plane right after it lands?" Vermeulen asked.

"No, sir. No vehicles allowed on the tarmac during taxiing."

"Where will he stop?"

"At the cargo area over there, sir." Ghosh pointed in the general direction.

Vermeulen grabbed his jacket.

"Thank you, Lieutenant."

Good thing he remembered their insignia.

———

PETROVIC'S STOMACH BULGED over jeans made for a man twenty years younger. The Hawaiian shirt revealed dark chest hair decorated with a gold chain. His bullet-shaped head was shaved except for a bushy mustache—he was a bruiser who'd gone to seed.

He stood by the cargo door of the Antonov and supervised a Nepali engineering platoon. Three soldiers pushed a pallet along a track to the rear gate, where a fourth put the pallet on a forklift and took it to a storage tent.

Vermeulen found the corporal in charge inside the storage tent. The man checked his ID, shrugged, and gestured to the two pallets already unloaded.

They were wrapped in plastic netting. The freight bill attached to each listed the number of boxes and their contents. Vermeulen checked each bill and counted the items on that pallet. They added up.

He pulled at the netting of the nearer pallet. It didn't budge.

"You want it off?" the corporal asked.

"Yes, I need to check the contents."

The corporal took a box cutter from his pocket.

"Get the fuck away from my cargo," a voice shouted from the entrance.

Vermeulen and the corporal turned. Petrovic had jumped to the ground and hurried to the tent.

"You better get the goddamn freight manifest signed before you open anything."

"What's the matter with you, Ranko?" the corporal said, brows raised. "You never gave a rat's ass about paperwork before."

"It's my cargo until the paper's signed," the pilot said. His eyes — the color of dishwater — were cold and menacing, and he had the stare of a street fighter. It reminded Vermeulen of all the bullies he had encountered from grade school on. He took an instant dislike to the pilot.

"Who the fuck are you?" Petrovic asked.

"Valentin Vermeulen, OIOS investigator." He pulled out his ID. "I don't need a signature. I can investigate anything I like."

The pilot stepped closer. At six feet six, Vermeulen towered over Petrovic, but the latter's bulk made him a formidable obstacle.

"You ain't getting near that cargo until the paperwork is signed."

"Okay, then let's get it signed," Vermeulen said. He turned to the corporal. "Just sign his manifest."

"I'm not allowed. The master sergeant does that, but he isn't here right now."

"So I won't be able to inspect the cargo until he returns?"

The corporal nodded.

"When will that be?"

The corporal hemmed and hawed. "I'm not sure. Probably not today."

Vermeulen shook his head. This wasn't going to be his day after all. He saw the sneer on Petrovic's face and turned to leave the tent. The corporal followed him.

Outside, he watched the forklift hoist a large aluminum container — wider and deeper than the pallets — from the plane.

"What is that?" Vermeulen asked the corporal.

"A refrigerated unit, sir."

"What's in it?" he asked, realizing too late that it was a dumb question.

"Perishable food for the troops. Meat, frozen vegetables, and the like."

Vermeulen nodded. What was that old saying? An army travels on its stomach. That was also true for UN peacekeepers. The UN could not feed a whole brigade from local resources. Hell, the locals barely had enough to feed themselves.

Petrovic climbed back into the plane. The white Toyota pickup assigned to Vermeulen waited outside the fence that enclosed the cargo area. He turned to it. Another wasted day on a lousy mission. Time for a drink.

"To the hotel, monsieur?"

Walia Lukungu's arm hung out of the window. He was one of the locals who'd been fortunate enough to snag a job with the UN. His driving skills, though, were questionable. Vermeulen had the feeling of sitting in a Formula One race car every time they went anywhere.

He was just about to nod when one of the soldiers inside the plane called to the corporal. The corporal answered, then shrugged.

"Anything the matter?" Vermeulen shouted from the open pickup door.

"No, sir. It's just that those chaps in Kampala have trouble counting past three. Now there's one refrigerated unit more than the cargo manifest says, but one was missing last week. It happens all the time." The corporal shook his head. "That's the trouble with contractors."

It took a moment before the significance of the corporal's comment sank in. Once it did, Vermeulen felt a familiar adrenaline rush. A clue. He ran back to the tent. The container hovered on the tines of the forklift. Its front consisted of a grille that covered the compressor and fan, and the large door was sealed with a plastic cable tie and bore some sort of label.

"I must check that extra unit. Now."

The corporal shook his head.

"You heard Petrovic. We can't open anything until the cargo is signed for."

"I don't care. I'll take responsibility for opening it."

Vermeulen signaled the forklift driver to place the unit on the ground. He pulled his pocketknife out and bent down to cut the plastic tie. A strong hand grabbed his shoulder and yanked him back from the container. Petrovic.

"Keep your fucking hands off that unit," he hissed, taking a boxer's stance.

"I won't and you can't stop me."

Vermeulen turned back to the unit. Before his knife reached the plastic tie, he felt a gun barrel against his head.

"Drop the knife and turn around slowly."

Vermeulen turned to face Petrovic, who kept pointing

the gun at him. The corporal and the other soldiers stood and gaped.

"Listen, asshole. You can't check the cargo until it's signed for. So why don't you go to your hotel, get some rest, find a whore, whatever, until that formality has been taken care of."

The sight of the pistol took the wind out of Vermeulen's sails. But he decided to play tough.

"What are you going to do? Shoot me?"

Petrovic's eyes narrowed.

"I will," he said. His tone left no doubt that he meant it. "'Courageous Pilot Prevents Pilfering of UN Supplies.' It'll play well in New York. And don't count on these guys helping you. They don't want any trouble. They want to go home."

Vermeulen swallowed. He had overplayed his hand. Without a weapon, he could do nothing. In a vain attempt to maintain his dignity he picked up his knife, straightened his jacket, and turned to the Toyota.

"Take me to Colonel Zaman, Walia."

———

THE CEILING FAN spun lazily. Small eddies in the smoke rising from his Gitane were the only indicators that the hot air moved at all. Stripped to his shorts, Vermeulen lay on the bed in his hotel room. His third bottle of Primus rested on his stomach. At least the beer was cold, even though it tasted like piss. He lifted the bottle to check the name of the brewery. *Brewed under license of Heineken.* Damn! You'd figure a former Belgian colony would at least have a decent Belgian beer, like De Koninck or Celis. Hell, he'd even settle for a bottle of Duvel.

He drew hard on his cigarette. The coarse tobacco crackled and sparked.

Colonel Zaman, commanding officer of this UN outpost, had been unavailable. His deputy, a timid paper pusher in a major's uniform, was afraid to make a decision. He rattled off the usual excuses: Can't order Nepali soldiers without talking to their superiors. Better wait until their master sergeant signs the manifest. Yes, the pilot was out of line, but he was right about his cargo. No harm done. The weapons, if they were there—the major made no effort to hide his skepticism—would still be there in the morning. Extra guards would make sure of that.

What was Vermeulen doing here? Chasing gunrunners? That seemed so futile. There'd be plenty whether or not he nailed that son of a bitch Petrovic and whoever worked with him. But would it come to that? Judging from his past experience, no.

He could easily write his report now. Inconclusive evidence, no witnesses, peacekeepers absolved—the usual bureaucratic-speak that declared victory even as it left everything unchanged. It would make everyone happy.

This job stank, Vermeulen knew that. More than once, he'd been ready to call it quits. But each case was a new opportunity, a chance that, this time, justice would be done. That's why he couldn't write the report yet. But his reservoir of hope was slowly running dry.

He lit another cigarette and watched the smoke curl upward until it reached the faint turbulences below the fan.

A door slammed down the corridor. The UN had chosen Bunia as the headquarters for the Ituri Brigade, so a bevy of aid organizations had descended here as well. Those with more money occupied several rooms the Hotel Bunia reserved for its important visitors. He'd seen a few at breakfast, B-list Hollywood personalities wearing brand-new safari clothing and big smiles.

More steps in the corridor. They slowed as they reached his door. He raised his head. A slight scraping on the floor. A quick retreat.

He jumped up, almost spilling the beer. A note was stuck under the door. He pulled the door open. The corridor was empty.

The note contained a single sentence: *Come to the Club Idéal at 9 tonight.*

He checked his watch. Eight thirty.

———

THE DRUMMER HAD played this beat a million times. Half asleep, he rested against the wall. His hands seemed to have a life of their own. The two guitar players were a little more animated, stepping out, swinging their guitars as they kept the soukous melody flowing at the right speed. Not that it mattered. Nobody was paying attention to the music. Two couples moved on the tiny dance floor, but to Vermeulen it seemed more like foreplay than dancing. Sure enough, one of the couples disappeared behind a ragged curtain, the girl squealing in pretend delight.

He found an empty table. The reek of sweat, cigarettes, and beer that had assaulted his nose began to fade into the background.

A man with a limp had waited for him outside the hotel and hustled him into a beat-up old Citroën 2CV. The man said, "Club Idéal," over and over until Vermeulen figured the ride would be no riskier than walking alone at night. Like all OIOS investigators, he was unarmed.

A girl in a blond wig, maybe seventeen, if that, wiggled her hips as she came to his table. Her breasts were barely concealed beneath a ragged tank top.

"Je suis Lily. Tu veux quelque chose?"

Lily's blond wig stood in startling contrast to her ebony skin.

He stared at her. Although there was no real resemblance, Lily reminded him of his own daughter. Gaby had run away at age fifteen after he divorced his wife. The police didn't care much. Runaways were common in Antwerp. So he searched for her himself. Staking out her friends, asking questions until he found her, in a hole not much different from the Club Idéal.

Lily's smile faded a little under his stare. She suddenly seemed self-conscious. He caught himself.

"Yes, a beer, please."

"Primus or Nile Special?"

Tired of Primus, he chose Nile Special.

The girl came back with the bottle and sat down at his table.

"You want company?"

He took a swig from the bottle and examined her again. *You should be doing homework,* he thought, *or working at a decent job.* His own daughter had finally turned a corner, gotten clean, and made it to the university. But the price had been estrangement. They hadn't spoken in five years. All he knew was that she worked for an import-export company.

Lily lingered a little and bent forward, hoping to change his mind by giving him a glimpse of her breasts. He shrugged and smiled apologetically. She got up, wiggled her hips under the impossibly short skirt, and rejoined the other girls by the bar.

None of the men in the bar was in uniform, but he knew most of them were UN soldiers or contractors. What else was new? Wherever there were soldiers, there were whores.

He finished his beer and noticed the beginnings of a pleasant buzz. One more and he'd be in the right spot. But he held back and lit a Gitane instead. Who knew what this meeting would bring?

A big woman waddled to his table. Of indeterminate age, she wore a brightly colored muumuu and an equally colorful cloth wrapped around her hair. She sat down. Close up, her round face showed the ravages of living at the margins in a poor country.

"My girls, you do not like them?"

He really didn't feel like defending his celibacy to the madam of the brothel. "Your girls all seem a little too young for their jobs."

She waved her right hand with a worldly flair. "Age, what is it? Polite men don't ask."

"I thought that applied only to women over thirty."

Her face lit up with a smile. "A gentleman in Mama Tusani's club! What a surprise. Let me buy you another beer."

She motioned to the counter. Lily brought another bottle and a glass with a milky fluid for Mama Tusani. She didn't leave.

Vermeulen clinked his bottle to her glass and took a swig.

"Nice place you got here," he said.

It was a blatant lie. She knew it but smiled anyway, swaying to the rhythm of the music. When the song ended, she leaned over.

"Please, go with Lily to the back."

He lifted his hands, angry. Mama Tusani took his hands and continued smiling for anyone watching.

"Please, it is important," she said in a tone quite unlike her smile.

He finally understood and got up.

The girl pulled him toward the curtain, giggling, clinging to him, rubbing his chest. He couldn't make himself play the part. To the rest of the crowd, he must have looked like a sixteen-year-old being dragged to his first sexual encounter.

They moved past ill-fitting doors through which unrestrained — and obviously faked — sounds of various stages of ecstasy could be heard. She pushed open the last one and pulled Vermeulen into a cubbyhole. The smell of sex and cheap perfume was overpowering. A filthy bed—reflected in a cracked mirror on the ceiling—took up most of the room. The couple next door was hard at work.

She sat on the bed and smiled. The door opened again and Mama Tusani slipped in. She whispered something to Lily, who began moaning loud enough to compete with the couple next door.

"You are here to stop the gun smugglers, no?" Mama Tusani whispered.

Vermeulen stared at her, speechless for a moment.

"How do you know?" he asked.

"Mama Tusani knows everything. When the men come here, they drink and talk. My girls tell me what they hear."

"Yes, I'm investigating the role of UN troops in illegal arms transfers."

"The plane that came today, it carried guns."

"Are you sure?"

"Yes, the pilot was here earlier. Every time, he comes here right from the plane. He brags to Lily. Says he can fool UN asshole in his sleep."

Lily nodded and smiled at him as she continued moaning.

"Why are you telling me?"

Mama Tusani looked at him. He felt her gauging his character. "My girls, they have a bad past. It's the war that made them so. They have no home to go back to."

"You seem to be doing all right."

Her face hardened.

"You think I like this life? I had a hotel once. The war destroyed everything. Yes, I run a whorehouse. But I keep the girls safe. And they earn some money."

Vermeulen felt a pang of shame.

"The guns make the war go on," she continued. "We want no more war. We want our lives back."

She stared into his eyes with a force that made him squirm. "The pilot, he's a bad man," she said. "He should not walk on this earth. Now go and do your job."

She turned toward the door. Lily simulated the sounds of the final stages of orgasm. At the door, Mama Tusani stopped.

"Go out the rear. The driver will take you back to the hotel."

———

VERMEULEN DIRECTED THE driver to the airport instead. The guard gave him an inquisitive look, but Vermeulen forestalled any questions by flashing his OIOS ID. The guard was appropriately awed—he even saluted.

Once they were inside the airport, it took Vermeulen a while to get his bearings. Twice, he pointed the driver in the wrong direction. The man, of course, knew the way and got them to the cargo area.

He got out of the car. A solitary lamp on a post cast a milky light. Contrary to the major's assertion, there were no guards. A simple padlock kept unauthorized people out.

He circled the fence, looking for a good spot to climb over. He grabbed the wire mesh with both hands and tried hoisting himself up but realized he was fooling himself. The fence was seven or eight feet high. The days when he could tackle anything that height were long gone.

Back at the padlocked gate, he thought about Mama Tusani's words. She was the first person in a long time who actually wanted him to do his job. Everyone else wished he and his investigations would just go away. Even those who had no stake in whatever swindle he was digging up feared that his reports would cast them in a bad light and upset the routines they had grown to like. Everybody had an interest in keeping the status quo.

He examined the padlock again. It was solid. The fence posts didn't move when he pushed against them. The latch was fastened to the post with large screws. He tugged on it. It didn't budge. A metal rod might be strong enough to force the latch open. He thought of a tire iron and turned toward the Citroën.

The driver tried to be helpful, but the trunk was empty, no spare tire and definitely no tire iron.

Vermeulen rifled through the contents of his pants pockets and found his penlight, his lighter, and his pocketknife. The small blade doubled as an emergency screwdriver.

He tried the first screw. It was fastened tightly. He twisted the knife with both hands. The handle dug into his palm. The screw budged a half a turn. He stopped and repositioned the knife. After five minutes, he had removed the first screw. Sweat streamed down his forehead.

The driver observed him for a while but then must have decided that breaking and entering were not his cup of tea. He and the car disappeared.

By the time there were two screws remaining, the knife had scraped his right palm raw. In anger, he kicked the gate. It creaked, and the latch rattled. He aimed carefully and put all the force he could muster into the next kick. The gate sprung open with the sound of screws being wrenched from wood.

The inside of the tent was dark. By the narrow beam of his penlight he made out five pallets in the rear. The refrigerated units stood closer to the front, their compressors humming. A tangle of power cords connected them to the outlets mounted on a pole to the left of the entrance.

The extra refrigerated container—he remembered the code number—sat closest to the entrance. Its door was still sealed with a plastic cable tie. Without hesitation, he cut the tie and opened the door.

A wave of putrid stench enveloped him immediately. The beer in his stomach gurgled uneasily, sending a wave of nausea upward. He pulled a handkerchief from his pocket and held it over his mouth and nose. His penlight revealed the source of the reek. The bags of once frozen food had swollen to resemble grotesque pillows. Many had burst. Mold blooms as large as pizzas covered the interior of the container.

It all fit together. This container was extra, and last week one had been missing. The plane had stopped somewhere, dropped off the container, and then picked it up a week later. Without electricity, the food'd be rotten, all right — a perfect cover for smuggling weapons.

The sound of a truck arriving stopped him. Doors slammed. Angry voices. They had discovered the open gate. He stuck the penlight in his pocket and slipped toward the rear of the tent.

Not a moment too soon. The door of the tent opened and the bright beams of flashlights danced across the tent fabric. He ducked behind a pallet.

"Hijo de puta," somebody swore.

"Fuck! Somebody opened the container!" Vermeulen recognized the pilot's voice. "Raúl, check if anyone is still here. The rest of you, get the guns out now. We gotta move fast."

A flashlight lit up the rear of the tent. Raúl came closer. Vermeulen's mind ran through his options. There were none. These men had guns; he had a little knife. No contest.

Raúl stopped on the other side of the pallet. His flashlight bounced across the dark reaches of the tent. Raúl stepped to the left. Vermeulen crawled to the right, keeping the pallet between them.

He was now in plain view of the men at the entrance, but they were busy tossing the rotten food on the ground.

Raúl walked toward the last pallet.

"*¡Nadie!*" he shouted to the front.

Vermeulen felt exposed. He crawled to the pallet on the left and knelt in the dark space between it and the side of the tent. The beam of Raúl's flashlight swung around. The beam stopped, lighting the space he had just left. Vermeulen's heart skipped. There, glinting in the beam, lay his penlight. It must have dropped from his pocket.

"*¡Mira!*" Raúl shouted and held the penlight in the beam of his torch. Vermeulen crawled behind the pallet Raúl had just left.

The men in front had started stacking the guns in a pile. They were in a hurry.

Another voice told Raúl to hurry up, they didn't have all night.

Raúl shrugged, pocketed the penlight, and joined the men up front.

Time was running out. Vermeulen had to stop them before his evidence disappeared. He knelt down and cut a long slit into the tent fabric. His escape prepared, he took his lighter and lit the plastic netting around the nearest pallet. The flame licked up quickly. The other pallets caught fire just as fast. He crawled out of the tent and held his lighter to the tent fabric. The nylon fabric burst into flames.

Voices shouted inside. In no time, flames erupted through the top of the tent. The soldiers raced to safety in a mad scramble. The tent had turned into a torch, lighting up the airport like a bonfire.

———

COLONEL ZAMAN STOOD up when Vermeulen was led into his office the next morning. His appearance evoked memories of the

Raj—a uniform that looked as if it had been ironed after he'd dressed; a dark mustache, neatly twirled at the ends; slicked-back dark hair with a few white strands that framed the pale olive narrow face; keen eyes and a sharp nose. He seemed distraught.

"Mr. Vermeulen? What can I do for you? We have to make this quick. I have to deal with the aftermath of a fire."

His clenched jaws told the whole story—endless investigations, reviews of procedures, new training protocols, a complete nightmare.

"I know. I was there. The objects of my investigation were in that tent."

The colonel shook his head.

His day has just gotten worse, Vermeulen thought.

"You were at the airport in the middle of the night? Why?" the colonel asked.

"I just wanted to make sure the cargo area was secured, as your deputy had assured me it would be. It wasn't."

"Did you see the fire?"

"Yes, I saw the flames when I arrived. I saw the pilot and several Spanish-speaking soldiers."

"Spanish-speaking, you say? Did you see any insignia?"

Vermeulen shook his head. The colonel made some notes on a pad.

"Did they find guns in the tent?" Vermeulen asked.

"Yes, AK-47s and MP-5s. All burned, of course. It took a while to get the fire extinguished."

"Have you ordered anyone arrested?"

"Arrested? Why? The cause of the fire is unknown."

"What about the people by the tent?"

"Lots of people were there, trying to douse the fire."

"I just told you who started it."

"But you don't know that. You only got there after the fire had started."

The truth began to sink in slowly. And when it finally hit, Vermeulen had to press his lips together to keep from screaming. Setting the fire had ruined his investigation. He knew who the culprits were but couldn't finger them unless he admitted to setting the fire. Which would mean the end of his job.

"You should at least arrest Petrovic," he said, sounding deflated.

"The pilot?" Colonel Zaman raised his left eyebrow. "Why?"

"Because the guns came on his plane. I need to question him." The colonel shook his head. Vermeulen knew what would come next.

"We don't know that. Besides, he's a civilian contractor. I can't arrest him on your say-so."

"My mission," Vermeulen said, trying to conjure gravitas out of thin air, "authorizes me to interview anyone attached to the UN operation here. That includes Petrovic."

The colonel sighed.

"You may interview him if you can find him, but I can't arrest him; I trust you understand that. Now, if you'll excuse me."

———

IN DAYLIGHT, MAMA Tusani's club was even less appealing. The bar still reeked of stale beer and tobacco smoke, but the shabby interior was no longer hidden by the darkness. An ancient tape player looped through a scratchy collection of American hip-hop. Some girls were hanging around the bar, but one o'clock in the afternoon was clearly not the main business hour.

Vermeulen had gone to the club after leaving Colonel Zaman's office. It was an obvious choice. He'd met men like Petrovic before. Despite their swagger, or maybe because of it, they were essentially stupid. Of course Petrovic would be at the club. One last screw before flying back to Kampala.

Mama Tusani stood behind the bar. She nodded and held up two fingers.

"Be careful, he's got a gun," she whispered.

He marched past the ragged curtain and ripped open the second door. Lily lay on the bed, her arms tied to the bed frame, her eyes wide with fear. Petrovic lay on top of her, pressing down hard.

Images of Gaby in that hellhole in Antwerp ran through Vermeulen's mind. His heart pounded and he had to stop himself from pulling Petrovic off the girl.

Petrovic smiled when he saw him.

"Vermeulen. What a surprise. Want to join the party? Lily here has many talents."

Petrovic's smile turned Vermeulen's blood to ice. The gangsters who held Gaby had smiled like that. The crooks he investigated smiled like that. Certain they were untouchable. Too often, they were right. But not this time.

"Get dressed, Petrovic, you're coming with me," he hissed through clenched teeth. His heart pounded.

"I'm not going anywhere," Petrovic said. He rolled to his side languidly. "Hey, Lily, let's show this guy a good fuck."

Petrovic's clothes lay piled at the foot end of the bed. Vermeulen bent down, rifled through them, and found the gun, a Beretta. He flicked off the safety and pointed the pistol at Petrovic. "Get dressed, Petrovic. Now!"

"Hey, careful with that," Petrovic said with a bored expression. "It doesn't suit you. I bet you never even fired one."

"You're wrong there. We shot all kinds of vermin on our farm. Now get up and get dressed."

Petrovic crawled to the edge of the bed and started putting on his underwear. "Tell me this is a joke. You haven't got anything on me."

"Oh, I've got plenty. I have all your departure and arrival times. You were late because you made unscheduled stops to pick up guns. I also know you stored them in refrigerated units because every time you brought an extra one, it had rotten food in it. I've put all the pieces together."

Petrovic pulled on his jeans, a sneer on his face. "That won't do you any good. You'll never make it stick. What court will hear your charges? I'll just walk away from this and fly somewhere else. No big deal. Africa always needs guns."

A rage Vermeulen hadn't known before erupted. It ruptured the dam that held back a sea of frustration accumulated over a decade. No need to think anymore. The flood swept away any hesitation. He saw everything—the room, Petrovic, Lily—with unearthly clarity. There was only one thing he could do.

"You're wrong again," he snarled, and stepped toward the bed.

Petrovic realized something had changed.

"What are you talking about?" he asked, his voice suddenly uncertain.

Vermeulen grabbed Petrovic by the shirt, pressed the Beretta's muzzle against his temple, and pulled the trigger. The side of Petrovic's head exploded. Lily screamed. A sick spatter of blood and tissue marbled the wall. Petrovic went limp. Vermeulen let the body slide onto the bed.

Briefly deafened by the gunshot, he took a handkerchief from his pocket and cleaned the gun. Then he opened Petrovic's right hand, placed the Beretta in it, stuck the index finger through the trigger guard, and closed the hand again.

Mama Tusani waited in the hallway.

He opened his mouth, grasping for an explanation. She put her finger on his lips.

"I'll take care of Lily. Go out the rear. The driver will take you back to the hotel."

He nodded and strode to the back door. A strange lightness took hold of his body. Tomorrow, he'd call his daughter.

THE UNREMARKABLE HEART

BY KARIN SLAUGHTER

June Connor knew that she was going to die today.

The thought seemed like the sort of pathetic declaration that a ninth-grader would use to begin a short-story assignment—one that would have immediately elicited a groan and failing grade from June—but it was true. Today was the day that she was going to die.

The doctors, who had been so wrong about so many things, were right about this at least: She would know when it was time. This morning when June woke, she was conscious of not just the pain, the smell of her spent body, the odor of sweat and various fluids that had saturated the bed during the night, but of the fact that it was time to go. The knowledge came to her as an accepted truth. The sun would rise. The Earth would turn. She would die today.

June had at first been startled by the revelation, then had lain in bed considering the implications. No more pain. No more sickness. No more headaches, seizures, fatigue, confusion, anger.

No more Richard.

No more guilt.

Until now, the notion of her death had been abstract, an impending doom. Each day brought it closer, but closer was never too close. Always around the corner. Always the next week. Always sometime in the future. And now it was here, a taxi at the foot of the driveway. Meter ticking. Waiting to whisk her away.

Her legs twitched as if she could walk again. She became antsy, keenly aware of her pending departure. Now she was a businesswoman standing at an airport gate, ticket in hand, waiting to board the plane. Baggage packed. Luggage checked. Not a trip she wanted to make, but let's just get it over with. Call my row. Let me onto the plane. Let me put back my seat, rest my eyes, and wait for the captain to take over, the plane to lift, the trail of condensation against the blue sky the only indication that I have departed.

How long had it been since the first doctor, the first test, predicted this day? Five and a half months, she calculated. Not much time, but in the end, perhaps too much to bear. She was an educator, a high school principal with almost a thousand kids in her charge. She had work, responsibilities. She hadn't the time or inclination for a drawn-out death.

June could still remember going back to work that day, flipping through her calendar—standardized testing the following month, then the master schedule, which no one but June understood. Then the winding down of the school year. Grades due. Contracts signed. Rooms cleaned. The school was to be repainted this year. Tiles replaced in the cafeteria. New chairs for the band room. Lockers needed to be rekeyed.

"All right," she had said, alone in her office, staring at the full days marked on the calendar. "All right."

Maybe she could fit it all in. If she could last four months, maybe she could get it all done.

So June had not taken her dream vacation to Europe. She had not gone skydiving or climbed a mountain. She continued to work at a job she had grown to despise as if what she did made a difference. Suspending students. Lecturing teachers. Firing a slovenly gym coach she'd been collecting a file on for the last three years.

Clumps of hair fell onto her desk. Her teeth loosened. Her nose bled. One day, for no obvious reason, her arm broke. She had been holding a cup of coffee, and the heat from the liquid pooling on the carpet in front of her open-toed sandal was the first indication that something was wrong.

"I've burned my foot," she had said, wondering at the dropped jaws of the secretaries in the front office.

What had forced her on? What had made her capable of putting on panty hose and pantsuits every morning, driving to school, parking in her spot, doing that hated job for four more months when no one on earth would have questioned her early retirement?

Willpower, she supposed. Sheer determination to finish her final year and collect her full pension, her benefits, after giving thirty years of her life to a system that barely tolerated her presence.

And pride. After all this time, she embraced the opportunity to show her suffering on the outside. She wanted them to see her face every day, to watch the slow decline, to note the subtle changes that marked her impending death. Her last pound of flesh. Her last attempt to show them that they were not the only ones who'd sustained damage. Jesus on the Cross had made a less determined departure.

There was no best friend to tell. No family members left to whom she could confide her fears. June announced it in a school-wide e-mail. Her hand had been steady as she moused over to the icon showing a pencil hovering over a piece of yellow paper. Compose. Send to all. No salutation. No tears. No quibbling. She was fifty-eight years old and would not live to see fifty-nine, but a sentence of death did not give her license to lose her dignity.

You should all know that I have inoperable stage-four lung cancer.

The first thing people asked was, Are you a smoker? Leave it to June to get the sort of disease that had a qualifier, that made strangers judge you for bringing on your own illness. And even when June told them no, she had never smoked, never tried a cigarette or even thought about it, there was a glassy look in their eyes. Disbelief. Pity. Of course she'd brought this on herself. Of course she was lying. Delusional. Stubborn. Crazy.

It was all so eerily similar to what had come before that by the end of the day, June found herself laughing so long and so hard that she coughed blood onto her blouse. And then the horrified looks had replaced the pity, and she was back in those dark days when her only comfort was the thought that the sun would rise and set, the years would go by, and, eventually, she would die, her shame taken with her to the grave.

Irony, June thought now. An incongruity between what might be expected and what actually occurs.

The lung cancer had quickly metastasized. First to her liver, which gave her an alarming yellowish pallor, then to her bones, so brittle that she was reminded of angel hair pasta before you put it into a pot of boiling water. And now her brain, the last thing that she could truly call her own. All cancerous. All riddled with tumors, cells multiplying faster than the palliative radiation and chemotherapy could keep up with.

The doctor, an impossibly young man with a smattering of acne on his chin, had said, "The metastasis are quite pronounced."

"Metasta*ses*," June had corrected, thinking she could not even have the luxury of dying without having to correct the English of someone who should clearly know better. "Five months." He'd scribbled something in her chart before he closed it. "Six if you're lucky."

Oh, how lucky June was to have this extra time.

The tumors in her brain weren't impinging on anything useful. Not yet, at least, so it would seem not ever. This morning, she imagined them as similar to the shape of a lima bean, with tiny, round bottoms that fit puzzle-piece-like into curving gray matter. Her speech was often slurred, but the gift of brain metastases was that oftentimes she could not hear her own voice. Memory was an issue, though maybe not. She could be paranoid. That was a common side effect of the myriad medications she ingested.

Short-term-memory loss. Palsy. Dry mouth. Leaky bowels.

Her breathing was borderline suffocation, the shallow gulps bringing wheezing death rattles from her chest. She could no longer sit up unaided. Her skin was cold, the constant temperature of a refrigerator's vegetable crisper, and, in keeping with the metaphor, its texture, once smooth and even, was now entirely wilted.

In the early days of her diagnosis, she'd had many questions about her impending death but could find no one to answer them. There were plenty of tracts in the doctor's office on keeping a good attitude, eating macrobiotic diets, and making your way back to Jesus, but June could find nothing that spoke frankly of the actual act of death itself. There must have been information online, but if June wanted to read endless paragraphs of poor-me navel-gazing, she could walk down to the reading lab and start grading creative-writing assignments. Besides, she could not overcome her long-held belief that the internet was designed to render human beings functionally retarded.

Years ago, when June had had gallbladder surgery, she had talked to other patients to find out what to expect. How long was the recovery? Was it worth it? Did it take care of the problem?

There was no one to talk with this time. You could not ask someone, What was it like when you died?

"It's different for everyone," a nurse had said, and June, still enough life to feel the injustice of her situation, said, "That's bullshit."

Bullshit, she had said. *Bullshit*, to a perfect stranger.

Five years ago, the air conditioner at the house had finally given up the ghost, and the repairman, a former student of June's who seemed disproportionately fascinated with the minutiae of his job, had described in great detail where the fatal flaw had occurred. Condensation had rusted the coil. The Freon had leaked, depriving the system of coolant. The hose to the outside unit had frozen. Inside the house, the temperature had continued to rise rather than fall, the poor thermostat not understanding why cooling was not being accomplished. Meanwhile, the fan had continued on, whirring and whirring until the motor burned out.

Cause and effect.

And yet, while June could easily find a semiliterate HVAC repairman to explain to her the process by which her air conditioner had died on the hottest day of the summer, there was no medical expert who could reveal to June the minutiae of death.

Finally, on one of the last days that she was able to leave the house unaided, June had discovered a book in the dusty back shelves of a used-book store. She had almost overlooked it, thinking that she had found some New Age tripe written by a pajama-clad cultist. The cover was white with the outline of a triangle inside a solid circle. The title was an idiotic wordplay she could have done without—*How Do You Die?*—but she found comfort inside the pages, which was more than any living being had offered her.

The following text will serve as a guide to the physical act of dying, Dr. Ezekiel Bonner wrote. *Though every human being is different, the body dies in only one way.*

"Well," June had mumbled to herself. There, finally, was the truth.

None of us are special. None of us are unique. We may think we are individuals, but in the end, we are really nothing at all.

June had taken the book home, prepared a pot of tea, and read with a pen in her hand so that she could make notations in the margins. At points, she had laughed aloud at the descriptions offered by Dr. Bonner, because the physical act of the body shutting down was not unlike that of her dying air conditioner. No oxygen, no blood flow, the heart burning out. The brain was the last to go, which pleased June until she realized that there would be a period in which her body was dead but her brain was still alive. She would be conscious, able to understand what was going on around her, yet unable to do or say anything about it.

This gave her night terrors like she'd never had before. Not believing in the afterlife was finally getting its own back.

How long would that moment of brain clarity last? Minutes? Seconds? Milliseconds? What would it feel like to be suspended between life and death? Was it a tightwire that she would have to walk, hands out, feet stepping lightly across a thin cord? Or was it a chasm into which she would fall?

June had never been one to surrender to self-pity, at least not for any length of time. She considered instead the day ahead of her. She had always loved making lists, checking off each chore with a growing sense of accomplishment. Richard would come soon. She could already hear him downstairs making coffee. His slippers would shuffle on the stairs. Boards would squeak in the hallway. The hinges would groan as the door was pushed open. Tentatively, he would poke his head into the room, the curiosity in his eyes magnified by the thick lenses of his glasses.

Her eyes were always open. The morphine wore off in the early-morning hours. The pain was like thousands of needles that pricked her skin, then drilled deeper and deeper into the bone as the seconds ticked by. She lay in bed waiting for Richard, waiting for the shot. She would stare at him as he stood at the door, his hesitancy a third person in the room. He would not look at her face but at her chest, waiting for the strained rise and fall.

And somehow, she would force air into her constricted lungs. Richard would exhale as June inhaled. He would come into the room and tell her good morning. The shot would come first, the sting of the needle barely registering as the morphine was injected into her bloodstream. He would change the catheter. He would wet a rag in the bathroom sink and wipe the drool from her mouth as she waited for the drug to take away the gnawing edge of pain. He would ignore the smells, the stench of dying. In his droning monotone, he would tell her his plans for the day: fix the gutter, sweep the driveway, paint the trim in the hall. Then his attention would turn to her day: Are you hungry this morning? Would you like to go outside for a while? Would you like to watch television? Shall I read you the paper?

And today, as always, he did these things, asked these questions, and June checked each item off her mental list, shaking her head to the offer of food, to the trip outside. She asked for the local paper to be read, wanting him here, unreasonably, after wanting him away for so long.

Richard snapped open the newspaper, cleared his throat, and began reading. "'A severe weather pattern is expected to hit the county around three this afternoon.'"

His voice settled into a low hum, and June was consumed with the guilty knowledge of what the day would really hold. It was a secret that reminded her of the early days of their marriage. They had both been children of loveless unions, parents who hated each other yet could not survive in the world outside the miserable one they had created. In their young fervor, June and Richard had promised each other they would never be like their parents. They would always be truthful. No matter how difficult, there would be nothing unsaid between them.

How had that facade cracked? Was it June who had first lied? The obfuscations had come in dribs and drabs. An ugly shirt he loved that she claimed had been ruined in the wash. A "forgotten" dinner with friends that she did not want to attend. Once, June had accidentally dropped a whole chicken on the floor and still put it in the pot for supper. She had watched him eat that night, his jaw working like a turning gear, and felt some satisfaction in knowing what she had done.

Had Richard done that to her as well? Had there been a time at the dinner table when he had stared at her while relishing the knowledge of his crimes? Had there been a night when he made love to her in this bed, his eyes closed in seeming ecstasy, as he thought not of June but of others?

"'The school board has decided to renew the contract with Davis Janitorial for the maintenance of both the elementary and middle schools,'" Richard continued.

Early on in this process, June had felt much derision for the simple stories told by the *Harris Tribune* to the twelve thousand residents of the small town. Lately, the articles had taken on the importance of real news—The Renewed Maintenance Contract! The New Bench Erected in the Downtown Park!—and June found herself thinking of all those foolish stories people told about near-death experiences. There was always a tunnel, a light up ahead they chose to walk toward or away from. June saw now that there was, in fact, a tunnel—a narrowing of life, making a story as simple as what the elementary school was serving for lunch that week take on infinite importance.

"What's that?" Richard was staring at her, expectant. "What did you say?"

She shook her head. Had she actually spoken? She could not remember the last time she'd participated in a real conversation beyond her grunts for *yes* or *no*. June was capable of speech, but words caught in her throat. Questions caught—things she needed to ask him. Always, she said to herself, *Tomorrow. I'll ask him tomorrow.* The Scarlett O'Hara of dying high school administrators. But there would be no tomorrow now. She would have to ask him today or die without knowing.

" 'Harris Motors has asked for a side setback variance in order to expand their used-car showroom. Those wishing to speak either for or against the proposal can—'"

His shirt was buttoned to the top, the collar tight around his neck. It was an affectation he'd picked up in prison. The pursed lips, the hard stare—those were all his own, conjured during the lead-up to the trial, when June had realized with a shocking sense of familiarity that for all their attempts, they had become the one thing they'd set out not to be: two people trapped in a loveless marriage, a cold union. Lying to each other to make the day go by quickly, only to get up the next morning and find a whole new day of potential lies and omissions spread out before them.

She remembered glancing around the prison visiting room, seeing the other inmates with the stiff collars of their blue shirts buttoned snug around their necks, and thinking, *You've finally found a way to fit in.*

Because Richard had never really fit in. Early on, it was one of the things she loved about him. Friends joked about his lack of masculine pursuits. He was a voracious reader, couldn't stand sports, and tended to take contrary political views in order to play devil's advocate. Not the ideal party guest but, to June, the perfect man. The perfect partner. The perfect husband.

Before her cancer diagnosis, she had never visited Richard in prison, not once in the twenty-one years since he had been sent away. June was not afraid of losing the hate she felt for him. That was as firmly rooted in her chest as the cancer that was growing inside of her. What scared her most was the fear of weakness, that she would break down in his presence. She didn't need a Dr. Bonner to tell her that love and hate existed on the same plane. She didn't need him to tell her that her bond with Richard Connor was at once the best and the worst thing that had ever happened to her.

So it was that the day she drove to the prison, not the day that she was diagnosed with end-stage lung cancer, was the worst day of June Connor's life. Her hands shook. Tears rolled down her cheeks. Standing outside the door to the visitors' area, she let the fear take hold and imagined all the horrible things that could make her weak before him.

The feel of his lips when he kissed her neck. The times she had come home from school, exhausted and angry, and he had cupped her chin with his hand or pressed his lips to her forehead and made everything better. The passionate nights, when he would lie behind her, his hand working her into a frenzy. Even after decades of living apart, after loving him and hating him in equal measure, she found the thought of his body beside her still brought an unwelcome lust.

He never closed drawers or cabinet doors all the way. He never put his keys in the same place when he got home from work, so every morning he was late for school because he couldn't find them. He belched and farted and occasionally spat on the sidewalk. He took his socks off by the bed every night and left them there for June to pick up. There was not an item of laundry he knew how to fold. He had a sort of domestic blindness that prevented him from seeing the furniture that needed to be dusted, the carpets that needed to be vacuumed, the dishes that needed to be washed.

He had betrayed her. He had betrayed everything in their lives.

This latter bit was the only reason June was able to walk through the visitors' door, force herself through the pat-down and metal detector, the intrusive rifling of her purse. The smell of prison was a slap in the face, as was the realization that five thousand grown men were living, shitting, breathing the same air in this miserable place.

What was she worried about—her nose wrinkling, her hand going to her mouth—that she'd get lung cancer?

And then Richard had shown up, a shuffling old man, but still much the same. Stooped shoulders, because he was tall but never proud of it. Gray hair. Gray skin. He'd cut himself shaving that morning. Toilet tissue was stuck to the side of his neck. His thick, black-framed glasses reminded her of the ones he'd worn when they'd first met outside the school library, all those years ago. He was in two of her classes. He was from a small town. He wanted to teach English. He wanted to make kids feel excited about learning. He wanted to take June to the movies that night and talk about it some more. He wanted to hold her hand and tell her about the future they would have together.

There was nothing of that excited eagerness in the old man who'd sat across from her at a metal table.

"I am dying," she'd said.

And he had only nodded, his lips pursed in that self-satisfied way that said he knew everything about June before she even said it.

June had bristled, but inside, she understood that Richard had always known everything about her. Perhaps not the dropped chicken or the ugly shirt she'd gladly sent to the town dump, but he could see into her soul. He knew that her biggest fear was dying alone. He knew what she needed to hear in order to make this transaction go smoothly. He knew, above all, how to turn these things around so that she believed his lies, no matter how paltry the proof, no matter how illogical the reasoning.

"I'm a good man," he'd kept telling her. Before the trial. After the trial. In letters. On the telephone. "You know that, June. Despite it all, I am a good man."

As if it mattered anymore. As if she had a choice.

The secret that horrified her most was that deep down, part of her wanted to believe that he was still good. That he cared about her, even though the hatred in his eyes was so clear that she often had to look away. She could snatch the truth from the jaws of a tenth-grader at twenty paces, but her own husband, the man with whom she'd shared a bed, created a child, built a life, remained an enigma.

June turned her head away now, stared out the window. The curtains needed to be washed. They slouched around the window like a sullen child. Her hands still remembered the feel of the stiff material as she had sewn the pleats, and her mind conjured the image of the fabric store where she had bought the damask. Grace had been eight or nine then. She was running around the store, in and out of the bolts, screaming, so June had finally given up, quickly buying a fabric she wasn't particularly fond of just to get the annoying child out of the store.

And then came the horrible realization that the annoying child would be in the car with her, would come home with her and continue screaming the entire way. Outside the store, June had sat in the blazing-hot car and recalled stories of mothers who'd accidentally left their kids unattended in their cars. The children's brains boiled. They died horrible, agonizing deaths.

June had closed her eyes in the car, summoned back the cool interior of the fabric store. She saw herself browsing slowly down the aisles, touching bolts of fabric, ignoring the prices as she selected yards of damask and silk. No child screaming. No clock ticking. Nowhere to go. Nothing to do but please herself.

And then her eyes popped open as Grace's foot slammed into the back of the seat. June could barely get the key in the ignition. More shaking as she pressed the buttons on the console, sending cold air swirling into the car, her heart stopping midbeat as she realized with shame that it was not the idea of killing her child that brought her such horror, but the thought of the fallout. What the tragedy would leave behind. Grieving mother. Such a sad story. A cautionary tale. And then, whispered but still clear, *How could she...*

Every mother must have felt this way at one time or another. June was not alone in that moment of hatred, that sensation of longing for an unattached life that swept over her as Grace kicked the back of her seat all the way home.

I could just walk away, June had thought. Or had she said the actual words? Had she actually told Grace that she could happily live without her?

She might have said the words, but, as with Richard, those moments of sheer hatred came from longer, more intense moments of love. The first time June had held little Grace in her arms. The first time she'd shown her how to thread a needle, make cookies, decorate a cupcake. Grace's first day of kindergarten. Her first gold star. Her first bad report card.

Grace.

June came back to herself in her dank bedroom, the sensation almost of falling back into her body. She felt a flutter in her chest, a tapping at her heart; the Grim Reaper's bony knuckles knocking at the door. She looked past the dingy curtains. The windows were dirty. The outside world was tainted with grime. Maybe she should let Richard take her outside. She could sit in the garden. She could listen to the birds sing, the squirrels chatter. The last day. The last ray of sunlight on her face. The last sensation of the sheets brushing against her legs. The last comb through her hair. The last breath through her lungs. Her last glimpse of Richard, the house they had bought together, the place where they had raised and lost their child. The prison cell he had left her in as he went off to live in one of his own.

"'A house on Taylor Drive was broken into late Thursday evening. The residents were not at home. Stolen were a gold necklace, a television set, and cash that was kept in the kitchen drawer...'"

She had loved sewing, and before her life had turned upside down the second time, before the detectives and lawyers intruded, before the jury handed down the judgment, June had thought of sewing as a metaphor for her existence. June was a wife, a mother. She stitched together the seam between her husband and child. She was the force that brought them together. The force that held them in place.

Or was she?

All these years, June had thought she was the needle, piercing two separate pieces, making disparate halves whole, but suddenly, on this last day of her life, she realized she was just the thread. Not even the good part of the thread, but the knot at the end—not leading the way, but anchoring, holding on, watching helplessly as someone else, some*thing* else, sewed together the patterns of their lives.

Why was she stuck with these thoughts? She wanted to remember the good times with Grace: vacations, school trips, book reports they had worked on together, talks they had had late at night. June had told Grace all the things mothers tell their daughters: Sit with your legs together. Always be aware of your surroundings. Sex should be saved for someone special. Don't ever let a man make you think you are anything but good and true. There were so many mistakes that June's own mother had made. June had parented against her mother, vowing not to make the same mistakes. And she hadn't. By God, she hadn't.

She had made new ones.

We didn't raise him to be this way, mothers would tell her during parent-teacher conferences, and June would think, *Of course you did. What did you think would happen to a boy who was given everything and made to work for nothing?*

She had secretly blamed them—or perhaps not too secretly. More often than not, there was a complaint filed with the school board by a parent who found her too smug. Too judgmental. June had not realized just how smug until she saw her own smirk reflected back to her at the beginning of a conference about Grace. The teacher's eyes were hard and disapproving. June had choked back the words *We didn't raise her this way* and bile had come into her throat.

What had they raised Grace to be? A princess, if Richard was asked. A perfect princess who loved her father.

But how much had he really loved her?

That was the question she needed answered. That was *literally*—and she used the word correctly here—the last thing that would be on her mind.

Richard sensed the change in her posture. He stared at her over the paper. "What is it?"

June's brain told her mouth to move. She felt the sensation—the parting of the lips, the skin stuck together at the corners—but no words would form.

"Do you want some water?"

She nodded because that was all she could do. Richard left the room. She tilted her head back, looked at the closed closet door. There were love letters on the top shelf. The shoe box was old, dusty. After June died, Richard would go through her things. He would find the letters. Would he think her an idiot for keeping them? Would he think that she had pined for him while he was gone?

She *had* pined. She had ached. She had cried and moaned, not for him, but for the *idea* of him. For the idea of the two of them together.

June turned her head away. The pillowcase felt rough against her face. Her hair clung to wet skin. She closed her eyes and thought of Grace's silky mane of hair. So black that it was almost blue. Her alarmingly deep green eyes that could penetrate right into your soul.

"We're almost out of bendy straws," Richard said, holding the glass low so that she could sip from the straw. "I'll have to go to the store later."

She swallowed, feeling as if a rock were moving down her throat.

"Does it matter to you if I go before or after lunch?"

June managed a shake of her head. Breathing, normally an effort, was becoming more difficult. She could hear a different tenor in the whistle of air wheezing through her lips. Her body was growing numb, but not from the morphine. Her feet felt as if they were sliding out of a pair of thick woolen socks.

Richard placed the glass on her bedside table. Water trickled from the straw, and he wiped it up before sitting back down with the paper.

She should've written a book for wives who wanted their husbands to help more around the house. *Here's my secret, ladies: twenty-one years in a maximum-security prison!* Richard cooked and cleaned. He did the laundry. Some days, he would bring in the warm piles of sheets fresh from the dryer and watch television with June while he folded the fitted sheets into perfect squares.

June closed her eyes again. She had loved folding Grace's clothes. The tiny shirts. The little skirts with flowers and rows of lace. And then Grace had gotten older, and the frilly pink blouses had been relegated to the back of the closet. What had it been like that first day Grace came down to breakfast wearing all black? June wanted to ask Richard, because he had been there too, with his nose tucked into the newspaper. As she remembered, he had merely glanced at June and rolled his eyes.

Meanwhile, her heart had been in her throat. The administrator in June was cataloging Grace the same way she cataloged the black-clad rebels she saw in her office at school: *drug addict, whore, probably pregnant within a year.* She was already thinking about the paperwork she'd have to fill out when she called the young woman into her office and politely forced her to withdraw from classes.

June had always dismissed these children as damaged, halfway between juvenile delinquents and adult perpetrators. Let the justice system deal with them sooner rather than later. She washed them out of her school the same way she washed dirt from her hands. Secretly, she thought of them as legacy children — not the sort you'd find at Harvard or Yale, but the kind of kids who walked in the footsteps of older drug-addled siblings, imprisoned fathers, alcoholic mothers.

It was different when the errant child, the bad seed, sprang from your own loins. Every child had tantrums. That was how they learned to find their limits. Every child made mistakes. That was how they learned to be better people. How many excuses had popped into June's mind each time Grace was late for curfew or brought home a bad report card? How many times did June overlook Grace's lies and excuses?

June's grandmother was a woman given to axioms about apples and trees. When a child was caught lying or committing a crime, she would always say, "Blood will out."

Is that what happened to Grace? Had June's bad blood finally caught up with her? It was certainly catching up with June now. She thought of the glob of red phlegm that she'd spat into the kitchen sink six months ago. She had ignored the episode, then the next and the next, until the pain of breathing was so great that she finally made herself go to the doctor.

So much of June's life was marked in her memory by blood. A bloody nose at the age of seven courtesy of her cousin Beau, who'd pushed her too hard down the slide. Standing with her mother at the bathroom sink, age thirteen, learning how to wash out her underpants. The dark stain soaked into the cloth seat of the car when she'd had her first miscarriage. The clotting in the toilet every month that told her she'd failed, yet again, to make a child.

Then, miraculously, the birth. Grace, bloody and screaming. Later, there were bumped elbows and skinned knees. And then the final act, blood mingling with water, spilling over the side of the bathtub, turning the rug and tiles crimson. The faucet was still running, a slow trickle like syrup out of the jar. Grace was naked, soaking in cold, red water. Her arms were splayed out in mock crucifixion, her wrists sliced open, exposing sinew and flesh.

Richard had found her. June was downstairs in her sewing room when she heard him knocking on Grace's bedroom door to say good night. Grace was upset because her debate team had lost their bid for the regional finals. Debate club was the last bastion of Grace's old life, the only indication that the black-clad child hunched at the dinner table still belonged to them.

Richard was one of the debate-team coaches, had been with the team since Grace had joined, back in middle school. It was the perfect pursuit for two people who loved to argue. He'd been depressed about the loss, too, and covered badly with a fake bravado as he knocked, first softly, then firmly, on her door.

"All right, Gracie-gray. No more feeling sorry for ourselves. We'll get through this." More loud knocking, then the floor creaking as he walked toward the bathroom. Again, the knocking, the calling out. Richard mumbled to himself, tried the bathroom door. June heard the hinges groan open, then heard Richard screaming.

The sound was at once inhuman and brutally human, a noise that comes only from a mortal wounding. June had been so shocked by the sound that her hand had slipped, the needle digging deep into the meat of her thumb. She hadn't registered the pain until days later when she was picking out the dress Grace would be buried in. The bruise was dark, almost black, as if the tip of June's thumb had been marked with an ink pen.

The razor Grace used was a straight-edge blade, a relic from the shaving kit that had belonged to June's father. June had forgotten all about it until she saw it lying on the floor just below her daughter's lifeless hand. Grace didn't leave a suicide note. There were no hidden diaries or journals blaming anyone or explaining why she had chosen this way out.

The police wanted to know if Grace had been depressed lately. Had she ever done drugs? Was she withdrawn? Secretive? There seemed to be a checklist for calling a case a suicide, and the detectives asked only the questions that helped them tick off the boxes. June recognized the complacency in their stance, the tiredness in their eyes. She often saw it in the mirror when she got home from school. Another troubled teenager. Another problem to be dealt with. They wanted to stamp the case solved and file it away so that they could move on to the next one.

Washing dirt off their hands.

June didn't want to move on. She couldn't move on. She hounded her daughter's best friend, Danielle, until Martha, the girl's mother, firmly told June to leave her alone. June would not be so easily deterred. She called Grace's other friends into her office, demanded they tell her every detail about her daughter's life. She turned into a tyrant, firing off warning shots at anyone who dared resist.

She studied her daughter's death the way she had studied for her degrees, so that by the end of it all, June could've written a dissertation on Grace's suicide. She knew the left wrist was cut first, that there were two hesitation marks before the blade had gone in. She knew that the cut to the right wrist was more shallow, that the blade had nicked the ulnar nerve, causing some fingers of the hand to curl. She knew from the autopsy report that her daughter's right femur still showed the dark line of a healed fracture where she'd fallen off the monkey bars ten years before. Her liver was of normal size and texture. The formation of her sagittal sutures was consistent with the stated age of fifteen. There were 250 ccs of urine in her bladder, and her stomach contents were consistent with the ingestion of popcorn, which June could still smell wafting from the kitchen when she ran upstairs to find her daughter.

The lungs, kidneys, spleen, and pancreas were all as expected. Bones were measured, cataloged. The brain was weighed. All appeared normal. All were in the predictable margins. The heart, according to the doctor who performed the autopsy, was unremarkable.

How could that be? June had wondered. How could a precious fifteen-year-old girl, a baby June had carried in her womb and delivered to the world with such promise, have an unremarkable heart?

"What's that?" Richard asked, peering at her over the newspaper. When she shook her head, he said, "You're mumbling a lot lately."

She couldn't tell from his expression whether he was annoyed or concerned. Did he know that today was the day? Was he ready to get it over with?

Richard had always been an impatient man. Twenty-one years in an eight-by-ten cell had drilled some of that out of him. He'd learned to still his tapping hands, quiet the constant shuffling of his feet. He could sit in silence for hours now, staring at the wall as June slept. She knew he was listening to the pained draw of breath, the in-and-out of her life. Sometimes she thought maybe he was enjoying it, the audible proof of her suffering. Was that a smile on his lips as he wiped her nose? Was that a flash of teeth as he gently soaped and washed her underarms and nether regions?

Weeks ago, when she could still sit up and feed herself, when words came without gasping, raspy coughs, she had asked him to end her life. The injectable morphine prescribed by the doctor seemed to be an invitation to an easy way out, but Richard had recoiled at the thought. "I may be a lot of things," he had said, indignant, "but I am not a murderer."

There had been a fight of sorts, but not from anything June had said. Richard had read her mind as easily as he could read a book.

He'd as good as killed her two decades ago. Why was his conscience stopping him now?

"You can still be such a bitch," he'd said, throwing down a towel he'd been folding. She didn't see him for hours, and when he came upstairs with a tray of soup, they pretended that it hadn't happened. He folded the rest of the towels, his lips pressed into a thin line, and June, in and out of consciousness, had watched his face change as if she were looking at it through a colored kaleidoscope: angry red triangles blending into dark black squares.

He was an old man now, her husband, the man she had never bothered to divorce because the act would be one more reason for her name to appear beside his in the newspaper. Richard was sixty-three years old. He had no pension. No insurance. No chance of gainful employment. The state called it compassionate probation, though June guessed the administrators felt lucky to get an old man with an old man's medical needs off their books. For Richard's part, June was his only salvation, the only way he could live out the rest of his life in relative comfort.

And she would not die alone, unattended in a cold hospital room, the beep of a machine the only indication that someone should call the funeral home.

So the man who had robbed her of her good reputation, her lifelong friendships, her comfort in her old age would be the man who witnessed her painful death. And then he would reap the reward of the last thing, the only thing, they could not take away: the benefits of her tenure with the public school system.

June chuckled to herself. Two birds with one stone. The Harris County Board of Education would remit a check once a month payable to Richard Connor in the name of June Connor. They would be reminded once a month of what they had done to June, and once a month, Richard would be reminded of what he had done to her.

Not just to her—to the school. To the community. To Grace. To poor Danielle Parson, who, last June had heard, was prostituting herself in order to feed her heroin addiction.

June heard a loud knocking sound, and it took a few seconds for her to realize the noise was conjured from memory, something only she could hear. It was Martha Parson banging on the front door. She'd pounded so hard that the side of her hand was bruised. June had later seen it on television; Martha held the same hand to her chest, fist still clenched, as she talked about the monster in their midst.

Grace had been dead less than a month, and the police were back, but this time they were there to arrest Richard.

Whenever June heard a child make a damning statement against an adult, her default position was always disbelief. She could not be blamed for doing this at the time. This was not so many years removed from the McMartin preschool trials. False allegations of child abuse and satanic sexual rituals were still spreading through schools like water through sand. Kern

County. Fells Acres. Escola Base. The Bronx Five. It was a wonder parents didn't wrap their children in cellophane before sending them into the world.

More girls stepped up for their moments in the spotlight: Allison Molitar, Denise Rimes, Candy Davidson. With each girl, the charges became more unbelievable. Blow jobs in the faculty lounge. Fingerings in the library. He'd let them watch adult movies. He'd given them alcohol and taken suggestive photographs of them.

June immediately pegged them as liars, these former friends of Grace. She thought with disgust about the fact that she'd had these girls in her home, had driven them to the mall and the movie theater and had shared meals with them around her dinner table. June had searched the house, the car, Richard's office at home and school. There were no photographs. The only alcohol in the house was a bottle of wine that had sat in the back of the refrigerator since June's birthday. The cork had been shoved down into the open bottle. She'd pried it out, and the smell of vinegar had turned her stomach.

If June Connor knew about anything, it was teenage girls. Half her school day was spent settling she-said arguments, where rumors and innuendo had been used by one girl to tear down another. She knew the hateful, spiteful things they were capable of. They lied as a way of life. They created drama only to embrace the fallout. They were suggestible. They were easily influenced. They were spiteful, horrible human beings.

She said as much to the detectives, to the media, to the women who stopped her at the grocery store. Anyone who met June Connor during that time got the same story from her: *I know these girls, and they are all lying for attention.*

For his part, Richard was outraged. Teaching was his life. His reputation was sterling; he was one of those teachers students loved because he challenged them on every level every single day. He had devoted himself to education, to helping kids achieve something other than mediocrity. The previous year, four of his kids had gone on to full scholarships at Ivy League schools. Twice he had been voted teacher of the year for the district. Every summer, former students dropped by his classroom to thank him for making them work harder than they had ever worked in their lives. Doctors, lawyers, politicians—they had all at some point been in one of Richard's English classes, and he had done nothing but help them prepare for their exemplary lives.

That first week was a blur; talking to lawyers, going to a bail bondsman in a part of town June had not known existed. There was an entirely different language to this type of life, a Latin that defied their various English degrees: *ex officio, locus delicti, cui bono.* They stayed awake all night reading law books, studying cases, finding precedents that, when presented to the lawyer, were dispelled within seconds of their meeting. And still, they went back to the books every night, studying, preparing, defending.

There is no bond tighter than a bond of mutual persecution. It was June and Richard against everyone else. It was June and Richard who knew the truth. It was June and Richard who would fight this insanity together. Who were these girls? How dare these girls? To hell with these girls.

June had often lectured Grace about responsibility. Like most children, Grace was a great subverter. Her stories always managed to shift blame, ever so subtly, onto others. If there was a fight, then Grace was only defending herself. If she was late with an assignment, it was because the teacher's instructions had not been clear. If she got caught sneaking out in the middle of the night, it was because her friends had threatened her, cajoled her into being part of the group.

"Which is more possible," June had asked, "that every single person in the world is conspiring to make you seem a fool, or that you are only fooling yourself?"

But this was different. June was vindicated. One by one, the girls dropped away, their charges dismissed for lack of evidence. The parents made excuses: The girls were not lying, but the public scrutiny was too much. The limelight not what they had expected. All of them refused to testify—all but one. Danielle Parson, Grace's best friend. Richard's original accuser.

The prosecutor, having tremendously lost face when the bulk of his case fell apart, would have sought the death penalty if possible. Instead, he threw every charge at Richard that had even the remotest possibility of sticking. Sodomy, sexual assault, statutory rape, contributing to the delinquency of a minor, providing alcohol to a minor, and, because the debate team had traveled to a neighboring state for a regional tournament, child abduction and transporting a minor for the purposes of sexual concourse. This last one was a federal charge. At the judge's discretion, Richard could be sentenced to life in prison without the possibility of parole.

"It's come-to-Jesus time," their lawyer had said, a phrase June had never heard in her life until that moment. "You can fight this and still go to jail, or you can take a deal, serve your time, and get on with your life."

There were other factors. Money from a second mortgage they had taken on the house would get them through jury selection. Obviously, Richard wasn't allowed back at work or within three hundred yards of any of the girls. The board had told June they were thinking of "transferring her valuable skills" to a school that routinely ended up in the news for campus shootings and stabbings. Then there were the signs left in their front yard, the burning bag of shit on their front porch. Nasty phone calls. Deep scratches in the paint of their cars.

"It's like Salem," June had muttered, and Richard agreed, making a comment that burning at the stake was preferable to being slowly drawn and quartered in front of a crowd of hysterical parents.

June decided then and there to dig in her heels. They would fight this. They would live in a homeless shelter if that's what it took to clear Richard's name. She would not let them win. She would not let this lying, cheating whore who had been her daughter's best friend take another life.

She was certain then that Danielle had had something to do with Grace's death. Had she taunted her? Had Danielle hounded Grace until Grace felt that picking up that straight razor and opening up her skin was the only way to save herself?

Leading up to the trial, June was consumed with such hatred for Danielle Parson that she could not look at a blond, slight, simpering teenager without wanting to slap her. Danielle had always been mouthy, always wanted to push the limits. Her mother let her dress like a whore. She skipped class. She wore too much mascara. She was a hateful, hateful child.

More obscure Latin: from *depositio cornuum*, "taking off the horns," came *deposition*.

The twenty-one years since Richard's conviction had given June plenty of time to reflect on what happened next. They were sitting at a table in the prosecutor's conference room. Richard and June were on one side of the table—he because he was the accused, and June because she would have it no other way—while Danielle, Martha, and Stan Parson sat opposite. The lawyers were in between, lined up like dominoes ready to knock one another over with objections and motions to strike.

June relished the prospect of confronting the girl face-to-face. She'd prepared herself in the mirror that morning, using her best teacher gaze, the one that caused students to stop in their tracks and immediately apologize even when they weren't quite sure why.

Cut the bullshit, June wanted to say. *Tell the truth.*

There was no such confrontation. Danielle would not look anyone in the eye. She kept her hands folded in her lap, shoulders drawn into a narrow V. She had that fragility some girls don't lose even when they cross into womanhood. She was the type who would never have to take out the trash or change a tire or worry about paying her bills because one flutter of her eyelashes would bring men running to her aid.

June hadn't seen Danielle since Grace's funeral, when the girl had sobbed so uncontrollably that her father had to physically carry her out of the church. Recalling this scene, June experienced a revelation: Danielle was acting out of grief. Grace had been her best friend for almost a decade, and now she was gone. Danielle wasn't hurt, at least not in the physical sense. She was mad that Grace was gone, furious at the parents who couldn't prevent her death. There was no telling what reasons had clogged her mind. She obviously blamed Richard for Grace's death. She was lost and confused. Children needed to know that the world was a place where things made sense. Danielle was still a child, after all. She was a scared little girl who didn't know that before you could get out of a hole, you had to stop digging.

In that crowded conference room, a tiny bit of June's heart had opened up. She understood fury and confusion. She understood lashing out. She also finally understood that the loss of Grace had left a gaping hole in the girl's chest.

"Listen to me," June had said, her voice more moderate than it had been in weeks. "It's all right. Just tell the truth, and everything will be fine."

Danielle had finally looked up, and June saw in her red-rimmed eyes that she was not angry. She was not vindictive. She was not cruel. She was afraid. She was trapped. The slumped shoulders were not from self-pity, but from self-loathing.

"It's my fault Grace died." Danielle's words were a whisper, almost too soft to be heard. The court reporter asked her to repeat herself as the girl's lawyers clamored to ignore the declaration.

"She saw us," Danielle said, not to the room, or to the lawyers, but to June.

And then, with no prodding from the prosecutor, she went on to describe how Richard had seduced her. The longing glances in the rearview mirror as he drove the girls to and from school. The stolen kisses on her cheek, and sometimes her lips. The flattery. The compliments. The accidental touches—brushing his hand across her breast, pressing his leg against hers.

The first time it happened, they were at school. He had taken her into the faculty lounge, deserted after the last bell, and told her to sit down on the couch. As Danielle described the scene, June moved around the familiar lounge: the humming refrigerator, the scarred laminate tables, the uncomfortable plastic chairs, the green vinyl couch that hissed out a stream of air every time you moved.

Danielle had never been alone with Richard. Not like this. Not with the air so thick she couldn't breathe. Not with every muscle in her body telling her to run away. June did not hear the girl's words so much as experience them. The hand on the back of her neck. The hissing of the couch as she was shoved face-down into the vinyl. The agonizing rip as he forced himself from behind. The skin shredded by his callused hand when he reached around to touch her.

Why hadn't she told anyone?

The lawyer asked this question, but June did not need to hear the girl's answer.

If June Connor knew about anything, it was teenage girls. She knew how they thought, what they did to punish themselves when something bad happened, even if that bad thing was beyond their control. Danielle was afraid. Mr. Connor was her teacher. He was Grace's father. He was friends with her dad. Danielle didn't want to lose her best friend. She didn't want to upset June. She just wanted to pretend it hadn't happened, hope it would never happen again.

But she couldn't forget about it. She turned it over again and again in her mind and started blaming herself, because wasn't it her fault for being alone with him? Wasn't it her fault for not pulling away when he brushed up against her? Wasn't it her fault for letting their legs touch, for laughing at his jokes, for being quiet when he told her to be?

Slowly, in her little-girl voice, Danielle described the subsequent encounters, each time shifting the blame onto herself.

"I was late with an assignment."

"I was going to miss my curfew."

"He said it would be the last time."

And on and on and on, and finally it really was the very last time because Grace had walked into Richard's office at home. She'd come to find out if her dad wanted some popcorn. She'd found instead her dad raping her best friend.

"That's why..." Danielle gasped, looking up at June. "That's the night..."

June didn't have to be told. Even if she had wanted to, there was no way she could clear that night from her mind. June had been working in her sewing room. Danielle and Grace were upstairs eating popcorn, lamenting their lost chance at the regional championship. Richard was in his office. Martha Parson called, looking for her daughter. Richard offered to drive her home but the girl chose to walk. Why hadn't June thought it strange that a fifteen-year-old girl would rather walk six blocks in the cold than get a lift from her best friend's father?

"It's my fault," Danielle managed between sobs. "Grace saw us, and..." Her eyes were nearly swollen shut from crying. Her shoulders folded in so tight that she looked as if she were being sucked backward down a tube.

There was a long row of windows behind Danielle and her parents. June could see Richard's reflection in the glass. His face was impassive. There was a glint of white from his glasses. She glanced down and saw that his hands were in his lap.

She glanced down and saw that he was enjoying the story.

By the time the deposition was over, June's jaw was so tight that she could not open her mouth to speak. Her spine was hard as steel. Her hands were clenched into fists.

She did not say a word. Not when the girl described a birthmark on Richard's back, a scar just below his knee, a mole at the base of his penis. Not when she talked about the obsessive way he'd stroked her hair. The way he had held her from behind and used his hand on her. The way he had seduced this fifteen-year-old child in the same way he had seduced June.

And June had thought of her words, long ago, to Grace: "Which is more possible," she had asked, "that every single person in the world is conspiring to make you seem a fool, or that you are only fooling yourself?"

June had left the prosecutor's conference room without a word to anyone. She drove straight to the school's administration offices, where they gladly granted her request for a temporary leave of absence. She went to the dollar store and bought a packet of underwear, a toothbrush, and a comb. She checked in to a hotel and did not go home until the newspaper headlines told her that Richard would not be there.

He had left the heat on eighty, he who had fastidiously turned off hall lights and cranked down the thermostat on even the coldest days. The seat was up on every toilet. All the bowls were full of excrement. Dirty dishes spilled over in the sink. Trash was piled in the corner of the kitchen. The stripped mattress held the faint odor of urine.

"Fuck you too," June had mumbled as she burned his clothes in the backyard barbecue.

The school board couldn't fire her for being married to an imprisoned sex offender. Instead, she was moved to the worst part of town, a job for which she was routinely called to testify in court cases of students who'd been accused of armed robbery, rape, drug trafficking, and any number of horrors. Her social life was nonexistent. There were no friends left for the woman who had defended a pedophile. There were no shoulders to cry on for the principal who had called the students raped by her husband a pack of lying whores.

Over the years, June had considered giving an interview, writing a book, telling the world what it was like to be in that room listening to Danielle Parson and knowing that her husband had as good as killed them both. Each time June sat down to write the story, the words backed up like bile in her throat. What could she say in defense of herself? She had never publicly admitted her husband's guilt. June Connor, a woman who relished the English language, could find no words to explain herself.

She had shared a bed with Richard for eighteen years. She had borne him a child. They had lost their child. They had loved together. They had grieved together. And all the while, he was a monster.

What kind of woman didn't see that? What kind of principal did not notice that her own husband was brutally sodomizing her daughter's fifteen-year-old best friend?

Pride. Sheer determination. She would not explain herself.

She did not owe anyone a damn explanation. So she kept it all bottled up inside of her, the truth an angry, metastasizing tumor.

"Another story about the weather," Richard said, rustling pages as he folded the paper. "Umbrellas are suggested."

Her heart fluttered again, doing an odd triple beat. The tightness in her chest turned like a vise.

"What is it?" Richard reached for the mask hanging on the oxygen tank.

June waved him away, her vision blurring on her hand so that it seemed like a streak of light followed the movement. She moved her hand again, fascinated by the effect.

"June?"

Her fingers were numbing, the bones of her hand slowly degloved. She felt her breath catch, and panic filled her—not because the time was here, but because she still had not asked him the question.

"What is it?" He sat on the edge of the bed, his leg touching hers. "June?" His voice was raised. "Should I call an ambulance?"

She looked at his hands. His square fingers. His thick wrists. There were age spots now. She could see the blue veins under his skin.

The first time June held Richard's hand, her stomach had tickled, her heart had jumped, and she'd finally understood Austen and Brontë and every silly sonnet she'd ever studied.

Love is not love which alters when it alteration finds.

This was the feeling she wanted to take with her—not the horror of the last twenty years. Not the sight of her daughter lying dead. Not the questions about how much Grace knew, how much she had suffered. Not the thought of Danielle Parson, the pretty young girl who could make it through the day only with the help of heroin.

June wanted the feeling from the first time she had held her child. She wanted the bliss from her wedding day, the first time Richard had made love to her. There were happy times in this home. There were birthdays and surprise parties and Thanksgivings and wonderful Christmases. There was warmth and love. There was Grace.

"Grace," Richard said, as if he could read her mind. Or perhaps June had said the word, so sweet on her lips. The smell of her shampoo. The way her tiny clothes felt in June's hand. Her socks were impossibly small. June had pressed them to her mouth one day, kissing them, thinking of kissing her daughter's feet.

Richard cleared his throat. His tone was low. "You want the truth."

June tried to shake her head, but her muscles were gone, her brain disconnecting from the stem, nerve impulses wandering down vacant paths. It was here. It was so close. She was not going to find religion this late in the game, but she wanted lightness to be the last thing in her heart, not the darkness his words promised to bring.

"It's true," he told her, as if she didn't know this already. "It's true what Danielle said."

June forced out a groan of air. Valentine's Day cards. Birthday balloons. Mother's Day breakfasts. Crayon drawings hanging on the refrigerator. Skinned knees that needed to be kissed. Monsters that were chased away by a hug and a gentle stroke of hair.

"Grace saw us."

June tried to shake her head. She didn't need to hear it from his mouth. She didn't need to take his confession to her grave. Let her have this one thing. Let her have at least a moment of peace.

He leaned in closer. She could feel the heat from his mouth. "Can you hear me, wife?"

She had no more air. Her lungs froze. Her heart lurched to a stop.

"Can you hear me?" he repeated.

June's eyes would not close. This was the last minute, second, millisecond. She was not breathing. Her heart was still. Her brain whirred and whirred, seconds from burning itself out.

Richard's voice came to her down the long tunnel. "Grace didn't kill herself because she caught me fucking Danielle." His tongue caught between his teeth. There was a smile on his lips. "She did it because she was jealous."

IT AIN'T RIGHT

BY MICHELLE GAGNON

I t ain't right, is all I'm saying."

Joe just kept walking the way he always did, shovel over his shoulder, cigarette clinging to his bottom lip.

"You hear me?"

He stopped and turned, lifting his head inch by inch until his eyes found my hips then my breasts then my eyes. A dust devil whirled away behind him, making the bottom branches of the tree dance like girls on May Day, up and down. He stared at me long and hard, and I felt the last heat of the day seeping into my skin and down through my bones, reaching inside to meet the cold that burrowed into my stomach early that morning.

"She's dead, ain't she?" With his free hand, Joe scratched his belly where the bottom of his T-shirt had pulled away.

"Just 'cause she's dead don't mean she should be put down like this."

He looked past me toward where the road met the hill and dove behind it, wheat tips glowing pink in the twilight. "What else we gonna do with her?"

We stared each other down while the shadows crept in and heat eased into darkness like air escaping a balloon. Night surrounded Joe's head, digging under his cheekbones and into his eye sockets, carving out the face that had been so handsome years earlier that I swore he could've been in pictures.

I turned and shuffled back to the house, kicking up pebbles and dust with my sandals, crossing my arms against the cold that radiated out like there was a snowball growing inside me.

He was gone a long time. The six o'clock news came and went, then *Wheel of Fortune* and *Jeopardy!*, and me checking the clock every five minutes, getting up from time to time to peer through our fading curtains. It was always so quiet at night, I swear the TV was the only thing keeping my head screwed on my shoulders.

Law & Order was on when he finally came in, bolted both locks, and went to the sink without so much as a word. Joe washed his hands for a long time. I stared at the screen, trying to figure out why some girl was crying over someone who from the look of things she hadn't much liked anyway. He plunked down beside me and made the same sigh as his beer when he popped it open.

"So it's done, then," I said.

"Yep."

And that was the last we spoke of it. But once that cold burrowed inside me, it seemed dead set on staying. It got so I couldn't watch Joe standing in a towel with the mirror steamed up, shaving in that slow, careful way he did everything without wanting to sock him over the head with something. I kept washing his clothes and making his dinner, but when he entered me I stared up at the ceiling and endured his gasps and cries without a word, both of us pretending there wasn't another person lying there with us, when both of us knew there was.

Winter made it better somehow, made it so I couldn't imagine her trying to claw through the roots and soil to the air. I knew she was done then, that she wouldn't be able to come after us, at least not till spring. I figured maybe we'd move, head to the city like we always said we would when we were young and such things still might just happen one day. I had almost put it out of my mind, even managed a smile for Joe when he showed up with a new scarf and mittens in my favorite periwinkle, when lights pulled into our driveway. The police didn't say much, just probed our eyes while they asked, *Ever hear what went on over there? Any word on who she was seeing?* Joe did most of the talking, smiling a little too large, taking so long to answer you could practically hear him sounding it out in his mind before the words left his lips. I thought, *Always so handsome in those uniforms, so shiny.* Then I caught myself twisting the dish towel around and around my hand.

"She's the type," I heard myself saying.

"What type, ma'am?" One of them was eyeing me now, the older one with the small mustache.

"Loose—you know. She'd head off with any Tom passing by—since the day she was born, dead set on getting outta here. I heard her say once she wanted to go to Vegas, see the lights."

"Vegas, huh." The two of them looked at each other and nodded, slapped shut their notebooks, and waved their way out the door. Joe leaned back on the couch again and started flipping through channel after channel: knives slicing meat, kids swinging on ropes, women cleaning their kitchens. He went through all five hundred twice and I saw he wasn't stopping anytime soon, so I got my new mittens on and went outside for more of that quiet I was always complaining about.

It was cold and crisp and the moon shone flat on the field with a strange dead light, all gray and unnatural. I started down the road without really thinking, 'cause if I had been I would've said to myself, *Sadie, the cops just been here and this ain't no way to behave,* but something about the moon and the quiet erased those thoughts and suddenly I was there. It looked the same as all the other fields. *This is why they put up markers,* I thought, tapping my feet to keep out the cold. *Otherwise no one knows where you last set foot on earth.* I tasted the salt before I knew I was crying and was suddenly on my knees tearing at the snow, periwinkle blue pounding at the crust then throwing handfuls of cold past my legs. *It should be red,* I thought, *I'll dig down until I see some red…*

And then Joe's hands were on my shoulders, and he was carrying me in those arms that looked too thin to hold anything heavier than a shovel, and I woke up in my bed, sun warming the curtains and the smell of coffee sneaking under the door.

After a knock-knock, Joe came in holding my favorite mug, steam licking his face, and he kind of smiled at me. He put the mug on the table and smoothed my hair back and said, "I know you didn't mean to do it. I made you, and I'm sorry."

We were fifteen again, and he was the only boy in the world for me, movie-star handsome standing on the side of the quarry, beads of water glowing on his skin before he dove in and came up laughing.

We were twenty, and married, and I was pregnant and he had a decent job, and we were moving to the city soon as we saved enough money.

We were thirty, still happy even though none of the babies had worked out, and his job was the same, and I had trouble breathing in summertime.

We were forty, and even though we had each done a terrible thing, he still bought me mittens and lied to the police and brought me coffee in the morning. And I thought to myself, *This is a good man.* And I said, "Let's move to the city." And we never spoke of it again.

SILENT JUSTICE

BY C. E. LAWRENCE

B less me, Father, for I have sinned."
Father Aleksander Milichuk pressed his fingertips hard against the sides of his forehead in an attempt to stop the throbbing in his right temple. Another Monday morning, another migraine on the way. He really needed to back off on the Sunday-night drinking at McSorley's. He wasn't as young as he used to be, as his mother was so fond of reminding him. Maybe she was right; he was nearing forty, and these days just a couple of drinks could bring on a wicked headache. He took a deep breath and cleared his throat.

"How long has it been since your last confession?"

"Three weeks." The voice on the other side of the confessional was a breathy tenor, the voice of a young person.

"Is it a venial sin or a—"

"A mortal sin, Father."

Something in the man's tone made him lean forward.

"And what was this sin, my son?"

The answer came in a low voice, barely audible.

"Murder, Father."

Father Milichuk sat up very straight on his narrow bench, his mind snapping into sharp focus. He was no longer aware of the throbbing in his head. Panicked, he tried to think of a response, but his tongue was dry as paper and stuck to the roof of his mouth. There was a rustling sound from the other side of the confessional, as though the man were removing something from a plastic bag. Crazy, improbable thoughts darted through the priest's head. *What if he brought a gun with him?* His knees shook as fear flooded his veins. *Say something!* He tried to remember if he had ever heard this voice before.

"Aren't you going to give me penance, Father?" The man's tone was patient, weary.

The priest was very good at identifying voices and was certain he had never heard this man's voice before.

"Uh, yes, of course," he sputtered finally. "Say twelve Hail Marys—" He stopped, stunned by the feeble inadequacy of his response.

The man on the other side of the booth chuckled sadly. "That's all?"

"H-have you confessed your sin to the police?"

"I'm confessing it to you."

"Yes, I know, but—"

"I don't want to go to prison."

"Who did you—kill?"

"It doesn't matter. I took a life; that's all I'm required to tell you. Give me absolution, Father. Please."

"It's just that—"

"Please." It was half entreaty, half threat.

The priest looked at the lattice of shadow cast by the metal grille between them, crisscrossed like miniature prison bars.

"All right," he said. "But—"

"Deus meus, ex toto corde paenitet," the man began, *"me omnium meorum peccatorum, eaque detestor, quia peccando..."*

He finished his flawless Latin recitation with a final "Amen."

"Now will you give me absolution?"

Father Milichuk could see no way out of it. Crossing himself, he began to recite the familiar litany.

"May our Lord Jesus Christ absolve you—"

"In Latin, Father—please."

The priest crossed himself again. His head throbbed, and his palms were sweating.

"Dominus noster Jesus Christus te absolvat..." The words seemed to stick in his throat. He coughed and managed to complete the prayer, crossing himself one final time. But he failed to find the usual comfort in the gesture; it felt futile, desultory.

"Thank you, Father." The man sounded genuinely grateful. Whatever else he was, the priest thought, he was a true Catholic who believed in the power of absolution.

"Say twelve Hail Marys," he began, "and—"

"I will, Father—thank you. God bless you."

"God be with you, my son."

Before the priest could say another word, he heard the door hinges creak open, then the sound of rapidly receding footsteps on the stone floor of the church. Father Milichuk peered out through a hole in the carved design of the door, but the lighting was dim and all he could make out was the figure of a man dressed in dark clothing walking quickly away. Medium height, medium build; he could be anyone.

One thing the priest was certain of was that the mysterious supplicant was a Roman Catholic, not Greek. His perfect Latin was spoken in the Roman way, and he had said "I have sinned" rather than "I am a sinner," which was the Greek manner. But why had he come here? St. George was a Ukrainian Greek

Catholic church; surely this man had a Roman Catholic church he attended regularly. The answer came to Aleksander Milichuk suddenly: The man had chosen a place where he wouldn't be known. His own priest was bound to recognize his voice and would perhaps pressure him to turn himself in. Here, he was guaranteed anonymity.

The priest sighed and leaned back in the cramped cubicle, which smelled of stale sweat and candle wax. He put a hand to his temple in an attempt to control the throbbing. What did it matter who the man was or where he was from? Aleks wasn't a detective, and it wasn't his job to hunt the man down. He felt the full weight of the sinner's guilt upon his own shoulders. Perhaps that was what God intended—maybe he was doing his priestly duty now more than ever before, but the thought made him feel only more anxious.

The rest of the day passed in a haze of meaningless activity. There were parishioners to call, schedules to arrange, events to discuss—choir practice, the Wednesday-night church supper, vendors for the annual Ukrainian festival. He wished he could drown himself in the barrage of mundane details, but all he could think of was the terrible secret he would be forced to carry to his grave. He considered the idea that the man was lying, but rejected that hopeful notion. Either he was telling the truth or he was the best actor in the world.

Aleks gazed idly out the window, but even the sight of the white blossoms on the mimosa trees failed to cheer him up. He sat at his desk staring blankly, his head buzzing with apprehension. Normally he would now start writing his sermon for next week's service, but he was unable to concentrate.

His secretary, the ever-intrusive Mrs. Kovalenko, noticed his mood.

"Are you feeling all right, Father?" she asked, one hand on her plump hip, the other clutching a freshly filled teapot. Mrs. Kovalenko was a great believer in the healing power of tea, and she had the persuasive ability of a used-car salesman combined with a Mafia enforcer. If she wanted to serve you tea, there was little you could do about it. He had briefly considered firing her for the sake of his bladder, but Mrs. Kovalenko was not the kind of woman you fired, so he had resigned himself to frequent visits to the bathroom.

"I'm fine," he replied, but his heart wasn't in it, and she continued to stand there studying him. "I just have a headache," he added when she didn't move.

She shook her dyed blond curls and clicked her tongue, then she brightened. "A good cup of tea is what you need," she proclaimed. "Straighten you right out."

"That would be nice," he replied; at least it might throw her off the scent for a while. She had nagged him about his drinking in the past, but he had cut down recently—partly because of the headaches. She busied herself gathering the honey and cream, bustling about the office happily humming a Ukrainian folk song. He knew she didn't speak a word of the language, but she liked to impress people with her knowledge of the culture, and had picked up a few songs and phrases here and there.

"I just bought this tea last week," she said as she poured him a steaming cup from the ornate ceramic pot, decorated with chubby, beaming angels. She had found it at the weekly yard sale on Avenue A and had presented it to him with great pride. Father Milichuk gazed at an especially porcine angel and sighed. He hated angels. The angel leered at him with a self-satisfied smirk; he yearned to smash the pot and erase the grin from its fat little face.

He made a point of telling Mrs. Kovalenko how delicious the tea was. "What's it called?" he said, taking a sip and smacking his lips.

"It's Russian caravan!" she declared, clapping her hands with delight. "From the new tea store around the corner. I'm so glad you like it."

In truth, it tasted like turpentine. But nothing tasted good right now, not even the butter cookies from the Polish bakery he usually adored. Still, to make Mrs. Kovalenko happy (and less suspicious), he choked down several cookies with his tea. They tasted like dust.

And yet when evening came, he left the church reluctantly. It would be even worse at home, when he had no happily bustling secretary, only his aged and morose mother. His father used to joke that his mother cooked like a Ukrainian but had the disposition of a Russian, dour and depressive, with occasional flights of high-spirited gaiety. She could be giddy as a schoolgirl, but her physical complaints could fill a medical dictionary. If it wasn't the lumbago in her back, it was the arthritis in her knees. She also enjoyed regaling Aleks with the health problems of her friends at the senior center. Illness was her chief conversational topic, and her eyes would brim with tears of delight as she reported the latest grim pronouncements her friends had received from various medical professionals.

"Do you know that Mrs. Danek's doctor told her that her heart valve could just pop like a grape? Like a *grape*, Sasha!" she would say, her eyes wide with amazement. She addressed him by his nickname but always called her friends by their last names, in the formal manner, which she thought indicated superior breeding.

He left St. George as the last rays of the sun slid across the windows of McSorley's Old Ale House, across the street. He resisted the urge to head straight for the bar—he would go there later, after his mother was in bed. He turned east and walked the half a block to his apartment, trudging up to the third floor on narrow, creaky stairs worn by decades of feet. The hall always smelled of boiled cabbage; the Polish couple on the second floor seemed to cook little else.

He unlocked the door quietly, in case his mother was napping. He often found her asleep in the big green chair, their fat orange cat purring in her lap. He opened the door to the smell of homemade soup and the sound of snoring. After his father died, four years ago, Aleks invited his mother to come live with him — not that he had much choice. It was expected that a good Ukrainian son would look after his mother. After all, he wasn't married and needed a woman's touch around the place, as her friends declared over coffee and cheese blintzes.

He hung his hat and coat on the rack and crept into the living room, where his mother lay in her usual position, mouth open, her snores rattling the windowpanes. Their orange cat was perched on top of the back of the chair and regarded Aleks through half-closed eyes. A white lace antimacassar had slipped from the top of the chair onto his mother's head. It sat at a rakish angle, like a lace yarmulke, the edges fluttering delicately with each racking snore. He stood watching her for a moment, then tiptoed to his room. He wanted to be alone with his thoughts.

It wasn't long before he heard a soft tapping at his bedroom door. Aleks opened it to find his mother smiling up at him. She was a tiny woman, barely five feet tall, but sturdy and stout, with the broad, rosy-cheeked face of a Slavic peasant. She wore her thick gray hair in a long braid, and her blue eyes were clear and sharp. In spite of her obsession with illness, Aleks felt she would outlive everyone around her.

"Hello, *myla*," he said, using the Ukrainian term of endearment. His mother liked that. "How are you tonight? It looked like you were having a nice nap."

She sighed dramatically. "I'm feeling badly today, Aleksander."

The heat rose to his face, and he fought to control his irritation. "You mean you're feeling *bad* today. If you were feeling *badly* you would be having trouble with your sense of touch."

She waved him away impatiently. "Don't carp at your sick old mother, Sasha. Lord knows I have enough to worry about with Mrs. Petrenko's boils acting up. I shall have to get up early tomorrow to make her my special poultice. She is counting on me; the doctors can do nothing for her, you know."

Aleksander Milichuk had no idea if anyone counted on his mother for anything, and he murmured a vague response. Perhaps the ladies at the senior center were enjoying her ministrations whether her remedies actually worked or not. Sometimes it was just pleasant to have someone who cared enough to go out of her way for you. That was one reason he kept Mrs. Kovalenko on as his secretary. She was an incorrigible gossip and a busybody, but she fussed and clucked over him in a manner that both irritated and pleased him.

Dinner tonight consisted of homemade split-pea soup, brown bread, and cheese. His mother was a superb cook and enjoyed cooking for her "little Sasha," just as she had for his father. Aleks knew that the standard Ukrainian diet was not the healthiest in the world, but there was little hope of training his mother in new cuisine techniques at this point in her life. He sometimes thought his father's overindulgence in his wife's excellent cheese and potato pierogi had contributed to his fatal heart attack— but in his darker moments, Aleks felt that his father had died of a broken heart.

As if reading his mind, his mother said, "I dreamed about her last night, Sasha." He gazed down at his soup, which was so thick that the croutons didn't so much float as perch on top of the viscous mass of dark green liquid.

"She came to me as I slept, Sasha—she looked just as she did that last day of her life."

He continued to stare at his soup. Ten years had passed since his sister, Sofia, had been killed by a hit-and-run driver, and yet the rage shivered within him like a wind that would not be stilled. His father had never been the same afterward. When the police failed to make an arrest or even come up with a viable suspect, he began to wither like an unwatered houseplant, until finally his heart gave out. Aleks coped with the loss by drinking too much, and his mother...well, she had her physical ailments to keep her company.

Ignoring his silence, she rattled on, as if helpless to stop. "When she comes to me like that, I know something is going to happen. Mark my words, Sasha, something will happen—something big."

"Yes, Mama," he said. He was too troubled by the events of the day to pay much attention to his mother's words. The last thing he needed was to think about his sister; it only made him angry. He refused a second bowl of soup and rose from the table. The cat lurked nearby, hoping for scraps of cheese.

"Are you going out tonight, Sasha?" his mother asked, slipping the cat a piece of cheese under the table.

"Just for a while," he replied, putting on his coat. "I told Lee Campbell I'd meet him at McSorley's for a drink."

"That handsome policeman friend of yours?" she asked, all smiles.

"He works for the police department, but he's a psychologist, not a cop."

"As you say, Sasha—but he is good-looking, you have to admit."

"Yes, Mama. Thanks for the soup—it was delicious."

"Don't be too late, Sasha. You're looking a little peaked."

"I won't—don't worry."

"And you won't have too many, will you, Sasha?"

"You know I've cut back lately, Mama."

"Promise?"

"I promise."

He kissed her and slipped out, locking the door behind him. Outside, the evening was crisp and sharp, the late days of April hugging the streets in a feathery embrace. It was the time of year when trees blossomed overnight and flower beds came alive with riotous bursts of yellow.

Inside the bar, Lee Campbell was sitting at a window table with four beers in front of him. Beer at McSorley's came two at a time, in heavy glass mugs wielded by stocky, red-cheeked waiters— fresh off the boat, if they were young, and former policemen if they were older. Their waiter was a retired cop Aleks had seen numerous times here, a burly man with the heavy shoulders and head of a mastiff. He nodded at the priest, which made Aleks unaccountably nervous.

Aleks slid into a seat across from his friend, resting his elbows on the ancient, scarred oak table. McSorley's Old Ale House was the oldest pub in continuous operation in the city, dating back to 1854. It hadn't changed much since then: the floors were still covered with sawdust, and the potbellied woodstove in the front room still huffed out heat during the cold winter months. Decades of dust lay on strands of abandoned spiderwebs hanging from ancient knickknacks over the bar. There was hardly an inch of bare space on the walls, which were crammed with photos, paintings, and mementos.

"Sorry I'm late," Aleks said, reaching for the icy mug of ale that Lee pushed across the table.

"I got us one of each," Campbell said, nodding at the twin mugs, one dark and one amber. Only a single beverage was available at McSorley's: ale. You could order it dark or amber, but either way you got two mugs of it.

"Thanks," Aleks said, drinking deeply. "The next one's on me."

"It's a deal," Lee said. "I have a head start on you already."

The two men had met at St. Vincent's in the dark days following 9/11. Aleks had had a series of anxiety attacks, something he'd never experienced before, and by the time he showed up at the hospital for psychiatric treatment, he needed very much to talk to anyone who would listen. Because of his position, he was used to giving comfort and advice to others but was not very good at taking it himself.

In the weeks after the attack, a lot of people needed help, so he wasn't alone. Psychiatric wards all over the city were seeing a record influx of patients. Lee Campbell was another patient at the St. Vincent's clinic, and they struck up a friendship. Campbell's position as New York City's only full-time criminal profiler was unique, and Aleks was drawn to the tall, charismatic Scot. After all, they each dealt with matters of morality, good and evil, though perhaps from different viewpoints. They had other things in common: Both loved music, had played rugby in college, and, to top it off, lived on the same block of East Seventh Street. And, as they liked to joke, both had difficult and devoted mothers.

But what really united them was shared tragedy. Each had lost his younger sister in a misfortune with loose ends, the loss like an open wound that would never heal. The driver of the car that killed Sofia had never been caught, but Lee's heartbreak was even worse, Aleks thought. His sister, Laura, had disappeared without a trace some years after the accident that took Sofia's life. When Aleks thought about this, he took some small comfort in the fact that at least he knew what had happened to his sister. Lee Campbell's tragedy had caused him to go from being a therapist to being a forensic psychologist, while Aleks had given up a promising career as an academic, turning from philosophy to the priesthood.

He looked forward to their monthly Monday-night meetings at the pub, where they talked about everything from Beethoven to Jakob Böhme, the seventeenth-century German mystic. Aleks had written his Columbia honors thesis on Böhme, and when he found Lee Campbell had read the German's work, it cemented their friendship.

And, Aleks thought as he gazed at those deep blue eyes, it didn't hurt that Campbell was a hell of a good-looking man. His mother was right about that, at least. Aleks had renounced ways of the flesh when he took his vows, but he had a weakness for Lee's kind of looks: curly black hair, blue eyes, and ruddy cheeks. He sighed deeply as he drained his first beer and started on the second.

"Are you all right?" Campbell asked.

"Why do you ask?" Aleks said. *Was it that obvious?*

"You look preoccupied. And it's unusual for you to show up late."

The priest gazed into the glass of amber ale and cleared his throat, a nervous habit. "I just, uh—I had a few last-minute things at the church, you know."

"Okay. I don't want to pry or anything."

"I had to take confession from someone, and—let's order another round, shall we?"

He flung a hand into the air, and the waiter gave a tiny nod of his massive head. Moments later, four more beers were thrust roughly in front of them, a few drops sloshing onto the table. The serving style at McSorley's was abrupt, bordering on surly. You would never find the androgynous, fey waiters here you saw elsewhere in the East Village. There were no metrosexuals working at McSorley's Old Ale House.

Father Milichuk took a long swig and wiped his mouth. The beer was good, bitter and cold and comforting. The room was already starting to haze nicely around the edges. He gazed at the words carved into the cabinet behind the bar: *Be good or be gone.*

"So," he said, setting the mug down on the table with a plunk, "how are things?"

Campbell smiled. "On one hand, I can sympathize with Sherlock Holmes when he claimed to be bored because there were no interesting criminals in London. On the other hand, it's creepy to actually wish for something bad to happen."

"But isn't something bad always happening?"

"Sure, but in most cases it's routine stuff the cops can handle without my help. It's only the really weird crimes where I get called in."

Father Milichuk drained his third mug and started on the next one.

"You're thirsty," Lee commented, raising an eyebrow.

"I guess I am." Aleks felt his secret gnawing at him, carving a hole in his soul. He felt an overpowering urge to share it with someone. "I don't suppose—" he began.

"What?"

"Can I ask you something?"

"Sure."

"When you were a therapist, if someone told you he had committed a crime, did you have to keep it confidential?"

"No. If I thought my patient was a threat to himself or others, I was ethically bound to report that to the police."

"Oh."

"Why do you ask?"

"No reason; I was just wondering."

He knew his answer was unconvincing and realized that perhaps he wanted it to be. His friend peered closely at him.

"What's bothering you, Aleks?"

"Well, we've talked about how our jobs are similar, and I—I was just wondering about that particular point."

"You mean the seal of the confessional?"

"Uh, yes."

Lee Campbell leaned his long body back in his chair and shook his head. "You're a terrible liar, Aleks. I knew the minute you walked in something was wrong. You don't have to tell me what it is—in fact, from what you've just said, I'm thinking you can't. But if there's anything I can do, let me know, okay?"

Aleks nodded, staring miserably at the empty glasses in front of him. He wanted more than anything to tell his friend everything about the mysterious supplicant and his cryptic confession. And yet he couldn't; he was bound by his sacred vows.

"I wish I could talk to you about this."

"It's okay," said Lee.

"It's making me question . . . well, everything."

"Your profession? Are you questioning that?"

Aleks took another long swallow and traced his finger in one of the deep hollows carved into the wooden table. "I don't know."

"You made a hard choice when you became a priest."

Aleks ran a finger over the lip of his mug. "Sofia's death changed everything. You must understand that better than anyone."

"Yes, but I haven't made the sacrifices you have."

Aleks gazed out the window and saw it was raining. He watched the thin, hard droplets slice through the soft pink blossoms on the mimosa trees. "I've never told anyone this before, but a few days after it happened, I was lying in bed one night, and I had a vision."

"In your sleep?"

"No, I was wide awake."

"What happened?"

"Sofia came to me. She was standing at the foot of my bed, and she glowed, as though she were made of light beams. And I felt a sense of utter peace and joy come over me like I had never felt before."

"Wow. Did she say anything?"

"No. She just smiled at me. And I knew that she was an angel, and that she was there because God had sent her to comfort me. Suddenly I saw the meaning of Sofia's death: I was being called by God to comfort those in need, people who had experienced the kind of anguish I had. I knew that if I answered the call, this sense of complete peace might be mine again someday."

"So you became a priest?"

"The next day I applied to seminary school, and I was accepted."

"And Sofia? Have you seen her again?"

"No. But sometimes I have a sense that she's nearby."

Lee raised a hand to signal the waiter for another round. Aleks took a deep breath. It was now or never.

"I, uh, don't suppose I could ask you a hypothetical question?"

"What is it?"

Is even that acceptable? Aleks wondered. If he told his friend the story of the mysterious confession as a hypothetical, would that violate the seal of the confessional?

He had never been faced with a dilemma like this before.

"You won't mention this conversation to anyone, will you?"

"Not if you don't want me to."

Aleks looked around the pub to see if anyone was listening in.

Luckily, Monday evening was the thinnest time at the popular watering hole. There were a few people in the back room, but only two other tables in the front room were occupied, one by a young couple too interested in each other to be eavesdropping. Sitting at the other table were half a dozen corporate types who looked as if they had been boozing ever since leaving work. Their jackets were slung on the backs of their chairs, their shirtsleeves rolled up, and their shiny faces were flushed from alcohol. Bursts of boisterous laughter erupted from their table from time to time.

He leaned in and spoke in a low voice.

"If one of your patients confessed to committing a terrible crime, would you report it to the police?"

"What kind of crime?"

Aleks looked down at his hands, which were trembling.

"Murder."

Lee Campbell sat back, obviously nonplussed. It was clear he knew that the question was not hypothetical for Aleks. Lee shook his head.

"If I had taken a vow to respect the seal of the confessional, no, I wouldn't."

"Even if it meant a murderer would go free?"

"Yes."

Aleks stared out the window; it was raining harder. He watched the pink mimosa blossoms fall under the cascading droplets, fluttering softly before surrendering to the pavement.

Lee Campbell leaned forward, resting his elbows on the ancient oak table.

"Is there any chance—in this hypothetical scenario—that this person is making up the entire thing just to screw with the priest's head?"

"I'm afraid not."

The waiter shot an inquiring look in their direction, and Aleks nodded, though he knew all the amber ale in the world couldn't fill the gnawing hole in his heart. He stared out the window at the soggy puddle of pink petals on the sidewalk, and knew it was going to be a very long night.

––––

AT HOME IN bed later, he watched car headlights flickering across the walls of his room, unable to sleep, tormented by the unwelcome knowledge locked inside his heart. Finally he arose and thumbed through his volume of the collected works of Jakob Böhme. His eyes fell on a passage from *Threefold Life of Man:* Man, Böhme said, "cannot see the whole of God's One," and "it follows that a part of it is hidden from him." In order to reach God, Böhme claimed, man had to go through hell itself.

These ideas, which had been little more than an intellectual puzzle to him when he was a philosophy student, now struck him as deeply personal. He felt as if Böhme were talking directly to him and that the key to solving his dilemma lay in Böhme's words, if only he could dig deep enough to uncover the wisdom there. Perched on the side of his bed, he turned the pages, searching desperately for something to help him. One quote in particular gave him some cause for hope: "What now seems hard to you, you will later learn to love the most."

Finally exhausted, he fell into a fitful sleep sometime before dawn. His dreams swarmed with disquieting images of masked murderers stalking their victims inside the stern marble interiors of churches, their steps echoing against the unforgiving floors. He followed them down endless corridors, but they always remained ahead of him, just out of sight. Finally he turned down one hallway to see his sister standing there gazing at him. She was glowing, as in his vision years before, but her large brown eyes were searching, beseeching him—to do what?

He awoke in a sweat, the book still in his lap, unable to shake the feeling that she wanted something from him. His eyes fell on the passage on the open page: "The anguished work of the creature in this time is an opening and a generation of divine power by which God's power becomes moving and working." He sensed the words had a deeper meaning for him, but he didn't know what they were.

Later that morning, after a quick breakfast, Father Milichuk dragged himself to St. George and took his usual place in the confessional. His hours were rigid: He was at his post every weekday morning from ten o'clock until noon. He had a wicked hangover, and that combined with his lack of sleep had put him in a foggy state of surreal, dreamlike consciousness.

It felt even more like a dream when the door to the adjoining booth creaked open. He slid open the wooden cover of the metal grate between the two sides in order to listen and was stunned by what he heard.

"Bless me, Father, for I have sinned."

It was the same voice Aleks had heard the day before. More weary, perhaps, and more wary—but the same. There was no mistaking it.

He tried to speak, but no words came out. Finally, he croaked out a response. "B-bless you, my son."

Jagged rays of light sliced through his field of vision, interrupting his sight—the familiar aura telling him another migraine was on the way. He pressed a hand to his forehead; he could feel the blood vessel in his head throbbing through his fingertips.

"What do you have to confess?" Aleks longed to peer through the metal grate separating them so he could see the man's face, but he could hardly bear to keep his eyes open. Pain sliced through his head, and he stifled a groan.

"I have committed another mortal sin."

"What is it, my son?"

"I have killed again."

Father Milichuk's intestines turned to ice. Cold sweat spurted onto his forehead, and he fought to control the buzzing in his ears.

To his horror, the man continued. "Not only that, Father, but I enjoy it. I like killing. Even now I'm thinking of the next time I can go kill again."

"My s-son," he said, hearing his voice shake, "you need help. Please—*please* tell the authorities what you have done."

The man laughed softly. "That's not likely to happen, Father. I'm not going to tell anyone else what I've done, and certainly not the police."

"Then why are you telling *me?*" Milichuk cried, his voice ragged.

"I enjoy talking about it. And my secret is safe with you." There was a pause, and then he said, "It is safe with you, isn't it?"

When Father Milichuk spoke, it was the voice of a dead man. "Yes. It's safe with me."

"Good," the man said. "I would hate to be the cause of your breaking your solemn vows to God." His tone was mild, but Aleks sensed the threat lurking beneath it.

The man went on to tell him the details of his crime. He preyed on prostitutes, he said, the unfortunate women who prowled Tenth Avenue near the entrance to the Lincoln Tunnel. Some were runaways whose families had no idea where they were; some were transvestites; and others were strung out on drugs, trying to earn enough money for their next fix. The man owned a nice car, and it was no problem getting them inside.

Once there, the women were his prisoners; he could do what he liked with them. When he described just what that was, Father Milichuk's stomach lurched and churned. The throbbing in his head crescendoed, and he vomited.

"Oh dear," the man said as the sour smell rose to engulf them. "I'm sorry. I'd better go so you can get cleaned up. I'll come back again soon—maybe even tomorrow."

Before Aleks could respond, he heard the door latch click open and then the sound of retreating footsteps.

But this time something inside him rebelled. He whipped out his handkerchief and wiped his mouth, then stuffed the hankie back into his pocket. With trembling hands, he ripped off his soiled cassock. Dropping it to the ground, he threw open the door to the confessional and charged out into the church.

He dashed down the aisle just as the man reached the front of the church. Not noticing his pursuer, the man pulled open the heavy front door. Daylight streamed into the foyer, and he was briefly silhouetted in a blinding halo of sunlight. Shielding his eyes as pain shot through his cranium, Father Milichuk staggered after him, following him out into the street, where the man headed west, toward Third Avenue.

To his relief, the man didn't look behind him as he rounded the corner to join the parade of people on the avenue. Aleks put his head down and shoved his hands into his pockets, losing himself in the crowd, just another pedestrian in New York. All the while he kept an eye on his quarry, following half a block behind as he headed for the Astor Place subway station. As before, the man was dressed in dark clothing—a straight black raincoat over gray slacks. His head was bare, with curly brown hair and a tiny bald spot in the back. Aleks focused on the bald spot, following it through the thick weave of bodies. As Aleks walked, Jakob Böhme's words echoed through his aching head. *God's power... moving and working...*

He followed his quarry past the Cooper Union Building to Astor Place, where people were lined up in front of the pumpkin-colored Mud Coffee truck, waiting for their caffeine fixes. The man took the stairs down to the uptown-subway track. Aleks hung back, head lowered, blending in with the crowd, keeping an eye on that bald spot. The jagged interruption in his vision narrowed his line of sight, and he held on to the railing as he stumbled down the steps, heart pounding.

Joining the swarm of people on the platform, he could see the man in the black raincoat ahead of him, peering down the track in the direction the uptown train would be coming from. Aleks slowed his pace, then strolled toward him in a deliberately casual manner. He stopped in front of a map of the subway and pretended to study it, glancing up from time to time to see if the man had moved. But he still stood in his spot, waiting patiently for the local train. Aleks stared at the map, the colored grid of the subway lines dancing in front of his eyes as he fought to focus, trying to control the blinding pain in his head.

There was a faint rumble from the tunnel, and a shaft of yellow light spilled across the tiled wall of the track. The train was arriving.

The crowd surged forward, a great mindless beast driven by force of instinct and habit. The priest saw his chance. After quickly slipping into the mosaic of bodies, he pushed through to the front until he was just behind the yellow warning line. Glancing out of the corner of his eye, he saw he was only two people away from the man with the bald spot. The rumble of the train was louder now, the wall awash with the headlights of the oncoming train.

It was now or never. *God's power... moving and working...*

Aleks weaved quickly between the people separating him and his prey until he stood directly behind the man with the bald spot. He was slightly taller than the priest, and smelled of Old Spice. Aleks leaned forward and whispered into his ear.

"Thy will be done."

Before the man could turn around, Aleks gave him a quick, hard shove in the small of his back. He watched as the man lurched forward, his hands clawing uselessly at the air, watched as he fell onto the tracks. The train was upon him before anyone could react.

There was a roar in the priest's head, and the sound of a woman screaming. The crowd recoiled, and a man yelled, "Someone call nine-one-one!" A young student standing next to him covered his eyes, and his girlfriend began to cry.

In the pandemonium that followed, nobody was in charge. Aleks fully expected to be apprehended, but no one seemed to know exactly what had happened. Everyone looked dazed, except for a man in a business suit who whipped out his cell phone and dashed up the steps two at a time. The priest followed him, gripping the railing to steady himself. To his surprise, no one came after him. He staggered out onto the street and sucked up a lungful of fresh air.

Out on Astor Place, there was a disquieting atmosphere of normalcy. Taxis shot up Lafayette Street, careening around the curve in the road where it turned into Fourth Avenue. The orange Mud Coffee truck still sat at the curb, dispersing the aroma of French roast into the surrounding air. With a final glance behind him, Aleks walked quickly toward the Cooper Union building, then cut through the small park in the back.

His cell phone rang. Panic tightened his throat; he thought wildly that the police had found him. To his relief, the caller ID read *Lee Campbell.* He pressed the Talk button with trembling fingers.

"Hello?"

"I'm just calling to see if you're okay."

Aleks hesitated. Above him, a moody gray cloud slid across the sky, obscuring the sun. A pigeon pecked at a few scraps of bread on the pavement, then cocked its head and gazed up at him with its bright orange eye.

"I'm fine," he said. "Thanks for asking."

His friend seemed unconvinced. "Look, I have some time later today if you want to get together."

"I have something I have to do, but maybe I'll call you later."

"Please do, all right?"

"Sure, thanks," Aleks said, and snapped the phone closed.

He headed east, toward the river. It was a quick ten-minute walk to Most Holy Redeemer Catholic Church on Third Street. He had been there several times, though not for some years now. He did not know the current pastor or any of his staff.

The front door was open, and his footsteps clicked a stark echo as he strode down the aisle to the back of the church. The air smelled of incense and lilies, and he was reminded that Easter was only a few weeks away.

He stepped into the confessional and closed the door behind him. Welcoming the dim lighting, he leaned back in the narrow cubicle. He could hear the sound of gentle snoring, then the rustling of the priest's garments as the man awoke.

Father Milichuk leaned forward, his face nearly touching the grate between them. He took a deep breath, relief coursing through his veins like holy water.

"Bless me, Father, for I have sinned."

EVEN A BLIND MAN

BY DARRELL JAMES

The Greyhound arrived in Atlanta, midafternoon, swinging into the terminal on Forsythe Street to let off passengers. A hiss of air brakes, a mechanical unfolding of accordion doors—it marked the end of the journey for Earl Lilly. Three days in the seat from LA, his dog, Melon, curled up at his feet.

He'd come on a mission, the way he thought of it. A copy of his granddaughter's last letter stuffed into his breast pocket. What had happened to her? And why the sudden cry for help? He had crossed the country to find out.

Earl waited until all the other passengers had disembarked, then called to his dog. "Up!" was all he had to say. And Melon— a cocker-terrier mix—came wearily to his feet and nosed his way out from between the seats.

The bus driver was waiting impatiently, one hand on the lever, wanting to close the doors against the August swelter. He eyed Earl in the rearview mirror.

Earl took his good-natured time. He strung his camera

around his neck and centered it just so, adjusted his dark glasses on his nose for comfort, gathered his carry-on bag, smoothed the front of his poplin jacket, and moved up the aisle toward the exit. He was making something of a show of it. And why not? He was seventy years old and a black man back in the South.

Melon followed, brushing at Earl's pants cuff.

As they reached the exit, Earl turned to the driver, keeping his gaze off and distantly focused. He pushed his dark glasses higher on his nose, giving the man his best Ray Charles sway-and-grin. "Thank you so much for the ride," he said.

The driver studied him with a puzzled look on his face. "You don't mind my asking...if you're blind, how do you use the camera to take pictures?"

"I let the dog take 'em," Earl said in a polite tone. Then he turned, leaving the driver to ponder that image, and stepped down off the bus. "Jump!" he said. And Melon made his leap of faith to the ground.

See, it was the dog that was blind, not Earl.

Earl led the way through the wash of hot diesel exhaust, across the bus paddock, to the street, where a row of taxicabs sat parked at the curb. The first two cars in the queue were manned by Middle Eastern drivers. They stood outside the vehicles, chatting near the sign that read TAXIS ONLY. They seemed wholly indifferent to his approach, indifferent to the possibility of a fare. At a third taxi, a black woman had already prepared the passenger door for arrival.

Now she was calling to Earl's dog, "Here, boy! Bring your daddy right on in. Let Loretta give you fine gentlemen a ride."

Earl crossed past the two Middle Easterners, who found need to voice objection now. Loretta flipped them off and waved Earl and his dog on over.

DARRELL JAMES

The idea that Earl was blind and that Melon was his service dog was a ruse they played routinely. It got them onto public transportation together and into the bars along Vermont Street back in LA. And so far, it had won them a few courtesies here in the South. Few seemed to question it. The dark glasses also served to shade Earl's aging eyes from the light. They were both getting old, he and Melon. They depended on each other for their respective advantages.

Earl folded himself into the backseat, saying, "Up," for Melon to join him. The dog found his place on the seat, and they both settled in for the ride.

"You know where Cabbagetown is?" he said as his lady driver slid in behind the wheel.

"Sho' do," Loretta said, cranking the engine. "I know where e'thing is. North to Buckhead, east to Conyers. You ain't really blind, is you?"

"How could you tell?"

She was looking at Earl in the mirror. "I seen blind folks; they's always hesitant. You seem to know where you goin'. Dog's somethin' else, though. Playing along like a regular little con man."

"He's the one that's blind," Earl said.

"You say! I saw the way he come jumpin' off the bus. Must trust his master somethin' fierce."

"We've been together for a while," Earl said.

They had come off Forsythe Street onto Memorial Drive heading east. It had been forty years since Earl had last been in Atlanta, the place of his birth. The city didn't seem much different really from what he remembered. Maybe a few more glass-and-chrome buildings was all. It still had the same shady streets, the same sleepy feel to it. LA, by comparison, never seemed to stop.

"What's your name, big man?" Loretta asked, nosing the cab through traffic.

242

"Earl... Earl Lilly... but most people call me Little Earl."

"Cause you so tiny and all," Loretta said, metering out the sarcasm.

"Yeah, 'cause of that," Earl said.

"So, what brings you two good-looking dudes to Hotlanta? Come to howl at the moon?"

"I think we're both a little too old to be howling at anything, except in pain. Actually, I'm here to find someone," Earl said. He fished a photograph from inside his jacket and passed it across the seat to her. "You ever seen this young lady?"

Loretta looked briefly at the photo, keeping an eye on the traffic ahead. "She a beautiful young woman. One of yours?"

"She's my granddaughter," Earl said. "I'm sure you get around; you ever run across her, by chance?"

"She look a little familiar. But then, I see a lot these young girls on the streets. They's all just faces after a time. Know what I mean?"

"I guess I do," Earl said.

"Still, I should remember this one. Pretty an' all." Loretta took a last look at the photo and passed it back. "What she do?"

Earl had little to go on, just the name of a gentlemen's club where his granddaughter worked and a return address on her letters, presumably where she lived. "She tells me she's going to school during the day. Wanting to become a physical therapist. And dancin' nights to pay her way. A place called Bo Peep's Corral. You ever hear of it?"

"Peep's? Yeah, I know somethin' about the place," Loretta said. Her response was heavy with disdain. "Might not look it now, but I used to dance there myself. Was a good-paying job, but I got fed up with the owner. Always trying to get me to do things I didn't want to do. If you know what I mean."

"Still the same owner?"

"Ray Tarvis," Loretta said, a nod to Earl in the mirror. "Redneck asshole from the word *go*. She dancin' there, huh?"

"That's what she tells me."

"Your grandbaby got a name?"

"India," Earl said.

"That her real name?"

"What she tells me."

"You don't know?"

"Actually, I didn't even know I had a granddaughter until a few months back. I've never met her mother—my daughter. I went off to prison a month before she was born. After I got out, my wife and I just never reconnected. Somehow, little India ran my address down and started to write to me. Says her mother is probably dead or eaten up by the streets."

"This town can do that," Loretta said, grim eyes looking back at him in the mirror. "Either you claim it or it claims you."

Earl considered the woman driver in the seat ahead of him. It appeared the town had claimed her. She may have, in fact, been pretty once. But she looked nothing short of used up these days. She was possibly only thirty-eight, thirty-nine, but could pass for fifty. She was painfully thin. Deep lines were etched in her forehead. Her eyes were darkly cratered.

"So, you were sayin'?" Loretta said.

"Well, I was getting letters from her almost every day. Exchanging pictures and the like. Then about four weeks ago they just stopped coming. Then I got one last letter asking for my help."

"Help in what?"

"That's just it. She didn't say."

"An' you jumped on a bus and rode all the way out—what? three, four days?—just to see what she want? You gotta be grandpappy of the year, sugar. Have to hand it to you."

"Well, I haven't had anyone in my life for a good long time. 'Cept Melon."

Melon lifted his head at the sound of his name. Earl gave the dog a stroke for reassurance.

"I was enjoying her letters," Earl continued. "Made me feel connected a little. See, my life hasn't been what you would call exemplary. You get to a certain age, you start adding up your markers. I added mine and found I didn't have all that many. I don't know how much time I've got left. Me or my dog."

"I guess I see what you sayin'."

"I'm guessing she needs money. I've got a little tucked away from my photography," he said, lifting the camera for her to see in the mirror. "I figure maybe she wants help with her tuition and all."

"You take pictures?"

"Photos of life on the streets. Things that just happen. Some of my work hangs in a gallery in Beverly Hills. It's all on consignment, but now and then one of them brings a price."

"Well, I hope financial support is all your grandbaby is asking for. 'Cause that joint, Bo Peep's, is no place for a fine little African princess like your granddaughter. You find her, you tell her to get her ass over to Starbucks or someplace. Or"—Loretta caught his eye in the mirror to make sure he was paying attention—"she end up like me. This here's Cabbagetown, you got an address?"

They had rolled into an aging area of the city known for the cotton mill that once turned out bags for the agricultural industry; Loretta told him all about it as she drove. There were remnants of shotgun houses along the streets—little box huts that looked like they might have housed dwarfs or something. They were intermingled with modern apartment buildings. The mill had been converted to lofts. "We becoming yuppies," Loretta said. "That number again?"

"Six-six-two," Earl said, consulting the envelope from his granddaughter's last letter.

"Here you go," Loretta said pulling the taxi to the curb.

Earl ran his eyes along the series of stores on the street; 662 was a glass-fronted building sitting right ahead of them. "That's a postal service."

"Yeah, it is," Loretta said.

They sat with the engine idling. Earl double-checked the address on the envelope and compared it to the numbers along the street. He'd come all this way to find a PO box.

"You want to try the club where she works?"

"She says she works nights. I'll have to wait until this evening," Earl said. "You know of a hotel? Something cheap for the night?"

"I think we can find you something," Loretta said.

Loretta routed them back a dozen blocks to the Savoy Hotel. It was a dingy old three-story, stuck between a liquor store and a dry cleaner's. Earl paid her across the seat back, then pulled Melon to the opposite side so he could slide out first. When he was on the sidewalk with his carry-on, he called, "Out!" and Melon obeyed, leaping blindly to the sound of Earl's voice.

"Can you wait till I see if they got a room?" Earl said to her, her window rolled down to see him off.

"Just tell 'em Loretta sent you. They'll have somethin', sugar. Say I pick you up around eight tonight. We go check out Bo Peep's together."

"You sure?" Earl asked.

"Yeah, you got Loretta's curiosity up. Have to see how this mystery turns out."

Earl nodded, and Loretta pulled away, leaving him and his dog alone on the sidewalk.

Earl took a moment to survey his surroundings. They were on

the dark side of town, as he thought of it, not far from where he had once lived. It was mostly cut-rate, by-the-week rooming, filled with the city's black aging and infirm. There were a few independent shops, their storefronts covered in gang graffiti, their windows secured behind iron bars. A pair of homeless men sat on the sidewalk leaning against the wall of the Savoy, their backs against the bricks. All this beneath the gleaming glass skyline that was today's modern Atlanta.

"I told you it'd be different. And not different. Didn't I say so?" Earl asked his dog.

Melon nosed against his pants cuff with a whimper, and the two made their way inside.

At the desk, Earl was greeted, more or less, by a kid with spiked hair. He told the kid Loretta had sent him.

The kid didn't seem all that impressed and didn't ask about the dog neither. But he handed him a card to fill out—his name, address, and phone number. "One night, thirty dollars."

Earl paid in cash.

"Number four, upstairs. Second door on the right." The kid slid a key onto the counter. He hadn't looked at Earl once during the entire exchange.

Earl took the key and made his way to the stairs, bag in hand. Melon followed, keeping Earl's pants cuff against his face. "Step-step..." Earl said.

They reached their room. Earl let them inside.

The space smelled of mildew and urine. The bedcovers were stained a permanent yellow. "Jump," Earl said. And, with unquestioning trust, Melon leaped onto the bed he couldn't see.

"My man," Earl said, feeding his dog a treat from his coat pocket.

Earl removed his dark glasses and laid them on the dresser. The last letter from his granddaughter had been unsettling. It had been more than just a call for financial assistance, as Earl had implied to his lady cabdriver. It had been a desperate cry for help. There was something troubling going on in her life, something he couldn't ignore.

Her letters had started coming earlier that year. First one was a polite introduction; he wrote back, and they'd grown into a pen-pal friendship as they learned of each other's lives.

India had been consistently optimistic in her letters, looking forward to a degree from a real college. A better life. Maybe outside Atlanta, she'd hinted. Leaving the idea hanging at the end of an ellipsis, waiting for his response.

Yeah, maybe he could help her find a job, he'd written. LA being "exciting" and all for a young woman.

The last letter had been nothing like the previous correspondence. It was one word. *Help!* Nothing more. It was in an awkward blocky print, almost as if a child or someone of limited education had written it.

Earl took his camera from around his neck and crossed with it to the window. Beyond the tattered curtains, the buildings cast their late-afternoon shadows across Mitchell Street. He focused, framing the shot to capture the disparity between the richest-of-rich and the poorest-of-poor. Maybe he'd do a series of photos on the theme. He clicked off four shots in rapid succession.

He'd been told on occasion that his work looked like crime scene photos. The style had come to be known as urban evidentiary, a term the good-looking Beverly Hills gallery owner had coined to give Earl's work a brand. Earl didn't know what it meant exactly. But he had to admit, most of his work had a haunting, disturbing quality. Maybe something of his past, his own life, was wrapped up in it.

Earl let the curtains fall shut. He was tired and had a dark sense of foreboding about his granddaughter. Melon was already lying quiet on the bed, maybe absorbing his dark mood from his master.

Earl crossed back to the bed and set his camera on the nightstand. He stretched out on top of the covers next to Melon and closed his eyes.

It was a little after four. He would nap until dark, then set out to find the girl.

Just as she'd promised, Loretta was waiting at the curb when Earl and his dog came out of the hotel. It was a little after eight.

She drove them north into midtown, telling Earl a little about the place they were headed. "Bo Peep's Corral, mostly just topless lap dancin' and all. But they's a VIP room where you can get just about anything you want, you got enough money. You best watch yourself, though. This place," she warned, "no place for a black man. This is still the South, sugar. And Peep's is filled with rednecks."

"I'll keep it in mind," Earl said. "I just want to see if she's there and know she's all right."

"Just the same," Loretta said.

They arrived at the gentlemen's club, which was in the trendier part of the city. A beefy young bouncer in a tuxedo that was tight across his chest stood, arms folded, at the entrance.

"Maybe I better wait," Loretta said.

"I'm not planning on any personal services. I won't be long."

"You want to leave your little buddy with me?"

"No," Earl said. "I almost lost him in a fire once. Now he goes where I go."

Earl slipped his dark glasses on and adjusted the camera around his neck. He withdrew a retractable white cane from his belt for good measure and extended it, then stepped out. "Jump!" he called. And Melon followed.

At the entrance, the bouncer stopped him with a hand on his chest. He lifted Earl's camera and looked at it; studied the dog at Earl's side a minute. "Okay," the bouncer said, and let them pass.

The place was dark and smoke filled. Heavy-metal music blared from loudspeakers. A tall brunette, undressed down to her G-string and high heels, was on the runway, grinding her pelvis provocatively against a brass pole mounted center stage. Young women paraded past in scanty attire. Waitresses—Bo Peeps, one and all—moved about the room in exaggeratedly short blue-and-white-gingham skirts and belly-tied blouses. Young white boys lined the runway, mesmerized by the woman above them on the stage. Others sat brooding at tables in the dark, beyond the lights.

Earl was the only black man in the place, he noticed. He tapped his way with the cane to the back. Melon followed at his cuff until Earl found a seat, then he curled up beneath his chair.

"What can I get you?" a waitress said, appearing almost magically and before Earl's butt had even adjusted to the hard chair. She was bent toward him, her tail jacked high by her spiked heels, showing lots of cleavage. A routine.

"Glass of water," he said, staying with his own routine, eyes off and distantly focused.

"There's a two-drink minimum. I'll have to get you two and charge them like they're beers," she said.

Earl nodded.

The waitress went off to get his order.

Earl sat, eyes skyward, pretending to use his ears to draw life from the sound-filled room. From time to time he would sneak glances at the faces of the young dancers who passed. There were two black girls among the exotic mix of women. One was just mounting the stage as the music shifted to a sultry beat, replacing the brunette who gathered up the tossed dollar bills on her hands and knees before slinking off, liquid-hipped, toward the back. The other black girl was just starting a lap dance for a table full of young professionals in suits and ties. The group cheered her on as she lavished attention on one of their comrades. Neither of these two women was his granddaughter, and neither was half as pretty.

Earl considered the possibility that there were other young women offstage, in the dressing rooms or someplace. And from where he was sitting, he could see through parted curtains into the VIP room. It was currently unoccupied. It occurred to him that maybe it was India's night off. But it was a Friday and more likely that all of the staff would be on duty. He waited. The waitress brought him his two glasses of water and Earl gave her a twenty without looking up.

Earl sipped his water.

"You want a dance?" a young blond woman asked, appearing over his shoulder. She was dressed in a sheer camisole and white lace panties. Earl waved her off without looking directly at her.

He sipped some more water and watched the room for signs of India.

Only minutes had passed when Earl noticed a man at the corner of the bar looking at him with interest. He was barrel-chested, balding, midsixties maybe, with a mass of dark chest hair showing through the open front of his Hawaiian shirt. Earl had the impression the man had been observing him for some time.

He pretended not to see. He sipped his water, eyes turned skyward.

But now the man was sliding off his stool and coming Earl's way. This was Ray Tarvis, the owner. Earl was sure of it.

The man pulled a chair close to his.

Tarvis said nothing at first. Then he nudged Earl to get his attention. "Hey!" he said.

"Who's there?" Earl asked.

"I'm the owner of this place," Tarvis said. "I noticed you're not interested in my girls dancing for you. You're not here to drink. I'm wondering to myself just what the hell a blind man gets from spending twenty bucks for water."

"I like the music!" Earl said, swaying his head in time to the beat.

"Yeah, well, you can get music a number of places, pop. But I don't allow cameras in my club."

"Don't intend to take no pictures," Earl said. "How could I?"

"Then what are you doing with it?"

"Was a present from my sister. A little joke among us. I like the way it feels."

"Uh-huh. Well, we don't allow dogs neither. I think you best go."

"You mean you don't allow Negroes."

"If you weren't fucking blind you'd see I keep a number of young black girls in my employ. I'm trying to be nice."

"Nice would be allowing me to stay," Earl said, not backing down.

"All right!" Tarvis said; his patience had run out. He rose to his feet, dragging Earl up by the elbow. "You can take your water with you. Just get out!"

Melon suddenly came out from under Earl's chair, baring his teeth and issuing a deep, sustained growl at the voice that had become threatening.

"It's okay, boy," Earl said. "We've worn out our welcome, as usual."

Earl extended his cane and moved off toward the exit, tapping his way between the rows of tables and chairs. Melon fell into formation at his cuff and together they left the club.

Tarvis followed them all the way through the door. He stopped just outside the entrance, next to the bouncer, and watched until Earl and his dog were inside the taxi and its door was closed. Then he smacked his bouncer upside the head and turned and went back in.

Loretta was slumped far down in her seat behind the wheel. "He gone?" she asked.

"He went inside," Earl said.

Loretta straightened. "Man told me if he ever saw me near his club again he'd kill me, no questions asked, and I believe him."

"He reminds me why I didn't come back to this town," Earl said.

"Why I should be gettin' out myself. No luck finding little India, huh?"

"I didn't see her."

Loretta turned worried eyes on him in the mirror. "Friday night, there's only one other place she could be."

"Where's that?"

"The Atlanta boys' club," she said.

"Boys' club?" Earl repeated.

Loretta threw a quick glance at the bouncer near the entrance, then turned to look at Earl directly across the seat. "I didn't want to tell you this till I was sure . . . but I been worried she might not be here."

"Why do you say that? And why do you—"

"Care?" Loretta said, finishing his thought for him.

Earl studied Loretta's eyes, the woman inside them. She was harboring pain, he could see it now. "It was you," he said. "You were the one who sent the last letter, not my granddaughter. But how would you know . . ."

Loretta lowered her gaze.

"You're..."

"Don't matter who I am!" she snapped, her eyes coming back to challenge his.

Earl examined the woman he'd only just met but now believed to be his daughter. He saw her in a somewhat different light than he had before. More determined than pathetic. More feral than beaten. "Where's India?" he said.

"They's a house out in Walton County, a cabin twenty miles from here, tucked way back in the trees. I was hoping we'd find India at Bo Peep's, and everythin'd be all right. But now my worst fear is she's out there with them."

"Them who?"

"The boys. They got this little club, see. An appreciation-of-little-black-girls club. Five of them, including Ray Tarvis. But they ain't throwing no charity benefit out there, huh-uh! They're mean and cruel and like to take their aggressions out on sweet young black females." She avoided looking at him.

"How do you know all this?"

Loretta brought her eyes to his now. There were tears streaming down her cheeks. "Kept me out there for nearly a year once."

Earl felt his heart cave in. The anguish in her eyes was born of deeply guarded pain. Melon stirred on the seat next to him.

"Why didn't you just go to the police?"

Loretta's eyes were pleading now. "Daddy, they *is* the po-leece!"

Earl stared at the daughter he'd never known. He recalled that his estranged wife's grandmother was named Loretta. He couldn't take his eyes off her, off the pained, crippled expression on her face. "Can you take me to this boys' club?" he said.

"I was so hopin' you'd say that. I had no one else to call; I got no one. And I wouldn't get two steps inside 'fore Tarvis would put a bullet in me and drop me in the bottoms someplace."

"I understand," Earl said. "The world can be a hard place. Just take me to her."

Loretta wiped at her tears and turned back to the wheel. In minutes, they were on the freeway headed east.

There was nothing left to say between them. Earl sat quiet in the back, Melon dozing next to him. Loretta kept her eyes on the road.

By the time they reached the outskirts of civilization, the moon had risen full above them. Loretta exited the interstate and followed back roads into the piney hillscape. Soon, she pulled off onto the gravel shoulder and brought her taxi to a stop.

"I don't see anything," Earl said.

"It's through those trees. I'd like to go, but they see me, they'll deal with both of us the same way, no questions."

"Get the car off the road, out of sight," Earl said.

Loretta produced a handgun. "You want to take this along."

"No, I'll handle it my way."

"There'll be a guard out front."

"Don't worry," he said.

Earl opened the door and stepped out with his cane and dark glasses in hand, his camera still strung around his neck. "Jump!" he called to Melon. And together, they set off through the trees—blind dog and seeing-eye master—to face whatever fate held for them.

"You stay close now," Earl said to Melon, putting his dark glasses on.

Melon gave him a whimper in return.

In minutes they arrived at a cabin set deep in the woods. There was a single light over the porch. A muscled young white boy in blue jeans and a tank top stood guard outside the door.

Earl came out of the trees, tapping with his cane, Melon at his cuff.

"The hell you doing, old man? You lost?"

"Come looking for Masta Tarvis," Earl said, laying it on thick.

"Yeah, well, you got the wrong place. This here's private property, so just turn your black ass around and head on back the way you came."

Earl never stopped walking. He continued tapping his way forward, ignoring the threatening glare, until he was face-to-face with the man.

The young guy was a good head shorter than him, Earl now realized, and probably half his weight. But Earl was also a good fifty years older. He couldn't let this boy get the first strike.

"Nigger, you deaf as well as blind—"

In one swift move, Earl came up with a right and drove a huge fist into the young man's face. It caught him square on the nose and dropped him like a loose sack of grain onto the porch decking. The force of the blow also drove pain up Earl's arm and into his shoulder, and for a second he thought he might cry out.

He rubbed at his shoulder until the pain subsided. "Stay," he said to Melon. Then he dragged the boy off the porch, letting his head bang on its way down the steps. He found a section of the telephone line leading up the side of the house and used a switchblade he found in the kid's boot to cut a long section of it free. He wired the kid's feet and hands and cut a slice of his shirt away and used it to gag him. Then he dragged the still-limp body into the trees and dumped it there. All the while, Melon remained on the porch.

Earl returned to him and let them both quietly inside.

The cabin was dark but for a wedge of light that spilled from a room at the end of a long hallway. He could hear men's voices, bawdy laughter and crude talk, over the wash of southern rock. He crossed down the hallway, the switchblade closed but cupped in his right hand. Melon followed.

Through the open doorway, Earl saw what he had feared the most. His granddaughter was on the bed naked and spread, tied to the bedposts. Four men were ganged around and over her. All were in their late fifties to early sixties; flabby white bodies, hairy backs and legs. They spouted crude epithets as they worked, prodding and jabbing with implements to coax some life into their crippled prey.

This was the Atlanta boys' club, minus one—Ray Tarvis— and they were preparing for another round.

Earl stepped into the room and tapped his cane hard on the floor twice. It brought four faces swiveling toward him.

"Jesus Christ!"

"What the fuck?"

"Who the hell are you?"

The protests came in unison.

Earl didn't respond. He raised his camera and clicked off a series of auto-shots in quick succession, capturing the men, their naked bodies, the implements in their hands, and the girl tied spread-eagle on the bed.

"Now, wait a minute," one of them said, stepping away from the bed, a bottle of Southern Comfort in his grip. The other men came to join him, the gang of them standing there, genitals dangling.

Earl snapped another shot.

There was a stunned moment in which no one moved. Earl was broader and at least a foot taller than any man in the room. But there were four of them. He no longer felt the need to keep his eyes distant. He slipped his glasses off and leveled a steely gaze their way.

Just then, Melon began to bark. Another man had entered the room behind Earl. "The fuck you doing here?"

It was Ray Tarvis, come to join his club mates for the festivities.

Earl put his glasses back on and stepped to one side, his shoulders in line with his flanking opponents'.

"Who the hell is this asshole? What's he doing with the camera?" the man with the bottle wanted to know.

"He's fucking blind!" Tarvis said. "He ain't seen a thing!"

"He sees enough to take pictures!"

Tarvis studied Earl more closely now, trying to peer beyond the lenses of his dark glasses.

Earl tipped the glasses forward on his nose and looked across them, let the man see the truth of the matter for himself.

"You're going out in a fucking box!"

Tarvis started forward, then—

Chick!

—the sound of the switchblade clicking open stopped him in his tracks. The other men had closed a step. They also halted.

"I see you all understand the language of the streets," Earl said. "I took it off your boy."

Earl pointed the knife alternately at Tarvis and at the gang of men.

Tarvis grabbed a heavy ashtray from a nearby dresser and hurled it in Earl's direction. It whizzed past Earl's head, missing by inches. Tarvis followed with a charge. "Give me the goddamned camera!" Tarvis cried, rushing Earl, head down like a bull.

Earl let the cane drop and caught the man about the neck with one big arm. The momentum of his charge rocked Earl back a step, but he used his size to quell the force. He wrenched Tarvis's head upward so he could see the bed, the girl, the savage damage that the men had inflicted. He still had the knife pointed toward the men.

"Take a good fucking look!" Earl said.

There was nothing but hate in the man's eyes. "Fuck you!" Tarvis said. "And fuck the little whore!"

Earl brought the blade around in a swift arc and buried it deep in Tarvis's stomach, just below the rib cage.

There was an expression of startled disbelief on Tarvis's face. Earl let it linger there a moment. Then he shoved the knife up hard beneath the ribs and held on until the light in Tarvis's eyes flickered and died.

Earl let him drop to the floor. Melon let out a chuff.

The others had remained fixed in place, unsure of Earl's prowess, perhaps, or just insecure in their naked vulnerability. But now they started forward as a group.

Loretta suddenly burst into the room. She had her gun out. Her eyes were wild with fear.

It halted their advance.

"Cut the girl loose!" Earl said to them.

A couple of the men moved to carry out his orders; the other two glared at him as if trying to say *We will remember you and there will come a time.*

Loretta handed the gun to Earl and rushed to her daughter's aid. The girl-child lolled, made dopey by the weight of Rohypnol or some other rape drug. But her eyes were aware and shifting between Earl and her mother.

Loretta dragged her to her feet, gathered her clothing, and dressed her as best she could.

When they were at the door and ready, Earl popped the small memory card from his camera and held it for the men to see. "You try to fuck with me or my family ever again, not only will this go to the media, but I'll come looking for each of you myself."

There was little of what could have passed for shame on the four white faces. Earl considered for one brief moment the idea of opening up on them with the gun. But the priority for now was to get his daughter and granddaughter to safety. "Are we clear on all this?" he asked, fixing his eyes on each of the men in turn.

"What about him?" one man asked, motioning to Tarvis lying on the floor in a pool of his own blood.

"I understand you're all members of Atlanta's finest," Earl said. "I'm sure you got ideas how to make a body disappear, make a crime as though it never happened."

Earl could see by their eyes they were already considering the possibilities. He backed his way to the doorway with Melon at his cuff. And with his daughter and granddaughter, he fled off into the moonlit Georgia night.

———

AT THE GREYHOUND bus terminal at four in the morning, Earl bought two one-way tickets to Los Angeles. His granddaughter was still docile and quiet, but she was starting to come around.

Loretta had managed to clean her up and get her properly dressed for the trip. And India herself had managed a smile.

"Take good care of our little girl," Loretta said. "See she get a good education."

"You sure you don't want to come with us?" Earl asked.

"It's too late for me," she said, pride overriding the sadness in her eyes. "Will you be all right?"

"I'll let you know. But I don't think the mystery of what happened to Ray Tarvis will ever be solved. A Jimmy Hoffa kinda thing. Still, I wish the rest of the bastard boys' club could receive some evens."

Earl studied his daughter, feeling a certain sense of guilt-layered pride. She was a survivor, at the very least. And though he couldn't change the past, he could give her some justice for the pain and humiliation both she and India had suffered.

Earl took Loretta's hand and folded the memory card from his camera into it. "What's this?" Loretta asked, looking down.

"It's a bit of justice," Earl said. "Put it in an envelope and send it anonymously to the *Atlanta Journal*."

Loretta brought her eyes back to his. "It'll stir up a hornets' nest that could come back on you."

"It doesn't matter," Earl said. "I'm an old man with an old dog and just as blind as I need to be. I'll take what comes."

Loretta gave him a strong hug and wished him and her daughter well. Then she turned toward her taxicab parked at the stand.

Earl put his arm around his granddaughter. And together they watched Loretta gather a waiting fare from the curb and drive away.

"Been some kind of visit, eh, Melon?" Earl said to the dog at his feet. "And we got a new member of the family to share our house with."

Melon chuffed and nuzzled India's ankle to show his approval.

"What about you?" Earl said to his granddaughter. "You ready for a new life?"

India gave what passed for a smile and boarded the bus ahead of him.

The driver was waiting to close the door against the heat.

Earl pulled his dark glasses from his inside pocket and slipped them on. He adjusted the camera around his neck, extended his cane, smoothed the front of his poplin jacket.

He was making a show of it. And why not?

Even a blind man could see he was seventy years old and a black man back in the South.

THE GENERAL

BY JANICE LAW

E ven after he went into a comfortable, if still bitter, exile in the north, the General hired only men from his own country. He trusted the loyalty of those who had been comrades and subordinates and the poverty of the others. Of the two, he regarded poverty as the surer thing, but the General was never without a sidearm, and the inner recesses of his handsome house—a glossy, glamorized version of the old stucco mansions of his homeland—held a small arsenal. He had enemies, some persistent, who had fled north a few years ahead of him. That political power was fleeting was a basic tenet of the universe.

Power of other sorts—the power of money, influence, personality—had proved more durable. Overseeing his silent, well-trained indoor staff and the ever-changing retinue of gardeners, pool attendants, and chauffeurs, the General felt as close as he was ever going to be to his old life of unquestioned authority. Dismissing a gardener for an ill-raked path or sacking a cook for a soup too cold or too hot satisfied impulses that he'd feared he was leaving behind when he boarded the plane, late and secretly, on the night the government fell.

But the north, with its labyrinth of immigration laws, had given him new levers to control his employees, and the General used them all, partly to avoid familiarity and partly for pleasure, because the General had loved only two things: power and his young son, Alejandro, a slim, dark boy of eight who reminded the General strongly of his late wife. Not that there was anything effeminate about the child, who played noisy soccer games at St. Ignatius and who could set the kitchen staff laughing the moment he returned from school, but from his earliest years, Alejandro had been thoughtful, and what he was thinking was not always transparent to his father.

Like his mother, the boy kept his own counsel, and he could be as quiet as he was noisy, spending hours reading in his room or playing one of his squeaking video games or frolicking in the far reaches of the garden and learning ungrammatical Spanish from the gardeners. He looked like his mother too, being rather pale, with eyes neither brown nor green, but a speckled amalgamation of the two. He had her nose, already quite large and angular; her full mouth; her thick, glossy black hair.

Watching him run joyously about on the playing field, the General had moments when some angle of jaw or cheek or hairline brought Maria back with a sharp, unwelcome ache. Aware of her own innocence, she had been as fearless as the boy, and she had paid for her carelessness when a motorcycle roared up to her limousine and the pillion rider loosed a burst of fire. The assailants had expected the General to be in the car, and though he'd escaped, he had known that his days were numbered.

Eventually, he fled north, where he had contacts, protection, assistance of useful kinds, and money. He hadn't gone into either the army or politics to remain poor. Now he lived in luxurious retirement; in exile, true, and with greatly diminished powers, but with vastly enhanced safety and comfort. Alejandro would grow up to be a citizen of this new and often enigmatic country, where power of many sorts would be available to him. The General had no doubt of that.

So he was as content as a man of his past and temperament could be. He raged sometimes—though never at Alejandro. The General was known to strike his kitchen staff and even his young and pretty mistress, who lived in an apartment a mile away from his home, but he did nothing worse. The past was gone and buried, and all that he had done and seen and ordered—for the good of his country and his party—was put to rest.

With wealth, a gated acreage, state-of-the-art alarms, and armed guards, the General could be confident that his life would run smoothly. It was therefore surprising that he allowed one irritant: Manuel, the gaunt, silent head gardener whom it had pleased the General to hire after precipitously firing the last one for burning the perfect turf with a carelessly placed glass tabletop.

Manuel was, naturally, one of the General's countrymen, an old, dark, sad Indian without papers. The General preferred illegals, whom he could pay next to nothing. But although his salary was minimal, the elderly gardener was permitted to live in the shed at the back of the yard.

Why the General arranged this is unclear, since he was cautious to the point of paranoia. Yet to save a few dollars on Manuel's salary, dollars that the General could well have afforded, having left the capital with a suitcase full of gold bars, he allowed a stranger, and a mysterious one at that, to live within his gates and beyond his immediate oversight.

There was no physical danger, of course. The General's two bodyguards, Hector and Jesus, were always vigilant. One or the other was perpetually on duty, and at some point, it would surely please the General to throw the old man into the street. Yet from a strict security standpoint, Manuel's residence in the garden, even briefly, was unwise.

If asked about this, the General would have said that Manuel was a wonderful gardener who would get the place into shape. The orchids, the lilies, the flowering cacti, the bananas, the bamboo, all the various ornamentals and tropicals thrived under his care. Every time the General went into his garden, he was reminded of his patio back in the capital and of evenings sitting with friends under the palms.

But, as with so many aspects of the General's life, the situation with Manuel was complex. Even in retirement, the General had considerable business dealings and still retained influence back home. He was absent a good deal, and Alejandro, who was lonely, had taken a great liking to Manuel and a great interest in the operation of the garden.

At home, the General would have put a stop to that at once. The son of the General was not training to be a gardener. But here, things were subtly different. The boy missed his adored mother and none of the housekeepers or cooks had won his heart to the degree the old gardener had. When the General was away, the boy spent hours down in the garden shed talking to Manuel and learning the mysteries of propagation and pruning.

One evening the General asked Alejandro what he and Manuel found to talk about, the old man being, as the General knew, quite illiterate.

"We talk about the plants," said the boy.

"Nothing else?"

"This and that. He comes from the highlands."

The General pricked up his ears at that, and it came into his mind to fire Manuel instantly.

"He says," Alejandro added, "that you were a great man at home, and one day I'll understand the sort of man you are." The boy gave a smile of such trust and sweetness that the General was disarmed. There were, after all, some good people in the highlands, faithful, sensible souls. Even there.

Just the same, he began to take a greater interest in Manuel and in what Alejandro was learning in the garden. He had the boy show him which plants he had pruned and how the small orchids—propagated, as even the General could see, with delicate skill—were progressing. Sometimes in the evening when Alejandro was in bed, the General would wander through his garden, smoking a thin cigar, thinking of this and that, of days in the capital when his power was supreme, and of earlier days in the mountains when his word, his every impulse, was law.

Often as he strolled along the immaculate paths, the General found his way past the plots holding chilies and cilantro, yams, jicamas, beans, tomatoes, and corn to the little potting shed. There was a pipe for water, and some fastidious former owner had installed a small toilet. Manuel or one of his predecessors had acquired a hot plate and a barbecue, and on some nights the General smelled bracing, peppery concoctions or, more rarely, the scent of meat or chicken bathed in herbs.

It was on these nights that the General thought of the backcountry, so terrible and beautiful, and of what he had done and ordered there. Sometimes, the smells were so intense, so delicious—as if they were the scent of memory rather than the cookery of an impoverished gardener over a few charcoal briquettes—that the General imagined a single mouthful of such food would restore him to his old headquarters deep in the past.

I'm getting old, thought the General one evening. He felt that it would be wise to fire Manuel that night, that very moment, and yet he did not. In fact, he found himself drawn more and more to the night garden and to the shed, which always seemed dark to him, though he knew for a fact that it was wired for power, and he sometimes saw a faint light emanating from it when he looked out his bedroom window at night. He told himself that he could have the power cable disconnected, just as he could fire Manuel. There were always gardeners in need of work.

One day, Alejandro had an orchid to show him, a minuscule cluster of green leaves. It was a hybrid, the boy said. A new one. If it turned out to be as beautiful as he hoped, it would be named for his mother.

The General looked at his smiling face and said, "What a splendid idea."

Nonetheless, when Alejandro went off to school, the General felt grumpy and out of sorts. Who was this gardener to remind him of Maria? He stepped onto the terrace and studied his lush foliage. The original garden had been too tidy and suburban for his taste. Now, without its ever looking sloppy or unkempt, the garden reminded the General of his native thickets and jungles. Though the birds' songs were different, there were moments when he felt at home, when he felt returned, almost. He traced the beginning of those moments to when Manuel had taken up residence in the garden.

It would have seemed a simple matter for the General to question the old man directly, but this he did not do. First, he was confident that the man would lie, on principle, if not out of fear, and second, it was surely beneath his own dignity to investigate one of his servants. If he had real questions, he would let Hector and Jesus handle the business; they would soon discover anything he needed to know about Manuel. Anything.

The awareness that this might be done consoled the General.

In his mind, having the power to do something ran a close second to actually doing it. Besides, Alejandro was often alone, and the General preferred for him to have a companion within the compound instead of running wild among the neighborhood boys with their motorized scooters and skateboards and their delight in surfing rough water.

Already the boy's English was full of slang and his Spanish corrupted. There could be no harm in the old gardener, and the General thought himself well enough protected by asking the occasional question.

"Manuel must be very patient," the General said one day. "He teaches you a great deal."

"He had a son once," Alejandro said. "A boy like me."

"And where is his son? Back home or here?"

Alejandro shook his head. "He did not grow up. He is dead."

"Ah," said the General. That explained much. Alejandro looked reflective, even melancholy, and the General thought it well to add, "So many children die back home. The peasants are ignorant of even the simplest care."

Alejandro did not answer this observation, and some delicacy kept the General from pressing him.

Another time, he asked Alejandro where Manuel came from.

"The highlands," Alejandro said. "He picked coffee and then he made gardens for the plantation owner."

"Do you know what village that might be?" The General kept his voice low. There were lots of coffee plantations, and he did not fear the answer. It would be too much of a coincidence. Still, even the idea was unwelcome.

Alejandro shrugged—a nasty habit he had picked up from the boys next door.

"Answer your father." Unintentionally, the General spoke so sharply that Alejandro flinched.

"I don't know."

"I was just curious," the General said, to pass over the moment.

"I can ask him," Alejandro said.

"It is not important," said the General, though now he greatly desired to know, to know that it was not Santa Lucia de Piedras. But he did not want to disturb Alejandro. There were surely other ways to find out.

One day, quite spontaneously, Alejandro said, "I think Manuel is very sad."

Sorrow was always a danger, and the General thought again of firing the old man. "Perhaps he would be happier in another job."

"I hope he never leaves us," his son said quickly. Oh, the boy was careless like that, just like his mother. *The innocent are careless,* the General thought, *trusting.* He felt a moment of fear — and then of anger. His son would have to learn caution. It would serve him right if he fired Manuel, but, weakened by his love for the boy, the General said, "I would be very sad if I lost you. The death of his son is why Manuel is sad."

"I think that is true. He can never forget what happened," said Alejandro, but his face told the General nothing.

"The child was ill, wasn't he? There was no one to blame."

"I don't know," said Alejandro. "Mother—" He started to speak, then stopped. The General looked at him sharply.

"Mother didn't die of illness."

"Evil men murdered your mother," the General said. "She was too trusting. She went out in the car when I had warned her—" He broke off, moved in spite of himself. Though there had been threats, she had never understood the hatred against him. Of necessity, he had kept her innocent of his life, and that innocence had killed her. To prevent Alejandro from meeting the same fate, the General had fled to the north, even though his prime impulse had been to seek revenge.

"A lot of people were killed at home," observed Alejandro.

Well, what had the General expected? There were stories in the Yankee papers, perhaps even in Alejandro's school lessons, for the General suspected that even St. Ignatius, chosen for its tradition and rigidity, was infected with new and liberal ideas. "Most of them deserved to die," he said. "The men who murdered your mother—death would have been too good for them."

"They got away, didn't they?"

"Things fell apart. We had many enemies. It was me they wanted to kill, because I defended our country."

He spoke passionately, and as if to console him—for the boy had a tender heart—Alejandro said, "I know. I know you were a great man at home. When I am older, I will study your career. You will be in history books."

The General was pleased; then it struck him that this was a strange phrase for a boy to use, even a bookish boy. He remembered again that Manuel had told the boy that his father had been a great man at home and that one day Alejandro would understand the sort of man he was. *Not if I can help it,* thought the General.

Still, he did nothing about the old man's residence in the garden, which bloomed ever more luxuriantly. *I am getting old,* thought the General, *I am succumbing to nostalgia.* He sat out on his terrace smoking and listening to the night sounds and imagining himself back in the capital. Or, and these were moments he both loved and feared, he sat in the darkness with only the torches lit and envisioned the highlands with the moon rising over the jungle trees of Santa Lucia de Piedras, and he saw himself turning toward the interrogation rooms. He'd always liked to work at night. Certain things do not belong with daylight.

Possibly, neither did Manuel. The General avoided the garden during the heat of the day, and even at night, when, courting a confrontation, he walked around the vegetable patch and passed the shed, the old man remained as invisible as if he were a figment of the General's imagination—or of Alejandro's.

But the latter idea was disturbing, for why should Alejandro have any knowledge of the villages of the hinterlands, villages he had never seen? Why should he imagine an old man who offered him the promise of seeing the General as he was? No, this was a warning, and the General had just resolved to fire Manuel and make the shed uninhabitable when Alejandro raced inside, crying that his friend had taken ill, that he must have a doctor.

"He is probably just drunk," said the General, and saw the shock in his son's eyes. Then there was nothing for it but to go down to the garden and see for himself.

Alejandro ran ahead, his anxiety for Manuel all too apparent. Perhaps the gardener really was sick; perhaps he could be sent to the hospital, or even home. The General gave a tight smile at that and entered the shed. The afternoon light came in over the potting bench, stacked with clean terra-cotta pots and shining trowels and containers of soil, sand, and peat moss.

The old man, very thin, very gray, was lying on a small cot in the shadows. The General saw at once that this was serious. "Get out of here," he told Alejandro. "It may be contagious." Then he took out his cell phone and dialed for an ambulance. "We will get you a doctor," he told the old man in Spanish.

One hand, brown, cracked, and callused, moved on the covers, a gesture of gratitude—or indifference.

"Should we notify someone?"

Again the gesture.

"At home?" In his interest and anxiety, the General leaned closer and whispered, "Where is your village?"

There was a long silence; the dark eyes, dilated by pain, studied his face. The General had almost given up when, in a whisper, his eyes closing, Manuel said, "Santa Lucia de P…"

The General took in a breath and stood up, but the old man had lost consciousness and did not seem to notice his agitation. In a few minutes, emergency medical personnel arrived with their screaming ambulance and carried Manuel out of the garden. When Alejandro pleaded to go with him—young as he was, he understood the necessity of insurance—the General realized that he would have to become involved.

The doctors kept Manuel in the hospital for a week, gave him intravenous fluids and antibiotics, took X-rays and ran expensive blood tests. They cured a variety of small illnesses common to the General's countrymen, but they could not touch the cancer that was taking his life. At the end of a week, the old man came back—ghostly pale and thin, scarcely capable of walking—and returned to his bed in the shed.

"We will have to send him home," said the General. "To his own family. A little money too," he added, to soothe Alejandro. "They will be able to take care of him better there."

"He has no one," said Alejandro. "His son is dead."

"He will have relatives; everyone has relatives."

But Alejandro shook his head, and knowing Manuel came from that ghost village, Santa Lucia de Piedras, the General did not argue. He wanted to close the discussion; even more, he wanted the gardener gone, and he walked into the garden. When he opened the shed door, he saw at a glance that the old man was dying. *What is one more casualty of Santa Lucia de Piedras?* the General thought, and considered calling a cab. He could have Manuel at the airport before Alejandro returned. But there were no papers; and after employing Manuel all this time, the General might have trouble with the *migra*. No, unless he took drastic action, he was stuck with the old man until he died. This knowledge spoiled the garden.

The General began to avoid the terrace in the evenings, and he closed the broad wooden shutters of the windows overlooking the rampant tropical foliage. Alejandro remained faithful. He visited Manuel twice a day, before he went to school and as soon as he returned home on the bus from St. Ignatius. He was forever begging the cook for special broths and bits of meat and even for the bottles of wine that appeared to be Manuel's preferred painkiller. All this the General saw with dread—and with anger, too, at being reminded of Santa Lucia de Piedras after so many years and in such a manner.

Now it seemed to the General that he had been right from the start, that Manuel's skill in the garden had returned him to his days of power and command, back to nights in the interrogation rooms, back even further, to a day of sun and blood and the smell of gunpowder and diesel fuel, back to Santa Lucia de Piedras, to what was now beyond explanation. The gardener had no right to awaken these ghosts, and when Alejandro reported that Manuel was feeling a little better and talking about some work in the garden, the General decided to act.

He waited until the boy went to school, but though he checked the garden periodically from his window, he saw no sign of the old man. Perhaps Alejandro had been wrong. Perhaps Manuel was worse; perhaps he was already dead. It was late afternoon before the General saw a thin, white-clad figure with a straw hat moving through the trees.

Manuel was using his machete as a cane, leaning heavily on it and sometimes grasping at branches to stay erect.

The old fool, thought the General. *He thinks he can show me that he can still work. He'll be asking for his pay next. If he's well enough to work, he's well enough to be on the first bus south. Whatever it costs will be worthwhile.*

In a rush of anger, the General went out onto the terrace and crossed the lawn toward the pool. Manuel's high cheeks were flushed, and his dilated and unfocused eyes were fathomless. He staggered a little when he saw the General, then straightened up and stared directly at him. In Manuel's shadowed eyes, the General was surprised to read rage and desperation without the slightest trace of fear. *We have both come a long way from Santa Lucia de Piedras,* the General thought, and he smelled blood on the hot afternoon breeze.

"How fortunate that you are out of bed," the General said. "I won't be needing you in the garden anymore. For Alejandro's sake, I will make arrangements to send you home."

"I will never leave you, General," Manuel said. His voice was low and hoarse, the voice of the rebels and criminals of Santa Lucia de Piedras, the General thought. He had done his duty. They had no right to haunt him.

"If you give me trouble, you will wind up in the gutter," the General said. He raised his voice so angrily that he did not hear the familiar wheeze and grunt of the school bus stopping.

"Give me back my son," said Manuel.

"You have no son."

"He was ten years old, a mere boy, no bigger than Alejandro."

"I know nothing of him." But the General remembered the bodies in the plaza, men and women and other, smaller corpses — they had spared no living thing, not even the chickens and donkeys. And what did a few peasants more or less matter? The hills were full of bandits and rebels.

"I was gone on the day of the massacre," said Manuel. "I came home to find them all dead."

"It was war," said the General. "It was an accident of war."

Now Manuel gave a thin, ghastly smile. "You drink blood," he said.

"That's enough." The General slipped his hand into his pocket for the stubby handgun that never left his side.

Manuel took a step toward him. He was so unsteady that he lurched against one of the ornamental planters beside the pool. "Give me back my son," he cried in a voice fit to wake the dead. "Before I die, give me my son."

He took another step, and it seemed to the General that the old man was covered in blood, that he had risen from the wet red ground of Santa Lucia de Piedras or from the filth of the interrogation room, that he was advancing irresistibly. The General raised his pistol, and, though he heard a cry at the very periphery of his awareness, he fired.

Manuel's hat was flung off; his white shirt blossomed red, and he collapsed at the edge of the pool, his blood spoiling the pure aquamarine of the water. He looked past the General and struggled to say one last thing, his throat already rattling: "You see now what your father is."

And the General knew, even before he turned around, that Manuel spoke to Alejandro.

A FINE MIST OF BLOOD

BY MICHAEL CONNELLY

The DNA hits came in the mail, in yellow envelopes from the regional crime lab's genetics unit. Fingerprint matches were less formal; notification usually came by e-mail. Case-to-case data hits were rare birds and were handled in yet a different manner—direct contact between the synthesizer and the submitting investigator.

Harry Bosch had a day off and was in the waiting area outside the school principal's office when he got the call. More like a half a day off. His plan was to head downtown to the PAB after dealing with the summons from the school's high command.

The buzzing of his phone brought an immediate response from the woman behind the gateway desk.

"There's no cell phones in here," she said.

"I'm not a student," Bosch said, stating the obvious as he pulled the offending instrument from his pocket.

"Doesn't matter. There's no cell phones in here."

"I'll take it outside."

"I won't come out to find you. If you miss your appointment

then you'll have to reschedule, and your daughter's situation won't be resolved."

"I'll risk it. I'll just be in the hallway, okay?"

He pushed through the door into the hallway as he connected to the call. The hallway was quiet, as it was the middle of the fourth period. The ID on the screen had said simply *LAPD data* but that had been enough to give Bosch a stirring of excitement.

The call was from a tech named Malek Pran. Bosch had never dealt with him and had to ask him to repeat his name twice. Pran was from Data Evaluation and Theory—known internally as the DEATH squad—which was part of a new effort by the Open-Unsolved Unit to clear cases through what was called data synthesizing.

For the past three years the DEATH squad had been digitizing archived murder books—the hard-copy investigative records—of unsolved cases, creating a massive database of easily accessible and comparable information on unsolved crimes. Suspects, witnesses, weapons, locations, word constructions—anything that an investigator thought important enough to note in an investigative record was now digitized and could be compared with other cases.

The project had actually been initiated simply to create space. The city's records archives were bursting at the seams with acres of files and file boxes. Shifting it all to digital would make room in the cramped department.

Pran said he had a case-to-case hit. A witness listed in a cold case Bosch had submitted for synthesizing had come up in another case, also a homicide, as a witness once again. Her name was Diane Gables. Bosch's case was from 1999 and the second case was from 2007, which was too recent to fall under the purview of the Open-Unsolved Unit.

"Who submitted the 2007 case?"

"Uh, it was out of Hollywood Division. Detective Jerry Edgar made the submission."

Bosch almost smiled in the hallway. He went a distance back with Jerry Edgar.

"Have you talked to Edgar yet about the hit?" Bosch asked.

"No. I started with you. Do you want his contact info?"

"I already have it. What's the vic's name on that case?"

"Raymond Randolph, DOB six, six, sixty-one—that's a lot of sixes. DOD July second, 2007."

"Okay, I'll get the rest from Edgar. You did good, Pran. This gives me something I can work with."

Bosch disconnected and went back into the principal's office. He had not missed his appointment. He checked his watch. He'd give it fifteen minutes, and then he'd have to start moving on the case. His daughter would have to go without her confiscated cell phone until he could get another appointment with the principal.

———

BEFORE CONTACTING JERRY Edgar at Hollywood Division, Bosch pulled up the files—both hard and digital—on his own case. It involved the murder of a precious-metals swindler named Roy Alan McIntyre. He had sold gold futures by phone and internet. It was the oldest story in the book: There was no gold, or not enough of it. It was a Ponzi scheme through and through and like all of them, it finally collapsed upon itself. The victims lost tens of millions. McIntyre was arrested as the mastermind, but the evidence was tenuous. A good lawyer came to his defense and was able to convince the media that McIntyre was a victim himself, a dupe for organized-crime elements that had pulled the strings on the scheme. The DA started floating a deal that would put McIntyre on probation—provided he cooperated and returned all the money he still had access to. But word leaked about the impending deal, and hundreds of the scam's victims organized to oppose it. Before the whole thing went to court, McIntyre was murdered in the garage under the Westwood condominium tower where he lived. Shot once between the eyes, his body found on the concrete next to the open door of his car.

The crime scene was clean; not even a shell casing from the nine-millimeter bullet that had killed him was recovered. The investigators had no physical evidence and a list of possible suspects that numbered in the hundreds. The killing looked like a hit. It could have been McIntyre's unsavory backers in the gold scam or it could have been any of the investors who'd gotten ripped off. The only bright spot was that there was a witness. She was Diane Gables, a twenty-nine-year-old stockbroker who happened to be driving by McIntyre's condo on her way home from work. She'd reported seeing a man wearing a ski mask and carrying a gun at his side run from the garage and jump into the passenger seat of a black SUV waiting in front. Panicked by the sight of the gun, she didn't get an exact make or model of the SUV or its license-plate number. She'd pulled to the side of the road rather than following the vehicle as it sped off.

Bosch had not interviewed Gables when he had reevaluated the case in the Open-Unsolved Unit. He had simply reviewed the file and submitted it to the DEATH squad. Now, of course, he would be talking to her.

He picked the phone up and dialed a number from memory. Jerry Edgar was at his desk.

"It's me—Bosch. Looks like we're going to be working together again."

"Sounds good to me, Harry. What've you got?"

DIANE GABLES'S CURRENT address, obtained through the DMV, was in Studio City. Edgar drove while Bosch looked through the file on the 2007 case. It involved the murder of a man who had been awaiting trial for raping a seventeen-year-old girl who had knocked on his door to sell him candy bars as part of a fundraiser for a school trip to Washington, DC.

As Bosch read through the murder book, he remembered the case. It had been in the news because the circumstances suggested it had been a crime of vigilante justice by someone who was not willing to wait for Raymond Randolph to go on trial. Randolph was intending to mount a defense that would acknowledge that he'd had sexual intercourse with the girl but state that it was consensual. He planned to claim that the victim offered him sex in exchange for his buying her whole carton of candy bars.

The forty-six-year-old Randolph was found in the single-car garage behind his bungalow on Orange Grove, south of Sunset. He had been on his knees when he was shot twice in the back of the head.

The crime scene was clean, but it was a hot day in July and a neighbor who had her windows open because of a broken air conditioner heard the two shots, followed by the high-revving and rapid departure of a vehicle in the street. She called 911, which brought a near-immediate response from the police at Hollywood Station three blocks away and also served to peg the time of the murder almost to the minute.

Jerry Edgar was the lead investigator on the case. While obvious suspicion focused on the family and friends of the rape victim, Edgar cast a wide net—Bosch took some pride in seeing that—and in doing so came across Diane Gables. Two blocks from the Randolph home was an intersection controlled by a traffic signal and equipped with a camera that photographed vehicles that ran the red light. The camera took a double photo — one shot of the vehicle's license plate, and one shot of the person behind the wheel. This was done so that when the traffic citation was sent to the vehicle's owner, he or she could determine who'd been behind the wheel when the infraction occurred.

Diane Gables was photographed in her Lexus driving through the red light in the same minute as the 911 call reporting the gunshots was made. The photograph and registration was obtained from the DMV the day after the murder and Gables, now thirty-seven, was interviewed by Edgar and his partner, Detective Manuel Soto. She was then dismissed as both a possible suspect and a witness.

"So, how well do you remember this interview?" Bosch asked.

"I remember it because she was a real looker," Edgar said. "You always remember the lookers."

"According to the book, you interviewed her and dropped her. How come? Why so fast?"

"She and her story checked out. Keep going. It's in there."

Bosch found the interview summary and scanned it. Gables had told Edgar and Soto that she had been cruising through the neighborhood after filling out a crime report at the nearby Hollywood Station on Wilcox. Her Lexus had been damaged by a hit-and-run driver the night before while parked on the street outside a restaurant on Franklin. In order to apply for insurance coverage on the repairs, she had to file a police report. After stopping at the station, she was running late for work and went through the light on what she was thought was a yellow signal. The camera said otherwise.

"So she had filed the report?" Bosch asked.

"She had indeed. She checked out. And that's what makes me think we're dealing with just a coincidence here, Harry."

Bosch nodded but continued to grind it down inside. He didn't like coincidences. He didn't believe in them.

"You checked her work too?"

"Soto did. Confirmed her position and that she was indeed late to work on the day of the killing. She had called ahead and said she was running late because she had been at the police station. She called her boss."

"What about the restaurant? I don't see it in here."

"Then I probably didn't have that information."

"So you never checked it."

"You mean did I check to see if she ate there the night before the murder? No, Harry, I didn't and that's a bullshit question. She was—"

"It's just that if she was setting up a cover story, she could've crunched her own car and—"

"Come on, Harry. You're kidding me, right?"

"I don't know. We're still going to talk to her."

"I know that, Harry. I've known that since you called. You're going to have to see for yourself. Just like always. So just tell me how you want to go in, rattlesnake or cobra?"

Bosch considered for a moment, remembering the code they'd used back when they were partners. A rattlesnake interview was when you shook your tail and hissed. It was confrontational and useful for getting immediate reactions. Going cobra was the quiet approach. You'd slowly move in, get close, and then strike.

"Let's go cobra."

"You got it."

———

DIANE GABLES WASN'T home. They had timed their arrival for 5:30 p.m., figuring that with the stock market closing at 1:00 p.m., Gables would easily have finished work for the day.

"What do you want to do?" Edgar said as they stood at the door.

"Go back to the car. Wait awhile."

Back in the car, they talked about old cases and detective bureau pranks. Edgar revealed that it had been he who had cut ads for penile-enhancement surgery out of the sports pages and slipped them into an officious lieutenant's jacket pocket while it had been hanging on a rack in his office. The lieutenant had subsequently mounted an investigation focused squarely on Bosch.

"Now you tell me," Bosch said. "Pounds tried to bust me to burglary for that one."

Edgar was a clapper. He backed his laughter with his own applause but cut the display short when Bosch pointed through the windshield.

"There she is."

A late-model Range Rover pulled into the driveway.

Bosch and Edgar got out and crossed the front lawn to meet Gables as she took the stone path from the driveway to her front door. Bosch saw her recognize Edgar, even after five years, and saw her eyes immediately start scanning, going from the front door of her house to the street and the houses of her neighbors. Her head didn't move, only her eyes, and Bosch recognized it as a tell. Fight or flight. It might have been a natural reaction for a woman with two strange men approaching her, but Bosch didn't think that was the situation. He had seen the recognition in her eyes when she looked at Edgar. A pulse of electricity began moving in his blood.

"Ms. Gables," Edgar said. "Jerry Edgar. You remember me?"

As planned, Edgar was taking the lead before passing it off to Bosch.

Gables paused on the path. She was carrying a stylish red leather briefcase. She acted as though she were trying to place Edgar's face, and then she smiled.

"Of course, Detective. How are you?"

"I'm fine. You must have a very good memory."

"Well, it's not every day that you meet a real live detective. Is this coincidence or..."

"Not a coincidence. I'm with Detective Bosch here and we would like to ask you a few questions about the Randolph case, if you don't mind."

"It was so long ago."

"Five years," Bosch said, asserting himself now. "But it's still an open case."

She registered the information and then nodded.

"Well, it's been a long day. I start at six in the morning, when the market opens. Could we—"

Bosch cut her off. "I start at six too, but not because of the stock market."

He wasn't backing down.

"Then fine, you're welcome to come in," she said. "But I don't know what help I can be after so long. I didn't really think I was much help five years ago. I didn't see anything. Didn't hear anything. I just happened to be in the neighborhood after I was at the police station."

"We're investigating the case again," Bosch said. "And we need to talk to everybody we talked to five years ago."

"Well, like I said, come on in."

She unlocked the front door and entered first, greeted by the beeping of an alarm warning. She quickly punched a four-digit combination into an alarm-control box on the wall. Bosch and Edgar stepped in behind her and she ushered them into the living room.

"Why don't you gentlemen have a seat? I'm going to put my things down and be right back out. Would either of you like something to drink?"

"I'll take a bottle of water if you got it," Edgar said.

"I'm fine," Bosch said.

"You know what?" Edgar said quickly. "I'm fine too."

Gables glanced at Bosch and seemed to register that he was the power in the room. She said she'd be right back.

After she was gone Bosch looked around the room. It was a basic living room setup with a couch and two chairs surrounding a glass-topped coffee table. One wall was made up entirely of built-in bookshelves, all filled with what looked by their titles to be crime novels. He noticed there were no personal displays. No framed photographs anywhere.

They remained standing until Gables came back and pointed them to the couch. She took a chair directly across the table from them.

"Now, what can I tell you? Frankly, I forgot the whole incident."

"But you remembered Detective Edgar. I could tell."

"Yes, but seeing him out of context, I knew I recognized him but I could not remember from where."

According to the DMV, Gables was now forty-one years old. And Edgar had been right: She was a looker, attractive in a professional sort of way. A short, no-nonsense cut to her brown hair. Slim, athletic build. She sat straight and looked straight at one or the other of them, no longer scanning because she was inside her comfort zone. Still, there were tells: Bosch knew through his training in interview techniques that normal eye contact between individuals lasted an average of three seconds, yet each time Gables looked at Bosch, she held his eyes a good ten seconds. That was a sign of stress.

"I was rereading the reports," Bosch said. "They included your explanation for being in the area—you were at the police station filling out a report."

"That's right."

"It didn't say, though, where your car was when it got damaged the night before."

"I had been at a restaurant on Franklin. I told them that. And when I came out after, the back taillight was smashed and the paint scraped."

"You didn't call the police then?"

"No, I didn't. No one was there. It was a hit-and-run; they didn't even leave a note on the car. They just took off and I thought I was out of luck."

"What was the name of the restaurant?"

"I can't remember—oh, it was Birds. I love the roasted chicken."

Bosch nodded. He knew the place and the roasted chicken.

"So what made you come back to Hollywood the next day and file the report on the hit-and-run?"

"I called my insurance company first thing in the morning and they said I needed it if I wanted to file a claim to cover the damages."

Bosch was covering ground that was already in the reports. He was looking for variations, changes. Stories told five years apart often had inconsistencies and contradictions. But Gables wasn't changing the narrative at all.

"When you drove by Orange Grove, you heard no shots or anything like that?"

"No, nothing. I had my windows up."

"And you were driving fast."

"Yes, I was going to be late for work."

"Now, when Detective Edgar came to see you, was that unsettling?"

"Unsettling? Well, yes, I guess so, until I realized what he was there for, and of course I knew I had nothing to do with it."

"Was it the first time you'd ever encountered a detective or the police like that? You know, on a murder case."

"Yes, it was very unusual. To say the least. Not a normal part of my life."

She shook her shoulders as if to intimate a shiver, imply that police and murder investigations were foreign to her. Bosch stared at her for a long moment. She had either forgotten about seeing the armed man with a ski mask coming out of the garage where Roy Alan McIntyre was murdered, or she was lying.

Bosch thought the latter. He thought that Diane Gables was a killer.

"How do you pick them?" he asked.

She turned directly toward him, her eyes locking on his.

"Pick what?"

Bosch paused, squeezing the most out of her stare and the moment.

"The stocks you recommend to people," he said.

She broke her eyes away and looked at Edgar.

"Due diligence," she said. "Careful analysis and prognostication. Then, I have to say, I throw in my hunches. You gentlemen use hunches, don't you?"

"Every day," Bosch said.

———

THEY WERE SILENT for a while as they drove away. Bosch thought about the carefully worded answers Gables had given. He was feeling stronger about his hunch every minute.

"What do you think?" Edgar finally asked.

"I think it's her."

"How can you say that? She didn't make a single false move in there."

"Yes, she did. Her eyes gave her away."

"Oh, come on, Harry. You're saying you know she's a stone-cold killer because you can read it in her eyes?"

"Pretty much. She also lied. She didn't mention the case in 1999 because she thought we didn't know about it. She didn't want us going down that path, so she lied and said you were the only detective she'd ever met."

"At best, that's a lie by omission. Weak, Harry."

"A lie is a lie. Nothing weak about it. She was hiding it from us and there's only one reason to do that. I want to get inside her house. She's gotta have a place where she studies and plans these things."

"So you think she's a pro? A gun for hire?"

"Maybe; I don't know. Maybe she reads the paper and picks her targets, people she thinks need killing. Maybe she's on some kind of vigilante trip. Dark justice and all of that."

"A regular angel of vengeance. Sounds like a comic book, man."

"If we get inside that place, we'll know."

Edgar drove silently while he composed a response. Bosch knew what was coming before he said it.

"Harry, I'm just not seeing it. I respect your hunch, man, I have seen that come through more than once. But there ain't enough here. And if I don't see it, then there's no judge that's going to give you a warrant to go back in there."

Bosch took his time answering. He was grinding things down, coming up with a plan.

"Maybe, maybe not," he finally said.

———

Two DAYS LATER at 9:00 a.m., Bosch pulled up to Diane Gables's house. The Range Rover was not in the driveway. He got out and went to the front door. After two loud knocks went unanswered he walked around the house to the back door.

He knocked again. When there was no reply, he removed a set of lock picks that he kept behind his badge in his leather wallet and went to work on the dead bolt. It took him six minutes to open the door. He was greeted by the beeping of the burglar alarm. He located the box on the wall to the left of the back door and punched in the four numbers he had seen Gables enter at the front door two evenings before. The beeping stopped. Bosch was in. He left the door open and started looking around the house.

It was a post–World War II ranch house. Bosch had been in a thousand of them over the years and all the investigations. After a quick survey of the entire house he started his search in a bedroom that had been converted to a home office. There was a desk and a row of file cabinets along the wall where a bed would have been. There was a line of windows over the cabinets.

There was also a metal locker with a padlock on it. Bosch opened the venetian blinds over the file cabinets, and light came into the room. He moved to the metal locker and started there, pulling his picks out once again.

He knelt on the floor so he could see the lock closely. It turned out to be a three-pin breeze, taking less than a minute for him to open. A moment after the hasp snapped free he heard a voice come from behind him.

"Detective, don't move."

Bosch froze for a moment. He recognized the voice. Diane Gables. She had known he would come back. He slowly started to raise his hands, holding his fingers close together so he could hide the picks between them.

"Easy," Gables commanded. "If you attempt to reach for your weapon I will put two bullets into your skull. Do you understand?"

"Yes. Can I stand up? My knees aren't what they once were."

"Slowly. Your hands always in my sight line."

"Absolutely."

Bosch started to get up slowly, turning toward her at the same time. She was pointing a handgun with a suppressor attached to the barrel.

"Easy," he said. "Just take it easy here."

"No, you take it easy. I could shoot you where you stand and be within my rights."

Bosch shook his head.

"No, that's not true. You know I'm a cop."

"Yeah, a rogue cop. What did you think you were going to find here?"

"Evidence."

"Of what?"

"Randolph and McIntyre. Maybe others. You killed them."

"And, what, you thought I'd just keep the evidence around? Hide it in a locker in my home?"

"Something like that. Can I sit down?"

"The chair behind the desk. Keep your hands where I can see them."

Bosch slowly sat down. She was still standing in the doorway. He now had 60 percent of his body shielded by the desk. He had his back to the file cabinets. The light was coming in from behind and above him. He noticed she had now lowered the muzzle to point at his chest. This was good, though from this range he doubted the Kevlar would completely stop a bullet from a nine-millimeter, even with the suppressor slowing it down. He kept his hands up and close to his face.

"So now what?" he asked.

"So now you tell me what you think you've got on me."

Bosch shook his head as if to say *Not much.* "You lied. The other day. You didn't mention the McIntyre case. You didn't want us linking the cases through you. The trouble is we already had."

"And that's it? Are you kidding me?"

"That's it. Till now."

He nodded at her weapon. It seemed to confirm all hunches.

"So, without a real case and the search warrant to go with it, of course you decided to break in here to see what you could find."

"Not exactly."

"We have a problem, Detective Bosch."

"No, you have the problem. You're a killer and I'm onto you. Put the weapon down. You're under arrest."

She laughed and waggled the gun in her hand.

"You forget one thing. I have the gun."

"But you won't use it. You don't kill people like me. You kill the abusers, the predators."

"I could make an exception. You've broken the law by breaking in here. There are no gray areas. Who knows, maybe you came to *plant* evidence here, not find it. Maybe you *are* like them."

Bosch started lowering his hands to the desktop.

"Be careful, Detective."

"I'm tired of holding them up. And I know you're not going to shoot me. It's not part of your program."

"I told you, programs change."

"How do you pick them?"

She stared at him a long time, then finally answered.

"They pick themselves. They deserve what they get."

"No judge, no jury. Just you."

"Don't tell me you haven't wished you could do the same thing."

"Sure, on occasion. But there are rules. We don't live by them, then where does it all go?"

"Right here, I guess. What am I going to do about you?"

"Nothing. You kill me and you know it's over. You'll be like one of them—the abusers and the predators. Put the gun down."

She took two steps into the room. The muzzle came up toward his face. Bosch saw that deadly black eye rising in slow motion.

"You're wearing a vest, aren't you?"

He nodded.

"I could see it in your eyes. The fear comes up when the gun comes up."

Bosch shook his head.

"I'm not afraid. You won't shoot me."

"I still see fear."

"Not for me. It's for you. How many have there been?"

She paused, maybe to decide what to tell him, or maybe just to decide what to do. Or maybe she was stuck on his answer about the fear.

"More than you'll ever know. More than anybody will ever know. Look, I'm sorry, you know?"

"About what?"

"About there being only one real way out of this. For me."

The muzzle steadied, its aim at his eyes.

"Before you pull that trigger, can I show you something?"

"It won't matter."

"I think it will. It's in my inside jacket pocket."

She frowned, then made a signal with the gun.

"Show me your wrists. Where's your watch?"

Bosch raised his hands and his jacket sleeves came down, showing his watch on his right wrist. He was left-handed.

"Okay, take out whatever it is you need to show me with your right hand. Slowly, Detective, slowly."

"You got it."

Bosch reached in and with great deliberation pulled out the folded document. He handed it across the desk to her.

"Just put it down and then lean away."

He followed her instructions. She waited for him to move back and then picked up the document. With one hand she unfolded it and took a glance, taking her eyes off Bosch for no more than a millisecond.

"I'm not going to be able to read it. What is it?"

"It's a no-knock search warrant. I have broken no law by being here. I'm not one of them."

She stared at him for a silent thirty seconds and then finally smirked.

"You have to be kidding me. What judge would sign such a search warrant? You had zero probable cause."

"I had your lies and your proximity to two murders. And I had Judge Oscar Ortiz—you remember him?"

"Who is he?"

"Back in 1999 he had the McIntyre case. But you took it away from him when you executed McIntyre. Getting him to sign this search warrant wasn't hard once I reminded him about the case."

Anger worked into her face. The muzzle started to come up again.

"All I have to say is one word," Bosch said. "A one-syllable word."

"And what?"

"And you're dead."

She froze, and slowly her eyes rose from Bosch's face to the windows over the file cabinets.

"You opened the blinds," she said.

"Yes."

Bosch studied the two red laser dots that had played on her face since she had entered the room, one high on her forehead, the other on her chin. Bosch knew that the lasers did not account for bullet drop, but the SWAT sharpshooters on the roof of the house across the street did. The chin dot was the heart shot.

Gables seemed frozen, unable to choose whether to live or die.

"There's a lot you could tell us," he said. "We could learn from you. Why don't you just put the gun down and we can get started."

He slowly started to lean forward, raising his left hand to take the gun.

"I don't think so," she said.

She brought the muzzle up but he didn't say the word. He didn't think she'd shoot.

There were three sounds in immediate succession: The breaking of glass as the bullet passed through the window. A sound like an ice cream cone dropping on the sidewalk as the bullet passed through her chest. And then the *thock* of the slug hitting the door frame behind her.

A fine mist of blood started to fill the room.

Gables took a step backward and looked down at her chest as her arms dropped to her sides. The gun made a dull sound when it hit the carpet.

She glanced up at Bosch with a confused look. In a strained voice she asked her last question.

"What was the word?"

She then dropped to the floor.

Staying below the level of the file cabinets, Bosch left the desk and came around to her on the floor. He slid the gun out of reach and looked down at her eyes. He knew there was nothing he could do. The bullet had exploded her heart.

"You bastards!" he yelled. "I didn't say it! I didn't say the word!"

Gables closed her eyes and Bosch thought she was gone.

"We're clear!" he said. "Suspect is ten-seven. Repeat, suspect is ten-seven. Weapons, stand down."

He started to get up but saw that Gables had opened her eyes.

"Nine," she whispered, blood coming up on her lips.

Bosch leaned down to her.

"What?"

"I killed nine."

She nodded and then closed her eyes again. He knew that this time she was gone, but he nodded anyway.

LEVERAGE

BY MIKE COOPER

I was counting on that pension." Joe Beeker looked up from his hands, knuckled together in his lap. "I need the money."

"We all need money," said the lawyer. He was younger than Joe, but so was everyone nowadays. He clacked at the silver laptop sitting open on his desk. "Doesn't mean they have to give it to you. The bankruptcy wiped out their obligations."

"I worked there thirty-seven years." And Joe knew he was marked from those decades: scarred fingers; flash burns on his arms; a small, weathered scar right under one eye. "On the line, mostly, and maintenance. Overtime every single week. You could look up my pay stubs."

"I'm sorry."

The office was small and undecorated, its window open to the parking lot off Mill Street. Humid summer air coming through the window oppressed the room rather than cooling it.

"I'll lose the house," said Joe softly.

"You'll get Social Security." The lawyer was trying to be helpful, Joe knew that. The youngster's tie was still snug at his throat, even if he'd rolled his cuffs back in the heat. He studied the computer screen for a moment. "And it looks like you've been at the same address for nearly four decades. Surely the mortgage is paid off by now?"

"We bought in 1972. Right after I got out of the service, with a VA loan. Marjo loved that house."

"And property taxes are certainly low around here."

"I had to take another mortgage." Joe looked away from the lawyer's disappointed sigh. "When Marjo got the cancer."

"Oh." The lawyer's sigh turned into a cough. "Insurance?"

"It wasn't enough." Joe shook his head. "I'm not complaining. She needed the nurse at home all those months. And the hospice. That's okay."

"I don't see anything in the file."

"She..." Joe felt his voice trail away. "Three weeks ago."

"I'm sorry," the lawyer said again. The fourth time since Joe had sat down.

"At least she didn't have to see me laid off. That would have killed her—" Joe stopped abruptly. "Never mind."

"Do your children...?"

"We never had any." Another old wound.

"Oh." The lawyer fussed a moment, then changed the subject. "The company's new owners are rehiring, I'm told."

"New owners?" For the first time, Joe couldn't keep his anger stopped up. "New owners? It's the same bastards, far as I can tell. They bought the company cheap, busted every single contract, sold off the inventory—and now they're starting up again. Yeah, they're rehiring. That's right. You know what they're paying? Six-fifty-three an hour. That's only one dollar more than I *started* at in 1974!"

"It's not quite that simple—"

"And you know what? I might have to take it, if I don't get the pension. I might have to take that fucking slop-hauler's wage, even though it's one-fourth what I was making a month ago, because I need to eat. I'm going to lose the house, probably get a boarding room over in Railton, listen to the bikers gunning their engines all night. But I need to fucking eat."

"I understand how you feel."

"No, you don't." But Joe's anger drained away. "That's okay."

"At least you can get unemployment during the layoff, if you're not applying for early SSA."

"They owe me the pension."

"Not anymore."

"And it's not even—you know how much I'm due? Thirty-seven years, paying in every single week? All I'm supposed to get is eighteen thousand dollars a year. Barely fifteen hundred a month. These *new owners*"—Joe heard his voice coarsen—"eighteen grand, they probably lose that at the cleaners. Loose change in their pants."

"Everything they did was completely legal."

"Legal." Joe slumped back in his chair.

"Believe me, if there was any possibility for a claim, I'd have filed already. Class action, in every jurisdiction Valiant has so much as driven his Lamborghini through." The lawyer seemed to have some anger of his own stored away. "But they've got two-thousand-dollar-an-hour attorneys out of Washington negotiating these deals and writing the agreements. It's bulletproof like plate armor. We can't touch them."

"Okay, it's legal." Joe looked out the window, at the late-afternoon sun and, far in the distance, a low line of clouds. "But it's not *right*."

———

Two weeks later, midmorning. Dim inside the community room with the lights off, but dog-day heat shimmered outside the windows. An air conditioner rattled and dripped, not doing much.

A dozen men and two women sat on metal folding chairs, filling a third of the room. The Rotary was coming in later, and their dusty flag stood in one corner. No one could hear the projected video very well, not over the air conditioner, and the facilitator had closed her eyes, fanning her face with the same copy of "Writing a Killer Résumé!" that was on everyone's lap.

"I still don't understand how they did it," Stokey said in a low voice to Joe. They'd taken seats in the rear. Long-forgotten memories: grade-school desks, ducking the teacher's eye, daydreaming.

"Leverage," he whispered back. "The lawyer walked me through it three times." No one in the room had any interest at all in the career-counseling service, but they had to show up to keep the unemployment checks coming.

"It worked because Fulmont had borrowed all the money, six or seven years ago," Joe said. Fulmont was the plant's owner, the third generation to run Fulmont Specialty Metals. "For the modernization—ISO 9000, all that? But when the economy tanked, it looked like we were about to go out of business, and Valiant's hedge fund bought up the debt."

"How can you buy debt?"

"Like Rico laying off his markers? Fulmont doesn't owe to First City National anymore, he owes to Valiant."

"Oh." Stokey squinted. "I guess."

"So then Valiant called the debt, drove us into bankruptcy, and the bankruptcy court let him cancel every single obligation the company had. Suppliers, customers, subcontractors—they all got totally screwed, and we lost our pensions. Everything went into Valiant's pocket."

Tinny music came from the video. On the screen, young,

well-dressed men and women strode through high-tech offices, smiling and making decisions and managing big projects.

"And then he opened the plant up again, only now everyone's getting paid minimum wage." Joe glanced at Stokey. He hadn't shaved either. "You could do better pumping gas at the interstate plaza."

"They ain't hiring."

"I know." Joe felt his shoulders sag. "I asked out there too."

"Valiant stole every penny that could be squeezed out of Fulmont," said Stokey. "No different than he took dynamite and a thermal drill down to the bank after hours. Except instead of trying to stop him, the judges and the courts and the sheriff, they were all right there helping him do it."

"Pretty much."

"That's how I see it. That's how you see it. That's how everyone in this fucking room sees it." Stokey was getting worked up. Joe noticed the facilitator's eyes had opened. "What country are we living in here? Russia? France? Who wrote these damn laws anyway?"

"The best politicians money can buy. You know that." Joe put a hand on Stokey's arm. "Forget it. Watch the movie."

Stokey subsided, grumbling, and they sat through the rest of the session. People got up wearily when it was done, chairs scraping on the worn floor.

"Next week we're doing social networking," said the facilitator, shutting down her computer. "We'll get you all going on Facebook."

Outside, the sun and heat was a hammer blow.

"Where you going now?" asked Stokey. He'd taken a Marlboro box out of his shirt pocket and was gravely considering the remaining cigarettes. Seven bucks a pack. Joe knew he was figuring how long he could stretch them out.

"Down the river, by the bluff. Thought I might shoot a deer."

"They ain't in season."

"There's no season on being hungry."

Stokey nodded. "Put some venison up for the winter."

"That's the idea."

They separated, going to their trucks, and Stokey drove off first. Joe sat for a few minutes, despite the heat, gazing at nothing in particular.

———

THE DROUGHT FINALLY broke, like it always did, and the weather turned beautiful again. Mid-September, the high school's first home game, and some of the nights were already cool.

On one of those nights, Joe ran into Stokey in the gravel parking lot out behind Community Baptist. Quarter to nine, mostly dark, right before the church food pantry closed up. Joe was walking out, carrying his paper sack of canned beans and margarine and Vienna wieners. Stokey hesitated, then started to turn away.

"It's all right," said Joe.

"I was just — you know."

"I've been coming every week. No shame in it."

"Yeah." But there was, of course. Stokey wasn't the only one to show up after dusk, at closing, hoping to avoid running into anyone he knew. Joe had nodded to two women inside, and none of them had spoken.

"Annie said we had to come." Stokey sighed. "I didn't want to. Didn't let her last week. But she insisted. So I said I'd do it."

"She trust you?" Joe tried to lighten it up, but Stokey just shook his head.

"It ain't right, taking handouts. It's not her job to be begging food."

"It's not begging."

"Same as."

They stood for a few minutes while Stokey finished a cigarette. Traffic noise drifted over from Route 87, across the soybean fields. The moon had risen, almost light enough to read by. Joe pulled a folded envelope from his shirt pocket. "Got this today," he said, running his finger along the torn edge. "From the bank."

"Uh-oh."

"Yeah." He looked at Stokey. "Foreclosure. I must have called six times since August, trying to talk them into a workout, but no go. They're taking the house."

"When?"

"Don't know."

"Harrell and his wife, they're still in their place. Haven't paid a dime since March. Sheriff's even been out, and Harrell just says he's working on it, shows another letter, and they let it go."

"Working on what?" Joe didn't know Harrell well, but once he'd seen him walking through the neighborhood at dawn, checking trash bags. "Buying Hot Lotto tickets?"

"It's a game. The bank, they don't really want to foreclose, because then they're stuck with it. People ain't exactly lining up to buy houses around here, you notice that? You could string them out for months, just like Harrell."

Joe *had* thought about it, but he shook his head. "That wouldn't be right."

Stokey grimaced. "What's not right is the whole fucking system. Everything's rigged for the fat boys."

The screen door at the back of the church banged, and a shadowed figure came out, carrying two sacks. A family allotment. Joe thought he recognized the woman, but she went by without greeting them, got in her car, and drove away.

"I'm leaving," Joe said.

"What?" Stokey looked up.

"Marjo's gone, my job is gone, the house is going. I got nothing to do here."

"Yeah, but—" Stokey didn't seem to know what to say. "Where?"

"Connecticut."

"*Connecticut?* What the hell for?"

"I'm going to..." Joe stopped. When he said it out loud, it sounded stupid.

"What?"

"Valiant lives there. His office is in New York City, but he lives in some little town in Connecticut. I want to talk to him."

"*Talk* to him?"

"Ask him why he did it. Ask him to make things right."

Stokey made a choking noise. He put his hands up, then dropped them. "Why the *fuck* would Valiant talk to you? Why would he even see you?"

"I'll make an appointment." Joe straightened up. "Look, he's another human being, right? We're all walking the earth. Maybe he just needs to see things clear."

"That's just plain—Valiant's *not* walking the earth, not the same one as you and me. He'll probably have you arrested. You can spend your golden years at Fort Madison."

"I don't think so." Joe shifted the sack of food he'd never put down. "But it doesn't matter. I've got nothing to do here. Seems worth a shot."

They fell silent. Stokey's energy faded. A light wind rustled the bean fields.

"You got to get in there," Joe said finally. "They're closing up, and Annie's waiting on you."

"Yeah." Stokey started to move off. "Hey, when are you leaving?"

"Tomorrow."

"Tomorrow? When are you coming *back?*"

"When it's done." Joe felt—not happy, but somehow...eager. "When it's done."

———

MANHATTAN WASN'T SO bad.

Joe had been there before, but not since he was in the service—for some reason he'd been shipped home via Germany, even though the West Coast was a lot closer to Vietnam. New York in the early seventies had been spiraling into chaos, bankruptcy, and gang violence, and that's how Joe remembered it. But the modern city was all clean streets and shiny buildings. He didn't recognize Times Square at all.

Valiant's firm had its offices on Park Avenue, the fortieth floor of a glass skyscraper called the Great Prosperity Building. Chinese characters on the largest logo in the atrium suggested the building was no longer owned by Americans.

"Mr. Valiant is out of the office this week," said the receptionist.

"How about next week?"

"Fully booked, I'm afraid."

The woman sat at her desk facing the elevator bank, but two husky young men stood by, one on either side, both staring at Joe. The carpet felt deep and plush beneath his feet.

He figured the bouncers were just guys who worked there, not real security. Their hands looked soft, and they didn't have that wary, hooded gaze Joe remembered from the MPs. But they'd been out in the foyer already when Joe stepped off the elevator.

He'd had to sign in at the main desk in the lobby, downstairs, and show a driver's license; he'd received a printed pass. The guard there must have called up. Somehow Joe didn't look right.

"Why don't you call him and check?" Joe said.

"I'm sorry, Mr. Valiant's schedule is very busy."

Back on the street, Joe stood on the small plaza, under a tree just starting to blaze orange. Early afternoon and people seemed to be on extended lunch breaks, sitting in the sun, tapping at smartphones, eating paper-wrapped takeout.

After a minute he walked back to his truck, drove around the block, and entered the garage underneath the Great Prosperity Building.

On the A level, closest to both the surface and the elevator, Joe coasted slowly, counting. Two Ferraris, five high-end Audis, BMWs, Mercedeses, several Range Rovers...and a single Lamborghini Gallardo, the distinctive rear end unmistakable.

The lawyer had mentioned the model Valiant owned. Before leaving town, three days earlier, Joe had looked through old *Car and Driver* issues at the library until he'd found it.

"I didn't even park," he told the attendant at the exit, "I got a phone call, have to go right back out."

"Ten minutes." The attendant was black, with an accent from somewhere far away. He pointed to the sign at the booth. "Five dollars."

Joe started to protest, then shrugged and dug out his wallet. No reason to attract more attention.

This time there were no good parking spaces on the street. Good thing he'd had the tank filled that morning in New Jersey, at a gas station near the highway motel he'd stayed at. Joe started driving around the block again, taking his time. Sooner or later a spot would open up, one with a nice view of the garage exit. He had all afternoon.

Valiant would have to leave the building eventually.

———

THE RESTAURANT SEEMED far too crowded, barely room to walk between the tables and people standing two deep at the short bar. Despite some kind of fancy cloth on the walls and a carpeted floor, it was noisy, with constant clatter, chattering, and glassware clinking.

"I'm meeting someone here at eight thirty," Joe said, glancing at his watch. He'd put on his old jacket and tie, good enough to pass under the dim lamps that barely illuminated a podium at the door.

"Certainly," said the maître d'. "Care for a drink at the bar?"

"That would be perfect."

Valiant was already at a small table, a woman probably twenty years younger sitting across from him. Joe had followed the Lamborghini straight here when Valiant left for the day, but Valiant used valet parking, and Joe had to take twenty minutes to find a spot on his own. He didn't want to leave any more obvious a trail than necessary.

"Seltzer," he told the barman after jostling his way to the front.

"Fourteen dollars."

He made the drink last. People drifted in and out. Finally, after a quarter hour, Valiant's companion stood and made her way to the restroom, in an alcove at the end of the bar.

When she came back out, Joe had maneuvered himself to stand where she had to brush past him.

"Excuse me?" he said, as politely as he could.

"Yes?" Up close she looked even more like someone accustomed to brushing off strange men in bars—flawlessly beautiful, dark eyes, precisely cut hair.

"I'm sorry. I don't know if I should even tell you this, but..."

"What?" She was on the verge of pushing through and ignoring him.

"While you were in there? I happened to see your fella—he's

the handsome man in the blue shirt, right? He, well, he put something in your wineglass."

That got her attention. "Say that again."

"I'm waiting for my date, she's coming down with one of her friends, so, you know, I'm just killing time. And I noticed, after you stood up—pardon me, miss, but I noticed *you* and I hope you're not offended by that. But after you left, your man, he took something out of his pocket and reached across the table and held it over your drink. Like he was dropping something in."

A long pause. The woman stared hard at Joe, then even harder at Valiant, who hadn't noticed her returning yet.

"Are you sure?" she said.

"I'm afraid so. But surely, if he's a good friend of yours—"

"I met him this weekend at a party." She made up her mind. "Thank you."

"Oh, no. Really, I'm sorry."

"Yes." And she walked straight out of the restaurant.

Joe finished his seltzer, placed the glass on the bar, and went into the dining area.

"Mr. Valiant?" He pulled out the woman's chair and sat down. "Mind if I join you for a moment?"

"Wha—"

"Don't worry, your companion won't be here for a few minutes."

"Who are *you?*"

"Joe Beeker." Joe held out his hand, not expecting Valiant to take it. "I used to work at Fulmont Metal."

Valiant looked around. Up close, he had presence—fit, strong, clear-eyed, with a haircut and clothes that even Joe could tell cost vast amounts of money. Someone accustomed to watching other people get out of his way.

"You're interrupting a private dinner," he said. "Leave now, or the police will haul you away."

"Yeah?" Joe said. "Do you *really* want to do that? Because I won't go quietly. I'll be hollering about how badly you treated us, stealing the company, stripping the pensions, cheating the suppliers. I'll bet there are forty cell phones with cameras in here. You'll be all over the internet in half an hour—and I'll walk, since I haven't actually done anything wrong." He paused. "Unlike you."

A smile flashed. "You're trying to threaten me?"

"Me? I just turned sixty-two. I'm a tired old man. I'm not threatening anybody."

Valiant shrugged. "What do you want?"

"Just to talk for a couple minutes." Joe looked closely at Valiant's eyes. "Mostly, I'm wondering, do you understand what you did to us?"

"I—"

"Deep down? Because I don't think a regular person would have gone there. I think you just don't realize the suffering you caused in order to make an extra few million bucks for yourself."

"Just business." Valiant looked toward the bar, frowning a bit, then drank from his wineglass. "You wouldn't understand."

"Oh, I—"

"Everything we did was perfectly legal. By the book."

"I keep hearing that."

"Your boss had run the company into the ground. What you don't get is, we saved the place. If we hadn't come along to fix it, the entire operation would have gone under, and *nobody* would be working anymore."

"Fulmont was doing fine until you called the debt."

"That was entirely within our rights."

"That was ruthless and unnecessary—except to give you an opening to loot the place." A waiter appeared, looking confused.

"Excuse me, sir, are you joining the party? And the lady...?"

"We're fine," Valiant said.

"Ah, shall I bring out the first course?"

"I'll let you know when."

"Very good." He slipped away, still frowning.

"You can't fix everything," said Joe. "Not completely. I know that. But at an absolute minimum, you need to give the pension back."

"Oh, go to hell." Valiant's patience had begun to wear.

"It's only six million dollars. Last year you boasted about earning, what, nine billion? You can afford it."

"It was all legal. There's no obligation."

"Legal." Joe sighed. "What you did—it was wrong."

He didn't get anywhere. Valiant sat obstinate for another minute, disregarding him. When the waiter came back again, with the maître d' for support, Joe stood up.

"Thanks for the time, Mr. Valiant," he said.

"If I ever see you again, you're going to jail."

"Beeker," said Joe. "With three e's. You need some time to think it over, that's okay. Let's say, by Wednesday? A public announcement. I'll be waiting."

"Fuck you."

Joe nodded. "Wednesday," he said again, and left.

———

NOTHING HAPPENED, EXCEPT that Valiant hired some bodyguards. They were at his house—Joe followed the Gallardo one evening, an hour's drive out of the city and into horse country, to see a blacked-out SUV waiting at the gate. In the morning the bodyguards arrived early at the office, and when Valiant went out for lunch, Joe saw at least one musclehead nearby the entire time.

On the other hand, they didn't actually drive with him. The sports car was a two-seater, hardly built for six-foot linebackers carrying automatic weapons. Joe thought about this, and he followed Valiant to and from his house for a few more days.

At a distance—a great distance. He wasn't going to be accused of stalking.

Thursday afternoon, Joe stopped waiting for Valiant's announcement and started thinking about plan B. He had to borrow a phone book from the desk guy at the motel—the room didn't have one, and pay phones seemed to have disappeared from the city. He'd never find this particular kind of shop back home, but Manhattan didn't disappoint: three choices in Midtown alone, and more in the boroughs.

New Yorkers seemed to like spying on one another.

———

"The lens is easy," said the clerk. He gestured at a glass case alongside the counter, its shelves crammed with glinting electronics. "You need wireless?"

"I don't think so." Joe remembered the combat radio he'd humped through Vietnam, twenty-three pounds of steel and plastic knobs. The equipment here would fit inside a pencil. "I can wear the recorder on my belt or something, connect it under my shirt."

"Sure. Pin-wire mike too—put it separate, different buttonhole or something, makes it harder to catch."

"You sure it can record everything someone says to me? Video too?"

"So long as you're facing them. The exact orientation doesn't matter much. A lens like this"—he held up a tiny crystal bead, two thin leads trailing away—"has a seventy-degree field of view. Looks a bit like a fishbowl on playback, but you'll see everything."

"Good." Joe pulled out his wallet.

As the clerk settled the components into a plastic bag, he said, "I ought to tell you, the courts don't accept this sort of thing."

"Excuse me?"

"If you're planning to catch someone, go undercover? It's not admissible. I'm just saying."

"Oh, that's not what this is about." Joe took the bag. "We're way beyond a court of law."

———

ON FRIDAY HE started late, checking out of the Rest-a-Way at noon and eating a full lunch at a diner off 280. By three o'clock he was in Connecticut, the truck parked in Old Ridgefork's municipal lot. The town was small and charming, with pottery shops and coffee boutiques on the renovated main street. Joe walked a few blocks north, to the edge of the town center, and sat on a park bench near a stoplight where Bluff Street crossed Main.

Late sunlight slanted across trees and Victorians. Children's shouts drifted from a playground a block away. Traffic was light but steady, a stream of cars headed mostly east. Old Ridgefork sat on one of the commuter arteries into Fairfield County, as Joe had determined from careful study of a state map.

Valiant had driven this way all three times Joe had tailed him home.

He sat for ninety-five minutes, and then he saw the Gallardo coming through town, a few blocks away.

Joe stood and began to walk along the sidewalk to the street corner, his back to Valiant. He could hear the car—the sort of whiny rumble that came from overpriced, overpowered Italian engines—and paced himself accordingly. When the Lamborghini was still a block behind him, Joe hit the pedestrian-crosswalk button, and the light turned red just in time to halt Valiant at the intersection.

Two feet away.

Joe turned, leaned over, and put his hand through the open passenger window to unclick the lock latch. In one smooth motion, he opened the door, slid in, and slammed it shut behind him.

"Hey, Prince," he said. "Light's green, you can go."

Valiant recovered, snarled, and twisted in his seat, reaching across in a lunge that was half punch, half grab. Joe pulled out his .45 and pointed it at Valiant's face.

"Settle down or I'll shoot you," Joe said.

Valiant froze.

"My service weapon." Joe held the Model 1911 comfortably, with his elbow against the door, keeping as far from Valiant as possible. "I wasn't supposed to take it, but no one was paying attention on those MAC flights forty years ago. New ammunition, of course."

"You're over the line."

"Yeah, I'm afraid so." Joe considered the handgun. "I suppose I really could go to prison for this."

"You will!"

"Maybe." Joe looked back at Valiant. "See, that's the difference between you and me—I own up to my responsibilities."

"What do you want from me?"

"I told you—the light's green. Start driving."

Valiant glared another moment, then put the car into gear and started up the road.

"Turn up here," said Joe. "Yes, there, on Valley Road. No need to bother anyone behind us."

They followed the winding road up a hill, soon leaving the scattering of houses that marked the edge of Old Ridgefork proper. Fall foliage had just started to turn, and the trees glowed in the setting sun. As they ascended, Joe could see a lake sparkling in the distance. "Slow down," he said. "Around this bend...yup, there it is. Pull in."

They stopped at a roadside historic marker—a faded metal sign standing on a wide verge so cars could pull over. The road was deserted. Valiant killed the engine at Joe's direction, and in the quiet they could hear birds and crickets.

"You rich assholes," said Joe. "Playing Wall Street games. Hundreds of us, you ruined our lives, and that was just at Fulmont. I figure you have thousands and thousands to answer for, all the deals you've done."

"I told you, we followed every single law, every single regulation." Valiant didn't look at the pistol.

"That's kind of not the point, which you still don't seem to understand."

"We kept that business alive."

"By screwing every single guy who worked there."

"At least they're working."

"Is that why you did it?"

"What?"

"To put us all on minimum wage? Take away our retirement? Force us to work until we die?"

Valiant breathed hard. "Why are you doing this?"

"I just want to understand."

"Understand?"

"You."

Cool forest air drifted through the open window, bringing a

smell of earth and fallen leaves. Far away, the sound of traffic on the state road was barely audible.

"Was it just money?" Joe said. "I really want to know. You can't possibly need another million dollars."

Valiant said nothing for a long moment.

"Well?" Joe moved his pistol slightly, bringing it back into the conversation.

"You just want me to explain myself?" Valiant seemed uncertain. "That's all?"

"If I wanted revenge, I'd have shot you already." Joe shrugged. "I thought about it. But what's the point?"

"So put the gun away!"

"Don't get any ideas," Joe said. "Self-defense cuts both ways."

Not actually true, but Valiant nodded.

A minute later he was talking, talking, talking.

"You worked at Fulmont a long time, didn't you? The rolling line, right? Not just pressing buttons, turning cranks. You think I don't know anything about the industry, but you're wrong. I study every detail before I make a deal. *Everything.* So I know about your job. It takes skill. Years, maybe, to get good at it."

Joe raised an eyebrow.

"That's the reason Fulmont's not in Mexico," said Valiant. "Or Indonesia, or Poland. Skills. You guys know what you're doing, and that can't be yanked up and dumped in some cheap, overpopulated free-trade zone."

"Thanks."

"Not my point. Look, you were good at your job, I bet. Spend years learning a craft, there's satisfaction in performing it. Real satisfaction. Doing a job and doing it well—that's what makes people happy."

Joe stared at him. "So why—"

"Because what *I* do is, I make deals."

314

"That's not the same thing."

Valiant shook his head. "I find value to unlock, synergies to realize. Ways to bring people together, so everyone comes out ahead. And I'm *good* at it, just like you're good at the milling press."

"Good at destroying lives?"

"Good at two-plus-two-equals-five. Seeing possibilities where no one else does and bringing them to life."

Not a single car had passed by. The sun was descending into a bank of purple.

"But you walk away with seven figures," said Joe. "And I have to eat day-old bread and government cheese."

Valiant frowned. "That's not my fault. That's how the world works. You make strap steel. I create billions of dollars of value. Billions! Of course I get paid more."

They fell silent. Valiant looked away. Time passed.

"I should tell you," Joe said finally. "You're on tape."

"Huh?" Valiant swung back.

Joe kept the gun steady but used his left hand to pull the camera lens from concealment in his shirt placket. He held it up, thin wires dangling.

"All recorded, picture and sound both."

"So what?" Valiant grimaced. "Take it to some prosecutor, he'll just laugh. I keep telling you, there's nothing illegal going on here!"

"I know." Joe let the lens fall. "I was thinking I'd put it on the internet. YouTube? Get some attention on what you've done. What you *are*."

After a moment, Valiant's face cleared. "Go ahead," he said. "Sure, post it. My lawyers can get a takedown notice in an hour. And even if they don't, who cares?"

"The rest of the world cares."

"I don't think so." Somehow he'd recovered every last sniff of self-confidence.

"You *want* yourself seen like this?"

"Sure." Valiant laughed. "All you'll be doing, really, is proving that I know how to find a bargain—and capitalize on it."

"That's..." Joe's voice trailed away.

"It's like free advertising. Asshole."

They sat silent, eyeing each other.

"So," Valiant said. "Now what?"

Joe wondered how he'd ended up here. He looked out the windshield, unable to hold Valiant's smirking gaze.

The setting sun pierced the cloud bank, and golden light dappled the trees below them. Joe sighed.

"I'm not sure." The 1911 was heavy in his hand.

"Well, I don't care. Do what you want."

Joe turned back. "Okay," he said.

He raised the pistol and shot Valiant in the heart.

———

"THE FBI TALKED to me," said Stokey. "And the state police. Even the DA—and I voted for him last year."

"Me too." Joe closed the iron firebox, adjusted its damper, and checked the thermometer poking out from the smokehouse planking. "Down in the courthouse. They took over the whole second floor, it felt like."

Hardwood smoke drifted from blackened vents. They were in Stokey's backyard, where he'd built the little smokehouse twenty years before.

"I told them you went up there." Stokey shifted uncomfortably. It was the first time he'd brought up the subject directly. "To see Valiant. You told me you were going."

"You did the right thing," Joe said. "I did tell you that, and I went to New York. Of course you had to tell them the truth."

"They're convinced you did it." Stokey looked at Joe square. "That you killed Valiant."

"Lots of guys wanted to."

The October morning was cool and overcast. Joe had shot a deer the day before—in season, permit and everything—and what hadn't been frozen, he and Stokey were turning into sausage and jerky.

"Did you?" Having finally asked, Stokey wasn't letting it go.

"They don't seem to have any evidence," said Joe. "Whoever did it, he probably walked away all bloody, but if he burned the clothing and got rid of the gun, there's no connection."

"But eyewitnesses—"

"Saw a man in a dark jacket and a hat. Worthless."

The wood smoke was sharp and clean. A couple dogs from the neighborhood had shown up and were now sitting out by the road, watching with keen attention.

Stokey gave up. "You taking your old job back?"

Joe studied the smoke rising, drifting slowly into the gray sky. "I don't think so," he said. "That wouldn't be right."

THE HOTLINE

BY DREDA SAY MITCHELL

R ukshana Malik wasn't angry when she was passed over for promotion at the London bank where she worked. It was true that Sarah, the successful candidate, wasn't as well qualified. It was also true that she was a bit younger, but Rukshana didn't want to draw any conclusions from that. After the selection process was over, her manager had given her a debriefing in which he explained that it had been a very close thing and that Rukshana still had a very bright future with the company—after all, she was only twenty-nine. He also suggested that the next time a position came up, she should go to him so he could prep her with some interview practice. Rukshana liked Jeff; he was a great boss. So she was disappointed and a bit puzzled, but she wasn't angry.

Her family was, though. They suspected that the reason she hadn't been given the promotion was that she was a Muslim who wore a headscarf. Her sister, Farah, asked, "This girl who got the job, what does she look like?"

"Well, she's young and blond..."

"And very good-looking, I imagine?"

"I suppose."

"Oh, wake up, Rocky." Farah waved her hands in the air. She was wearing her pale blue soft leather gloves with the fancy fringe at the end and the three white buttons on the tops, one of her newest fashion accessories.

"It's not like that; they have strict policies on race, religion, gender, and the rest of it."

Her sister sighed and shook her head with pity. Sometimes it was easy for her to forget that Rukshana was the older of the two, and an outsider could be forgiven for not realizing they were related at all. Farah wore her faith lightly, dressed in Western clothes, and was a party girl with dark brown eyes that flashed and sparkled like her gold jewelry.

The following week, Rukshana was called away from her desk to see a guy from Personnel. As soon as he told her that she was a highly valued member of the staff and a key member of the team, she knew what was coming, and sure enough she was right. He went on, "Unfortunately, in today's harsh financial climate, tough decisions have to be taken . . ."

Rukshana was let go, but she still wasn't angry. She was handed a letter that included a nice payoff and a glowing reference, and all her coworkers said that they were sorry to see her leave. But she was nonetheless let go. She was in tears as she cleared her desk and didn't see an angry Jeff appear from his office.

"Is this true, what I've heard?" he asked.

"Yes."

"This is outrageous. I'm going up to Personnel, they're not getting away this." He started walking toward the elevator.

She grabbed his arm and dragged him back. "Please, don't. It's all right, honestly."

"I don't care."

He stormed off, and she didn't see him again before she left. Farah was equally angry when Rukshana told her what had happened. "You should sue the bastards."

"For what?"

"Like Marlon Brando said in *The Wild One,* 'Whaddya got?' There's race, religion, gender—sue them for all three. Make them pay. Drag their arses through the courts, embarrass them in public, chuck dirt at them, and make them wish they'd never heard your name."

"It's not worth it."

Farah was genuinely baffled. "What's the matter with you, Rocky? Why aren't you angry? I'd be fizzing if people treated me like that."

"I'm just not angry."

And it was true—she wasn't. She was upset, scared, shocked, and confused. London could be a tough city at the best of times, and when you had no job and bills to pay, it was a very frightening place indeed. But she still wasn't angry.

That evening she got a call from Kelly, her best friend at the bank. "Rukshana, I can't believe they've done this to you. You've got to get them back."

Not another person telling her to sue...

"You can't take an employer to court for letting you go. That's not how it works."

"I'm not talking about the bank. I'm talking about Jeff and that bitch Sarah."

Confused, Rukshana answered, "It's got nothing to do with Jeff and even less to do with Sarah."

There was a long silence before Kelly said, "Oh, of course, maybe you don't know..."

"What don't I know?"

"About Jeff and Sarah. About them having a bit of slap-and-tickle."

Rukshana was horrified. "They're not having an affair. He's married with kids; he's got a photo of them on his desk, he's always going on about his family."

"Oh, Rukshana, puh-leeze—you can't be that naive. They're carrying on, everyone at the bank knows that."

"I didn't know that."

Kelly hesitated. "Well, people didn't like to tell you gossip, what with you being a Muslim and everything—they thought you wouldn't like it."

Rukshana was disgusted. She loved gossip. Kelly went on to tell Rukshana what everyone knew. "It's been going on for months. They think it's a big secret, but of course everyone knows. That's why he fixed it for her to get the job, to keep her sweet. Then he advised Personnel to get rid of you, so in case you sued them about missing the promotion, they could say you were just bitter because you'd been fired. That's what everyone's saying happened."

"That's what everyone's saying?"

"That's what everyone's saying. He was on your interview panel, wasn't he? He goes up to Personnel every five minutes, doesn't he? Every lunchtime at noon, Jeff and Sarah meet up. He goes out and waits a couple of streets away, and then five minutes later she follows and they get a cab to some Holiday Inn, where they do their dirty business. Then at two o'clock on the dot, he comes back, and five minutes later, she arrives on her own so no one will guess that they're at it. I mean, can you imagine? It'd take a lot more than a promotion to persuade me to shag that fat ugly bastard. Talk about lie back and think of England. Rukshana? You've gone very quiet. Are you still there?"

Rukshana was still there. She was just very, very angry.

RUKSHANA DIDN'T DO anything the following day because she was still too angry; she wanted a clear head when she decided what to do next. Twenty-four hours later she was still too angry but had decided to ring a couple of lawyers anyway to see if she had a case against the bank. They were a bit skeptical but thought she might be able to do something on discrimination grounds. They were less sure about Kelly's preferred option, that Rukshana sue Jeff for being a lying, cheating, disloyal, fat ugly bastard who'd taken her job away. Rukshana was glad the lawyers didn't advise that. She didn't want to sue anyone; that wasn't what she was after.

She couldn't relax. The only person in the house during the day was her granddad. He was in his eighties. He got a little confused sometimes, but on other occasions he was very sharp. Whatever—she didn't feel like chatting. She tried doing a little housework to calm down. That didn't help, but she did it anyway. In Farah's room, she picked up the clothes her sister had scattered around after she'd come in from a party the previous night. Rukshana held a miniskirt against her hips; it really was immodestly short. A few months ago, their cousin had come from Pakistan to visit and had shared a room with Farah; what a culture shock it must have been for her. Their cousin refused to leave the house without wearing a burka, so when she went out, she was covered in black, only her eyes visible to the outside world. When she returned to Pakistan, she'd left one of her burkas behind, and it was still sitting on a shelf, possibly meant to serve as a reproach to her wayward cousin. Rukshana picked it up.

From the bedroom window, she could see the towers of the City, London's financial district, looming over the rooftops;

down below those towers was the bank where Jeff and Sarah were having a good laugh at her expense. She looked at the clothes in her hands and then out over the city, and she bit her lip.

Rukshana knew what she was considering was a serious criminal offense and that she'd go to prison for several years if she was caught. She'd have to get everything right and not make any mistakes. There were a lot of things that could go wrong, and there was her family to think about. Then she thought about Jeff appearing from his office and telling her how outrageous her sacking was and how he wasn't putting up with it. She gripped the clothes tightly in her hand. Every single day she spent staring out the barred windows of a prison cell would be worth it. Jeff was going to pay. She smiled and whispered to herself:

"It's on."

———

IT WAS A Thursday. Rukshana had everything prepared and all the timing worked out. She was wearing one of her sister's short skirts, a low-cut top, and ballet shoes on her feet. In her shoulder bag were silver high heels, a pair of fashionably outsize Jackie O. sunglasses, and her cousin's burka. Out in the hall was the family bike that she'd oiled and left ready. And she'd picked the day very carefully.

Her grandfather was a cricket fanatic. He was already in his armchair with various fruit juices and nibbles in easy reach, getting ready for the first day of the England-Pakistan match being played in London. Every ball would be shown on the TV, along with the replays and analyses. Rukshana knew her grandfather; he wouldn't be moving from that spot all day. He might briefly go upstairs for a call of nature, but even that wasn't certain. Where cricket was concerned, he had very firm bladder control.

And there was a house rule—no one disturbed Granddad when the cricket was on. Knocks on the door went unanswered, the phone was left to ring, and any attempt to start a conversation was ignored.

When the first ball of the match was bowled, Rukshana looked up at the clock on the wall. It was half past eleven. She had thirty minutes to complete the first part of her plan.

"I'm just going upstairs to read a book."

She was met with silence. Out in the hall she put on her cousin's burka and wheeled the bike out onto the street. Very, very gently, she pulled the front door shut. She mounted the bike and began pedaling, the burka wrapped around her, only her eyes visible. She rode to the end of her street and turned onto the main road that led to the City.

On a typical day in London, you could see almost anyone dressed almost any way, but even so, a woman cycling in a burka was unusual. Truant schoolkids laughed as she flew by. Some drivers did double takes when they saw her, which were quickly followed by contemptuous stares directed not at her but at her burka. Rukshana almost wobbled on her bike, she was so shaken by the response to her clothing. She'd heard women in her family talk about how they were sometimes insulted and verbally abused on the street when they wore their burkas, but Rukshana hadn't thought it was as bad as this. And—perhaps it was inevitable—one guy leaned out of the window of his van and yelled "Terrorist!" when she stopped at a traffic light. She threw off her shock. She began to feel mad and bad. She felt like an outlaw.

It took her twenty minutes to arrive at her destination, a quiet side street two blocks away from the bank where she'd worked. She parked the bike, locked it up, and checked the street. There was no one looking. She pulled the burka off over her head and put it in her bag before swapping her slippers for the high heels. She put on sunglasses. She used a mirror to apply some makeup and arrange her long raven-black hair so that it waved and flowed around her face. She smiled at her image. She looked fantastic, nothing like her normal headscarf-wearing self. She couldn't help thinking that she could give her sister a run for her money in the looks department.

Unsteadily at first, but with growing confidence, she clip-clopped down the street on her heels and then turned onto the main road. With her new look, she might as well have been in a different country. The same sort of male drivers who had given her dirty looks when she'd been on her bike were now slowing down to admire her bronzed legs. When a man leaned out of a van's window and shouted, "Oi, oi! Do you fancy a portion, sweetheart?" Rukshana avoided eye contact and kept walking. She wondered if it was the same man who'd shouted "Terrorist!" at her fifteen minutes earlier.

She walked the two blocks. On the left was the bank, and on the right was a small park where the staff sometimes went to eat their lunches. Rukshana took a seat on a bench that gave her a view of the entrance to the bank. She crossed her long bare legs and looked at her watch. It was 11:55 a.m. She'd made it. A bicycle courier walked past her wheeling his bike; he clocked her legs, and she heard him whisper "Asian babe" as he went by. She smiled and looked at her watch. It was noon. She looked over to the entrance and sure enough, just as Kelly had foretold, Jeff emerged from the bank and walked down the steps. He adjusted his tie and ran his fingers through his hair a few times before trotting off and turning down a side street.

Five minutes after that, Sarah too came out of the bank. She turned and walked down the same side street Jeff had. Rukshana shook her head and whispered, "Bastards." Then she stood up, adjusted her hair again, and walked across the road. There were hundreds and hundreds of employees in this building, so she was sure she would get away with it. On the steps of the bank, she took a deep breath and said to herself, "This is it," before walking into the lobby.

In front of her was a security gate that you needed a swipe card to pass through. To the left of it sat Mark, a security guard, a big barrel of a man in a peaked cap. She fished around in her shoulder bag and took out her now-invalidated employee swipe card along with another one that she used for her local library. She wriggled her shoulders like her sister and giggled at Mark; he smiled back. When she got to the gate, she used her library card to try to get through. A red light flashed and the machine honked at her. She tried again. Another red light and another honk. She looked at Mark helplessly and waved her swipe card at him. Like a middle-aged knight, he got out of his chair and came over to help.

The bank had strict procedures about access. Mark's role was to examine her card and see whether there was a problem and, if necessary, refer her to the security office. But Rukshana knew Mark well. His view was that strict procedures didn't apply to ditzy, sexy women with long legs. And today, Rukshana was a very ditzy, very sexy woman with very long legs. Mark towered over her.

"Is there a problem, miss?"

"Oh, yes, Mark," she breathed. "My card is always letting me down."

Mark slipped his own security card into the machine, and there was a green light, a ping, and the gate swung open. She squeezed his arm.

"Oh, Mark, you're such a sweetie…"

Mark saluted and Rukshana walked through with the almost

physical sensation of his eyes drilling into her backside. She walked to the elevator and went up to the fifth floor, taking out her sister's blue leather gloves and putting them on. When the doors slid open, she was face-to-face with Renata, a colleague who knew Rukshana as well as Rukshana knew her. Rukshana stiffened; everyone who might have recognized her, with or without her headscarf, should have been out at lunch. Renata smiled at her.

"Do you really need those sunglasses in here, dear?" For a few seconds Rukshana thought it was all over. Renata held the elevator door open for her and said, "If you don't get out, you're going back down." Rukshana got out, fingered the sunglasses, and stammered, "G-got to look cool..."

Renata got in the elevator, smiled, and said, "You look very cool, darling. You'd better watch out or you'll have that sleazy lecher Jeff after you."

The elevator doors closed. Rukshana hurried down the corridor to Jeff's office and peered in the window. It was empty. With her gloved hands she pulled the handle and went inside. She sat at his computer. On the screen was a website featuring romantic breaks for two in Paris: *The city of love...a weekend of amour... for that special person in your life...*

Rukshana had the feeling it wasn't Jeff's wife who would be going. She took a list out of her handbag and began typing in the web addresses of radical Islamic websites, one after another, so that a casual observer of Jeff's computer history might think Jeff spent all his time looking up death-to-the-infidel!, death-to-the-great-Satan!, death-to—well, death-to-pretty-much-everyone-really! websites. Then she changed his screen saver from a sugary snapshot of Jeff's wife and kids to a photo of a radical Islamic cleric.

She decided to skip the elevator and took the stairs down to the lobby. Mark didn't wait for her to try her card this time; he jumped up smartly and opened the gate for her, assuming her card still wasn't working. She gave him a long, sultry look with the promise of the East in it—a look her sister had perfected—and with that she was back out on the street.

She walked the two blocks to her bike and changed into her burka and ballet shoes. She checked her watch. It was 12:40 p.m. She had to move. She pedaled furiously away from the glass and glitz of London's financial district to a poorer quarter of town and parked her bike in the yard of a disused workshop. Over her loomed a minaret. She walked a couple of streets until she was standing in the shadow of the tower.

Al-Nutjobs Mosque. That wasn't its real name, of course. It was called Al-Nutjobs by the British newspapers; they claimed that every Muslim extremist in London was a regular there, but the members of the Muslim community weren't so sure. Their view was that most of the people who hung out at Al-Nutjobs were undercover newspaper reporters, police spies, and operatives from various Western intelligence agencies. Whatever the case, Rukshana knew the street was plastered with CCTVs and other forms of surveillance and that all the local public phones were bugged. She had to be very, very careful.

She walked up to the pay phone opposite the mosque. She checked that her gloves were on and then went inside. She picked up the phone, put some coins in, and called the special police antiterrorist hotline. When she got through, she faked an Indian accent, the sort that had been thought very amusing on British comedy shows in the 1970s but that in these more liberal times wasn't considered funny anymore.

"Please, please, this afternoon, bombs, bombs! *Bombs!*"

Rukshana explained in her accent that she'd overheard a campaign being planned in Al-Nutjobs, and the ringleader was an undercover white convert who worked at—and she gave them all Jeff's details. As the operator desperately tried to keep her on the line, Rukshana shouted, "Please, please, this afternoon, bombs, bombs! *Bombs!*"

She hung up and walked smartly down the street. Rukshana collected her bike from the disused workshop and checked her watch. It was 1:15 p.m. Time was short. As she jumped on the bike to pedal back to the bank, a siren wailed through the air. Shit—she hadn't expected the cops to move that quickly. A police car screamed down the street heading toward the mosque. Rukshana didn't look back as she cycled to the bank. Once there, she parked her bike in the same spot as before, took off her burka, and slipped into her heels.

Her old bench opposite the bank was still available, and she sat down and checked her watch. It was 1:55 p.m. She was just in time. At 2:00 p.m. precisely, just as Kelly had said he would, Jeff appeared and walked back into the bank. Five minutes later, Sarah arrived, looking a little red-faced and with her clothes askew, and followed him in. Now Rukshana just had to wait.

If you reported any ordinary crime, the police would assess the evidence and decide what, if anything, to do. If you reported a terrorist bombing from a pay phone outside Al-Nutjobs, the police couldn't wait. They couldn't investigate the threat to see if it was serious; they couldn't weigh things up. They had to act fast and worry about it later.

At 2:15 p.m., the police acted. In the distance Rukshana heard sirens, and then more sirens as other police vehicles joined the chorus, and then they all came around the corner, brakes squealing, lights flashing, careering down the street. A police van mounted the pavement and juddered to a halt; it was followed by police cars and motorbikes. The doors to the van flew open and a half a dozen cops in black-and-white-checkered baseball caps, submachine guns slung over their shoulders, jumped out. Pistols were pulled from holsters; safety catches were disabled. The police raced up the stairs and into the bank. Other vehicles arrived, and soon there were so many flashing blue lights, you might have thought you were at a carnival.

Five minutes later, Rukshana rose to her feet to enjoy the view. Jeff was dragged down the steps, being frog-marched by two burly cops. He was thrown to the ground and spread-eagled; one cop kept a pistol to his head while the other cop pressed his knee into Jeff's back and handcuffed him. Down the steps came another officer holding Jeff's computer. Then the doors to the bank flew open as two policemen tried to stop Sarah from running after Jeff. She screamed, "Leave him alone, he hasn't done anything, what's the matter with you?"

Rukshana winced as Sarah punched one of the policemen in the face, after which Sarah was bundled to the ground, long legs akimbo, and thrown into the back of a van. Then the two suspects were driven away.

Rukshana sat back down. An old teacher of hers had once quoted a French saying: Revenge was a dish you ate cold. Perhaps that was true. But it certainly filled up the belly.

———

"Oh, Rukshana, you should have been there!" Kelly rang that evening to tell Rukshana about the day's events. "The cops turned up and nicked Jeff. And they took Sarah away too, it was so funny."

Rukshana put on her best sympathy voice. "Poor Jeff…"

Kelly couldn't believe it. "Poor Jeff? After what he did to you?"

The following evening Kelly updated Rukshana. "It was all a hoax! The police released Jeff in the small hours without charge. Now we've had a team of detectives in all day trying to find the hoaxer. They're drawing up a list of suspects. It'll be pretty heavy for the guy who did it. The police don't take too kindly to that sort of thing—the cops say it'll mean jail time for the culprit. That won't help Jeff, of course, now that it's all out about him and Sarah. The bank's really embarrassed. Word is that when it's all calmed down, they're going to sack him. And Sarah."

"Poor Jeff."

"Poor Jeff? You have more reason to hate him than anyone…" There was a long pause before Kelly added, "I don't want to worry you, Rukshana, but I think you might be on the list of suspects, what with being let go." There was another long pause and then Kelly asked, "It wasn't you, was it?"

"Of course not."

"That's what I told the police! A nice inoffensive Muslim girl like Rukshana—no way was it her. The thing is, though…I'm not sure they believed me."

———

It was the following Tuesday, the last day of the cricket match between England and Pakistan. The commentators agreed it was going to be a thrilling finish, and Rukshana's grandfather was in position in his armchair for it. Rukshana was jumpy. Every time she heard a noise outside, she got up and looked through the window. Then at about noon it happened. A silver sedan pulled up outside her house and a man got out and walked up the garden path. There was a knock on the door.

Rukshana's grandfather snapped, "Ignore it."

Instead Rukshana ignored him and went to the door. She opened it to a man with a flashy suit, sunglasses, and slicked-back blond hair. He'd obviously modeled himself on a character from an American cop show. He showed her some ID.

"Rukshana Malik?"

"Yes."

"Detective Constable John Martin, Metropolitan Police. I'm investigating a very serious crime and I'd like to ask you some questions."

She looked into his eyes. He knew. And what's more, he knew that she knew that he knew — but could he prove it? Rukshana had been ultra careful. She'd made sure she was unrecognizable in the burka and in her sister's clothes. She'd burned all the evidence and left the bike on the High Street, where some kids had promptly stolen it. She'd worn gloves. She had a story worked out and she was sticking to it. She knew what to do; she watched the same American cop shows as DC John Martin.

"You'd better come in."

John Martin said good afternoon to her grandfather and was ignored for his trouble. Rukshana whispered, "He's watching the cricket, he doesn't like to be disturbed."

"I see."

They sat down on a sofa. John Martin went through the preliminaries, explaining why he was there and giving Rukshana the chance to avoid wasting everyone's time.

"Is there anything you'd like to tell me about the events of last Thursday?"

"I'm sorry, I don't know what you mean."

John Martin sighed. He knew. But could he prove it?

"Could you tell me where you were last Thursday?"

"I was here all day with my granddad."

John Martin looked over at the cricket fanatic. "Could you confirm that, sir?"

Martin was ignored. Rukshana explained, "He'll confirm it when the cricket's over."

John Martin was disgusted. "I'm sorry, I'm not waiting seven hours for the cricket to finish."

Rukshana shrugged her shoulders. "I'm sorry."

John Martin moved on. "You must have been very disappointed to be passed over for promotion at the bank?"

"Not really, no."

John Martin feigned surprise. "Not really?"

"I'm a person of faith, Detective Constable. Do you know what that means?"

John Martin looked blank. Islamic theology obviously wasn't his strong suit. Rukshana went on. "I accept everything as part of the divine plan. So, no, I wasn't disappointed."

"Very commendable, I'm sure. But you must have been a little upset when you were let go? Angry?"

She smiled at him. "That's for atheists, I'm afraid."

John Martin had the feeling he was being put down, but he pressed on. "Were you aware that the successful candidate was having intimate relations with your manager?"

"Jeff and Sarah? I certainly was not. I had no idea. People don't pass gossip on to me. It's because I'm a Muslim, you see."

John Martin pursed his lips and produced a photo from a file. He handed it to Rukshana. "Do you know who that is?"

It was a CCTV still photo from the lobby of the bank. It showed Rukshana at the security gate in her heels, short skirt, low-cut top, and sunglasses. Rukshana passed it back.

"No, sorry."

John Martin passed it back to her. "Have another look. Rack your brains."

Rukshana studied it again before handing it over.

"Still no."

John Martin moved in for the kill. "It's you, isn't it?"

Rukshana feigned outrage and tugged at her headscarf. "Certainly not. I'm a good Muslim. That girl looks like a prostitute. Totally inappropriate clothes for any decent Muslim woman."

John Martin passed her another photo, asked her if she recognized the subject. This one was a CCTV still of Rukshana in her burka outside Al-Nutjobs. But Rukshana had hit her stride. "I doubt her own mother would recognize her. If it was a woman, of course; perhaps it was a man in disguise? We don't wear burkas in this house."

John Martin played her the tape of the phone call to the antiterrorist hotline. When it was finished he said, "That was you, wasn't it?"

"It sounds more like a white comedian making fun of Asians. There's too much of that sort of racism in our society. I don't know why the police don't crack down on it."

And so it went on. For an hour, John Martin probed and Rukshana parried. But Rukshana could see the detective was getting frustrated. He knew, okay, but he couldn't prove it. Eventually, John Martin accepted a cup of tea and a couple of Samosas that he found "very tasty." Then, with obvious reluctance, he returned to the attack.

"Our inquiries have revealed—oh, I say, good shot!"

John Martin was looking over Rukshana's shoulder at the cricket. A young Pakistani batsman had just hit the ball clean into the cheering crowd. Granddad turned around and said to him, "What about that kid, eh? What a prospect!"

John Martin returned to his questioning, but he began going around in circles. He admitted the photos could have been of anyone. He also confessed there was no fingerprint evidence and that the tape didn't really prove anything. He admitted—off the record—that the police had quite a list of people who didn't much like her ex-boss Jeff, so they had a lot of others to interview. In fact, some of his fellow officers suspected Jeff's wife was the real culprit, and, frankly, they didn't blame her. The wife was certainly a more promising suspect than a nice Muslim girl like Rukshana.

"Okay, Miss Malik, I think we're about finished for now."

But as he got up to go, he noticed something on the mantelpiece. He walked over and picked up the large pair of sunglasses that Rukshana had worn the previous Thursday when she'd framed Jeff. They were sitting where she'd left them when she'd gotten back. John Martin looked at the shades and then fished out the CCTV still of Rukshana in the bank lobby and studied it. They were obviously the same distinctive pair. Rukshana felt her stomach tense. She'd been so careful, and now this...

But before John Martin had a chance to ask Rukshana for an explanation, her granddad snapped, "What are you doing with my sunglasses?"

"Your sunglasses?"

"Yes. They're medicinal, I use them to cut out the glare from the TV."

Granddad got up, took the sunglasses from the cop's hand, and put them on. He looked quite natty in them. John Martin was not convinced.

"You use them to cut out the glare from the TV?"

"That's right."

"So why weren't you wearing them when I came in?"

"I was. But I take them off when we have visitors. I don't want to look like a prat, do I?"

"I'm sorry, sir, but..."

Granddad angrily turned on the unfortunate police officer. "Are you calling me a liar? And by the way, the girl is right—she was here all day last Thursday and I was here all day watching cricket in my sunglasses and I'd like to see you prove otherwise. Now, why don't you clear off and catch some real criminals?"

———

WHEN JOHN MARTIN was gone, Rukshana sat down in the front room by her grandfather.

"So you were listening then?"

"I can listen and watch cricket at the same time. I'm not stupid. And that was a very foolish thing you did. You could have gone to prison."

"I know. And thanks, Granddad. For backing me up."

Her granddad nodded and then said, "If you'd wanted revenge on someone, you should have spoken to me. I know all about that. When I was a child, a British prime minister came to our village and was a little bit rude and arrogant." Rukshana's granddad forgot the cricket for a moment and became lost in thought. Then he added, "Now, that was a revenge story . . ."

BLOOD AND SUNSHINE

BY ADAM MEYER

Most people don't believe in pure evil, and neither did I until I met five-year-old Dylan Brewster.

Before I ever laid eyes on Dylan, I saw his nanny. She was barely older than I was, clearly much too young and pretty to be anyone's mother. Her lush blond hair was pulled back in a ponytail, her toned arms pushing a heavy stroller. A few-months-old baby in a pink onesie was strapped inside.

"Can I help you?" I asked, trying for a mix of helpful yet suave. Not easy when your hands are covered with finger paint and you're wearing a yellow T-shirt that says SUNSHINE SUMMER CAMP.

"Is this the Dolphin room?" she asked, turning back as if she'd lost something, or someone. About halfway down the hall I saw him: a small, dark-haired boy with his head stuck in one of the cubbies that lined the hall. "Dylan! Come over here, please."

He did, and there's no denying he was awfully cute. Long, straight hair cut in a neat line over his forehead, and a nose that looked like a button in a snowman's face. He wore plaid sneakers so small I could've swallowed one whole.

"Hi, Dylan," I said, kneeling down to look him in the eye. "I'm—" But he marched past me and into the classroom where the rest of the Dolphins were busy playing. This was midmorning during my third week of camp, but it was the first time Dylan had come.

"Sorry we are late," the nanny said, and there was a precision in her words that hinted at a faint accent. "We had some trouble getting out today."

"Trouble?"

The nanny glanced down at the baby in the pink jumper, then at Dylan. "Sometimes he acts a little"—she wriggled her fingers, searching for the word—"a little crazy."

"That's okay. I act a little crazy myself sometimes."

At first I wasn't sure she got the joke, but then she smiled. "I'm Britta."

Before I could get my name out, Rebecca bellowed it from behind me. "Eddie! Where on earth have you—oh." The frown on her face dissolved as soon as she saw Britta. "You must be Dylan's caretaker."

Britta nodded and Rebecca put on one of her biggest, phoniest smiles. She was in charge of the group and I was her assistant. She was pretty old—early thirties, at least—and a full-time kindergarten teacher, which seemed to require that she speak to virtually everyone as if they had the intelligence of a five-year-old. Especially me.

"Eddie, why don't you go in and get the morning snack ready. Would that be all right?"

I glanced at the wall clock—it was half an hour before our usual snack time—but I didn't argue. She clearly wanted to get rid of me, and maybe even embarrass me in front of Britta.

"Yes, ma'am," I said, saluting Rebecca. She didn't look amused, but Britta did, and that was even better. I washed my hands, then slipped back into the room and saw the dozen boys and girls in our Dolphin group hard at play. Some had clustered in the toy kitchen, and others finger-painted at the child-size tables. The last few kids were in the corner stacking wooden blocks into what looked like a fort.

Dylan stood to one side, watching the block builders. I crouched beside him, lining up plastic cups for apple juice.

"We're glad to have you here at camp with us," I said. "Have you had a good summer so far?"

"I went on a trip."

"Oh, yeah? Where'd you go?"

His eyes narrowed, his gaze still on the kids with the blocks. "Ug-land."

At first I wasn't sure what he meant. And then I got it: England. "Was it fun?"

He shrugged. "It's *far*."

"It sure is."

I was from Queens and had never been farther than Newark. It burned me that kids like Dylan got to take trips overseas they didn't appreciate while I worked all summer just to cover the cost of college textbooks. But that was how it was. Upper West Side kids like Dylan had nannies and European vacations and summer camp, and kids in Astoria didn't.

"You want to help me pour the juice?" I asked.

"I wanna build a galley," Dylan said.

I wasn't sure what a galley was, but I let that go and unscrewed the top of the juice bottle. "Sure, go build whatever you want. I'm sure the other kids will let you play with them."

"I wanna do it myself."

I sharpened my tone. "Dylan, we all have to play together here. But if you ask nicely—"

Clearly Dylan had no intention of asking, nicely or otherwise. He was already headed right for the play area, and by the time I'd put down the apple juice and gotten over to him, it was too late. He had stomped right through there, blocks tumbling down and flying every which way.

Amber—one of the block builders—threw up her hands, showing off the Band-Aids stuck to each of her elbows. It was lucky the falling blocks had missed her because she always seemed to be getting hurt. "He knocked down our house."

"That's not very nice," I said, pointing a finger at Dylan.

At first, he looked defiant, and then his face crumpled and tears appeared. "They said I couldn't play with them."

"Now, that's not true," I said. "You just went right over and—"

"Enough," Rebecca said from behind me. I turned around. She looked sharply at me and then put on a smile, her mood changing as abruptly as Dylan's. "It's cleanup time, everyone."

The kids grumbled, but then Rebecca held up a bag of sugar cookies, and that got them motivated. "Maybe you should finish pouring the juice now," she said to me, using the same tone she had with the kids. I grabbed the juice bottle and glanced over at the doorway.

Britta was there. Her big blue eyes were aimed at me, and I smiled, but she missed it and focused on Dylan, who watched the other kids clean up while he stood by, doing nothing. Britta turned from him, her expression hard to read. It was only when she wheeled the stroller away that I recognized the emotion.

It was relief.

———

The Sunshine Summer Camp was housed on the top two floors of a private elementary school on Central Park West and Seventy-Fourth Street. We had everything an urban camp for little rich kids needed: a rooftop swimming pool, an indoor playground, and classrooms chock-full of educational toys and games. A far cry from the Boys' Club camps where I'd spent the summers of my early years, and a relatively easy way to make some cash before I headed back to Binghamton in the fall.

Or at least it had been, until Dylan showed up.

My next run-in with him happened during afternoon nap time. All the kids gathered their blankets from their cubbies and spread them out through the classroom while I stood watch. Rebecca had gone to lunch.

The kids were supposed to lie down without talking or moving, which of course isn't easy when you're five. Unlike Rebecca, I tried to be understanding when they began to stir. First Amber raised her Band-Aided elbow and said, "I'm thirsty." Then Michael, who would wear only green socks, complained that Royce had kicked him. No surprise there. Royce never stopped moving, even when he was flat on a blanket half asleep.

After settling everyone down, I put on a CD, *Peter and the Wolf.* As the gentle music filled the room, the children seemed to relax. I did too. I pulled out my cell phone to check my e-mail — a no-no with Rebecca around, but she wasn't there — and I saw a movement from the corner of my eye. Dylan was upright, gathering a stack of blocks from the shelf beside him.

The other children watched, wide-eyed. Royce leaped up, eager to get in on the action. "Can I play too?"

"Nobody's playing," I said, storming over to Dylan's blanket.

But he didn't seem to hear me. He continued to pile up the blocks, one after the other, making a tower as high as the table beside him. Then he added a long block and balanced it across the top, the tower threatening to topple.

I snatched away this last block and glared. "Put these back."

"I don't want to." There was no anger, just a simple declaration.

"If you don't, you're going to have a time-out."

This was a punishment the kids dreaded as much as losing pool time. But Dylan was unfazed. He reached out to the shelf and found another block the same length as the one I had just taken away. He added it to the top of his column of blocks to form what looked like an upside-down L.

"See, it's a galley."

I had no idea what he was talking about and I didn't much care. Besides, I felt the eyes of all the other kids on me. If I didn't establish authority over Dylan, and fast, they'd think I was a pushover.

"You need to listen to me," I said firmly. "No playing during nap time."

He looked up with eyes as dark as charcoal. "But my galley isn't done."

"Trust me, it is," I said.

Music swelled from the boom box, the soaring violins that represented the wolf's arrival. Dylan smiled then, as though he knew something I didn't, and it made me so angry I started to pull my hand back. I wasn't really going to hit him, of course, it was just my anger getting the best of me. And then I heard the door open.

When Rebecca walked in, my hands were back at my sides, and Dylan looked at her. "Eddie and I made a galley."

"That's very nice," she said, but the look on her face was stern. "But Eddie knows there's no playing during nap time."

"Of course I know that, but—"

Rebecca gave me a sharp look that said she didn't care what I had to say and shook her head. Disappointed. Dylan had made a fool out of me once more, and I didn't much like it. But then, it was my own fault. I promised myself that I wouldn't let him take advantage of me again.

———

DYLAN WAS ON his best behavior for the rest of that week, at
least until the encounter with the ice vendor. It was a Friday, and
the promise of the weekend was bright—I'd finally have some
time with my old high school friends and away from camp. I
stood on the hot Manhattan sidewalk, the sun crisping my skin.
There were kids all around, being herded by their mothers and
nannies.

A middle-aged street vendor was selling Italian ices in paper
cups. I waited in line behind some of the campers and then
ordered a pineapple ice. I'd just taken my first lick when I heard
a familiar voice. Britta. She was calling after Dylan, who'd
stormed toward the ices cart. She was a dozen feet behind him,
struggling to push the stroller over a large sidewalk crack.

"Tell the man what you like," she said, wheeling up to the
cart.

"Chocolate," Dylan said.

"No chocolate," the vendor said in what was barely English.
"You want grape?"

Dylan closed his hands into fists. "No, I want chocolate."

The vendor looked at Britta with concern. He didn't want to
be the cause of a full-fledged tantrum in the middle of Seventy-
Fourth Street. "No chocolate."

I glanced at Britta, who looked like she was about to have a
meltdown of her own, and then at Dylan. "I've got pineapple.
It's pretty tasty. You want to try some?"

"I don't know," he said.

"Go ahead. I think you'll like it."

I held out my soggy paper cup. Dylan took it and lapped up a
mouthful of pineapple ice.

"It's good," he said, surprised. "I want one of these." Instantly, the vendor began to scoop pineapple ice into a cup. Britta gave me a look of pure gratitude.

"Thank you."

"Of course. Anything to help."

"How has he been doing?" she asked quietly, adjusting the bonnet around the doughy face of Dylan's baby sister. Dylan was a few steps away.

I shrugged, playing coy. "Pretty good, mostly. What's he like at home?"

She shook her head sharply, which I took to mean *Don't ask*. I wanted to know more, but just then Dylan inserted himself between us, still sucking on my pineapple ice. He looked sharply at Britta.

"He won't let me make my galley."

I smiled. "Yup, I'm Mr. Mean, all right." I tousled Dylan's hair and leaned in closer to Britta. She smelled of baby powder and suntan lotion and looked as beautiful as any girl I'd ever seen. "What's this galley he keeps talking about?"

She turned away, and I couldn't tell if she didn't know or if she felt this wasn't the moment to tell me. I wanted to press her further, but I didn't have the chance. Something cold and sticky began to dribble onto my leg, and I saw that Dylan had turned over the paper cup and was pouring pineapple ice on me.

"Goddamn it, what the..." Glancing at Britta, I let the anger sputter out, smiling instead. "Lost your grip, huh, little guy?"

Dylan said nothing, just let the paper cup fall to the ground. He reached out to the vendor to take his own cup of ice and began to lick it with relish.

"I'm so sorry," Britta said. "Let me buy you another one."

"No need," I said, and I was about to say *Why don't you make it up to me by going out with me sometime,* but then the baby started to squawk. I noticed that Dylan was beside her, one hand around his ice, the other inside her stroller. He must've pinched her or hit her and made her cry.

You little bastard, I thought, but I kept that smile right on my lips, still sticky from pineapple ice.

"Let's go," Britta said, spinning the stroller away from me. As I watched them head down the sidewalk, Dylan looked back, only once, a faint smile on his lips.

———

EARLY THE NEXT week, a heat wave settled over the city. Temperatures soared into the high nineties, and the humidity was off the charts. The kids moved sluggishly through our barely cool classroom, and even Royce hardly stirred during nap time. No one showed any signs of energy all day until it was time to go up to the pool.

The aboveground pool sat on the rooftop and was filled with just enough water to reach most kids' chins. There was an area on the far side of the roof for those who didn't like to swim, with a sprinkler and a sandbox. Rebecca and I switched off which of us went in the pool, and that day was my turn.

She sat on a wooden picnic bench beside a mound of towels, wiping sweat from her face. I couldn't help but smile. Although the water only came up to my belly button, it was deliciously cool.

"Look at me," squealed Amber, whose soggy Band-Aids hung from her elbows. "I'm going underwater."

She ducked her face at the surface, went just deep enough to splash her nose and some of her round cheeks.

"That's great," I said. "Do you want to maybe try putting your *whole* head under?"

"No." Amber giggled. "That's too scary."

"You want to see scary?" I asked, ducking underwater and

sticking my elbow up like a shark fin. Amber splashed away, giggling. When I rose, Dylan tugged at my leg.

"You want to see me swim?" he asked.

Dylan was like a little duck, one of the few kids who could swim. Dutifully, I watched him churn across the pool as I tossed a beach ball back and forth with Amber and a couple of the other kids.

After a few minutes I got tired of Dylan's swimming and turned away. "You're not watching," Dylan whined, and Amber threw the ball at me again but missed.

The ball drifted toward Dylan. He grabbed it and hurled it over the side of the pool, onto the roof.

Amber leaned out. "Hey, someone get the ball!" But everyone else was on the far side of the roof, out of earshot, including Rebecca.

"I'll get it," I said, going right for the ladder since I was closest. I didn't even think about it, really. It wasn't a big deal. I'd have my hands on the ball in five seconds and be right back in the pool. What could possibly happen?

My feet had barely touched the hot rubber that covered the roof when I heard a shriek from behind me. At the sandbox, Rebecca had whirled and spotted me outside the pool. Anger crossed her face.

"Who's watching the kids?" she shrieked.

I was halfway up the ladder when I saw Dylan holding Amber's head underwater, her hair floating like kelp. I broke the surface with a crash, landing inches from the two kids. Dylan let go of Amber instantly and swam away.

I picked her up, wiped tendrils of hair out of her face, and made sure she was breathing okay. I felt Dylan brush by my legs, circling like a piranha.

"Shhh, it's okay," I told Amber, leaning her against my shoulder.

But she just cried, rubbing her eyes with her hands. The wet Band-Aids had fallen off her elbows.

"You are in very serious trouble," Rebecca said, and Dylan and I both looked up at once. I didn't know if she meant me or him.

———

APPARENTLY SHE'D MEANT me. "That's goddamn unacceptable, leaving those kids in the pool alone." I'd never heard Rebecca curse before. Of course at the moment, our kids had gone off with another group, so we were alone by the pool. "Somebody could've drowned in there."

"Yeah, like Amber," I said. "But only because Dylan was holding her underwater."

"Don't be ridiculous. The kids were horsing around, that's all. Which would've been fine if someone were supervising." She shook her head at me. "This is it, your last free pass. Don't screw up again."

I nodded and went to the bench where I'd stashed my clothes. As I started to slip on my sneakers, I noticed that one of the laces was gone. I looked around inside the sneaker and under it, but I couldn't find the lace. Was this some trick the kids were playing on me? But I didn't have time to dwell on it. I had only fifteen minutes until afternoon snack.

———

I STAYED IN the city after work that day and saw a movie, a comedy. I was glad to get some laughs, but my good mood didn't last. Soon I was standing on the sweltering subway platform, my anger starting to resurface. Then I noticed a familiar figure at the edge of the platform. Britta.

"How's the nanny business?" I asked.

She smiled when she saw me, and my bad mood disappeared again in an instant. "Pretty good."

"Seems like a tough job. Dealing with Dylan, I mean."

She opened her mouth to answer, then closed it. After a moment, she said, "He's...how do you say it? Hands full?"

"Hands full is right," I said, and we both laughed. "How long have you worked for his family?"

"Three months. My friend worked there before me. She told me not to take the job, but..." She shrugged. "I need the money."

"Tell me about it." I looked down at the end of the platform, then back at her. I wanted to find out more about Britta, who she was and where she came from, but I couldn't stop thinking about Dylan. I was still haunted by that image of him holding Amber's head underwater. "Have you ever wondered if he might be...dangerous?"

I thought about a case we'd studied in criminal justice during spring semester, involving two seven-year-old boys who had murdered a toddler. We discussed whether they should be punished as severely as teenagers, or even as adults, despite their age. Their attorney had argued they were too young to know what they had done and should be released, but the court disagreed. The boys were sentenced to juvenile detention until the age of twenty-one, which some of my classmates thought was extreme.

Not me. I believed they were stone-cold killers. They wouldn't stop. As soon as they got out, they'd just do it again.

"Dangerous? No, not little Dylan." Britta shook her head emphatically, but there was uncertainty in her eyes.

A train rumbled at the edge of the tunnel, its headlights blasting through the dark. I turned to Britta.

"So I was thinking...do you want to get together sometime? For coffee? We could even talk about something besides Dylan."

She smiled, beaming at me. "Yes. I would certainly like that."

———

AFTER THE POOL episode, Dylan was on his best behavior for the next two days, and I started to think that maybe I was wrong about him. Maybe he wasn't such a bad kid, and I had just overreacted.

And then there was the incident with the Star Wars figures.

Kids weren't supposed to bring their own toys to camp, but I didn't see it as any big deal. He'd brought them out of his cubby during afternoon playtime, and since Rebecca hadn't noticed, I didn't say anything.

"This is me," he said, holding out an Anakin Skywalker figure. "And this is you."

Apparently I was Darth Vader.

When I reached for the figure, Dylan pulled it away. "Huh-uh," he said with a fake babyish voice. "It's mine."

He sat at one of the tables and moved the figures across an imaginary starscape. Ignoring him, I let myself get drawn into the kitchen area by Amber, who served me an imaginary breakfast of pancakes and ice cream. "Delicious," I said, spooning it up.

And then I heard Dylan call my name. "Eddie! Eddie!"

I looked over but all I saw was Royce jabbing his paintbrush furiously at the easel, creating a splotchy mess, and Michael painting a picture of a dog the exact same shade of green as his socks.

"Eddie!" I heard for the third time, and when I finally saw him, I was shocked.

Dylan had built his favorite shape, the tall tower with a single long block on top, only this time he had added something else to it. My missing shoelace. Dylan had tied one end of it along that top block and the other end of the lace hung down, forming a makeshift noose around the Darth Vader action figure.

"You're on my galley," he said, smiling.

And I thought: *gallows. He's been saying* gallows. He must have learned about them on his family vacation to England, during a visit to some medieval castle or other. Now instead of a fort or a spaceship or anything a normal kid would create, the little son of a bitch was making a gallows, just so he could threaten me.

I charged across the room, my arm pulled back, and Dylan flinched as though he thought I might hit him. I didn't. Instead, I swatted the blocks aside, watched them scatter across the floor. A couple of the pieces flew toward the easel and landed at Royce's feet. He stared at me in utter shock. Rebecca whirled and stared at me. But I ignored her and looked right at Dylan.

"You knocked down my galley," he said, his lower lip starting to quiver.

"Yeah, well, fuck you and your goddamn galley."

I was about to say more when Rebecca stomped over, kicking aside one of the fallen blocks. "Eddie, get your stuff and go." That was all she said, that I was fired.

When I got down to the lobby, I went into the bathroom and splashed cold water on my face and then ducked into a stall, where I tried to throw up. But I couldn't. I was angry and confused. I went through it all, trying to imagine what I should have done differently, but I knew that things had had to end like this. Dylan had made sure of it.

I sat in the stall for an hour, maybe more, and tried to calm myself down. Dylan was dangerous. He was sick, truly sick. At least I wouldn't have to see him again, but what about Britta? What if he tried to hurt her to get back at me? Or one of the kids I really cared about, like Amber?

I couldn't allow that. I wouldn't.

I slipped out of the bathroom, but instead of going for the exit, I ducked into the shadows of the sprawling lobby. Behind me, the basement door had been propped open and I stepped inside the stairwell and peered out from there. I heard the murmur of restless adults waiting for the elevators to come down. Through the faint noise, I soon heard the voices of eager campers, including some of mine: Amber and Michael, Royce and Cory.

I stepped out from the shadows and saw Britta leaning wearily on the baby stroller and talking to Rebecca. I wanted to wait for Rebecca to go away so that I could explain to Britta what had really happened with Dylan. I felt sure that she would understand.

In the stroller, Dylan's sister opened her mouth in a wide O and began to wail. Britta fumbled around in the stroller, opening and closing zippers, muttering. Finally, she found a bottle and stuffed it in the baby's mouth.

"Let's go," Dylan said, tugging at Britta's hand. "I want an ice."

"Just one minute," she said, turning back to Rebecca.

Dylan began to push his sister's stroller in circles around the lobby. Britta watched casually, listening to Rebecca, nodding. I wondered what kind of lies my former boss was telling her. Would Britta even want to go out with me after what she'd heard?

Dylan wheeled closer to me. It was almost as if he knew I was there. But no, he must not have, because he jumped when I put a hand on his shoulder.

"You think you're so smart, don't you, you little shit."

Dylan was as solemn and obedient as if he were standing in a church pew.

"I am smart," he said.

"Not as smart as me."

I hadn't thought about what I would do next, not really. It

just happened. I grabbed the stroller from Dylan and started walking, looking down at the baby cocooned inside, sucking on her bottle, swinging her tiny fists, Dylan must have looked like that once too, I thought, so helpless and small. No one ever would've suspected what he would someday become.

"Where we going?" Dylan asked in surprise as I wheeled the stroller through the basement door.

"You're going away, my little friend," I said, and then the baby dropped her bottle. It rolled into the corner of the stairwell and she started to scream, but only for a moment. I had no choice but to act, so I did. I pushed. The whole thing took maybe three or four seconds and then the baby was quiet, the sound of Dylan's tears filling the void.

I don't know what happened next. I was already gone, out the service door, then walking calmly down the sidewalk. But I imagine that Britta and Rebecca ran over, and so did everyone else who was there, and they all covered their mouths in horror. I see the baby lying at the bottom of the basement stairs, covered in blood, head cracked open like a coconut. Dylan must've stared down at her in disbelief as Britta shook him by the front of his shirt and said, *Why did you do this?*

No, it was him.

It was who? Rebecca would have asked.

Eddie did it. Eddie, not me! He pushed her, he hates me, he did it!

But as everyone knew, I had left camp at least an hour earlier. The police interviewed me several times, but they weren't suspicious. Dylan was the guilty party. Of course, no charges were filed, since Dylan was only five and no one could—or wanted to—prove that he had purposely pushed the baby down the stairs. It was probably just an accident. Some blamed the janitor who'd left the basement door propped open, while others blamed Britta for not watching the kids more closely.

I went back to college that fall and I met a girl, one even prettier than Britta, and joined a fraternity. I had a lot of friends and a good life and whenever I thought about Dylan, I felt a little sadness mixed with relief.

Dylan's story got lots of coverage in the papers. I read that he was hospitalized for a while and faced a barrage of psychiatric tests and behavioral evaluations. They must have prescribed him tons of pills. Someone who saw Dylan on the street three or four years later told me he was like a walking zombie, so drugged up that he wasn't capable of hurting anyone. Not even himself.

I also heard that no matter how many times Dylan was asked, he wouldn't admit to pushing his sister down the stairs. That's too bad, because, as I'm sure someone must have told him, confession is good for the soul.

IN PERSONA CHRISTI

BY OREST STELMACH

Two days before the killers came for Maria, a gang of teenagers rampaged across church property. I was washing the liners under my prosthetic arm when I heard them. Their whistles and shouts came from everywhere, as though they had the rectory surrounded. It was just past dusk, too dark to see clearly out the window. All I could detect were amorphous black images, vaguely human, flitting in and out of my field of vision.

Manuel, Maria's thirteen-year-old son, was the first to come downstairs. As always, he spoke with facial expressions and physical gestures, as opposed to using his tongue. He hadn't said a word to me since he and his mother had moved into the rectory, two months ago. Given his father had recently been hanged to death over the course of an hour while a block of ice melted beneath his feet, I wasn't surprised. He stood now at the base of the stairs, his deceased father's gold watch around his wrist, lips quivering and eyes bulging, begging me to tell him his mother and he weren't in danger again.

A Catholic priest must be a father. He is a spiritual provider and protector in the image of God, in the person of Christ. The role of father is my favorite part of being a priest, the one that comes most naturally to me and gives me the most joy.

I walked up to Manuel and put my arm around him. I spoke to him in Spanish. "Don't worry, son," I said, as though he were my own child. "There's nothing to fear. I'll take care of you."

When I opened the front door, the clucking and crowing stopped immediately. The sight of a six-foot-three, two-hundred-twenty-pound, one-armed and one-legged priest limping on his prosthetic limb as an empty sleeve dangled at his side sent the boys scurrying. All I could hear was the sound of feet pounding the asphalt as they escaped into old Dillon Stadium, across the street.

"You boys go on now," I said. "And don't come back. This is a church, you know."

The screen door was against my back. When I turned and swung it open, the springs let out a long, eerie squeak. It was followed by the sound of a teenage male voice from the direction of the stadium.

"You need me to hear your confession, Father?"

After a few howls and laughs, more footsteps followed and the voices faded. I went back inside and explained to Manuel that the hooligans were just a bunch of bored kids. He calmed down and returned to his room to finish his homework. His mother, Maria, taught violin at the local university during the day and studied English at home at night. She was in her room listening to language tapes on her headphones and had missed the entire event.

After reattaching my prosthetic arm, I called the police and reported the incident, just to establish a record in case the next time the kids decided to break into the church and steal an icon or a chalice. It took ten minutes for a police cruiser to arrive. That didn't surprise me.

Once Bermuda usurped Hartford as the insurance capital of the world, the companies moved out and the drug gangs moved in. Now Hartford is just a waypoint between Boston and New York City, and you need a different kind of insurance to walk around at night. With the Kings of Solomon in the South End, 77 Love in the North End, and city and state budget crises, the police are spread thin. There are precious few resources to dedicate to the eastern fringe of the city near the defunct Colt's gun factory and Dillon Stadium, where the old Hartford Knights used to play semipro football back in the day. The oldest Catholic church in Hartford, however, still stands on a tiny wooded lot, serving a small but devoted parish whose members live in the projects nearby.

After I told them what happened, the patrolmen stared at me as though I were a self-indulgent moron. They exuded the arrogance of the armed and immortal. One of them looked like Mr. Clean, with a shaved head and a physique that could double as a battering ram. His partner was long and wiry, with an untrustworthy-looking pencil mustache that he might have lifted from an uncooperative nightclub owner.

Their eyes told me I was wasting their time. There were serious crimes being committed in other parts of town.

A priest must be a mediator. Just as Moses revealed the law to Israel, the priest brings the human family together through eternal redemption. In this case, though, I needed to redeem myself for appearing to be a pain in the ass in the cops' eyes.

"I didn't mean for you to come out," I said. "I didn't dial nine-one-one. I told the dispatcher not to send anyone if you were busy."

They continued glaring at me, as though motives mattered little in their world. "Hot June night, Father," Mr. Clean said.

"Probably kids from Franklin Avenue, Father," Pencil Mustache said. "They break into the stadium to party. They never hurt no one. But we'll drive around and take a look for you."

"Yeah, Father," Mr. Clean said. "We'll take a look."

The police car radio squawked. They jumped inside, answered the call, and peeled out of the driveway, lights flashing and siren blaring. They took off toward the center of town, away from the stadium. Understandably, there was no time to drive around, no time to take a look.

Maria was at the base of the stairs with her arms wrapped around Manuel when I went back inside.

"Why were the police here, Father Nathan?' she said. "Are they here to deport us? Are we being sent back to Mexico?"

"No, no one is sending you back to Mexico. Would you make us some tea, Maria? I can't stop thinking about that *tres leches* cake you made. Is there another piece left in the fridge?"

Twenty-two years ago, Maria's mother was my teacher at the Consultoria Española y Lingüística in Santa Volopta, Mexico, where I studied Spanish and worked with Mother Teresa of Calcutta's Missionaries of Charity. Maria was nine years old at the time.

Santa Volopta lies within the Golden Triangle of the Chihuahua state, the most violent territory in the world outside of actual war zones. Not all the violence is a result of the drug trade. Over the past ten years, 937 women have been murdered, their bodies tossed in random dumps and ditches. Although no arrests have ever been made, high-level policemen and prominent citizens are suspected.

At age eighteen, Maria married a lawyer in Volopta. When he

became the municipal prosecutor, he launched an investigation into the murders of the daughters of Volopta; it led to his own assassination. Maria's mother called me immediately after his body was found, put her daughter and grandson on a plane, and sent them to live with me in Connecticut. She didn't trust the municipal or federal governments. She was certain her son-in-law's murderers, the drug czars, and the high-level officials responsible for the killings of the daughters of Volopta were one and the same. In Maria's mother's mind, her daughter and grandson were as good as dead if they stayed in Mexico.

From the moment Maria and Manuel arrived, my goal was to provide a spiritual and physical home for them while they integrated themselves into the community and began new lives. The gossipers in the parish, of course, didn't want to see it that way. It was far more entertaining to contemplate a priest violating his vow of celibacy with the beauty living beneath his roof.

As soon as Maria started appearing in church, attendance and contributions at Mass increased. A dozen men, single and married alike, received a thunderbolt of devout inspiration and started showing up daily. When I turned from the altar to bestow a blessing during morning Mass, I would catch one or more of them trying to steal a glance at her from a side pew. She possessed an elegance that could make men sob in anguish because they would never touch her. Her hair fell past her shoulders in silken strands that shone under the ceiling lights like onyx.

She tended to gaze at the ground, either because she didn't want to encourage any suitors or because she was desperate to disappear. This habit lent her an air of innocence. When she looked up, there was a gentleness and purity in her oval face and chestnut eyes that took one's breath away.

It didn't take long for the comments to start.

"There they are," a widow said. "The Thorn Birds."

"His third leg still work?" a former altar boy said.

"If it didn't, it does now," his friend replied.

I am forty-five years old. I've been a priest for seventeen of those years, and over time, it has been my observation that ethical and moral standards are deteriorating, nowhere more so than in the Catholic Church. And no one has disappointed the faithful more than the Catholic priest. As a result, people have become cynical. It's just a profession, they say; there is no special calling. For some folks, it's unimaginable that a heterosexual man such as I would not lust for a woman such as Maria, would not lie in bed wrestling with temptation every night.

And yet, I must insist: I do no such thing. I do not think of her in the way that other men do. I do not want to touch her. I do not want to possess her. I pray only for her and her son's health and salvation. Seeing them alive and healthy at Mass fulfills me in every way. Such is the joy of priesthood: contentment beyond the scope of sexual fulfillment. In the twenty-one years since a priest gave me a prayer book and changed the course of my life forever, I've said the Lord's Prayer three million, six hundred, and sixty-six times. That is how much prayer it has taken me to reach such a state of contentment.

I was not always this way. There was a time in my youth when I would have broken doors down to get to Maria, and no one would have tried to stop me. I was once the golden boy, a star collegiate baseball player with a bazooka for a right arm, a flame-throwing pitcher drafted in the third round by the New York Yankees. I had all the girls I wanted, and then the only one I ever needed died in a car accident when I was behind the wheel.

The day before the killers came for Maria, the same gang of kids tried to break into the church. They attempted, unsuccessfully, to jimmy open the padlock to the front door with a tire iron, and they ran away when I limped over from the rectory. I wished I could have caught one of them and had a discussion with him, helped him channel his energies into something more useful, such as the boys' baseball team I coached in the Rotary league. It consisted of misfits and orphans, the shunned and unwanted. But this gang of kids was too fast for a one-legged priest.

"Hey, Father," the same boy said from his hiding place in the stadium across the street. "You need me to hear your confession, Father?"

It was just past 9:00 p.m. when I got back to the house, sweat rolling down my cheeks from one minute of exertion. That's all it took on a sultry June night. Manuel was waiting for me at the bottom of the stairs, like the first time. After reassuring him there was nothing to fear, I dialed 911. I didn't want to bother the cops, but I had no choice. The kids had tried to enter the church. The church belonged to everyone, but its safekeeping was my responsibility.

This time it didn't take the cops ten minutes to get there. It took them twenty.

"Doesn't look serious, Father," Mr. Clean said as we studied the old wooden door to the church.

"See the dent here?" I said, pointing to a welt in the church's door. "That's where they pushed off with the tire iron."

Pencil Mustache tilted his head at me. "Just kids, Father. You actually saw them, though. Like, with your own eyes. Right, Father?"

"Yes, Officer. I saw them. I may have only one arm and one leg, but I still have vision in both eyes."

Sirens sounded in the distance. The radios attached to their belts squawked. One of them answered the call, barked a clipped response into the microphone, and nodded at his partner. "We'll write it up, Father," Mr. Clean said.

"Yeah. And we'll drive around and take a look for you," Pencil Mustache added.

"Yeah, Father. We'll take a look."

They rushed back into their cruiser and peeled out of the driveway, lights flashing and siren wailing. They took off toward the center of town, away from the stadium. Understandably, once again, there was no time to drive around, no time to take a look.

The day the killers came for Maria, I was driving back home from the hospital when I spotted Manuel huddled with two older teens along the far side of the stadium. The teens were more than a foot taller than Manuel. They wore inscrutable expressions, knapsacks, and black bandannas wrapped around their foreheads like headbands. I had to swerve away from a telephone pole at the last second to avoid a head-on collision when I remembered I was driving a car.

When Manuel got home, I went to his room and asked him if he felt like a game of catch. He didn't answer exactly. Instead, he shrugged, grabbed his glove, and shuffled out the door with his head hanging.

Since losing my right arm, I have become more proficient at throwing with my left, though my pitching wouldn't remind pro scouts of Goose Gossage's anymore. My prosthesis is a trans-humeral one, commonly known as an AE because it replaces the arm above the elbow. Both the hand and the arm are myoelec-tric, meaning a battery-powered device converts the electric signals of my muscles above the arm into movements of the prosthesis. It offers the strongest grip of any type of prosthetic; that's the upside. The downside is the time lag between my

muscles signaling a movement and my replacement parts react-
ing. Consequently, some of Manuel's throws sailed past me even
though they were within my reach. Although I saw the ball
coming, I was a second slow when I tried to catch it.

After half an hour, we were both drenched and went back
inside. There is no air-conditioning in the rectory and it doesn't
cool down until midnight, at which point the attic fan finally
begins to help. The kitchen seemed hotter than the yard. I
poured each of us a tall glass of lemonade from the pitcher that
Maria had fixed that morning and asked Manuel to sit down for
a moment.

A Catholic priest must be a teacher. He helps his parishioners
understand the Church and deal with conflicts and adversity. I
am less comfortable with my role as Manuel's teacher because a
great teacher should fully comprehend his student's life. Maria's
mother told me that Manuel had been hiding in a closet and
witnessed his father's murder. Since I can't truly comprehend
what the boy has been through, I'm uncertain if I can establish
an authentic bond with him.

He guzzled half the glass and gasped for air when he was
done. Sweat trickled down his cheeks. His lungs heaved gently. I
took a big swig of lemonade myself to celebrate seeing him
diverted from his recent realities.

"When I was driving home, I saw you walking from school
with those two boys," I said.

He choked on air.

"It's okay, it's okay," I said. "I just want you to understand two
things. Those bandannas they were wearing around their heads?
That's the fashion accessory of choice for members of the Aztec
Rulers. You know who the Aztec Rulers are?"

Manuel shook his head, but his eyes flickered in a way that
told me he was lying.

"They're an international gang that specializes in drugs and illegal-weapons distribution. You hear what I'm saying, right? Drugs and illegal weapons."

He acknowledged me with a slight nod.

"Good. I'm telling you this just to make sure you understand that they may or may not be who they appear to be. But whether or not they're Aztecs, they are welcome here. Everyone is welcome here. Especially friends of yours. Okay?"

He finished his lemonade. As he stood there with the glass tipped to his mouth, I thought there was something different about him, but I couldn't tell if it was his physical appearance, his carriage, or just my imagination.

That evening I listened to confessions after Mass, as was customary on Friday nights during the summer. I heard seven in a row, and then I waited fifteen minutes to make sure there weren't any stragglers, engrossing myself in a series of obscure prayers for wayward souls written by Saint Ignatius of Constantinople. I was drifting on a parallel plane of consciousness, meditating on missing and lost parishioners, when the kneeling bench creaked on the other side of the confessional screen.

At first, the person didn't say anything. English and Spanish are spoken in equal measure in my parish, so I usually have to guess which language to use to break the silence in cases like this. Now, however, there was no guesswork involved. They say a priest's chastity increases his sensory strength. I'm not sure that's true, but I smelled Maria's rose perfume as soon as she arrived. The hint of lily, vanilla, and white musk gave her away.

"In the name of the Father, and of the Son, and of the Holy Spirit," I said in Spanish.

She repeated the Trinitarian formula. "Forgive me, Father, for I have sinned." Her voice cracked with emotion.

I let a few seconds pass. "Yes?"

She could barely get the words out. "It's been four weeks since my last confession. But my last confession was a lie."

I let a few more seconds go by. "Why was it a lie?'

"Because I was unfaithful to my husband. I was unfaithful to my husband…with one of the men that had him killed."

As she sobbed, I dreamed of stepping out of the confessional, lifting her in my arms, and comforting her like a man. This pleasant vision flitted in and out of my mind in a nanosecond and was usurped by the reality that a priest must be a judge. He has jurisdiction over the penitent, and the power to forgive sins.

The role of judge is my least favorite. As a priest, I relish the opportunity to help the penitent heal, but as a man, I've never fully forgiven myself for one particular sin, so I am insecure about sitting in judgment of others.

After absolving Maria of her sins, I waited a few more minutes to let Maria say her penance before turning off the lights and locking the church. I saw her walking to the rectory ahead of me, and as she passed under the streetlamp at the corner of the church lot, the light illuminated her figure. I couldn't help but notice her hips gently sashaying in the fabric of her capri pants. And once again I insisted to myself that I did not think of her in the way that other men did. I did not want to touch her. I did not want to possess her. I did not love her more for having the strength to confess to her transgression.

When I got to the rectory, I locked myself in my room and prayed for her and her son's health and salvation, and for the strength to keep my vows. As I prayed, it occurred to me that if Maria knew who was responsible for her husband's death, she and her son might be in constant mortal danger.

By 11:00 p.m., the lights were off in Maria's and Manuel's rooms. The prosthesis on my leg is a transfemoral one, commonly known as an AK, because the leg was replaced above the knee. It also uses a myoelectric, battery-powered device that works with a time lag. I have to put on additional socks intermittently because the fit fluctuates during the day. I was taking off the last pair in preparation for my nightly stretching routine when I heard a car door close.

My bedroom sits atop the living room at the front of the rectory. I peeked through the curtain and saw a Lincoln Town Car parked across the street. I assumed it was a livery car—no one actually *buys* a Lincoln Town Car—and looked around to see if some well-heeled party animal was taking a leak along the fence after a night of drinking at Black-Eyed Holly's up the street. I didn't see any such person.

Instead, a man got out of the driver's side. He was short and squat and dressed in a suit. He was looking toward the church when a second man appeared in my line of sight, coming from beneath my window, presumably from the steps to the rectory. He was tall and lean and also dressed in a suit, with a fedora on his head. The tall man went to the car, where the short man whispered something to him. Beneath the light of the streetlamp in front of the house I could see their dark complexions. It occurred to me that while no one bought a Lincoln Town Car, people did rent them. At airports. When they were in town on business.

The men reached inside their suit coats, pulled out guns, and headed down the walkway toward the door to the rectory.

I scrambled to my feet, grabbed the phone, and dialed 911.

I cupped my hand over the phone and kept my voice at a whisper. "This is Father Nathan, from St. Valentine's Church on Huyshope Avenue."

"Yes, Father." It was the same dispatcher as before. Muted voices barked in the background. "What is the nature of your emergency?"

"Two men with guns. They're here. They've come for Maria and Manuel. The woman and the boy who are staying with me."

A siren sounded on her end. "Please hold, Father."

An unbearable number of seconds followed. I held my breath to try to hear what was going on outside, but the sound of my heartbeat filled my eardrums.

When the dispatcher finally picked up again, a combination of sirens, screaming, and static echoed from her end. "I'm sorry, Father. Are these the kids that have been bothering you all week?"

"No. They're not kids. They're two men with guns. They came in a Lincoln Town Car. They're assassins. The woman who's staying here—her husband was a prosecutor who was murdered in Mexico. They're here for her. For her and her son."

"Please calm down, Father. These men, are they in the house?"

"No. Not yet."

"Officers will respond as soon as possible. Please keep the doors locked—" A knock on the front door.

I hung up the phone and limped down the stairs, cursing the creaks in my prosthetic leg. When I got to the foyer, I faced the door and held my breath.

Three more short knocks followed. It was a smart move, I thought. A church was a shelter for all. A priest's first instinct was to open his door to anyone who needed assistance. Why break into a house when you can wangle an invitation?

It took the cops ten minutes to arrive the first time, twenty minutes the second time. It seemed, based on the background noise during the call with the dispatcher, that the natives were restless this evening. The odds the cops would arrive faster than the previous two times were zero.

I didn't own a gun. The closest thing I had to a weapon was a butcher's knife. But the idea of using it, the thought of sinking a blade into another human being's flesh, was unimaginable under any circumstances.

Sweat streamed down my back and created an itch beneath my cassock but I didn't dare scratch it. A minute passed. Still, I didn't dare move, for fear of making any kind of noise. Perhaps I'd misread the situation. Perhaps they weren't killers. Perhaps I could will them away with my thoughts.

Something clattered outside the living room.

I forced my feet to move, crept around the corner into the living room, and hid behind a curtain. A night-light cast a semicircle of light beside a red-velvet couch. Above the sofa, the window rattled gently. They were checking to see if a window was open. Why break a window if you can slide it open?

They were killers. They were here for Maria and Manuel.

These words should have motivated me. They should have summoned an adrenaline flow and spurred me to action. But they didn't. Instead, I stood solemnly in place, resigned to my fate.

It simply wasn't in me. Twenty-three years ago, a stranger had groped my girlfriend's breasts as we filed out of a rock concert at the Civic Center. When we got outside, I broke his jaw with a single punch. Unbeknownst to me, he followed us to a bar in his monster truck, and when we parked, he drove his vehicle through the passenger door. Matilda died and I lost two limbs, all because I raised my hand to another man. I couldn't do it again. Two decades of meditation and three million, six hundred, and sixty-six repetitions of the Lord's Prayer had absorbed all my rage.

The glass broke inward with a muted crack. I remained behind the curtain, feet frozen in place, my vision wet and blurry. One of the men reached inside with a gloved hand, wiggled a shard of glass free, and removed it. After he repeated the process several times, a third of the window was gone. In sixty seconds, they would slip into the house.

"Kill the cripple and the boy," one of the men whispered, "but not the woman. She's dessert."

Images of the killers raping Maria and then strangling her with their bare hands flashed before me. I slipped out from behind the curtain and headed straight for the kitchen closet. Swinging the door open just a smidge so the rusty hinges wouldn't squeak, I thrust my good hand inside in search of my Hillerich & Bradsby bat. No luck. I felt the broom and mop handles but no stick.

Another crack in the adjoining room told me the window was half gone. I had thirty seconds, if that. I lowered my reach and got the fire extinguisher. Better than nothing, but not what I wanted. I raised my hands six inches and grasped again. Pay dirt. The cold, hard wood felt good as soon as it hit my hand.

I pulled the bat out of the closet. It was a vintage 1967 Roberto Clemente model, 36 inches long and weighing 36.4 ounces, a gift from my high school coach in Rockville after I hit thirty-four home runs in thirty games my junior year.

I slipped into a nook between the living room and the staircase. The killers could not get upstairs without passing me, and they wouldn't see me until it was too late. I'd drop the first man with a tomahawk swing and pulverize the second one's skull with an uppercut blast. I hadn't crushed a baseball in decades. There was nothing like the sensation of hitting the ball square on its sweet spot, the thud of the wood generating maximum force, the satisfaction of slamming one out of the park.

Abraham waged war. Abraham was a warrior.

Joshua laid siege to Jericho. Joshua was a warrior.

A priest must be a warrior.

I must be a warrior.

I couldn't see the window from my hiding place, so I had to rely on sound and shadow. I heard a scratching noise, followed by a gentle thud. One of them was inside. The short one, I suspected. The second man made almost no noise. He had the first one to help him. The living room was small, and there was only one way to go.

The night-light cast ghoulish shadows on the wall. The ghouls moved.

They were upon me faster than I expected. I raised the bat with both hands high in the air. As soon as I saw the first man—the short one—I swung downward with all my strength. My left hand led, but the right arm seemed slow to react—of course it was; the prosthetic lagged—and then it just stopped. In midair. My left arm fought to bring the bat down but it wouldn't move.

My prosthetic arm was locked. It had malfunctioned.

The killer saw me. He jumped back. The taller man with the fedora came into view. The three of us stood there for a couple of seconds, frozen in mutual disbelief. A priest, posing like an ax murderer for a wax museum, and two assassins, silencers attached to the barrels of their guns.

The short one laughed. It was the deep, resonant laugh of a lifetime scoundrel and smoker, coarse enough to sand wood without touching it. The tall one chuckled like the calculating kind of person for whom genuine laughter was too frivolous. They raised their guns in tandem and pointed them at me, grins etched on their faces.

Gunshots exploded. The floor shook. Pain racked my eardrums.

I opened my eyes. I hadn't even realized I'd closed them.

The killers lay on the ground, the left sides of their chests riddled with multiple bullet holes.

Manuel appeared in the stairwell, arms outstretched, clutching a gun with both hands. When he spoke for the first time, his voice had a youthful pitch, but his delivery was shockingly composed.

"Leave my mother alone," he said.

When I saw Manuel's arms stretched out, I realized how his appearance had changed and figured out what I'd failed to detect when we'd shared a glass of lemonade in the afternoon. His wrist was bare. His father's gold watch was gone. He'd met the Aztecs to trade his father's watch for a gun.

By the time Maria arrived, hysterical, I'd removed my prosthetic arm from the socket and the gun from Manuel's hands. I'd taken an EMT course and knew how to check for a pulse. I found none in either man. Manuel had shot each of them through the heart. They were dead.

The rage I'd managed to build receded quickly. A sense of calm fell over me, as though I'd gone on a trip I'd detested and now I was back home.

If the police saw that Manuel shot two men, he and his mother could be deported to Mexico. After all, he'd shot them with an illegal weapon, and he wasn't an American citizen. In Mexico, they would die. In America, they would live.

A priest I knew from seminary lived in upstate New York. He was a friend and kindred spirit. We would create new names and birth certificates. Manuel and Maria would start new lives. No one would know their past. Manuel's father's killers would never find them.

I took the gun and wiped it down with the end of my cassock to make sure Manuel's fingerprints weren't on it. Then I fired two shots with my left hand into the wall behind the place where the killers had stood.

Maria screamed at me, "What are you doing?"

"Gunpowder and cordite leave burn marks," I said. "Especially when fired at close range. If the burn marks are on my fingers, no one will bother checking Manuel's hands. Why would they? It was my gun. I bought it from persons unknown."

A siren sounded in the distance. Its blare grew gradually louder.

A Catholic priest must be a father. He is a spiritual provider and protector in the image of God, in the person of Christ: *in persona Christi*. The role of father is my favorite part of being a priest, the one that comes most naturally to me and gives me the most joy.

I stepped closer and put my arm around Maria and Manuel. "Don't worry," I said, as though they were both my children. "There's nothing to fear. I'll take care of you."

THE HOLLYWOOD I REMEMBER

BY LEE CHILD

The Hollywood I remember was a cold, hard, desperate place. The sun shone and people got ahead. Who those people were, I have no idea. Real names had been abandoned long ago. Awkward syllables from the shtetls and guttural sounds from the bogs and every name that ended in a vowel had been traded for shiny replacements that could have come from an automobile catalog. I knew a guy who called himself LaSalle, like the Buick. I knew a Fairlane, like the Ford. I even knew a Coupe de Ville. In fact I knew two Coupe de Villes, but I think the second guy had his tongue in his cheek. In any case, you were always conscious that the guy you were talking to was a cipher. You had no idea what he had been and what he had done before.

Everyone was new and reinvented.

That worked both ways, of course.

It was a place where a week's work could get you what anyone else in the country made in a year. That was true all over town, under the lights or behind them, legitimate or not. But some got more than others. You were either a master or a servant. Like a distorted hourglass: Up above, a small glass bubble with a few grains of sand. Down below, a big glass bubble with lots of sand. The bottleneck between was tight. The folks on the top could buy anything they wanted, and the folks on the bottom would do whatever it took, no questions asked. Everyone was for sale. Everyone had a price. The city government, the cops, regular folks, all of them. It was a cold, hard, desperate place.

Everyone knew nothing would last. Smart guys put their early paychecks into solid things, which is what I did. My first night's work became the down payment on the house I've now owned for more than forty years. The rest of the money came with a mortgage from a week-old bank. And mortgages needed to be paid, so I had to keep on working. But work was not hard to find for a man with my skills and for a man happy to do the kind of things I was asked to do. Which involved girls, exclusively. Hollywood hookers were the best in the world, and there were plenty of them. Actresses trapped on the wrong side of the bottleneck still had to eat, and the buses and trains brought more every day. Competition was fierce.

They were amazingly beautiful. Usually they were better-looking than the actual movie stars. They had to be. Sleeping with an actual movie star was about the only thing money couldn't buy, so look-alikes and substitutes did good business. They were the biggest game in town. They lasted a year or two. If they couldn't take it, they were allowed to quit early. There was no coercion. There didn't need to be. Those buses and trains kept on rolling in.

But there were rules.

Blackmail was forbidden, obviously. So was loose talk. The cops and the gossip columnists could be bought off, but why spend money unnecessarily? Better to silence the source. Better to make an example and buy a month or two of peace and quiet. Which is where I came in. My first was a superhuman beauty from Idaho. She was dumb enough to believe a promise some guy made. She was dumb enough to make trouble when it wasn't kept. We debated disfigurement for her. Cut off her lips and her ears, maybe her nose, maybe pull every other tooth. We figured that would send a message. But then we figured no LA cop would stand for that, no matter what we paid, so I offed her pure and simple, and that's how I got the down payment for my house. It was quite an experience. She was tall, and she was literally stunning. I got short of breath and weak at the knees. The back part of my brain told me I should be dragging her to my cave, not slitting her throat. But I got through it.

The next seven paid off my mortgage, and the two after that bought me a Cadillac. It was the eleventh that brought me trouble. Just one of those unlucky things. She was a fighter, and she had blood pressure issues, apparently. I had to stab her in the chest to quiet her down, and the blade hit bone and nicked something bad, and a geyser of blood came out and spattered all over my suit coat. Like a garden hose. A great gout of it, like a drowned man coughing up seawater on the sand, convulsive. Afterward I wrapped the knife in the stained coat and carried it home wearing only shirtsleeves, which must have attracted attention from someone.

Because as a result, I had cops on me from dawn the next morning. But I played it cool. I did nothing for a day, and then I made a big show of helping my new neighbor finish the inside of his new garage. Which was a provocation, in a way, because my new neighbor was a dope peddler who drove up and down to Mexico regular as clockwork. The cops were watching him too. But they suffered an embarrassment when we moved his car to the curb so we could work on the garage unencumbered. The car was stolen right from under their noses. That delayed the serious questions for a couple of days.

Then some new hotshot LAPD detective figured that I had carried the knife and the bloody coat to my neighbor's garage in my tool bag and that I had then buried it in the floor. But the guy failed to get a warrant, because judges like money and hookers too, and so the whole thing festered for a month and then went quiet, until a new hotshot came on the scene. This new guy figured I was too lazy to dig dirt. He figured I had nailed the coat into the walls. He wanted a warrant fast, because he figured the rats would be eating the coat. It was that kind of a neighborhood. But he didn't get a warrant either, neither fast nor slow, and the case went cold, and it stayed cold for forty years.

During which time two things happened. The LAPD built up a cold-case unit, and some cop came along who seemed to be that eleventh hooker's son. Which was an unfortunate confluence of events for me. The alleged son was a dour terrier of a guy with plenty of ability, and he worked that dusty old file like crazy. He was on the fence, fifty-fifty as to whether the floor or the wall was the final resting place for my coat, and my coat was the holy grail for this guy, because laboratory techniques had advanced by then. He figured he could compare his own DNA to whatever could be recovered from the coat. My dope-peddling neighbor had been shot to death years before, and his house had changed hands many times. None of the new owners had ever permitted a search because they knew what was good for them, but then the sub-primes all went belly-up and the place was foreclosed, and the hotshot son figured he could bypass the whole warrant process by simply requesting permission from whatever bank now held the paper, but the bank itself was bust and no one knew who controlled its assets, so I got another reprieve, except right about then I got diagnosed with tumors in my lungs.

I had no insurance, obviously, working in that particular industry, so my house was sold to finance my stay in the hospital, which continues to this day, and from my bed I heard that the buyer of my house had also gotten hold of my neighbor's place and was planning to raze them both and then build a mansion. Which got the hotshot son all excited, naturally, because finally the wrecking ball would do the work of the warrants no one had been able to get. The guy visited me often. Every time he would ask me, how was I feeling? Then he would ask me, wall or floor? Which showed his limitations, to be honest. Obviously the coat and the knife had exited the scene in the dope dealer's stolen car. I had put them in the secret compartment in the fender and left the key in the ignition when I parked the car on the curb. They were long gone. I was fireproof.

Which brought me no satisfaction at all, because of the terrible pain I was in. I had heard of guys in my situation floating comfortably on IV drips full of morphine and Valium and ketamine, but I wasn't getting that stuff. I asked for it, obviously, but the damn doctor bobbed and weaved and said it wasn't appropriate in my case. And then the hotshot son would come in and ask how I was feeling, with a little grin on his face, and I'm ashamed to say it took me some time to catch on. Everyone was for sale. Everyone had a price. The city government, the cops, regular folks, all of them. Including doctors. I have no idea what the son was giving the guy, favors or money or both, but I know what the guy wasn't giving me in return. The Hollywood I remember was a cold, hard, desperate place, and it still is.

ABOUT THE AUTHORS

Alafair Burke is the author of seven novels, including the best-selling thriller *Long Gone* and two mystery series, one featuring NYPD detective Ellie Hatcher and one featuring Portland deputy district attorney Samantha Kincaid. A former prosecutor, she now teaches criminal law and procedure at Hofstra Law School and lives in New York City. She welcomes e-mails from readers at alafair@alafairburke.com.

Lee Child was born in 1954 in Coventry, England, but spent his formative years in the nearby city of Birmingham. He went to law school in Sheffield, England, and after part-time work in the theater, he joined Granada Television in Manchester for what turned out to be an eighteen-year career as a presentation director during British TV's "golden age." But after being let go in 1995 as a result of corporate restructuring, he decided to see an opportunity where others might see a crisis, so he bought six dollars' worth of paper and pencils and sat down to write a book, *Killing Floor,* the first in the Jack Reacher series. It was an immediate success and launched the series, which has grown in sales and impact with every new installment. Lee spends his spare time reading, listening to music, and watching the Yankees and Aston Villa and Marseille soccer. He is married with a grown-up daughter. He is tall and slim, despite an appalling diet and a refusal to exercise.

Michael Connelly's latest novels are *The Fifth Witness*, featuring Mickey Haller, and *The Drop*, with LAPD detective Harry Bosch. His books have been translated into thirty-five languages and have won the Edgar Award, Anthony Award, Macavity Award, *Los Angeles Times* Best Mystery/Thriller Award, Shamus Award, Dilys Award, Nero Award, Barry Award, Audie Award, Ridley Award, Maltese Falcon Award (Japan), .38-Caliber Award (France), Grand Prix Award (France), Premio Bancarella Award (Italy), and the Pepe Carvalho Award (Spain). Michael was the president of the Mystery Writers of America organization in 2003 and 2004 and edited both the MWA anthology *The Blue Religion* and the Edgar Allan Poe anthology *In the Shadow of the Master*. He lives with his family in Florida.

Mike Cooper is the pen name of a former financial executive. Under a different name, his short stories have received wide recognition, including a Shamus Award and inclusion in *The Best American Mystery Stories*. His new novel, *Clawback,* has just been published by Viking. Mike lives outside Boston with his family. Visit his website at www.mikecooper books.com.

Brendan DuBois of New Hampshire is the award-winning author of twelve novels and more than a hundred short stories. His latest novel, *Deadly Cove,* was published in July 2011 by St. Martin's Press. His short fiction has appeared in numerous magazines and anthologies, including *Playboy, Ellery Queen's Mystery Magazine, Alfred Hitchcock's Mystery Magazine,* the *Magazine of Fantasy and Science Fiction,* and *The Best American Mystery Stories of the Century,* edited by Tony Hillerman and Otto Penzler. His short stories have twice won him the Shamus Award from the Private Eye Writers of America and have also earned him three Edgar Allan Poe Award nominations from the Mystery Writers of America. Visit his website at www.BrendanDuBois.com.

Jim Fusilli is the author of six novels; his latest, *Narrows Gate,* is a gangster epic set in the first half of the twentieth century in the

Italian-American community of a gritty waterfront city in the shadow of Manhattan. A resident of New York City, Jim is also the rock and pop critic of the *Wall Street Journal*. His book *Pet Sounds,* described as "an experiment in music journalism," is his tribute to Brian Wilson and the Beach Boys' classic album.

Michelle Gagnon is the author of *The Tunnels, Boneyard, The Gatekeeper,* and *Kidnap & Ransom.* Her bestselling thrillers have been published in North America, France, Spain, Argentina, Denmark, Norway, Sweden, Finland, and Australia. In 2012, she will release two young-adult novels: *Don't Turn Around,* under the HarperCollins Teen imprint, and *Strangelets,* with Soho Crime. She lives in San Francisco, California.

Darrell James is a fiction writer with residences in both Pasadena and Tucson. His short stories have appeared in numerous mystery magazines and book anthologies and have garnered a number of awards and honors, including finalist for the 2009 Derringer Awards. His first novel, *Nazareth Child,* was published in September 2011 by Midnight Ink/Llewellyn Worldwide Publishing. His personal odyssey to publication appears in the *Writer's Digest* book *How I Got Published,* along with essays by J. A. Jance, David Morrell, Clive Cussler, and many other notable authors.

Janice Law is a novelist who frequently commits short mystery stories. Her first novel, "The Big Payoff," was nominated for an Edgar, and her stories have been reprinted in *The Best American Mystery Stories, The World's Finest Mystery and Crime Stories, Alfred Hitchcock's Fifty Years of Crime and Suspense, Riptide, Still Waters,* and the fabulist anthology *ParaSpheres.*

C. E. Lawrence is the byline of a New York-based suspense writer, performer, composer, poet, and prize-winning playwright whose previous books have been praised as "lively" (*Publishers Weekly*); "constantly absorbing" (starred *Kirkus Review*); and "superbly crafted prose"

(*Boston Herald*). *Silent Screams, Silent Victim,* and *Silent Kills* are the first three books in her Lee Campbell thriller series. Her other work is published under the name of Carole Bugge. Her first Sherlock Holmes novel, *The Star of India,* has recently been released in England by Titan Publishing. Visit her website at celawrence.com.

Dennis Lehane grew up in the Dorchester section of Boston. Since his first novel, *A Drink Before the War,* won the Shamus Award, he has published, with William Morrow, eight more novels that have been translated into more than thirty languages and become international bestsellers: *Darkness, Take My Hand; Sacred; Gone Baby Gone; Prayers for Rain; Mystic River; Shutter Island; The Given Day;* and *Moonlight Mile. Mystic River, Shutter Island,* and *Gone Baby Gone* have been made into award-winning films. Dennis Lehane and his wife divide their time between St. Petersburg, Florida, and Boston. Visit his website at www.dennislehanebooks.com.

Steve Liskow is a member of both Mystery Writers of America and Sisters in Crime and serves on panels for both groups. His stories have appeared in *Alfred Hitchcock Mystery Magazine* and several anthologies, and his novels include *Who Wrote the Book of Death?, The Whammer Jammers,* and the newly released *Cherry Bomb.* A former English teacher, he often conducts writing workshops throughout central Connecticut, where he lives with his wife, Barbara, and two rescued cats. Visit his website at www.steveliskow.com.

Rick McMahan is a special agent for the Bureau of Alcohol, Tobacco, Firearms and Explosives. The year 2012 marks his twentieth in law enforcement. Rick's work takes him to counties across central and southeastern Kentucky, including Bell County, the area featured in "Moonshiner's Lament." His mystery stories have appeared in various publications, including the Mystery Writers of America anthology *Death Do Us Part.* He also has a story in the International Association of Crime Writers' forthcoming collection of crime fiction from around the world.

ABOUT THE AUTHORS

Adam Meyer is the author of the suspense novel *The Last Domino*. His short fiction has appeared in *The Year's Best Horror Stories, 100 Wicked Little Witch Stories,* and other anthologies. He also wrote and directed the independent feature film *Two Fireflies* and has written television series for Fox, the Discovery Channel, and the History Channel. A native New Yorker, he now lives in Washington, DC. Visit his website at www.adsasylum.com.

Dreda Say Mitchell is a novelist, broadcaster, journalist, and freelance education consultant who describes herself as a "complete busybody." She is the author of five novels. Her debut novel, *Running Hot,* was awarded Britain's 2005 CWA's John Creasey Dagger for best first crime novel. She has appeared on BBC television's *Newsnight* and *The Review Show* and has presented BBC Radio 4's *Open Book.* She was the 2011 chair of the Harrogate Crime Writing Festival. Her commitment and passion for raising the life chances of working-class children through education has been called inspirational and life-changing. Visit her website at www.dredasaymitchell.com.

Michael Niemann has traveled widely through Europe and southern Africa. He has published the short story "Kosi Bay" in *Mysterical-E* and a number of nonfiction items on global and African affairs. A native German, he now lives in southern Oregon and is busy finishing up a novel featuring Valentin Vermeulen. Visit www.michael-niemann.com.

A Stanford graduate and former (vengeful) plaintiff's trial lawyer, **Twist Phelan** writes the critically acclaimed legal-themed Pinnacle Peak mystery series published by Poisoned Pen Press. Her short stories appear in anthologies and mystery magazines and have won or been nominated for the Thriller, Ellis, and Derringer awards. Twist's current project is a suspense novel set in Santa Fe featuring a corporate spy. Visit her website at www.twistphelan.com.

Zoë Sharp opted out of mainstream education at the age of twelve. She created her highly acclaimed ex–Special Forces–turned–bodyguard series heroine Charlie Fox after receiving death-threat letters in the course of her work as a freelance photojournalist. Sharp lives on the edge of the English Lake District, where she and her husband, a nonfiction writer, built their own house. She blogs regularly on her website, www.zoesharp.com, and on the award-nominated www.murderati.com.

Karin Slaughter has written eleven books that have sold twenty-five million copies in thirty languages. A *New York Times* bestselling author, Karin's books have debuted at number one in the United Kingdom, Germany, and the Netherlands. She lives in Atlanta, where she is working on her next novel.

Orest Stelmach is the author of the thriller *The Boy from Reactor 4,* the first in the Tesla trilogy, and the historical mystery *Lady in the Dunes,* the first in a series set in 1950 Provincetown featuring Father Sean Kale. A Connecticut native, he went to kindergarten speaking only Ukrainian. He still tries to use as few words as possible. Orest and his wife divide their time between Connecticut and Cape Cod. Visit him at www.oreststelmach.com.

Anne Swardson is an editor-at-large with Bloomberg News in Paris and a former European economic correspondent for the *Washington Post.* "River Secret" is her first published work of fiction. She is also the author of a mystery novel. Like "River Secret," it is set in Paris, where Anne has lived with her husband and two children for fifteen years.

ABOUT THE MYSTERY WRITERS OF AMERICA

The Mystery Writers of America, the premier organization for established and aspiring mystery writers, is dedicated to promoting higher regard for crime writing and recognition and respect for those who write within the genre.

COPYRIGHTS

MULHOLLAND BOOKS

You won't be able to put down these Mulholland books.

YOU *by Austin Grossman*

MYSTERY WRITERS OF AMERICA PRESENTS: VENGEANCE *by Lee Child and Mystery Writers of America, Inc.*

FIFTEEN DIGITS *by Nick Santora*

THE CUCKOO'S CALLING *by Robert Galbraith*

POINT AND SHOOT *by Duane Swierczynski*

MURDER AS A FINE ART *by David Morrell*

ANGEL BABY *by Richard Lange*

THE SHINING GIRLS *by Lauren Beukes*

KILLER AMBITION: A RACHEL KNIGHT STORY *by Marcia Clark*

SKINNER *by Charlie Huston*

WEAPONIZED *by Nicholas Mennuti with David Guggenheim*

THE DEMANDS *by Mark Billingham*

SHAKE OFF *by Mischa Hiller*

Visit mulhollandbooks.com for your daily suspense fiction fix.

Download the FREE Mulholland app.